THE GUARDIAN OF THE CHAPEL

THE WARRIORS OF TIR NAN OG

BY ALISON SCOTT

The muinntir bell rang as if it would never stop. Ciarnan shouted and pointed to the Sound where the longships lay. Gil saw flickering lights flowing down the hill from the muinntir to the pier. One flame bobbed out towards the dim far shore: the ferryman crossing the Sound. Ciarnan and Donal pulled Ismail and Gil toward the path. The nun hastened Danni and Rachel after. Gil looked back at the stone High Cross, dark against the last light of the sky, and ran, knowing with strange certainty that much would happen to him, and all, before he stood by it again.

Grey clad brothers raised torches above the pier. Floki, Hakon and Palamedes leaned into the night, watching the light cross the water. A thin shout rode the wind across to Hy. Gil wondered, who travelled so late on Christmas Day? The light wavered as the traveller was taken aboard and the ferryman hastened back.

Two brothers hauled in the boat and between them the stranger staggered ashore: young, dirt-caked, blond hair matted, a handsome face gashed from cheek to chin. One arm hung, blood-soaked, by his side. Beneath his cloak of many-colored wool shone the dull gleam of battered chain. Bloodied and broken, he seemed the image of fallen Camelot.

And yet there was a fierce fire in his eyes when he searched the faces around him. His gaze fell on the white-bearded figure of the Ab. "Good Father," he whispered and clutched his wounded arm, "The raiders camp beneath Ben More. They come at dawn for the Warriors of Tir nan Og."

First edition

Pro Christo Domino

Hrolf's Isle I pledge her;
Black cattle, silver bere.
A bed of Irish linen,
A hearth of Irish song.
All she forsakes;
And for a brother's sake
Seeks the dragon way.
Ireland of the prayer houses
Must wait its day.
Backs bend; at my word
My sea-swan spreads her wings.
Heads bow, monkish voices sing
Te Deum, spared my sword.

from *The Saga of Floki Magnusson*
circa 900 (?) AD

On the lion and the viper you will tread
And trample the young lion and the dragon.

Kethuvim

PROLOGUE

Gil saw Crazy Ivan coming, a long way off. Even silhouetted by the late summer sun, his lanky height and loping stride were unmistakable. Gil and Aaron were at the far corner of Safe Haven's grounds, under the big oak tree by the wall. Aaron liked it because he could hide there at visiting time. Gil liked it because he could keep his roommate company while still watching the door from reception, in case anyone came. He stood up.

"Hey, bro," he said gently. "You okay here? I've got a visitor." Aaron glanced at him quickly, nodded vigorously, and returned his attention to arranging twigs and acorns into another of his hugely intricate 3-D designs. "That's a cool one," Gil said. Aaron nodded again without looking up and Gil trotted quickly across the wide, sunny lawn to meet Ivan.

Ivan grinned slowly, seeing him coming. Gil broke into a run, and halted, panting, in front of him. "What did she say?"

Ivan nodded. "Now, hold on," he said. "Let's start with hello."

Gil shrugged apologetically. "Hi, Ivan." Then he stopped and said, surprised, "You're wearing a suit!"

Ivan grinned again. "Didn't work. Got frisked coming in anyway. Sorry. No drugs." He held out empty palms.

Gil laughed and pointed to the headband with the eagle feather taming Ivan's long hair. "Probably that." He smiled ruefully. "I think they'd be happier if I *did* do drugs. Like, that explained everything."

"Conventional people like conventional answers."

"Is she going to get me out?"

Ivan's grin faded.

"Didn't she listen to you?" Gil said. He felt his lip tremble.

"Well, Gil," Ivan said slowly. "I was never your mom's favorite person. She kinda felt I led your dad astray." He paused, his dreamy eyes suddenly intent, "Tell you something – no one ever led your dad *anywhere*. He had a rod of iron up his ass. Still...." he shrugged.

Gil shook his head. "She likes Sophia. Sophia believes me. Can't Sophia convince her?"

"Sophia believes Elvis is alive, Gil. Not your best witness." He paused and mumbled, "Your mom says Sophia's in denial. Because of losing Danni and Percy."

"Fairchild's got to her," Gil said coldly.

"Yeah," Ivan dragged the word out. "It's shrink-speak." He paused again and said, "He's just doing his job, Gil. He's not your enemy."

"He is my enemy."

"Choose your battles, Gil. Going head-to-head with the clinic director isn't getting you out of here."

"But if she believed me," Gil cried desperately, "She'd believe Dad was alive. Doesn't she want to?"

Ivan was quiet a long time, hands in the pockets of his unaccustomed suit. "Hope's a bummer, Gil. It's got an edge on it like that sword you brought back, and it cuts two ways. She gave it up, once. Picking it up, again, now, means risking losing it all over again. It's like closing her fingers on that blade."

Gil nodded uncertainly. He looked far across the grounds to the oak tree where Aaron's curly dark head was yet bent over his weird sculpture. Gil felt something tug at him, like he was being pulled down into Aaron's strange, fearful world. "Ivan?" He felt his lip tremble again and his voice waver, "You *do* believe me, don't you? You're not just—"

"Humoring you? Sure I am, dude. Everyone knows you're crazy as a bedbug. Who am I to argue?" Gil grinned shakily. Ivan put hand on his shoulder. "Want to know why I believe you?" he said. "I'll tell you. Your dad was too damn good a kayaker to drown like that. Sure, it was a brutal day. But he ate days like that for breakfast. I never saw your dad make a mistake. He was so cool, so together. They call me crazy; but he did stuff I wouldn't touch. He just made it look sane."

He looked up into the tree-tops, squinting at the sun. Then he said quietly, "And we looked for him, Gil. Brian and I know that river like the back of our hands. We know the places you'd get snagged up. We find dead deer in them every year. Once we even found a fox. But we never found your dad."

Gil shivered slightly. Ivan kept his gaze on the treetops. After a long while, he said quietly, "Up home, Gil, we're newcomers. Men have lived there for thousands of years. Mountain men. River men. And, sometimes, when I'm out in the woods, or on the river, alone, I kind of feel them."

"Are you scared?" Gil said, uneasily.

"Nah. They're not ghosts or anything. They're alive, like me. But time is kind of standing in the way. And every now and then it stretches real thin, like the knees of a worn pair of jeans. Now, they weren't some kind of holy nature-saints like Sophia's shaman would tell you. They ballsed up just like us. But this was their world and they knew the place – so I kind of listen to them. Like when I go to some new river, I listen to the local guys who know it.

"So, hey, I'm out on the river above some hairy piece of water, and I kind of feel a nudge of birch bark up against my boat. And that's when I take out and portage."

"I never thought you ever portaged."

"Sure I do. I just never tell anyone. Ruin my rep." He grinned. "Easier than portaging a longship, anyhow."

Gil smiled and nodded.

"So," Ivan said, "if I'm rubbing shoulders with these old Iroquois, out hunting deer, in their world; why shouldn't you meet up with Vikings and knights hunting the Holy Grail, in theirs? So yeah, dude," he gave Gil his long, slow smile, "I *do* believe you."

The smile made Gil decide, all at once, to push his luck. "Want to try believing one more thing?"

"Shoot," Ivan grinned.

So Gil told him, then, about the Change-Things: the selkies,

Floki and his mother Shony, who could turn into seals, and about the blessing of Cille Aidan's Wandering Pool that gave Ismail and Rachel and Danni, their Other selves, of stag and hawk, and wild goose.

Ivan plucked a bit of long grass while he listened and twisted it around a finger. After a long while, he said, "That shaman of Sophia's – he talks about how his ancestors in their sweat lodges used to do these trances," he paused and grinned, "Far as I see, he's Polish from Brooklyn, but, hey, maybe they have sweat lodges, too. Anyhow, they'd sort of become animals – eagles, bears – in their trances…"

"It's not a trance," Gil said quietly. "It's real. I've seen it. And I've been it."

"You…?" Ivan dropped his piece of grass and his eyes opened wider. "For real?" Gil nodded. "So, what kind of…?"

"Just a cat," Gil said.

"Just?" Ivan took hold of both of Gil's arms and facing him, laughed aloud. "Dude, sometimes you blow my mind!" A look of wondering calculation crossed his face. "So, can you, like, do it?"

"Here?" Gil shook his head sadly, hearing Aidan: *Change-Things are gone from that world.* "Do you think I'd still be here if I could?"

The end-of-visiting-time bell rang. They started walking back to the clinic, Ivan still shaking his head in amazement. At the door, he said, "Hang in, Gil. I'll keep working on her." He turned to go, and then stopped. "Nearly forgot. Sophia sent this for you. She found it with your stuff." He reached into his pocket and held out his hand. A small green pebble nestled on the palm. "She thought it might be magic," he said with a grin. "Like that stone with the hole in it, the bird brought."

Gil smiled and shook his head. "There isn't any magic," he said. "It's just a pebble. From the beach on Hy."

"The island you sailed to?" Ivan said. "On the Viking's ship?"

"*Silver Dragon*," Gil murmured. "Floki's *Silver Dragon*." He turned the pebble in his fingers; smoothed by the tides and green as Janetta's sea-green eyes. His mind filled with memories of the island; the hummocky pasture where Lionheart grazed, the grey church and white strands, the high-cross on the windswept hill.

The ringing bell faded on the summer air and the vision faded, too, blurred as if shrouded in smoke. He barely heard Ivan's goodbye.

CHAPTER ONE

All the way from Pentland, they had hugged the rugged coast, following a map drawn only in Floki's mind. The weather had been harsh, the wind often against them. A whole day was lost sheltering from a gale. When Gil stole a glance at his compass, Floki laughed and told how he'd sailed this way, first, as a boy so small that his father bound him to a shield, lashed firm to the rail, lest the waves sweep him overboard.

To Gil it seemed impossible for any man, no matter how experienced, to remember the numberless rocks and islands and hidden bays of a land so wild and desolate. Everywhere, thickly wooded shores rose to steep craggy hills, and beyond, mountains draped in cloud and mist. For three days, they found no sign of human life at all. But then, on the fourth, as they approached a rocky headland, they smelled smoke.

Floki wrinkled his nose at it and cast Bjorn a grim look. Cautiously, they rounded the headland and saw before them a scattering of stone buildings tucked into a curving bay.

"A village!" Danni cried. "People!"

But Ismail shook his head and said, "No more." He bent his ear toward the shore. "Listen."

Gil heard a distant moan drift across the sheltered water. A black, shaggy cow stumbled amidst the houses, bellowing mournfully.

"She cries to be milked," Ismail said. "But there is no one left." His voice was calm, but a flash of anguish crossed his face. Gil saw then that each of the buildings was roofless and fire still smoldered in the ruined heaps of thatch.

Floki signaled Hakon and the two longships turned

together, spilling the wind from their sails. Then with their steersmen holding steady, and their oarsmen ready at their places, the cousins jumped together into the shallow sea. Floki looked up at his ship's deck. His eyes swept his crew and then settled suddenly on Gil. "Come."

Startled, Gil pointed an uneasy finger at his own chest. "Me?" he asked uncertainly.

Floki gave him a pained look. "Do I ask what I do not wish? Of course, you." He turned to Ismail and his voice softened, "And you, Saracen. Who knows? I may need a real swordsman."

Gil winced, but Ismail shrugged and offered a lopsided grin of solidarity as they hurriedly collected their shields and swords from the armor kist, and followed Floki over the ship's side.

The water was chest-deep and icy cold. Gasping, Gil struggled ashore, his sodden boots slipping on weed covered stones. The stiff wind off the sea plastered wet clothes against freezing skin as he stumbled up the narrow strand.

Hakon and Floki strode swiftly through the rough grassland beyond. By the time Gil and Ismail caught up, they were at the edge of the blackened village, standing still and quiet, their hands on the hilts of their swords.

There was no sound but the moaning of the cow and the cries of sea birds, but the air was thick with smoke and a bitter stench caught in Gil's throat. Hakon glanced uneasily at the boys and turned back to his cousin. "Leave them here," he said.

"They must learn," Floki answered. He went on, and reluctantly, Hakon beckoned Gil and Ismail to follow.

The black cow stood with tossing head and dragging udder before the doorway of a burnt-out byre. An overturned wooden stool lay at her feet and, beside it, the body of a man. Gil glimpsed blood-stained white hair and something wet and grey amidst it, before Hakon turned him quickly away. Shaking, he stumbled on after Floki, casting a hurried glance at Ismail. The African boy's smooth brown face was expressionless, his stride as purposeful as the Northman's.

A woman lay before a small roofless house, shrouded in her grey cloak; one bare, blood-smeared arm reaching desperately for a fallen, shawl-wrapped bundle. The wind lifted strands of long, lifeless hair and loosened the shawl from the bundle, revealing something white and broken. Gil thought it a doll, crushed by a boot, before he saw the blood.

He looked up in horror at Floki. The Northman's cold, grey eyes met his for an instant. He nodded toward the waiting ships. "Go back, if you wish," he said quietly. "This is not the worst you will see."

But Gil shook his head, and striving to imitate Ismail's remote calm, muttered, "It's okay."

They clambered over a stone wall and through a pen where dead sheep were scattered in wind-plucked disarray, and a slaughtered pony-foal sprawled pathetically, limbs splayed, soft nose buried in blood-soaked turf. Gil shut an image of Lionheart from his mind and hurried past.

Hakon moved suddenly to block the doorway of the next building, but it was too late. Gil had seen already what lay, half-buried under fallen roof-beams, in the still-smoking ash. Brutally exposed to the pale winter light, charred and consumed by flame, only their rough outlines defined them as human.

"More children!" Gil cried despairingly. "Why do they kill little children?"

Ismail looked away. Hakon ran a rough hand through his black hair. Floki said, "Children, yes. But not small. They were your age."

"My age?" Gil's eyes returned unwillingly to the black shapes. "But they're tiny."

"It is what fire does," Floki said. "I have seen burnings." Ismail nodded solemnly. Floki raised his eyes to the broken gable of the house. "They were as you. Four. Like yourselves."

Gil's stomach churned and he held his hand over his mouth. "Was it Northmen?" he whispered.

Floki still studied the blackened stone. "Northmen make slaves of children. They do not murder them." He paused and said quietly, "These men had other work to do." He looked out over the wreckage of the little village. "And for the sake of four, all die."

"Because of us!" Gil cried, understanding at last. "It was a mistake. It was meant to be us. They were killed because of us.

Because of our quest…." Floki said nothing. "But we agreed to it…." Gil stared, sickened, at the bodies. "And they didn't agree to anything!"

Floki met his eyes for a long, pitiless while, and said, "No man agrees to be born, Warrior. And few agree to die. But all men die in the end." With a last grim glance at the mounds in the smoking ash, he raised his gaze to the surrounding hills. Then suddenly, he spun about, and gripped Gil's arm, and Ismail's, too. "Now!" he cried. "To the ships!" He thrust them toward the strand. "Run!"

Gil heard a shout, looked up, and saw four mounted men gallop over the crest of the nearest ridge. Five more followed, and then, from the opposite side of the little bay and its village, too many more to count.

Then he was running, faster than he'd ever run in his life. Ismail was beside him, and the two Northmen right on their heels. "Sail!" Floki shouted, as they splashed wildly into the sea. The oarsmen leant hard on their oars, and the steersmen swung the dragon prows seaward and the sails bellied full. Erling caught Gil's arms as he struggled to mount the slippery strakes and hauled him on deck. Bjorn plucked Ismail from the sea by his shirt and the seat of his pants. Both ships were ploughing white foam when their masters scrambled back aboard.

Floki looked back, once, at the fast-receding village, and took the steering oar himself. Only when they had rounded two more headlands and the village was but a faint smoke-smudge on the horizon, did he step back, and let Erling hold the course. Danni whispered, "Gil? What happened? Was it Vikings?" He looked at her for a long time, in silence; then he turned his face away.

After that, they seemed to sail with a grimmer purpose, and on that fourth night, they did not put in to the shore, but anchored at a distance from the land, and slept uncomfortably, crowded aboard their ships.

On the fifth day, on a grey winter morning, they came to a low dark island, nestling close to another. The sail was lowered. Oarsmen took their places, and then, as powerful oar strokes drove the bare-masted longships into the island's lee, fields of fresh-tilled earth and green pastures dotted with black cattle appeared, and among them, buildings of wood and stone, enclosed by a stone boundary wall. On a low rise in the center, stood a grey stone, thatched roofed church. A weary cheer rose from the oarsmen as they rested thankful eyes on the safe refuge of the *muinntir* of Hy.

It was more than a day since they'd eaten warm food or dried themselves by a fire. Everything aboard the ship was cold and wet and smelled of ponies and unwashed men. Gil's hair hung in grimy tangles; his eyes stung from sea water. The cloak in which he wrapped himself was stiff with salt spray. He stared hungrily at the snug buildings and tidy fields of the *muinntir*.

The thin blue smoke of turf fires hung above the island and the sweet scent drifted across the sea. Distant figures, all in grey, stopped their work in the fields to stare at the approaching longships. Floki shouted a greeting and the words, carrying clearly across the open water, were answered by a returning shout. Grey-clad figures emerged from doors and hurried in from the fields, in response to the ringing bell. The air was full of the sound of farm animals, caught up in the excitement of their masters. A whole flock of small, four-horned sheep and a cluster of shaggy black goats grazed near the shore. There were chickens and ducks and geese, and somewhere a dog barked.

In a field beyond the church, a herd of bristly-maned ponies, buff and brown and black, galloped around and around, whinnying greetings to their shipboard kin. On the deck of *Silver Dragon*, their own ponies whinnied back. "Look!" said Rachel, patting Frosti, "New friends."

Gil cast a dire look at Lionheart, remembering introducing him to their pack-pony, Lucy. *Oh, great. Your two favorite things: "new" and "friends."* Lionheart's ears flattened and he rolled one white-rimmed eye.

The foreshore of Hy boasted a sturdy stone built jetty, thrusting out into the sea, offering a sheltered mooring on either side. As the longships glided to rest beside it, two lines of grey-habited brothers of Hy waited silently. Erling and Svein tossed ropes down to the jetty. Two of the waiting brothers caught them with seamen's ease.

With both ships firmly moored, Floki turned to his crew, solemnly unbuckled his sword belt and laid it down. There was a muttering among the Northmen, but, one by one, they followed suit. Bjorn's black brows descended and his mustached mouth twitched in a scowl, but he, too, divested himself of his sword, and the axe he carried, tucked through his belt.

Gil took his sword belt to their armor kist, struggling to put the smoldering village from his mind. "Warrior!" Floki shouted. "The Ab of Hy desires your exalted company." Gil turned and stared. *Silver Dragon*'s master waited, one foot on the rail of his ship, bowing flamboyantly to him.

"Mine?"

"For what other purpose have I moored my ship in this holy place? Shall I let the good father hear my confession and give him nightmares in his sleep?"

"I'm coming!" Gil dropped the sword into the kist and pulled out the leather satchel. Slipping the strap over his shoulder, he ran to Floki.

"Ah, the book. The beautiful book, which, alas, I cannot read." Floki grinned and then, ignoring the gangplank the brothers had raised, leapt grandly across the water to the jetty. Gil longed to do the same, but thought better, and trotted meekly down the gangplank, instead.

A lean man with a kindly face stepped forward. He lowered his hood, revealing a fringe of grey-speckled black hair, and bowed gently to Floki. Floki spoke to him in a language that Gil had never heard before. When the man turned to Gil, Gil shook his head. But Rachel ran down to his side and addressed the brother in a seamless flow of Latin, to which, beaming happily, he replied.

Floki grinned and slapped Gil's back. "Have no fear," he said. "A true Northman speaks with his sword."

Danni and Ismail hurried to join them, leading the ponies from their pen. Lionheart whickered and rolled his eyes. Gil ran back up the gangplank and took the pony's lead.

You forgot me.

Gil shook his head. *I will never be so lucky. Please, please, don't make any more of an idiot of me here.* Lionheart reared again at the edge of the gangplank, but then, with an unnerving, scuttling jump, he careered down it, to the jetty. The others followed tamely, behind Danni and Ismail, while Palamedes led his warhorse and Lucy off Hakon's *Storm Serpent*. The animals jostled together on the jetty and Lionheart's ears flicked flat.

Then, suddenly, two very young brothers appeared, their faces boyish, pink-cheeked in the cold, wet air. They smiled at Gil and his friends and, chatting in their strange language, reached at the same time for the ponies' bridles.

Danni handed over Frosti and Freya's lead reins to one of the boy-monks. The other then leapt up onto the charger, Doombearer's, back. Clutching his mane with one hand and digging his barefoot heels into the huge animal's flanks, he reached down and caught up Lucy's and Chocolate's reins, and reached for Lionheart's too. Gil shook his head wildly, but the boy laughed, and holding the leads all in one hand, led the three ponies away. Lionheart followed, docile as a lamb, at Lucy's side.

Aren't you even going to kick her?

After they feed me. Lionheart flicked sly ears and trotted past.

The lean man who had first spoken to Gil led them from the shore toward the church, halting at the foot of a small, grassy rise. A wooden hut, scarce bigger than Gil's own little cell at Cille Aidan, perched on its rocky summit, a wisp of blue smoke rising above. With a silent bow, the lean monk stepped aside, and gestured for the children to go on alone. Gil tucked Aidan's gift tighter under his arm, squared his shoulders, and mounted the rocky path.

The route led them to the side of the hut, which was blank-walled and windowless. Gil cautiously rounded a corner, and then another, before finding a wicker door, propped open with a stick, letting in the faint wash of winter sunlight. Out of the doorway flew four white doves. In a whirr of white wings, three of the birds fluttered over their heads, but one struck out alone, across the island, toward the grey glint of the sea.

From within the tiny building, a voice spoke, in soft English. "Here are three who will come and go and one who will stay forever. Come!" proclaimed the voice happily. "Come! Have I not waited since Saint Lucy's Day, for your coming?"

Rachel's brows drew close in puzzlement, but Gil ducked warily through the low door, and stood peering blindly into the darkness. Gradually, shapes grew out of the smoky haze. A blackened oil lamp glowed above a plain table strewn with books. A carved wooden cross hung on one wall, a little bench for kneeling set beneath it. At the back of the room, a turf fire burned, and in the smoky shadows beside it, sat an old, old man in the robes of the brothers of Hy.

His face was craggy and lined. His hair, where it wasn't shaved short, was a pure, snowy white; so, too, the beard that reached almost to the rope belt of his habit. But his brows were thick and black, and beneath them, his eyes, blacker still, glowed like coals as, unblinking, they probed Gil's face and that of each of his companions.

The old man's right hand lay motionless on his knees. His left rested gently on the tall, carved *bachall* that leant against his low chair. Somehow, here, it seemed like the staff of a king, and the white-haired monk looked as Gil imagined a king would look, indeed, a king like Arthur. Very slowly then, the Ab set the *bachall* aside and reached out the hand that had held it to Gil, keeping his other resting on his knees. The craggy face broke into a smile. "I beg you, forgive my little brother. He rises with me to sing the Night Office, but he is yet young, and so now is weary, and must sleep."

With a gentle gesture he indicated his right sleeve. Gil suddenly saw, nestled within the folds of the worn grey cloth, a tiny kitten, as grey as the cloth itself, curled contentedly asleep. "Oh!" Danni shrieked, "Look!"

Rachel rushed forward, brushing Gil aside. "There's more!" She pointed to a frayed wicker basket beside the fire. Both girls ran to the fireside and knelt beside the basket, lifting kittens out and passing them back and forth. When even Ismail joined in, crawling under the Ab's table to capture a small striped beast, Gil shrugged and bent down and picked up a black one that was climbing his leg anyhow.

"Yet another takes his rest upon my books." The Ab pointed to one more, white and grey, that was sprawled across the pages of an open volume on the table. "In all, there are seven. And even now their mother makes happy converse with their father, once again." He smiled and added drily, "Would that the minds of my scholars were as fertile."

Gil grinned and rubbed the black kitten's ears. But then, even as he did, he felt a sudden alarming urge to bat it with a paw, roll it over a few times, and chase it into a corner.

That's awful! I'd never do that! That would really scare it!

They need to be scared. It's good for them. The Cat hairs at the nape of his neck rose and he felt the twitch of a phantom tail.

Gil dumped the kitten in Rachel's lap. "Here, you take it!"

The Ab spoke suddenly. "Come," he said. His voice was sad and regretful. "Gladly would I have you play with kittens forever. But you have been called to a darker game. Come, let me see you." His face fell solemn as they lined up in front of him, Danni yet clutching a kitten in her hands. Then, as they stood there, he closed his eyes as if, somehow, he saw them better that way. He was silent for a long while and then, when he spoke, his voice was soft and distant. "A pure soul, a clear eye, a loving heart, and true courage. These four are all that are needed."

He opened his eyes and they crinkled as he smiled, but there was sadness in the smile, too. "But still, you are very young." He leaned forward. "Do you understand why you are here?" he asked suddenly.

"To bring the Holy Grail to King Arthur," Danni said at once, meeting his gaze with her bold brown eyes.

"And Arthur back to your world," said Rachel.

"But why?" pursued the Ab. "Why do this?"

"For peace?" Ismail murmured cautiously. "That war ends?"

"Ah. For peace indeed." The Ab's old face creased kindly, "Well spoken, young soldier. For peace cannot be – not in our world, nor in yours – until Arthur returns. But before peace," he shook his head slowly, "There is the sword."

He sighed and looked very solemn. Then he leaned forward, again, still careful not to disturb the kitten curled on his sleeve. "Do you understand the danger you are in?" he asked intently. "How lawless the land to which you travel?" Gil thought of the burnt village and nodded. "How heartless and cruel your adversary?" The Ab spoke with such intensity that Gil's confidence wavered. But again, he nodded and said, "Yes."

"Even here," the old man said urgently, "You are not safe. The Usurper respects neither man nor God, though he makes pretense to win favor when it suits him. Beyond our boundary wall, all pretense ends. Once you leave here, you leave all protection behind. Do you understand?"

For a third time, Gil nodded and bowed his head.

"Very well," the Ab said, and when Gil looked up, he thought he saw approval, as well as sorrow, in the old man's eyes. "This last answer, I must have." His gaze drifted across each of their faces. "Do you take up this task with a free heart? Do you go willingly into this danger?"

Gil straightened his back, looked once into the eyes of each of his friends, and saw there the same fear and the same resolve. "Yes," he said. "I do. We do."

The Ab's eyes locked with his own and Gil felt the old man could see right into his heart and mind, uncovering every secret. But then the old monk smiled and said firmly, "So be it then. The guardians do not look for perfection, but the willingness to seek it. You will go.

"But first," he added, his mood visibly lightening, "You must accept our hospitality. The Dark Time has come, and with it comes the holy day of Our Lord's Nativity. Then, our fast ends and you will share with us our great feast. Meanwhile, provisions will be made ready and your horses shod. Then, shielded by our prayers, you will set out at the end of Christmastide. A fortuitous time for a fateful journey." He stroked his sleeping kitten solemnly, his face set in lines of sorrow. But the panic that welled in Gil's heart had another cause. Horses? Shod? Lionheart? Shod?

Then the Ab inclined his white head, and a smile twitched at the corners of his mouth. "It is long years since I was a child," he said. "But there is a thing that I remember. Children are always hungry. Nor have they any need of fasting, since the mere hours between breakfast and the midday meal are heavy penance. And so," he said, his smile broadening, "Just as soon as your sails were sighted, tables were made ready, and even now groan with as much hearty fare as our island can provide."

He grew solemn again. "But I have asked you many questions. And you have answered most fairly. Are there questions, now, that you would ask of me in return?"

Gil's mind was too full of the prospect of food to think of anything else, but Rachel's voice rang out clearly in the little room. "How did you know," she asked, "That we set sail on Saint Lucy's Day?"

"Ah," the old man leaned back, his dark eyes assessing Rachel shrewdly. At last, he said, "Now, what better day would you have set out into darkness? Santa Lucia, whose very name means 'light'?" He paused, still studying Rachel. "Will that suffice as an answer?"

"Yes," she said politely, "But not to my question."

The Ab erupted in a peal of laughter, somehow too rich and vigorous to come from such an ancient body. "Here is one not to be trifled with," he said gleefully. Then he indicated the door, standing open, behind them, "This little house has a most pleasant outlook, has it not?" They all turned then, and Gil saw that the open doorway framed a wonderful view of sea and sky, green island and white surf. "And from this little house," the Ab said gently, "When I look out over the sea, sometimes I do see wondrously far."

As far as Einar's Holm? Gil wondered, but then Ismail spoke, in his soft, hesitant voice. "May I ask a question, too?"

"Most certainly," said the Ab. His dark gaze rested intently on the African boy. "And having learned my lesson with your sister of the clear eye, I promise to answer as worthily as I can." He bowed his head humbly toward Ismail, and Ismail bowed respectfully back.

"The guardians," he said. "They ask only we seek perfection?"

"That is so," said the Ab.

"But who is it, who asks?" Ismail said, his eyes wide with uncertainty. "Always we hear of them, but never are we told who they are."

"Who are the guardians?" The old man's dark brows arched in amazement.

"Forgive me," Ismail said. "I know little. I am never at school."

The old man shook his head, smiling curiously. "But why do you ask me? Surely it would be wise to ask them?"

Ismail's eyes remained, trustingly, on the Ab's face, but he shook his head slowly. "How do we ask them," he said, "When we do not know them?"

"You have known them and you will again." The Ab's eyes crinkled with gentle mischief, but he said no more. Somewhere nearby, a bell rang. The old man rose, still cradling the sleeping kitten on his sleeve. "Ah, little brother," he addressed it, "The bell rings the ninth hour, and I must join my monks, and so your sleep is at an end." With that, he scooped it up with his free hand and deposited it in the basket, where it sat blinking aggrievedly at its abandonment. "How wisely our Good Lord fashions the world," he said, "that an Ab must beg favor of a kitten, and thus be reminded of his place." He took up his *bachall* and stepped toward the open door and the children all followed him.

"Wait!" Gil cried. He pulled the leather satchel in front of him. "Aidan sent this for you."

"Then I must see it, at once." The old man smiled gently and, ignoring the ringing bell, took the satchel from him with a small bow, and then carried it to the table, laid it down, and withdrew the contents. "Ah," he murmured, stroking the silver banded, gilded cover, "Here indeed is a treasure." Rachel, Danni, and Ismail pressed forward to see. Rachel looked accusingly at Gil, for keeping the book hidden, even from her.

"It was a secret," he muttered.

"At least I could read it!" she whispered.

The Ab drew her forward. "Look now." Reverently he opened the book, displaying the first wondrously colored page. The Ab's old eyes studied the script hungrily, his lips gently moving as he read. The bell outside rang on, and he straightened suddenly. "I must go." He turned to Gil, "My heartfelt thanks to brother Aidan for this great treasure, and to you for bearing it here."

"It's for letting us stay here," Gil murmured awkwardly.

The old man smiled. "But we shelter you as we shelter all, by our Lord's command. As well my brother knows. Besides," he added quietly, "we all make common cause." He paused, serious for a moment, but his eyes crinkled with amusement. "Still, I am most honored to accept this great gift which has eluded both salt sea and marauding Northmen, to come to Hy."

Gil nodded, glad to have fulfilled his promise to Aidan. He stepped back to allow the Ab to pass, and then followed his friends out into the darkening day. Only when he was standing once more before the little hut, did he realize that the old man, striding away toward his church, had again spoken of things he could not possibly have seen.

Several of the monks followed their Ab to the church, but the lean man who had spoken first remained below, with two others, beside Hakon, Floki, and Palamedes, while the rest of the Northmen sat, cloak-wrapped, in patient huddles on the ground. One of the three figures was slender and female, wearing a dress and tunic of the plain grey of the brothers' habits, and, over her head, a white veil.

When he reached the waiting escort, Gil saw the woman was quite old, with a gentle face and bright blue eyes. Rachel was attempting a halting conversation but the woman knew no English, and Rachel's Latin wasn't working too well, either. At last, the woman pointed away to a distant thatched building on the low horizon, then placed her palms together. Resting her cheek on the back of one hand, she closed her eyes, produced two loud snoring sounds, and then collapsed in a wave of giggles.

"I've got it!" Danni cried. "We sleep there!" She pointed to the faraway buildings. "Come on," she grabbed Gil's arm and dragged him forward. "She wants to show us where we sleep." But a look of horror crossed the veiled woman's face and she cried out in her own language, raising her hands comically to thrust Gil away.

Ismail laughed. "No," he said to Danni, shaking his head. "You sleep there."

"They're nuns, Danni," Rachel added wearily. "It's a convent."

Gil smothered a laugh. Then, someone tapped his shoulder. He turned and saw that the young monk, who had boldly ridden Doombearer, had returned. His companion ran to join them, too, and both chatted happily at Gil and Ismail in the indecipherable language of Hy. Ismail pointed helplessly to their translator, on the path to the convent with Danni and their nun. Gil's heart sank. He tapped his chest, grinned determinedly, and announced, "I'm Gil." He pointed to Ismail. "He's Ismail."

The young monk looked puzzled for only a split second. Then his freckled face brightened and his blue eyes sparkled with recognition. He pointed to his own chest and said, "Ciarnan," and then, turning to his companion, who was taller and darker, with sharp brown eyes, he declared, "Donal." He waggled his finger back and forth between them, and said, "Cousins!"

It was soon clear to Gil that although Ciarnan's English was pretty basic, and Donal's non-existent, both boys were accustomed to a world of many tongues and skilled at signs and mime. Using both, they shepherded Gil and Ismail before them, gesturing to Hakon and Floki and Palamedes and all the Northmen, to follow.

They passed the church, from which came beautiful singing, and went on until the whole party was gathered around a stone building surmounted by a great cloud of blue turf smoke. Gil breathed in the sweet scent of the burning peat, and better still, the rich aroma of roasting meat.

Wide plank doors stood open at the front of the building, revealing a great cooking fire set into a stone rimmed pit. Beneath soot-crusted roof beams, a pair of massive bearded monks turned a spit laden with meat and stirred the bubbling contents of giant black cooking pots. Delicious baking smells rose from griddle loads of golden bannocks.

The Northmen all grinned at each other and muttered happily of feasting. But Floki laughed. "Tighten your belts and reef in your tunics, my good friends," he said. "This is not Odin's longhouse, but a Christian one, and they are fasting, as is their tiresome habit. You'll wait till Christ's Mass for your meat."

And, indeed, while Gil and Ismail were served a rich bounty of mutton, cheese, butter, honey, and ale, the rest received bowls of thin broth and dry bannocks for their meal. Morose Northmen swallowed their soup in single gulps and sniffed suspiciously at wooden mugs of water. Even the young monks, Ciarnan and Donal, who couldn't be much older than themselves, kept their fast. Gil stuffed down his meat and cheese as quickly as he could, and, grinning guiltily at Floki, sipped his ale.

"Oh, for the pagan halls of our fathers," Floki murmured in response. And, elaborately marking Lord Yesu's sign across his forehead and chest, he raised his meagre soup bowl and drained it dry. Still, after the meal, he set his crew to work clearing a field of stones, in return for the monks' hospitality, while Gil and Ismail explored the *muinntir* with their two young guides.

Ciarnan dragged them into the shadowy interior of the church and Donal proudly showed off his own place in the two parallel rows of benches before the lamp lit altar. Raising his hood, he seated himself in a dramatically prayerful posture, until Ciarnan punched him, and they both broke into giggles and fled with their guests, out the door.

Looking warily over their shoulders for disapproving elders, the boys showed them the refectory, with two long tables awaiting the monks' common meals and the scriptorium where a dozen brothers worked, too intent on their writing to notice the intrusion. A long, narrow building, with rows of straw mattresses laid on the floor, served as the monks' dormitory. But, in the guesthouse across the courtyard, wooden platforms raised the modest beds above the cold stone. Gil's sheepskin roll of clothing already lay on the foot of one, and Ismail's on another.

A row of stone and wood plank sheds stood beyond the cobbled courtyard. At one, a monk scraped a stretched animal hide. Beneath the thatched roof of another, a red-haired brother skinned bark from a tree-trunk with an axe.

The last in the line of workshops was a weaver's shed and, beyond, another stone building stood alone, hazed in smoke like the kitchen. When they drew closer, Gil glimpsed the flickering of a huge fire and heard a fearsome ringing of metal on metal, like the clash of a hundred swords. Through the open door he saw a sweat-soaked, mighty-armed brother, hammering a red-hot horseshoe against a black anvil. Beside him, a great, shadowy plough horse stood placidly enduring the trial by fire that waited soon for Lionheart.

Past the fiery forge, they joined a faint path that passed through a gap in the boundary wall and climbed onward to the highest point of the island where, from a windswept, grassy hill, they could see all of the *muinntir* spread out below: fields and farm buildings, turf cuttings and pasture, and the rambling stone wall that enclosed it all. Gil looked beyond, taking in the whole island from shore to shore; the crashing surf of the wild Western Sea on one side, the Sound sheltering their longships on the other.

On the hill's very summit stood a great stone cross, carved all over with birds and animals, ships and chariots, angels and men. Ciarnan leaned against it, clutching the wind-blown fabric of his habit tight around himself. He held up his hand to the cloud-cloaked setting sun and traced its course across the sky and then held up one index finger. He pointed at a carved stone ship on the cross and made the same two gestures.

"A day's sail?" Ismail guessed quietly.

Then Ciarnan pointed into the darkening mist and said, "Eire. Ireland." He indicated himself, with a tap on his own chest and then Donal.

"It's where they come from," Gil said and Ismail answered him, "One day's sail."

Ciarnan gazed toward the invisible land with such wistful longing on his young face that Gil understood instantly. *He's homesick. Like us.* Quickly, he made the "one day" gesture, himself, then indicated Ciarnan and Donal, and then pointed down to the *muinntir.* Holding several fingers in the air, he raised his eyebrows questioningly.

Ciarnan looked baffled, but Donal jumped in then, grinning, and mimed first, digging in the ground, then casting seed, then swinging a scythe, and last, kneeling down, warming his hands by a fire. Looking up, he smiled and held up one forefinger. Ismail shouted, "Yes! Plough, sow, harvest, fallow. One year." He grinned at Ciarnan and nodded vigorously.

Ciarnan smiled. He raised all the fingers of both hands, curled them into fists, and then raised six, again. Then he pointed at Donal. "Sixteen!" Gil said. "Donal's sixteen." Ciarnan smiled again and repeated the finger-counting but stopped at fifteen and pointed to himself. "And Ciarnan's fifteen," Gil said to Ismail. Quickly he counted off fourteen fingers for himself, and for Ismail, too.

They stood in a ring, then, smiling. Then Ciarnan nodded solemnly, and pointed again at the stone cross, this time to a crowned figure of a man. "Pater," he said, then hesitantly, "Father?" And he pointed sadly to the mist that hid Ireland. Then Gil understood that Ciarnan's father was an Irish king, but Ciarnan missed him the same as any boy missed his father. The same as Gil missed his own.

Below, the bell of the *muinntir* began to ring and the Irish boys looked at each other in alarm. Turning to Gil and Ismail, they made prayerful postures and pointed urgently down the hill. Gil grinned. But he wanted to stay in this high, windy place a little longer. So, he did the prayer thing himself, then shook his head and sat down on the ground below the stone cross. At once, Donal sat down, too. Smiling happily up at Ciarnan, he pointed toward the ringing bell and shook his own head. But Ciarnan reached down and hauled him back up onto his feet. Grinning and waving, he dragged his reluctant cousin away to his monastic duties.

The bell chimed a last time, and then Gil and Ismail were alone with only the sounds of the wind and the distant sea. Gil stood up again, and they walked together along the top of the low grassy rise, enjoying the feel of dry land beneath their feet. Gil stopped a hundred feet from the stone cross, looked back at it, and then out to sea and the veil of mist. "Ships must sail to Ireland all the time," he said to Ismail. "Why do they stay?"

"Because they make vow," Ismail said simply. "Like we make vow."

Gil nodded. They had vowed to Aidan, and now to the Ab of Hy, that they would make their quest. Most of all, they had vowed to each other and to themselves. Still, he wondered if any vow would keep him here if he too were but a day's sail from home. But the sea that lay between him and Greene Mountain Falls was wider than any in all this world. *Three who will come and go.* He heard the Ab's strange words again. *And one who will stay forever.*

"What if it isn't Danni?" he said suddenly, to Ismail. Ismail shook his head, confused. "What the Ab said, about us...or the birds...."

"About us," Ismail said. "The birds are like Aidan's stone. He sees us."

Gil nodded, uneasily. "So, one of us will stay."

"Perhaps." Ismail kicked a loose stone, then looked up, out to sea.

"Would you mind?" Gil said. "If it were you, would you mind staying? You'd be fine here," he added quickly. "You know how to live here, better than all of us."

"I have sister, brother," Ismail said.

"But," Gil shrugged awkwardly, "If you didn't. If there was no one...." Ismail's eyes narrowed, as if in pain, and Gil was sorry, at once, he had said it.

But then Ismail answered, "If there was no one; this is beautiful world."

"Oh, yes," Gil said softly, looking over the soft green island and the dark, mysterious sea, and thinking of all the wild, empty land he had seen from the deck of *Silver Dragon*. *I could stay*, he thought suddenly. It was like opening a window in his heart and seeing a part of himself he had not known existed. Immediately, he was swamped with guilt.

Mom's there. All alone. Still looking for me like we looked for Dad. No time has passed. A day. Two, three. It's all new, fresh.... But as much as he said it, he couldn't feel it. The months that had passed and the things he had seen and done were real. And they were like a wide sea, too, opening between him and home.

Below, in the dusky pastures, a cow lowed mournfully. Gil saw Ismail wince. "The sound of the village," he murmured.

Ismail smiled sadly. "The sound of *my* village," he said. "Believers come. Kill everything. People, goats, chickens, cattle. All dead. One cow, alone, her calf dead, her udder full...it is sound of my village, too, when all are dead."

He remembered how Ismail had wept as he told his story to Aidan. And then he remembered something else. "'John,'" he said. Ismail's face whipped around, his eyes widening with dismay. "You said your name was John. And Aidan said...."

"It is Believers' name. They say I must have Christian name."

"Christian?" Gil whispered. "The Believers were Christian?"

Ismail shrugged. "The jackal may call himself lion. It does not give him mane."

"But this place!" Gil pointed at the tall stone cross, his anger growing, "The Ab. Aidan! They're all Christians. And Christians killed your parents?"

"Aidan did not kill my parents," Ismail said. "Nor anyone here."

Gil stared silently at his friend, trying to subdue the waves of anger surging through him. At last, he muttered, "I don't think I could ever be that forgiving."

Ismail raised his eyes and coolly met Gil's. "You do not forgive, you become jackal, too." Gil stepped back. Ismail smiled gently. He sat down on the ground and beckoned Gil to sit, too. After an awkward pause, Gil joined him. They sat cross-legged, like little kids, their cloaks wrapped around themselves for warmth, both looking out to the endless Western Sea.

"I am nine when Believers come, first." Ismail said in his soft voice, "They take me from village. Say, I am soldier now. Christian now. Must say Christian prayers. But I am little kid. Carry gun all day, but cry at night for mother, father. Say Believers' prayers. But in here," he touched his chest, "I keep old prayers, too. But sometimes, now, I forget words. So, I pray and I hope my father with Allah. And he say, Allah, that is my son. He not clever. But I not there to teach...." He stopped talking, suddenly. Tears streaked his face, but he grinned and jumped up. "Hey, I am hungry again. Maybe time for supper?"

Gil did not move. "The pure soul," he said. Ismail cocked his head quizzically. "The pure soul. The Ab said four things: a clear eye, a loving heart, a pure soul, and true courage. Those were the four things we needed for the quest. And Rachel has the clear eye, and Danni must have the loving heart. And you – I think you have all four, really, but most of all, you must be the one with the pure soul."

Ismail shook his head. "No," he said. His eyes were dark.

"Yes." Gil stood up. "It's you. Nobody could forgive like that...."

"No," Ismail said again. "It is not me!" And when Gil opened his mouth to argue, he lowered his voice, and touching his hand again to his chest, whispered, "In here is secret. You know this secret, you not my friend. Never be my friend again."

"No," Gil said. He stepped back again. "That's not true! Whatever you say, I'll be your friend. I'm your friend forever."

Ismail shook his head with certainty. "No. You see what is in here, you will not be. You do not know."

Gil stared at the African boy, bewildered. His hands balled into fists, and then, unclenching them, he lunged forward and shoved Ismail back with his palms. "Don't tell me!" he shouted, and he shoved him again. "Don't tell me I don't know what I think. Don't treat me like a little kid. Just because your life has been harder than mine. Okay, I come from a rich country and kids don't have to be soldiers…." He dropped his hands to his sides, realizing Ismail would let him shove him all day and not fight back. "But still," he whispered, "I lost my father, too."

"But he is not dead," Ismail said, puzzled. "You find his knife."

Gil shook his head wearily. "His knife which had been here twenty years. Twenty years alone in this place?" He shrugged hopelessly.

"Maybe not alone," Ismail said cautiously. "We make friends. Ciarnan and Donal are friends. Maybe he make friends, too?"

The words hit Gil like a double thunderclap. First, the shock of the idea itself: that his father, too, might have found people to live with, might have changed and learned things and grown used to being here, just as he had. And second, the shock of knowing he didn't want it to be true. For if, in a handful of months, a treacherous love for this world had grown in his own heart, what of his father? Gil turned his back on Ismail and strode away.

"Wait!" Ismail called.

Gil stopped and looked back. His friend was silhouetted against the pale sky, a slim, wind-whipped figure beside the great stone cross. He hesitated, then turned again and began to run, away from Ismail, away from the *muinntir*, away from everyone, stumbling blindly toward the white seaward strand.

He only stopped when the surf was crashing at his feet. Sweating and breathing hard, he heard Ismail's cautious footsteps on the wet sand, following a respectful distance behind.

"Don't pretend you couldn't have caught me in the first ten feet," he said.

"Hunter does not try to catch in ten feet," Ismail answered softly, at his back. "Hunter lets animal run. Then tries to catch."

Gil grinned wryly and flopped down on the white beach, just above the high tide line. "Well, this animal has run." He lay on his back, staring at the winter sky. His hand brushed the bone handle of the knife at his belt. He withdrew it from its sheath and held it up, catching the cold sea light.

"What happens if we stay here really long?" he said. "Like, this whole thing takes years. We grow up here, even."

"Like, twenty years?" Ismail said. Gil looked quickly, but Ismail was staring at the grey and white sea.

"Yeah, maybe."

"Your father does not forget you," Ismail said.

"I was talking about us."

"But he does not. He remembers forever. He is your father. He never forgets. Whatever world."

Gil flopped back on the sand. When he sat up, he slid the knife back into its sheath.

The beach was scattered with small green pebbles. He gathered a clutch of them and then stood and tossed them, one by one, splashing into the sea. He looked out, beyond where they fell, to the West, where Tir nan Og was meant to be. He kept the last, smooth and cool, in his fingers and put it in his pocket. "You were wrong," he said. Ismail's look was guarded. "I will be your friend. Always. In any world."

Far away, the bell of Hy called evening in. Together with the African boy, Gil set out across the island for prayers.

CHAPTER TWO

By Christmas Eve, Gil and Ismail had roamed every foot of the island, exploring all its low hills, every shining beach. But they never saw Danni or Rachel. Secluded behind the convent's forbidden boundary wall, they were as unreachable as if yet at Cille Aidan.

Each day, Floki set his Northmen to work for the monks building an oratory, a little prayer house, between the graveyard and the sea. When Gil and Ismail strayed too close, they found themselves hauling barrows of stone through sleet and snow. Gil rubbed freezing hands against his tunic before lifting each stone. Bjorn and two of Hakon's Shetlanders were setting roof beams in place. Floki stood on an overturned barrow, chipping at the doorway's lintel stone with a mallet and chisel.

A burly man with a forked, braided beard unloaded a rumbling heap of boulders beside Gil. "Slave's work," he muttered loudly. Gil said nothing. He was happy to do something for Hy, though he had heard the Northmen grumbling about the labor, the meagre meals, the lack of ale. "I am oarsman," the man announced. "Swordsman." He cast a pointed glance at Floki. "Who sails to build prayer houses?" Floki's lips twitched in a smile, but he continued chipping at his stone. The man leaned over and gave Floki a little shove. "When I sail with your father...."

Floki dropped his mallet and chisel, leapt down from the barrow, caught the grumbling Northman by his plaited beard and flung him back against the newly built wall. Pinning him there with his sinewy forearm against his throat, he released the man's beard and gestured toward the graveyard. "Where would you lie, this winter, Freystein," he whispered, "Beside pretty Helga? Or beside the bones of monks?" The man struggled, gagged, and pointed frantically at his throat. Floki eased his grip. "Answer!"

"Helga," The man wheezed. "Helga."

Floki released him. "Then build prayer houses." The Northman stumbled back to work, rubbing his throat. Floki took up his mallet and chisel and climbed back onto the barrow. "You sail with me, now, Freystein," he said with a smile.

Gil crept cautiously back to his heap of boulders. Floki watched him and then laughed. "They work hard, Warrior," he said, "And then they sleep hard; before they dream of their women and the treasures they think lie in that church." He nodded toward the monks' chapel. Then he gave Gil's head a friendly cuff, caught him by the back of his tunic, the way a cat might catch a kitten, and hauled him up onto the barrow. "What think you of my hand work?" he said.

A row of neatly chiseled marks marched across the lintel stone; straight lines, branched lines, lines set at angles. "Runes?" Gil said, remembering Shony's stones.

Floki grinned and tracing his finger left to right, read out: "Floki Magnusson Made This"

"Will they like that?" Gil said uneasily.

Floki shrugged. "I think they cannot read it, any more than I can read their Latin. And, if they can, they will pray all the harder, knowing I was here." He laughed again, slapped Gil's shoulder, and looked up. Ciarnan and Donal approached warily. "Your holy brethren seek you," he said. "Shall we be proper Northmen and murder them, or shall we be friends?"

Gil winced, but then Floki called to the two boy monks in their own language and their faces broke into grins. They chatted happily with him in the Irish tongue, and Floki turned back to Gil and Ismail and translated. "Go with them. Your horses will be shod now, for your journey."

Gil and Ismail followed the Irish boys to the ponies' field. Gil remembered the clash of iron, the red-hot metal, and the flying sparks of the blacksmith's fire. "Does it hurt, shoeing horses?" he whispered.

"Not unless they kick you," Ismail grinned. But when they got to the field, Lionheart was not among the herd of animals gathered companionably at the gate.

"He's gone!" Gil cried.

"Not far," Ismail smiled. "It is island. Small island."

Gil paced the field, scrambling through mist-drenched gorse bushes and clambering over stone outcrops, and found no small buff-colored pony. He remembered the dead foal in the burnt village, and wild imaginings arose, of raiders and wolves and horrible heaps of pony hair and bloodied bones. And then he glimpsed the pale, buff-colored thing, low down on the ground, beside the grey boundary stones. "Lionheart," he whispered. Struggling through the gorse and brambles, he forced himself to look. Before him a very whole and alive Lionheart chomped grass at the bottom of a pony-deep ditch. He glared down in exasperation. *Didn't you hear me?*

The pony stopped munching. He flattened his ears and dropped his head and hunched his back. His tail drooped in abject misery. *You forgot me.* Press-ganged by Floki, Gil hadn't checked the ponies this morning.

Ciarnan and Donal looked after you, he said guiltily.

They beat me. With sticks. Lionheart hunched his back rounder, looking as if someone was beating him still.

Gil turned with dismay, to where Ciarnan and Ismail were rounding up the other ponies. He took one furious step toward the distant Irish boy, but then he stopped and looked carefully at Lionheart. *Show me where he hit you.*

All over.

You don't look hurt.

I'm furry. I'm hurt under my fur. Lionheart edged backwards out of his ditch and scrambled agilely up onto the bank, before resuming his beaten pony pose. He raised his head, and, seeing Ciarnan and Ismail gathering the ponies together, shook his mane in fright. *There!*

Each of the boys held their arms out wide and in his left hand Ciarnan held a long, thin switch, which he tapped lightly along the ground. Ahead of him, Chocolate, Freya, and Frosti trotted placidly. *That?* Gil stared, disbelieving. *That's the stick?*

He turned his back in disgust and walked away. *We're going now.*

The ship! I hate the ship!

Not the ship. The blacksmith.

Aware that Lionheart had never seen a blacksmith, Gil slid the bridle over his head, and held on tight as they made their way to the distant, smoke-shrouded forge. Ciarnan and Donal led the first pony in. Gil broke into a run.

Behind him, Lionheart launched into a happy trot, chanting, *Not the ship! Not the ship!* to the rhythm of his own unshod feet. Then suddenly he gave a loud whinny and the lead rein jerked tight around Gil's wrist, pulling him half off his feet. Lionheart pranced backwards, eyes rolling wildly. *Fire!* He shook his mane and pulled at the lead.

Gil saw the glow of the blacksmith's great fire, flickering and fierce, even in the morning light. He stepped closer to the terrified pony and patted his neck. *It's okay. It's safe fire. It's in a pen.*

Lionheart pressed his nose against Gil's chest. *I want my field.* Gil sighed and rubbed his ears. Ismail appeared, and undoing his headband of rough cloth, retied it carefully around Lionheart's face, covering both eyes. The pony stood quite still. *Night happened.* He didn't seem at all surprised.

"Fine," Gil said aloud. "Whatever makes you happy."

When he reached the forge with his blindfolded pony, Donal was holding Freya, while the blacksmith hammered a glowing horseshoe with great clanging blows. Lionheart jumped a foot in the air, broke free of Gil's hold and careened backwards, into Frosti and Chocolate. Chocolate lashed out with a hind hoof, just missing Ismail's leg. Frosti shied into Lucy and Ciarnan struggled to hold both.

Gil backed Lionheart out the open door and led him, still blindfolded, up the hill. The ringing of the blacksmith's hammer faded. The pony stopped trembling. He blew air through his nose, shook his mane, and bent one rear leg, shifting his weight comfortably onto the other. Lowering his nose to the ground, he leaned gently against Gil. *Are you going to sleep?*

It's night, Lionheart snuffled contentedly.

Gil jerked the blindfold off. *Right,* he said to the blinking pony, *Now it's day. And we're going to talk.* Lionheart turned his head, saw the fire again, and flicked his ears back and forth. Gil grabbed one ear. *Right. You're scared of the fire. And the ship. And the sea. And Doombearer's feet. And now you're scared of the blacksmith. Well, hear this:* He drew the ear down and whispered right into it. *I do not care. You are going to get shod. We're going through the forest and over the mountains and there are no roads and no nice soft Cille Aidan grass, but lots of big, pointy rocks. And if you don't have shoes on, your hooves will fall off and your legs will wear down to your kneecaps and you'll look even stupider than you do now!*

Lionheart rolled a wary eye back and flicked his free ear. Gil grabbed it and holding both, pulled the pony's face close to his own. *Now. We are going to the blacksmith. You are getting a shoe on every one of your stupid feet.* Lionheart lowered his head, pulled both ears free and flattened them, mean as a snake. *Or I ride Lucy and you are a pack horse.*

Lionheart kept his ears flat for a long, silent moment, then one flicked up and then the other. *Can I have night back?*

Deal, said Gil. He put the blindfold back on and Lionheart stepped meekly behind him and followed him back to the forge. Donal and Ismail pushed him sideways and Gil and Ciarnan worked together to lift one leg. Lionheart stood trembling haplessly on the remaining three, while the blacksmith hammered the glowing metal into shape. *I want my tree.*

Four feet later, Gil led Lionheart back to the field, patted his neck, fed him an apple, and released him with the others. He danced away skittishly into the dusk, his new shoes striking sparks off the stones.

Looking down, then, on the sheltered Sound and the longships brooding by the pier, Gil saw the Northmen's fires flickering into life. The wind had risen again and rain fell in murky sheets. For all their grumbling, they would be glad not to be out on the wild Irish Sea.

At Vespers, the mist rolled in from the Sound, swallowing the hills, and by the last hour, Compline, the *muinntir* was wrapped in a black shroud. Gil and Ismail found the church only by following the ringing bell. Shivering in the damp cold, backs aching from the prayer house stones, they stumbled gratefully afterwards back to their beds.

But then the bell rang once again, dragging Gil from a dreamless sleep. With a groan, he pulled his sheepskin tighter. A rough hand jerked it off and a familiar laugh answered his protest. "Floki?" Gil muttered. "Is it morning already?"

"It is midnight, friend. And our holy hosts are again at their unending prayers. Not even Lord Yesu can find peace in this place."

Outside, the sky had cleared and the night was starry and mild. The Milky Way shone like a pearly river through the stars, so brilliant that Gil could see his shadow on the ground. As the *muinntir*'s brethren hurried silently to their church, a formless dark wave of Northmen shuffled up from the shore.

Two flickering points of red wound down from the distant convent; two brothers carrying flaring torches either side of a column of nuns. Gil looked eagerly for Danni and Rachel among the white veils glimmering in the dancing light. But when the party arrived in the cobbled courtyard before the church, a woman at the front caught his, and everyone's attention.

She was tall and slender, with a beautiful pale face and though her brown hair was half-concealed by a white veil, she was clearly not a nun. Her rich clothing glowed in jewel colors in the torchlight; a dress of deep green velvet beneath a crimson hooded cloak, trimmed with glistening black fur. The white veil was held firm by a circlet of gold, and her fingers, clutching her cloak, glittered with jeweled rings.

The Northmen crowded closer, muttering their admiration. Floki silenced them with a sharp word and shoved two aside as the woman moved toward the door. Then, suddenly, she stopped and stood staring intently at Gil. She spoke softly and the torchbearers came so close that Gil felt the warmth of the flames on his face. The woman reached and touched his cheek. "It is you!" she cried wonderingly. "The Knight of the River!" A murmur of surprised interest swept the watching Northmen.

Gil stammered, "I'm just Gil. Gil Lake."

The woman smiled. "Alas, she did not know your name, but, oh, she knew your face!" She touched his cheek again. "And remembered it and told of it, as only a lover can. I would know you anywhere."

"Warrior!" Floki laughed delightedly behind him. "You are found out! Confess yourself, now. A whole *muinntir* listens!"

The bell rang, then, a final peal. The woman stepped hurriedly back to the waiting nuns. "We must go now, and hear Christ's Mass." Her eyes returned to Gil. "But come to the High Cross at the ninth hour, tomorrow, and I will tell you how bravely she pledges her troth!"

"Who?" Gil shouted after her. She looked back and shook her head with a puzzled laugh, as if she thought he teased her.

"Why, your own sweet, devoted lady," she cried. "My brother's daughter, the Lady Janetta de Troye."

"Wait!" Gil called, but she was gone into the candle-glimmer of the church, the nuns hurrying after. Danni and Rachel, swept along in their ranks, cast him looks of amazement as they passed.

The last of the Northmen had entered the church when Gil shook off enough of his confusion to follow. As he stepped beneath the stone lintel, a great voice spoke from the darkness, "You are greatly honored."

Sir Palamedes' white smile glinted in the starlight. "She is the Lady Griselle, widow of the noble knight, Sir Ewaine, who died most valiantly for Arthur." He glanced toward the church where the monks' voices rose in song. "When kings fall, those who serve them face a harsh reckoning. She chose exile. Her brother, a less honorable course. Go, and pray for them both."

On Christmas Day, when the great feast was finished and the prayers of None sung, Gil bolted for the hill, with Ismail, Ciarnan, and Donal trailing behind. When they reached the High Cross, the ridge was empty but for the wind. Ismail sprawled in the heather. "I eat too much and you run too fast." He pointed to the low, cloud-covered sun. "Now we wait long time."

To keep warm, they all played an Irish game, with curved sticks and a leather ball, on a grassy space below the stone cross. At last, four slender figures appeared, mounting the path to the meeting place. Wrapped in her velvet cloak, the noble lady strode easily, as if, for all her fine garments, hills were not new to her. The gentle nun walked in front, and Rachel and Danni followed a few paces behind.

Donal took the playing sticks and the ball and stepped back behind his cousin. The lady stopped at the foot of the stone cross and beckoned Gil closer. Laying both hands on his shoulders, she studied him as she had done outside the church. "Yes," she whispered. "It is you. I have known this face too long to be mistaken. A whole year has passed since she saw you first, upon Saint Lucy's Day, and since then she has painted me your picture in words, a hundred times over."

The lady laughed gently, "If we walked in the forest, she would find a hazelnut, or a burnished leaf. 'Look, there! The exact color of his hair.'" She caught a tangle of Gil's in her slender fingers. "Or, in summer, a harebell, a midday sky, a lochan's water and, 'Behold, my lady Aunt, the perfect shade of his eyes! All nature was her palette, and all Christendom, as well! Once, she found you in the triptych upon the Holy Altar: 'Look, Good Aunt, the Sainted John is his very brother.' Heaven help her! Or you will be Lord Yesu, next!"

She laughed again and then she lowered her head and smiled gently. "Forgive me, I make jest of you. But it is no jest to be young, nor foolishness to be in love. I was both, once, and now, though my youth and my love share the one grave, I do not forget!" Her voice dropped low. "And now, I meet you at last! But, by the Lord, I did not expect one so young! Still then, she is young, too, and to her, you will appear a man. And, indeed," she said solemnly, "You have been summoned to a man's task."

"But how did she see Gil?" Danni protested suddenly. "Gil wasn't even here then. He didn't come at all till Candlemas...."

"But I saw her," Gil said. "At the river. And she saw me. She saw me before any of us ever came."

"Through the stone?" Danni said.

"In a vision," the Lady Griselle said simply. "My niece could see through the veil even as a child. Those like her often do."

"Like her?" Gil asked uncertainly.

She smiled at him, but her eyes were sad. "She is both good and fair. A white rose of Alba. They do not bloom long."

The words cut like a knife to Gil's heart. He felt as if the people around him were slipping away, fading into grey mist. He heard the wind moaning around the stone cross, like a human voice. And he knew that in the same moment of finding his green-eyed girl, at last, he was hearing her whisper goodbye.

"But come," the lady said. "She is yet young, and so are you, and there's much to be done before your journeys end." She sat down at the foot of the stone cross, her knees drawn up like a child's and her velvet skirts pooled around her, held out her arms, and gestured that they sit beside her. "Come, I shall tell you how all this has come to be.

"When I was young," she began, "as young as you are yourselves, my father brought me to Camelot to serve the queen, while my brother, a young esquire, served the king. Ah, then," she smiled again, "all were young. My lady Guinevere, and Arthur and his knights. It was the springtime of our lives, just as this is the springtime of yours. Our days were filled with dancing and music-making and hunting the wild deer. There were tournaments, and a dozen knights begging to bear my favor. And though I lived among warriors, there was no war. Because Arthur and his great table of peace had put an end to war."

She leaned back against the carved stone cross, smiling. "And then," she said, "on one golden day of Pentecost, Lance'lot came, riding into the tournament, mastering his wild charger with one hand, his other raised to salute my lady Guinevere; her colors upon his helm! And he himself, dressed all in green, the colors of the forest from which he had come. And to which he would go, as if to become a great tree, himself, for no one ever saw the place he came from, or the place he made his home.

"Some whispered he was not man at all, but spirit, a ghost-knight returned from Tir nan Og, to ride again with men." She smiled wisely. "But he was a man. I knew. And my lady knew. And so, we made sport of love, like giggling servant maids." She smiled again, sorrowfully. "But kingdoms do not rest on the fate of serving maids. Our foolishness was discovered, and Camelot was divided. Some took the part of the king, some of his errant queen, and the knights of the brotherhood drew swords upon each other.

"My own sweet love fell beside the king. For him, Camelot had no end. But for those who must yet live, it lay in ruins. The knights scattered. Some sought fortunes in other lands. Some turned to banditry. Some made war, yet, on each other. A brave few kept their pledge to Arthur still. But Arthur was gone, to Tir nan Og, or Heaven, we knew not which. And Lance'lot was gone, too, into the Great Forest of Caledon, because he had destroyed the very thing he loved, the kingdom he had sworn, at Arthur's table, to defend.

"My good lady, in her penitence, took the veil of the Grey Sisters and there, indeed, she remains, as goodly a nun as she was a lover, and a queen."

Danni suddenly looked up boldly and said, "Is it true Lance'lot visits her still?"

The Lady Griselle looked away, over their heads. "If he does, I do not know. And if I knew, I would not speak." She reached over her shoulder and laid the fingers of one hand lightly upon the carved cross. "Even this old stone might have ears, and its carved saints, mouths to speak. If there is one man on earth Jocelyn Guidbairn fears, it is Lance'lot. He owes him his stolen kingdom, true, but a fiercer foe he will not meet."

She returned her gaze to their faces. "When good makes war on good, evil always wins. And so, into the ruins came the Usurper, dressed in gold and promising gold to all who did his will. As for us, we lived as prisoners, because we had loved Arthur, until my widowed brother moved to buy good favor back and pledged his hapless daughter, still a child, to wed our unwelcome king.

"But though the Usurper is the handsomest of men, his heart is black, and hers, being pure, saw through to its dark core. And as she approached the age of marriage, she pleaded for release. My brother, wed again, now, to Ingirid from the North, would not listen. And so, this wise stepmother sent the girl to me, to seek secret refuge with the sisters who sheltered our fallen queen. For though the Usurper could lay waste to castles, their sanctuary was beyond his power. Did he but set foot there, every hand in the kingdom would take up a sword.

"It was the Sunday of Our Lord's Passion, when we fled.

And on that very day the raiders returned with the Holy Fool. They led him through Camelot, mounted backwards on a donkey, in sinful mockery of Our Lord. The taunting crowds were our shield, as, dressed in servant's clothing, we made our escape. At the sight of the poor tormented child, my lady wept as desperately as he, and it took all my strength to drag her away.

"Outwith the walls, two palfreys waited, held by a brave good brother, as young as they," she gestured towards Ciarnan and Donal, "And then, we were away, into the forest that I knew so well. But she did not cease weeping until we reached the convent bounds." The Lady Griselle leaned back against the stone cross, wrapping her arms around her knees, and sighed. "And then," she said slowly, "She was safe; from her father and from her suitor, both.

"The forest was searched, as far as the Grey Mountains, and the Grey Mountains as far as Glen Alban. Word was sent north to Pentland and Orkney and the Kingdoms of the Danes. And south, to Dalriada, and Ireland. But, of course, she was not found.

"Summer came. And my young niece, like any caged bird, began to fret and beat her wings against her bars. "'Oh, good lady Aunt, I shall die within these walls, if I cannot be free, and run and ride among the trees and hills. I dream, day and night, of the taste of wild raspberries. If I could have but one?' And she would cling to my arm and look up into my face, so pitifully. And being childless, myself, I believed her.

"Our palfreys were saddled, and we rode out beyond the convent bounds, on the most perfect summer day. 'One hour,' I said, and we rode to the meadow where the raspberries grew. And, of course, she rode like no nun, and indeed, no lady, but like a rowdy boy, her disguising veil flying wild behind her, and soon vanished from my sight. When I reached the clearing in the forest that we sought, she was gone, her grey palfrey gone, too. Only her white nun's veil remained, left where it had fallen on the ground. And the raspberries, trampled all around.

"The Knight himself was away, searching in far Northumbria, when she came back to Camelot, bound between brutal guards.

And thus, they led her through the gates, as they had led the Fool, to the same prison, among the beasts. When Guidbairn returned and found his lady there, he slew her guards before her face. And pretending great distress, he begged her to come away with him, out of her prison to a far more golden cage."

The lady smiled sadly. "Beyond the walls of Camelot, there lies the gated Forest of Pentecost, where we hunted, of old, and beside it stands an ancient, ruined tower. There, in those happier days, King Arthur's falconers set a mews, to shelter his hawks in the molt. Within its walls lies a garden as perfect as that of Eden, with every kind of fruit tree and rose and vine, now all grown wild. And there, he proposed to keep his unwilling bride, until she was old enough to wed.

"But she would not go without her Fool. And the Fool, in turn, would not leave without the beasts which had befriended him. And so, to win her favor, all were moved to the tower mews by the Forest of Pentecost. And there the Usurper comes to court her, every day. For he is proud and would have a willing bride."

The *muinntir* bell began to ring. The midwinter dusk had settled on the sea and the land below. The lady jumped up from her seat beneath the cross, wrapping her cloak close. "I must go." She beckoned Danni and Rachel. "But first, you must have these." She took a ring from the smallest finger of her right hand, and a silver bracelet from her left wrist. She slid the ring onto Danni's finger and the bracelet onto Rachel's slender arm.

"These gifts of our good Queen Guinevere, I give now to you. All knights of Arthur will know that you have them from me. They will win you protection wherever you go. Come! The bell calls us to prayers and it rings as if it will never stop!"

But Ciarnan shouted suddenly and pointed down to the Sound where the longships lay. Gil saw a flow of flickering lights, moving down the hill from the *muinntir* to the pier, as if the Northmen's fires had taken life. He scoured the dark water for sign of a ship and saw a feeble flicker of flame separate from the land and bob out toward the dim far shore. Ciarnan pulled him toward the path. Donal was already running ahead. The nun, too, gathered her little party, like straying sheep, hastening them downward. Gil broke into a trot beside Ismail.

But then he stopped and turned to look back at the stone cross, dark against the last light of the sky. Something strange and sure told him that much would have happened to him and to all, before he stood by it again. With a mix of excitement and regret, he left the peaceful hilltop and broke into a run.

He caught the others where the paths for the *muinntir* and the convent diverged. Danni and Rachel were already hurrying away, with the sister and the Lady Griselle, who turned once and raised her hand in farewell.

Ciarnan and Donal ran on past the *muinntir* buildings, down toward the sea. Gil and Ismail followed to the shore, where a crowd of grey-clad brothers stood above the pier, holding the flickering torches he'd seen from the hill. Floki and Hakon were amongst them, and Palamedes' huge shape was at the fore. All peered outward to the moving light on the water; a torch held high above the rowing boat that ferried the brothers back and forth across the Sound.

A thin shout from the dark land, beyond, rode the wind across to Hy. Gil wondered who travelled so late, and on Christmas Day? The light reached the far shore and flickered as the traveler was taken aboard. Then, a moment later, the flame and the dark shore separated, as if the ferrymen were leaving in great haste. When the boat nudged into the island pier, the traveler was helped off the ferry by two oarsmen. Two other brothers ran down the steps to assist, and between them, the stranger staggered ashore.

Gil saw a young, dirt-caked man, with blond curly hair and a handsome face gashed from cheek to chin. One arm hung, blood-soaked, by his side. With the other, he clutched the long cloak of many-colored wool, wrapped around his shoulders. Beneath it shone the dull gleam of battered chain. Torn chausses sagged from his weary legs. Bloodied and broken, he seemed the image of fallen Camelot. And yet there was fierce fire in his eyes as he searched the faces before him. Then his gaze fell on the white-bearded figure of the Ab.

"Good Father," he whispered, and clutched his wounded arm. "The raiders camp beneath Ben More. They come, at dawn, for the Warriors of Tir nan Og."

CHAPTER THREE

B reathing hard from the wild run across the hill, Gil and Ismail felt blindly for the door of the Chapter House. Rivulets of water poured from the turf roof, splashing their faces. The girls huddled in the darkness behind them, clutching their hastily gathered belongings. Gil's hand closed on the iron door latch.

"We can't go in there," Rachel protested. "We're girls."

"It was the Ab who sent us to get you." The heavy door swung open. Within, the driftwood fire flared in the sudden draft of cold air and doves rustled and fluttered in the sooty rafters above. Floki, standing in the center of the circular room, turned to face them. The monks leaned forward from their low perimeter bench. The Ab, who sat on a raised chair opposite the entrance, put his *bachall* aside and extended his arm and beckoned them to his side. "Now let us continue our discussion," he said, with a gentle nod.

Floki returned the nod with a respectful bow. "I am a man of few words," he said innocently. "They come at dawn. We meet them at dawn."

A man rose from the shadows and Gil recognized the stranger, a warm cloak wrapped around his shoulders and his wounded arm bandaged. He inclined his head briefly toward the Ab and then addressed Floki. "They are many," he said. "Two dozen and more. Well mounted and well-armed."

Floki's white grin flashed. "And we are two longships of sixteen benches, each. I bring sixty men. Though half would be plenty. Or half again. For we are Northmen."

"But this is Hy," the Ab said gently, "And there will be no fighting here."

Floki lowered his head in response and stood as quietly obedient as any of the brothers. When he looked up, his face wore an expression of earnest sorrow. "With respect, good Father," he said, "That choice lies with those who gather beneath Ben More."

The Ab smiled kindly. "No," he said. "That they come lies in their hands. That we fight them lies in ours. And we will keep Our Lord's peace." He closed his fingers around the *bachall*.

"Then you will die here, good Father. And your brothers with you."

"That may be so," said the Ab. Floki studied the old man warily. The Ab leant forward. "You but travel through our island," he said.

"And it is your home. I understand," said Floki, "But…."

"You understand little, young friend." The Ab softened the words with his gentlest smile. "It is not our home," he said. "We are travelling through this land, just as you. Each day we journey from dawn to dusk, seeking always the place of our resurrection. Perhaps tomorrow we will find it here."

The monks nodded peacefully. Ciarnan appeared quietly determined. Donal's lip was trembling. Gil looked up at the Ab, "If they don't find us here, will they leave Hy alone?"

"They may," the Ab said mildly. "If they were Northmen, they might be content with fat lambs and treasure."

"They are not Northmen," Floki cut in impatiently. "And we have seen their work."

"But if we sail right now, you can say we were never here," Gil offered hopefully.

The Ab shook his head. "Swords may wound the body," he said. "Lies wound the soul."

Floki raised empty palms to the roof beams. "Give up!" he said. "I know this kind, with their fasting and their praying. They would as soon die as live. You can argue till the end of time and not move them." He kicked loose cinders into the fire.

"No matter," Hakon said quietly from his place on the bench. "Odin himself could not sail on a night like this."

"But how will they sail?" Rachel asked suddenly, "Even at

dawn, if they come with horses over land?"

"They will have ships to meet them," Hakon explained. "Light ships, travelling lightly crewed, to ferry them across."

"Landsmen!" Floki cried scornfully. "And their ships, landsmen's ships. Let us meet them, and by dusk the maas' beaks will pluck their eyes!"

"My good young earl," the Ab said sorrowfully, "You have shared our bread and slept beneath our roof. Do not, I beg you, spill blood on our shores." He leant forward and said gently, "Come now. I have a suggestion that might serve all well. I propose that you ready your ships in every way, this night, and sail from here at the very first glimmer of dawn. Sail north, back the way you came. That way, you will ensure no meeting with the foe."

"It is not my custom," Floki said, "To show men my back."

"Have patience," the Ab said, still gently, "As they cross the Sound, you will change course, turn southerly, and circle our island. By the time you turn your prows landward, again, the pursuers will be fruitlessly searching Hy. And by the time your ruse is realized, our young warriors will be riding the oak wood of Argyll."

Floki laughed coldly. "And when the ruse is discovered, and they have roasted one of your good brethren over a fire, and he has told them our route, how long before the oak wood is strewn with bones?"

"They may roast us if they wish, but no man of Hy will speak." The Ab's smile was as gentle as ever but his voice was hard as steel.

Then Palamedes rose to his feet, "And the warriors ride neither alone, nor undefended, but with me!"

"But they are two dozen," Hakon said quickly and graciously, "And you are one."

"Five," Danni said, meeting Floki's eyes boldly. "Who shed first blood aboard *Silver Dragon*?" Floki smiled for the first time. "And with Palamedes ..." she went on, but Floki laughed suddenly and cut her off.

"Sir Palamedes speaks fine words. But words are like sea spray, blown by every wind."

Palamedes' brows lowered and his black beard bristled. "Do you question my honor?"

"Never, sir," Floki grinned, "for that way lies certain death. I question only the great generosity by which you pledge your lance, when all know it is pledged already to your fabled prey, for one whispered word of which, you will abandon every other cause."

"That's not true!" Danni cried. "Palamedes would never abandon us."

But Palamedes bowed his head in solemn regret. "The older vow must be first served. Like my father and grandfather, I seek first the Questing Beast. Should its path cross mine, I must follow, at once." Danni's eyes widened with hurt. "My lady, the Beast is a matter of honor. I would lay down my life to please you, but not my honor."

"So go," Danni shouted angrily. "Go chase the stupid thing and keep your stupid honor. We don't need you. We'll go alone."

Sorrow and dismay settled on the faces of all the watchers. The Ab leaned forward, resting his elbow on his knee and his bearded chin on his palm. Then he straightened up and grasped the *bachall* as if about to make a final judgement. But Floki spoke first. With his pale eyes set on Danni's face, he said, "I will go with you."

Hakon stood up. "You will ride the oak wood?" he asked uncertainly.

Floki laughed. "I am no landsman, to scuttle about in the bracken and wear my arse sore on a nag's back. I will take them by the seaways through Glen Alban, and to the very heart of the Forest of Caledon, and land them beneath the Falls of the Fugitive. But two days ride, then, from Camelot."

"Narrow waters make easy prey of longships," said Hakon

"*Silver Dragon* is no one's easy prey," Floki returned instantly. "Her belly is filled with Northmen. They are hard to swallow. Still, if your rowing benches empty at the first adversity, so be it. Sail on to Ireland. My thirty men are all I need."

Hakon smiled in return and turned to the watching audience of monks. "When we were young," he said cheerfully, "Boy-cousins together, we climbed the cliffs of the High Island, one summer's day, gathering birds' eggs. And when his sack was full," he gestured to Floki, "so pleased was he with his plunder that he turned from the cliff and stepped off into empty air!"

"What happened?" Danni cried, staring at Floki.

"He fell," Hakon's smile broadened, "A ship's mast height, into the sea." He illustrated a tumbling figure with the fingers of one hand and soft laughter filled the room. "He had forgotten the dangers that lay all around him." Hakon looked back at his cousin. "As I fear he forgets them now."

"And I fear," Floki returned, "you remember dangers too well, like a woman in her dotage, seeing terrors by the fire."

Hakon's eyes narrowed, but he kept his calm smile. He looked at Danni and Floki where they stood now, side by side. "Set your course with care, cousin. Falling Star or Odin's Sword, all sway to the winds of the heart." He nodded gently at Danni as he spoke. Then he turned abruptly to the Ab. "I sail at dawn, with Floki Magnusson." He bowed his head. "I beg your blessing, Father, on us all."

The Ab studied the young Northman for a long thoughtful while, then raised his eyes to the gathered company. "So be it," he said quietly. The old man rose, and lifting the *bachall* high, spoke his Latin blessing over their heads. At the final word, Floki strode to the door and disappeared into the night.

Provisions were swiftly gathered in the torch-lit courtyard, and sea kists loaded onto carts. Ciarnan thrust a burning brand into Gil's hand and led him and Ismail to the pony field. Slumbering shoulder to shoulder with Doombearer, Lionheart was a small, contented shape casting a huge furry shadow in the flickering light. With a pang of guilt, Gil slipped the bridle over the pony's head.

Gil and Ismail made their beds that night, huddled under sheepskins, beside the pier. The ponies whickered nervously in their shipboard pen. The girls sheltered in their black tent beneath the mast. Gil lay shivering and wakeful, until at last he gave up, and, wearing his sheepskin as an extra cloak, crept through the sleeping shapes of Northmen to the fire. Squatting on his haunches, he warmed his face and hands and looked wistfully seaward for a glimpse of dawn.

"You keep guard?" said a soft voice, approvingly. Gil spun around. "I keep guard, too," Floki came into the circle of firelight and crouched beside him, "of my ship and my lady, with empty hands." He held them out, with a self-mocking laugh. Then he picked up a charred length of driftwood that had fallen from the fire and held it up, like the Ab's shepherd's staff. "That is better. Now I fight my battles like the brave men of Hy."

"They are brave," Gil said angrily.

"They are brave fools," said Floki. "Still, I like their courage, if not their foolishness."

"I don't want them to die."

"They are old men who seek death." Floki flicked his driftwood *bachall*, kicking up embers. "Besides, all men die."

"Ciarnan and Donal aren't old. And they're my friends."

Floki shrugged. "They have damped the fires of love and battle. Why live?" He stood up and flung the driftwood into the fire. "Enough. I weary of it." He strode off into the darkness of the shore. The fire flared and lowered. Gil heard a rippling splash. He stared at the place where the Northman should have been, and the Cat hairs prickled on the back of his neck.

He huddled closer to the fire, and somehow slept then, and awoke with the kindly face of the Ab of Hy looking down on him. The soft thud of oars settling into oarlocks stirred the still air. "Arise, little brother, your ship seeks the morning star." The old man pointed to one bright star, set high in a sky turned from black to the deepest blue. Dawn was coming, and with it, their foe.

Gil scrambled to his feet. Ismail was already helping Bjorn cast sand over the remnants of the fire to disguise their presence here. He joined them, layering green gorse branches over the hot ash. When he turned from the task, Ciarnan and Donal waited beside the Ab. They stepped forward shyly, holding out a small wooden bowl and a leather sack. Ciarnan mimed opening the sack and pouring. Gil turned the wooden stopper, and as Ismail held the shallow vessel, white milk gushed into the wood. Ciarnan smiled. "Breakfast."

The milk was still warm, creamy, and sweet. Gil offered it to Ismail, who drank also, and then stopped the milk-skin, to save the rest for the girls. The bell began to ring, and, smiling sadly, the Irish boys slipped into the darkness. The Ab's hand rested on Gil's shoulder. "I, too, must be at my prayers."

Gil looked up, then shook his head fiercely. "It's all wrong!" he burst out. "You helped us, and now, when there's danger, we're leaving you alone!"

"Alone?" The old man's face lit with joyful radiance. "We are never alone! Angels and saints stand guard over Hy! Sky, sea, and rock plead our cause with the Lord! What evil can befall us?" He leant on his *bachall* and smiled down on Gil.

"Warrior!" Floki called from the ship's deck. Gil turned and saw the Northman dimly outlined against the greying sky, his foot resting impatiently on the gangplank. "Do you sail? Or take holy vows?"

"I sail!" Gil answered, but he looked back to the Ab. He felt tears stinging his eyes.

"What do you fear, little brother?" the old man said. "That your passing this way hastens our path to Heaven?"

"Sail or swim!" Floki shouted.

The Ab raised a gentle hand to the Northman, then turned back to Gil. "But for that cause, should you not rejoice?" He smiled. "Go now. Before we try the patience of our good young earl."

But even as he spoke, Floki kicked the gangplank free, sending it crashing to the pier. "Swim, then!" he growled and thirty oars dipped seaward with one muffled splash.

"I'm coming!" Gil ran down the pier, cloak flying, stumbled over the discarded gangplank, and leapt out wildly for the moving ship. He missed by a yard but caught the rail with his outstretched hands and hung on, scrabbling with his feet against the sea-drenched wood. Laughter echoed from above and then Bjorn Break-Neck grasped his tunic with both huge hands, hauled him over the side, and dumped him on the deck.

Gil stared up past the bare mast to the grey dawn, as *Silver Dragon* slipped from the shore. Then he staggered to his feet, rubbing skinned bloodied hands against his tunic. Though the sky above their heads was clear, on all sides the Sound was blanketed with low mist. A few yards off their steering-board,

Storm Serpent rode like a phantom, cloud-shrouded. Her oars cast thin lines of white foam on the black sea. Ahead, their own dragon prow probed blindly into a wall of grey.

Gil turned for a last glimpse of the Ab. But the swirling mist had already swallowed the shore. Nothing remained of Hy but a low, wild strand of rock and foam and the steady sweet chiming of its bell. The bell rang on and on. Gil laughed and said to Ismail, "Someone's late for prayers."

"It rings too long for prayers," Ismail answered. Gil looked at Floki. The blond Northman stood at his steering oar, tense with concentration, his eyes on the mist-hidden sea and his head cocked towards the bell.

"They're guiding us around Hy!" Gil cried.

Floki nodded grimly. "And the raiders to their own shore. I like their courage this morning even more."

The chiming of the bell faded, growing thinner and thinner. At last, when it was the faintest, barely perceptible sound, brought to their ears by vagaries of the wind, Floki leant on his steering-oar and brought the prow around to the west. Then they rode seaward into nothingness, amidst black rocks and white shoals, the barking of unseen seal-folk, and the crying of seabirds in the mist. Twice Floki shouted for silence, and the two ships drifted, oars raised, until a murmur of waves on sand gave warning of the hidden shore. Then he called again, and his grim-faced seamen dipped wary oars once more.

Suddenly Danni, standing high up on the railings of the pony pen, cried, "Look out!" and pointed wildly. Gil whirled and saw a great spike of rock looming in their path. Muttered curses rose from the oarsmen as they slipped by. But Floki grinned. "Odin be praised!" he cried and swung his oar hard across the steering-board. Once again, the dragon prow came around. Hakon followed, and the two longships circled Floki's landmark and rode onward into the mist.

Gil drew his compass from his pocket and studied it in the growing light. He found north and read their bearing: south-southwest. But with neither map nor any glimpse of land, it told him nothing. "What says your Falling Star, Warrior?" Floki said, grinning. "Have you a better course than mine?"

Gil shook his head and put the compass away. "Your course is best."

"My course is set by the good men of Hy," Floki answered quietly. "Without them, this day, even Floki Magnusson feasts the crabs. Listen!" Gil listened and heard again the chiming of the bell, faint and muffled. "It is far now," Floki said, "Land lies between."

"I know," Gil answered, because he had heard the bell like this, when he and Ismail crossed the island the day they came. He strained his eyes for a glimpse of that place, but the mist hid all. Gradually the sound of the bell grew louder, and then softer again, and lastly, slipped behind as the oarsmen drove their ships southward along the seaward coast of Hy.

"We have left their waters, now," Floki said. He called to Erling and handed him the steering oar. Then he jumped down, into the body of the ship. Pulling back a covering of black cloth, he revealed the stack of arms, forsaken on their arrival day at Hy. Retrieving his own, he slung his shield around his neck, and strapped the sword belt around his waist. One by one, the rowers left their oars, armed themselves, and returned to their places.

"Now," Floki murmured, "We journey alone." He took the steering oar from Erling and altered course so that the rising wind shifted behind them. Svein beckoned Gil and Ismail to help hoist the great square sail. The wind filled it, even as it rode up the mast, and Silver Dragon surged forward.

Gil peered ahead, but could see nothing but veils of mist, though on either side he glimpsed foam-rimmed rocks rushing past. Behind, Hakon had raised sail, too, but his was warily reefed and he fell quickly back. Waves slapped fiercely beneath Silver Dragon's bow, casting freezing spray onto the deck. Ismail crouched at the foot of the mast and wrapped a hanging loop of coarse rope tight around his hands. "He is bold," he murmured, nodding towards Floki, leaning far out over the steering board, drenched with spray and laughing at each crashing wave.

Gil braced himself against the rail, thrilled and terrified in equal parts. And then, over the sound of wind and water, he heard the chiming of the bell. "Floki," he shouted, but in that instant, the Northman flung his oar savagely over the steering-board and the *Silver Dragon* slewed sideways, burying her rail in the sea.

Gil sprawled full length on the decking. Foaming water swept over him, tumbling him, crashing and banging, into a jumble of kists and oars and boots. With a grating roar, the wave pulled back to the sea, dragging Gil with it. He slammed into the low rail, and fought to hang onto it, as the rushing sea clawed at his tunic and cloak. Then something powerful caught him, dragging him back to the light.

"Ho!" a huge voice roared. "Twice I catch same fish!" Gil looked blearily into Bjorn Break-Neck's fierce wolf-grin. Then, shaking water from his hair, he sat up. *Silver Dragon* wallowed clumsily in cross-seas. Across a bare thirty feet of green sea, a wall of jagged black rock soared up, so tall its summit vanished into the mist. Streamers of cloud closed in again, blotting out the fearsome cliff. Svein pinched Gil's arm as Gil peered fruitlessly into the greyness. "Hrolf's Rock," he muttered in a voice tinged with fear.

"I make you swim," Floki said, with a courteous nod. "I am sorry."

Gil glimpsed a shadowy presence in the grey oblivion, before the cliff face vanished again. "How did you see it?"

Floki shook his head gravely. "I do not see. I hear the bell of Hy. But I cannot hear the bell beyond Hrolf's Rock…so I am in wrong place." He paused. "I am wrong." And then, miming the sudden thrusting of the oar, he said, "And so I turn. And then I see Hrolf's Rock."

A collective sigh went round the ship. Over the low muttering of their excited voices, Gil heard again, far off, the sweet notes of the bell. "It's still ringing," he said.

Floki stared into the grey mist. "The good men of Hy watch us, even now."

"Angels and saints stand guard over Hy," Gil whispered.

Floki looked grim. "They will need angels and saints," he said. "As will we, if we do not leave this place." Then he shouted orders in his own tongue, and his crew hastened to take up their oars, while Bjorn and Svein lowered the great sail, and set to reefing it to half its height.

"Hail, cousin!" Hakon's voice burst out of the mist as *Storm Serpent* glided into view. "By what cause do you humble your sail?" he called innocently. He pointed at the looming shadow of the rock, breaking again into view. "Surely not that pebble in the sea?"

"Nay, cousin!" Floki waved gaily at the rock, too. "I wish to gather birds' eggs!" He smiled at Hakon. "Come climb with me!"

Erling and Svein shouted gleefully. Hakon peered up at the mist-wrapped cliff. "You climb," he said modestly. "I stay here." He held out the hem of his tunic, "Like a good wife, catching eggs in my skirt." He grinned broadly at his cousin and made a little curtsy. Around him, his crew cheered and thumped their shields and pointed at Floki, "Climb! Climb!"

Floki's own shipmates joined in, laughing and chanting, "Birds' eggs from Hrolf's Rock!"

"Who's Hrolf?" Rachel asked suddenly.

"A great Viking captain," Svein said, grinning. "Who did not see Hrolf's Rock!"

"Hey!" Erling cried, "raise sail again! We make it Floki's Rock!" Floki stood, smiling quietly, taking their mockery with good humor. Then, suddenly, Danni stretched up on the pony pen and pointed beyond their stern, to where the island lay, hidden in cloud. The mist had changed color, as if the sun was rising over the island. But the island lay north of them now, where no sun rose. The ruddy glow spread outward, along the low base of the clouds. Silence fell, as all eyes turned toward the reddening sky. "What is it?" Danni cried, and as she spoke, the bell stopped ringing, cut off short.

"It is fire," said Floki. "They are burning Hy."

All laughter died and the crews of both ships stood watching solemnly. Gil's mind filled with visions of the place and the people they had only just left. "I wish we'd never, ever gone there," he whispered, staring at the terrible red glow. "Look what we've done!"

Floki slapped the steering oar into Erling's hand and leapt down onto the deck. He strode to the armor kist and returned to Gil with his shield and sword. Flinging the shield onto the deck, he drew the sword from its scabbard, thrust the hilt into Gil's hand and raised it high. "For Hy, who we have wronged! See, now! Here is how a Northman makes repentance! For Hy!"

A roar of war cries rose. "For Hy! For Hy!" Gil heard the loudest and angriest rise up in his own throat, and he smiled grimly at Floki as he sheathed his ready blade. The two longships set out again, under tight-reefed sail, into the grey nothingness. Anger vanquished Gil's fear and he peered eagerly into the mist for a glimpse of some stray landsman's ship upon which to wreak their vengeance. Then Svein Snaggle-Tooth shouted and pointed at the heavens. Over the top of the mast, blue sky broke through the layers of mist. And in it, floating like an island in a second, sky-bound sea, a mountain glistened with sunlit snow.

"Ben Buie!" Floki cried, triumphantly. "The Yellow Mountain." Entrusting the longship to Erling, he climbed up on the landward rail, staring hungrily at the snowy landmark. Gil saw another, more distant, peak appear, then vanish into the mist again. "And there, the Fort of the Winds." Floki held both arms out as if encompassing the two great hills within them. His face was intent with concentration, his pale eyes half-closed, reading the map in his mind.

Gil stared at the young Northman, awed by his uncanny skill. Then suddenly he shouted, "Floki! Quick!" He stumbled across the moving deck and climbed up to the rail beside Floki, his father's compass in his hand. "Let me show you! Let me show you another way!"

Floki turned sharply. His eyes narrowed when he saw the compass in Gil's outstretched hand. "I've seen your Falling Star," he muttered. "I have little time...."

"I know," Gil returned. "So don't waste it, okay?" Floki grasped a shroud and faced Gil, as if he was considering throwing him in the sea. "Just listen and look," Gil said. He held the compass before the Northman's darkening face.

"This arrow flies to your North Star." He pointed firmly at the compass needle flickering around the N. "Night or day, cloudy or not, always it finds the North Star. Okay?" Floki nodded gruffly. "So, the mountain is, like, halfway between that letter, that's called 'N,' and that one, that's 'E.'" He pointed midway between North and East. "And if you sail that way, you sail right at the mountain. Whether you can see it, or not."

Floki took the compass from Gil's hand and laid it on his own. "So, there, now, lies the Yellow Mountain," he said. "And there the Fort of the Winds. And I would keep the Yellow Mountain at this shoulder," he shrugged his left, "Until I pass the Small Islands. And the Fort of the Winds there, until I meet the Firth. And so," he pointed to the East on the compass and then extended his arm, eastward, toward the right of the dragon prow, "There is my course." He turned his sharp eyes to Gil. "Is that so?"

"Got it in one," Gil murmured. Floki saw his surprise and smiled. "So, will you use it?" Gil said cautiously.

Floki shrugged. "This is a clever toy. But I am Floki Magnusson," he said. "I sail this sea from boyhood. Why do I need a toy from Tir nan Og?"

"Because," said Gil, raising exasperated eyebrows, "you just nearly sailed into Hrolf's Rock!" He ducked and grabbed a shroud of his own. But Floki suddenly grinned and slapped Gil's shoulder, not quite hard enough to tip him into the sea.

"I use your Falling Star! And the first rock we hit, we name for you!" He grinned again and jumped down to the deck and strode back to his steering oar, compass in hand. Gil returned to his place and braced himself against the rail as *Silver Dragon* ploughed on into the mist. The Northman's new-found faith in the toy from Tir nan Og was almost as unnerving as the wild ride toward Hrolf's Rock.

But then the light grew stronger and shadowy shapes appeared in the distance. The mist rapidly thinned and swirled apart before them, and beside them, and above. Blue sky broke through and winter sunshine flooded down. A whole landscape suddenly appeared; great snow-covered hills, and forests of noble pines and snow-laden oaks; on either side of a long expanse of blue water. All was so crystal clear in the white winter light, that but for the grim, grey cloudbank on the sea behind them, it was impossible to imagine how they had been so lost.

Gil and Ismail scurried to help Bjorn release the reefed

sail. Behind them, Hakon's *Storm Serpent* emerged from the cloudbank, her own sail already billowing free. With white foam tumbling beneath their bows, both ships surged forward to where the blue water narrowed into a great cleft in the hills.

Floki beckoned Gil. "It is a fine thing, your Falling Star," he said. "But now we enter Glen Alban and a swaddled babe could sail unguided here!" He returned the compass to Gil as carefully as if it were made of gold and turned back to steer his ship in the old, well-proven way.

Gil left him, and scrambled up on the pony pen beside Danni, watching the passing shore. A herd of stags stood high on a snowy hill. Above, an eagle circled icy cliffs. "Maybe this is Heaven," she said. Gil smiled and tried to soak himself in beauty of the land, but his mind returned relentlessly to Hy. A jumble of images rose up: the blacksmith wrestling with Lionheart, the Ab's grey kitten, Ciarnan and Donal playing beneath the great stone cross. Flames licked at the edges of each memory. What still stood? Who was left of those who had gathered in the Chapter House on Christmas night?

All men die. He looked back to Floki at the steering oar. All men did die. For a fleeting moment he remembered that he belonged to a place a thousand years in the future and every man and woman, every bird and beast he knew here was already a thousand years dead. *But I'm here, now*, he thought angrily, *And for me it is today.* He returned his eyes to the water and the shore again, searching intently for any sign of human life. What he had once feared, now he yearned for. "Let them come," he whispered. "Let them come."

The water narrowed and the mountains grew higher and the land wilder, but he saw nothing but deer and birds, fish and otters. No dogs barked; no cattle lowed. No smoke rose. It was easy to imagine no man had ever trod here. But as the light faded, Floki and Hakon stationed archers at bow and stern, watching the silent hills.

The mountain tops turned pink, then dusky blue. Stars came out and the air turned bitterly cold. Gil felt his damp clothing begin to stiffen and freeze. He wrapped himself in his sheepskins and yearned for landfall and the night fire. But when they beached the longships in a sandy cove and released the ponies and Palamedes' warhorse to graze on rough marsh grass, Floki pointed across the narrow water to the dark opposing shore. "Fire is a beacon," he said to his unhappy crew, "And smoke a bold flag. Will you trade your lives for one night's warm belly?"

The Northmen settled then in the lee of snow-covered rocks, grumbling and eating cold, dried meat. When Floki called two, Ragnvald and Arnkel, to stand first guard, grumbling veered toward rebellion until Floki laid his hand on his sword hilt. Arnkel, a lean youth with a long, wispy moustache, threw the remnants of his unpalatable dinner into the snowy woods and, wrapping his cloak tighter, trudged off down the narrow strand. Gil ran after him and caught his sleeve. The youth turned and gave him a black look.

"I'll stand first guard," Gil said. He pointed at the shore and his own sword, miming defense. Arnkel blinked, and then suddenly understood. He gave Gil a friendly punch and turned back to the gathered company. But Floki spoke one curt word, and Arnkel stopped in his tracks. "I told him I'd do it," Gil said quickly.

Floki raised an eyebrow and nodded toward *Silver Dragon*, resting on the sand. "That is a fine longship that you master," he said.

Gil shook his head, "I don't...."

"No," growled Floki. "Nor do you undo my orders. This is rough country," he added. "I want men watching my ship."

"So how do I become a man if you treat me like a boy?"

Floki gave Gil a slow smile. "I spoke those words to my father!" he laughed. "He sent me to the women's house, but I had seen fewer winters than you." He held up four fingers and laughed again. "Go guard my ship," he said and walked away.

Gil raced to the ship and retrieved his chain hauberk and padded undercoat. He took up his shield, adjusted his sword belt and returned to the beach. Waving goodnight to Ismail, he strode to a well-placed rock outcrop at the edge of the forest and swept strand and sea with his gaze. *Come*, he begged silently. *Just come.*

Overhead, the sky turned from deep blue to star-filled black. A last sliver of waning moon rose and the snow gleamed softly on the hilltops. Silence quickly fell on the camp, as the Northmen curled resignedly in their cloaks and slept in the bitter cold. But Gil's eyes and ears seemed as sharp as his cat Other's, and his imagination was alive with expectation of battle. Scene after scene of confrontation passed vividly through his mind, but each ended the same: his foe, disarmed and begging for mercy. And Gil raising his sword, "Here is the mercy you showed to Hy!" and striking the fatal blow.

Something rustled amid the snow laden branches at his back and his heart surged with terror and joy. He whirled, peering into the oak forest, sword in hand. But the shape that hurtled out of the darkness came not from in front or behind, but above. A weight hit Gil's shoulders, hurling him to the ground. His sword flew from his hand. A wiry forearm pinned his throat to the snowy ground and strong fingers clasped his long hair, jerking his head back. "If I am enemy, this arm is sword," said Ismail. "And you are dead."

"What?" Gil cried. He stared up into the darkness.

"I follow footprints in snow. Go in forest. Climb tree." Ismail's smile, dimly illuminated in the starlight, was sheepish. Gil kicked at him furiously and struggled to escape. Ismail released his hold.

"Right," Gil muttered. "So why did you do that? Just to show me up? Well, guess what? I know you are super-cool warrior-man. So, what's new?"

Ismail spoke very quietly. "I do not do this to humble you. And you are better with sword than me. I do this to warn you."

Gil shrugged his bruised shoulders. "Fine. I'm warned. Next time I look in trees."

Ismail shook his head. "You fight me. If I not quick, you kill me. You very sorry."

"Not that sorry," Gil muttered.

Ismail laughed. "No," he said seriously. "Very sorry. So, I warn you. Know who you fight. Know why you fight."

"Oh, I know," Gil said grimly. "I do know."

"Yes. You seek vengeance," Ismail answered at once. "But

who do you avenge? They who would have no vengeance? Or you, for the hurt in your own heart?"

Gil looked away at the mountain tops, glowing coldly in the night. "I don't want vengeance," he said. "I want justice."

Ismail smiled again in the starlight and shook his head. "Beware, my friend. Even the Believers seek justice, once."

CHAPTER FOUR

Gil woke at first light, with Ismail standing beside him, warily holding out his wooden bowl, filled with milk. "Wait for the girls," he croaked, rubbing his aching throat. His face was too stiff with cold to smile. Fresh snow lay in a soft layer on his sheepskin bedroll. The masts and spars of the beached longships were plastered white and each carved dragon bore a white mane of snow. He stood up, stamped numb feet, and shook out his frozen sheepskins.

Danni and Rachel came skidding and sliding down the icy gangplank. Ismail held the bowl out. They passed it from one to the other, each drinking a few sips, until the milk was gone. Ismail scrubbed the bowl in the snow and wrapped it inside his bedroll. Gil rinsed the empty milk-skin in the sea-loch and put his gift away, and with it, his memories of Hy.

The light was strengthening, and the Northmen were re-floating their ships. Gil and Danni found the ponies standing in a row, heads down and tails to the blizzard, covering over like four-legged snowdrifts. Lionheart was nearest, and right beside him was Lucy. "They're friends now!" Danni cried.

"He's using her as a windbreak." Gil slipped the bridle over Lionheart's head, and defeated by the weather, the pony trotted willingly up the gangplank and into his pen, huddling beneath the mast as beneath his beloved tree.

The ships rode easily out into the rising tide and resumed their journey inland. The day was grey and cold, with blowing snow and the wind in their faces. With reefed sails, they tacked against it, crisscrossing the roughening water from shore to shore. The wind rose further and the water grew narrower. The

sails were lowered and both ships went on, under oars. The girls
retreated into their black tent and Gil and Ismail huddled beside
the warm ponies. Floki wrapped himself in furs, standing at
his steering oar. Only the hard-working rowers were immune.
Gil looked at Ismail, shivering beside him, and pointed toward
Bjorn wielding his great oar. "Maybe he'd like a break?" Ismail
nodded vigorously. Ducking his head against the wind, Gil
struggled across the sleet-covered deck to the black-bearded
Northman. "Can we help?" he shouted. He pointed at the oar
and back at Ismail and himself and made rowing gestures.

"You?" Bjorn pointed at Gil and then at Ismail. He flung his
head back and laughed.

"We can!" Gil said. "Together." He pointed to Ismail and
himself again and held up two fingers. Bjorn gestured toward
the tent where the girls sheltered. He clutched his rough black
hair into two girlish bunches and pointed at Gil.

"We're not girls," Gil said evenly. "And we can row." Bjorn
just glowered and hauled on his oar. But then Floki spoke
suddenly, his tone both good-natured and firm. Bjorn looked
up at his captain and then back to Gil and Ismail. He raised his
oar, stood up, and stepped back from the rough kist on which
he had been seated. Though, as Gil and Ismail jumped in to take
his place, he bunched his hair again, grinned, and stuck out his
tongue.

"We'd better make this good," Gil whispered to Ismail.

Ismail nodded. "You know how to do this?" he said
hopefully.

Gil stared, alarmed. "Don't you?"

"You start, I follow," Ismail grinned.

"Right," Gil gripped the oar grimly, and dipped the long
blade into the sea. There was a loud crack of wood on wood
and a curse from the man behind him. Bjorn was on his feet
again, twirling prettily in his cloak like a huge-footed girl. Gil
gritted his teeth and drove the oar into the water. He felt Ismail
adjusting his hands, finding the position. Within three strokes
he had the rhythm and was putting all his wiry strength to the
task.

Warm at last, they rowed vigorously, oar blades flashing

and bow wave surging, Hakon's ship, driven hard at their side. Shouts of rivalry and defiance flew back and forth as *Storm Serpent* slipped behind. Bjorn began chanting a song, pounding the mast with his fist while the Northman bellowed out the rhythmic words. Danni and Rachel scrambled from their shelter, cheering and clapping along.

"More oarsmen!" Bjorn shouted. But he laughed good-naturedly as Hakon's ship fell back. Above, the sky cleared to a cloud-streamed blue. Gil's spirit rose with the soaring mountains, revealed, white and glistening, all around. But his hands grew numb and his shoulders burned with a fiery ache. Beside him, Ismail bit hard on his lip and half closed his eyes, straining to keep pace with the Northmen. At last, when Gil was certain he could not bear another stroke, Bjorn gripped his arm with a bear-paw hand, stilling the oar. "Good oarsmen! Make Vikings! Rest now."

Sweat-drenched, Gil grinned at Ismail, and together they surrendered the oar and staggered to their feet. But Svein jumped up from his seat, bowed, and offered his. Cheers went round the ship and the song grew insistently louder, until Gil and Ismail slid reluctantly into Svein's place. Ismail winced as their first stroke clashed blades both fore and aft. A new pain blossomed beneath Gil's shoulder and throbbed in time to the Northmen's song.

He counted strokes, swearing to quit at fifty. But when he reached it, Ismail was still rowing hard, so he struggled on. At a hundred, the stinging in his hands overtook his aching shoulder. At a hundred and fifty, he'd lost all feeling in his arms, and at a hundred and fifty-nine, Svein thrust his yellow-toothed grin into his face and said, "I take now." Gil dropped the oar with a groan of gratitude, leaned back to stretch his shoulders and fell off the kist. He lay flat on the deck, luxuriating in its sleety comfort.

"Hail, oarsman!" Gil squinted warily up at the enormous hulk of Bjorn above him. "Arnkel waits!" Bjorn grinned, as Arnkel unwound his weedy length from his oar.

Ismail, lying flat on the deck beside Gil, opened his eyes and moaned, "Next time you have idea, I not hear." He dragged

himself upright and limped after Gil to Arnkel's bench. Gil's
blistered hands took up the oar. "Next time I have idea," he said,
"I not hear."

But they had made only three more oar strokes when Floki
suddenly called a halt, and sent Arnkel back to his oar. Gil
stumbled clear of the ranks of oarsmen as, with a series of quick
orders, Floki mounted archers at bow and stern, called Hakon
into line behind them, and slowed his oarsmen to a controlled
and wary pace.

Gil looked ahead, for the first time since he'd taken his place
on Bjorn's rowing kist. The great rounded shoulder of the tallest
of the snow-covered mountains loomed just above them. And
before them, the long, blue sea-loch ended in a thickly forested
shore. A blank wall of snow-weighted trees barred their way.
Silver Dragon altered her course slightly, approaching the land
on a wide, shallow curve, and suddenly a gap appeared between
two sandy points revealing a blue, freshwater river, frothy and
rock-filled, flowing from the forest land into their last remnant
of sea.

"In there?" he whispered. He turned and looked at Floki,
and then back at the river. As he watched, Floki altered course
again and drove straight for the river's mouth. Gil braced
himself for the crunch of wood on sand, but the ship slipped
through the gap with water under her keel and surged onward
into the river's flow. The rowers cursed and bent hard to their
oars, as the strong current battered their prow. And then they
were within the river's course, beneath sparkling, snow-bent
branches leaning from ice-fringed shores.

Danni and Rachel ran from one rail to the other, delighting
in the beauty of the winter Forest of Caledon. Gil relaxed against
the armor kist, soaking up the pale sunlight. Sheltered by the
trees from the icy wind, he felt warm and secure. "I could do
this forever!" he said to Ismail. "As long as someone else rows!"

Ismail was crouched warily beside the mast, his eyes
sweeping the landscape behind, to where *Storm Serpent* followed
in their wake, and forward, to their course between the walls of
trees. "If I am hunter," he said quietly, "I set trap here."

Gil sat up straight. His hand, resting lightly on the armor

kist, tightened its grip. *Narrow waters make easy prey of longships.* Suddenly, he imagined each tree hiding a waiting bowman, each rock, armored warriors. Not one, but two archers now stood, back-to-back, at prow and stern of *Silver Dragon,* and Hakon's ship was similarly defended. And although Floki never took his eyes from his complex course through rocks and rapids, Erling stood beside him, arrow set to bow-string, his gaze sweeping the forested shore.

Gil stood up cautiously, conscious of his body as a target, and then swiftly crossed the deck to where Rachel and Danni sat basking, as he had, in the sun. He pointed to their black tent. "Go in," he said, "It isn't safe."

Danni stared at him. "If you think I'm going to miss the best part...." she began. But suddenly there was a grinding crunch and *Silver Dragon* shuddered to a halt, her oarsmen tumbling like children onto the deck. An arrow whispered past Gil's ear and thudded into the mast.

"To arms!" Erling shouted. Bjorn and Svein jumped down into the river, struggling waist-deep in the current to free the grounded bow, while a dozen rowers thrust against the rocky bottom with long poles. Each man was shadowed by another with a shield, while the steering-board rail was lined with bowmen, arrows set, seeking the hidden foe.

Danni ran to the armor kist and dug out her own bow and quiver. Gil ran to join her. With the bow in his hand, he climbed up onto the rail, just as a second arrow flew from the forest. Floki fended it with a scornful shield, his eyes on the wall of trees. "There!" he shouted, pointing. Gil saw a brief movement among the snowy branches. A dozen arrows flew from the longship. There was a sharp cry of pain, and Floki pointed again. A second flight of arrows, Gil's and Danni's among them, rained down.

Branches cracked and swayed, and snow avalanched from the dead brown oak leaves. A horse whinnied, as if the attackers were hastening in retreat. Gil heard Lionheart's excited whicker. *Oh, great. Now he decides to be friendly.* Then, with a ferocious battle cry, Palamedes, mounted bareback on Doombearer, launched himself over the side of *Storm Serpent,* and splashing spray on every side, thundered toward the shore. Black hair and beard flying, he plunged into the forest and disappeared amid the snowy trees. Shouts of terror told that he had found his quarry.

"Come!" Ismail struggled to lift the gangplank, "We must go too!" Gil ran to help, while Danni scrambled over the bars of the pony pen and onto Frosti's back. Arnkel joined Gil and Ismail, and between them they slid the heavy ramp over the side and into the shallows.

Water rushed over it, but Danni was already urging Frosti down its precarious length. Riding bareback, her skirt hiked up and brown bare legs clinging to the pony's wet fur, she galloped ashore, drew her sword, and followed Palamedes into the forest. Rachel and Freya were right on her heels. Ismail and Gil ran for their own mounts. Chocolate clattered down the ramp and Lionheart followed, too caught up in the others' excitement to remember to balk. The moment the pony's hooves touched the shore, Gil urged him toward the forest. Behind, Northmen poured off both ships.

At the edge of the trees, Lionheart reared and shied and then, with a snort of terror, plunged through a lacy veil of branches into an eerie, snow-filled world. Sounds of distant battle reached Gil's ears, sharp clashes of steel, shouts of effort and anger, the snorting of horses. But the forest, like the sea-mist over Hy, hid all. Everything he had learned about fighting seemed useless among the great silent trees and the innocent sparkling snow.

Looking down, he saw small hoof prints and a channel through the drifts that lay belly-high on a pony. *Danni.* He dug his heels into Lionheart's furry flanks and drove him forward. Ahead, sunlight poured down through a break in the trees. When he reached it, he found a small clearing and, beyond, a wall of young firs. The hoof prints passed through the clearing, but Lionheart shook his mane and shimmied backwards. Gil thudded the pony's sides.

Lionheart extended a tentative hoof; then jumped back. *It crackles.*

"Ice," Gil whispered. The clearing was a frozen marsh. But

the ice had held Frosti. He urged Lionheart forward. *Quick.*
Faster is safer. But at the far edge, a yard from the safety of trees,
the pony stopped again. *Go! Go!*

Cat-thing. Lionheart snorted and rolled his eyes.

Gil peered at the snowy ground. No cat. No cat prints.
There's nothing. He kicked Lionheart's ribs hard. *Go!*

Lionheart shied, skidding on the snow-covered ice. It
creaked and snapped. Ominous black water rose around his
hooves. *Above! Above! Cat-thing in the tree!*

Gil's own cat-hairs rose on the nape of his neck. He
remembered Ismail's ambush, the night before and his eyes
flew upward to the dark fir branches. It wasn't a cat-thing he
saw, in the split-second before the attack, but a lithe, swarthy
boy who leapt, knife in hand, onto Lionheart's back.

Lionheart screamed, lunging backwards. With a crackling
splash, the ice gave way, and his hind legs plunged into icy
water, up to his haunches. Both Gil and the boy tumbled off,
and for a moment were mutually occupied scrambling out of
the breaking ice, onto the snowy bank. Then, with firm ground
beneath his feet, the boy rushed forward, knife hand extended.
But this time he met the point of Gil's sword.

They both froze, eye to eye over threatening steel. Gil saw a
thin young face, wild blue-green eyes, straggling black hair tied
back with a headband like Ismail's. The boy wore a rough grey
shirt, and a ragged garment of many-colored wool, wrapped
round his waist like a skirt, and over his shoulders, like a cloak.
His legs and feet were bare in the snow.

Pity rose in Gil's heart for his fear and his poverty, and he
hesitated. Instantly, the boy drove forward with his blade. Gil
swung hard, catching the long knife just below the hilt. The
boy yelped in pain as the blade flashed through the sunlit air
and vanished in a drift of snow. Clutching his bruised hand, he
turned terrified eyes to Gil. Then he sank down on his knees in
the snow, bowed his head, and waited to die.

Gil shook his head slowly and stepped back, but the boy
just cringed and closed his eyes. Lionheart whinnied suddenly,
and half-turning, Gil saw Arnkel striding quickly across the
snow-covered ice, sword raised high. "No! Stop!" he cried, as

the Northman pushed past Lionheart's muddy wet flank, to reach the kneeling youth. Arnkel laughed then and sheathed his blade. He slapped Gil's back.

"You catch!" he grinned. "You kill!" He bowed and stepped graciously out of the way.

Gil groaned inside. *Trust a Northman to remember his manners.* He looked down again at the cowering boy. *So, this was battle,* he thought sadly. Blundering around in the snow, his whole body aching still from rowing, wet, cold, and now, expected to commit murder. "I'm sorry," he whispered. He raised his sword and looked down once more at the boy. Suddenly, he saw him anew, in grey monks' robes, playing ball beneath the Great Cross of Hy. *He's just like Donal.* But he was the enemy, one of the Golden Knight's raiders who put Hy to the torch. Half closing his eyes, he lifted the blade above his head.

"Halt! Halt!" a huge voice thundered. Gil whirled, sword scything innocently through the air. Out of the forest burst two horses, galloping nose to tail. At the front, a skinny brown animal bore a ragged knight wearing a battered hauberk, but no helm. On its tail was Doombearer with Palamedes astride, stripped of his knightly courtesy, eyes ablaze with the lust for battle.

"Halt!" he roared again at his quarry. Hunted and hunter thundered out onto the frozen marsh, their weight splintering the ice, plunging both horses belly deep in black water. With three lunging leaps, they bounded across, leaving a cold, black channel behind. As they vanished again among the trees, a third horse and rider appeared in the clearing.

"Ismail!" Gil shouted, "Watch out!" But Ismail drew Chocolate to a skidding halt at the edge of the open water, dismounted, and ran lightly across the unbroken edge, toward Gil. A clash of steel sounded from the forest, then shouts and grunts as Palamedes and the ragged knight battled, out of sight. Arnkel strode off through the screen of trees. The clanging of swords grew faster and louder, and then a terrible scream knifed the cold air, rose to a shriek of agony and then cut off short.

Everything fell silent. Gil could hear his own breathing and was aware of some vague movement to his side but could think of nothing but the unseen source of that one, awful sound. Lionheart snorted and stamped. Gil turned distractedly, then froze in astonishment. The boy was there again with the knife, grinning and bold. "Huh?" Gil cried, as his adversary lunged forward and even as he raised his belated shield, he thought, *What a stupid way to die and what a stupid last word.*

And then the boy just stopped. His eyes filled with confusion and he waved his knife hand weakly and dropped the knife again into the snow. Then he slid forward and down into a silent heap with a sword half-buried in his blood-soaked back. Ismail stepped forward, over the body of the boy, and grasped Gil's shoulders, shaking him furiously. "Never turn your back to enemy!" he shouted. "Never. Never!" he was so angry that tears stood in his eyes. He shook his head and turned away.

Gil was trembling as if Ismail's hands were still shaking him. He looked down at the bloody, dead heap on the ground. "He dropped the knife. He gave up!"

"You turn your back, he find it again. This is not game. No one gives up."

"But he was so afraid of me," Gil murmured. "He was a boy."

Ismail shrugged. "I am boy," he said, without emotion. And, without emotion, he put his foot on the dead boy's back and with one firm yank, drew out his sword. It made a wet-meat sound and Gil felt something queasy rise in his gut. Ismail crouched and wiped the blade clean on the pristine snow and returned it to its scabbard. Gil looked at the long red blood smear in the snow and the queasy thing swept up his gullet like a hot snake, and suddenly he was puking his guts out all over the snowy ground.

I want to die, he thought. Then, *No, I want to go home. Home. Oh, please. Home.*

"Is okay," Ismail said softly, patting his back as gently as he patted a frightened pony. "First time. First time, I do this, too."

Then, Arnkel returned, the grin on his face assuring them that the victory had gone to Palamedes. His eyes fell on the body in the snow and his grin broadened. "Warrior!" he gave

Gil's shoulder a friendly shove. Gil shook his head and turned his clammy face away.

A wild crashing of branches and a high, frantic whinny signaled the approach of horsemen. Gil and Ismail ran back to their ponies, leapt aboard, and drew swords in readiness. Then, distinctly, in the place in his head where he heard Lionheart, Gil heard a pony voice crying out in terror. *I'm alone! I'm alone!* And out of the forest burst Frosti, rider-less and blind with panic. He skidded out onto the ice, stumbled, and fell, plunged half into the water and scrambled out again. Ismail sent Chocolate after him, and at the far edge of the clearing he grasped the runaway's loose flapping reins and drew both animals to a halt.

Frosti stood, fore-legs splayed, soaked with sweat and marsh water, his breath freezing in the cold air, eyes rolling with terror. *Where's Danni?* Gil cried but got only a picture of Frosti running and alone.

"We follow tracks back," Ismail said. He tossed the trembling animal's reins to Arnkel and urged Chocolate into the forest. Gil sheathed his sword and galloped after him, with Arnkel following on Frosti, his long legs wrapped comically around the pony's belly. The snow made easy work of the trail, though low-hanging branches and thickets of gorse soon slowed the ponies to a trot. Twice they crossed the paths of other horses; a group of four, and another, solitary rider. But Ismail led on, unerringly re-tracing Frosti's flight.

Lionheart whickered suddenly and there was an answering familiar whinny, ahead. Gil saw sunlight, and suddenly they burst into another clearing, with snow and marsh grass and a smooth stretch of hidden ice, at the edge of which two riders faced each other in deadly combat.

One was tall and bearded, dressed in a hauberk of dull chain, and a many-colored cloak, like the dead boy had worn. He rode his big brown horse easily, but warily, circling his opponent, shield raised, sword ready. The other, though small and slight, rode so gracefully and wielded sword and shield with such confidence that Gil's first thought was that the pair were evenly matched. Then he caught a quick glimpse of a long auburn braid, and a Stooping Hawk device on the shield. Driving Freya straight at the brown horse, Rachel lunged forward, sword held high to meet her foe. Steel clashed furiously on steel, once, twice, three times.

Gil thudded his heels into Lionheart's flanks. "Go! Go!" He charged into the clearing and in the same instant the bearded rider's blade spun in a bright arc from his hand, vanishing into the snow. The man stared, in a brief moment of total astonishment, then seeing Gil, Ismail, and Arnkel thundering out of the forest, spun his horse to flee. Rachel whirled Freya, too, shield raised, and then a brilliant smile lit up her face. "Gil! Ismail!" Ignoring her disarmed opponent, she beckoned urgently toward the wall of trees beyond the clearing. "They've got Danni."

Gil turned Lionheart, without breaking stride. Splashing through marsh and cracking ice, he shouted, "Ismail! You lead!" Ismail galloped to the edge of the forest, trotted swiftly back and forth and then, picking up the trail, urged Chocolate into a dark gap between the trees.

But Arnkel veered instead to cut off the escape of Rachel's defeated warrior. "No time!" Gil shouted. "Leave him!" Arnkel ignored him. Catching up with the bearded man, he hurled himself from Frosti's back onto the brown horse's rump, unseating its rider and tumbling with him into the snowy marsh. Pulling his soaking adversary upright, Arnkel spun him around and landed a firm kick on the seat of his pants. The man sprawled, face-down, in muddy water. "Now I leave!" Arnkel grinned, mounted the brown horse and followed Gil into the forest with Frosti, rider-less again, at their heels.

The tracks of a single horse, weighed down by a double load, meandered erratically through the trees and thickets. Hoof prints sank deep in the snow and in one place the drifts were churned and flattened, and footprints appeared. Ismail got down and studied them. "Two people, one big, one small. Push, shove, struggle. Here," he pointed, "Mount again." He jumped back up on Chocolate and followed the continuing track. "They not go fast," he assured Gil. "We catch soon." And he slowed his pony to quiet their passage.

Then, ahead, they heard a shout and a curse and a sharp cry of pain. Ismail kicked Chocolate into a gallop and the others followed, dodging and ducking wildly through the trees. Suddenly, a tall black horse loomed in the shadows of a great fir. On its back was a big, powerful knight, with a flowing red beard and hair, and mounted before him, pinned in place by one huge arm, was Danni. Wriggling sharply around, she bent her head and fastened teeth into her captor's bare wrist. He howled and shook her off and Gil saw on his face a weary puzzlement, like he'd started something he had no idea how to finish.

Danni glimpsed Gil, around her captor's shoulder, and with a flash of delighted triumph, re-doubled her efforts, kicking and biting and struggling all the while to reach her sword. The red-bearded man let go of his reins and grasped both her hands in both of his. And then, as he held them up, a look of astonishment crossed his face.

Slowly shaking his head, he released her hands and pointed at one of them. Then he leapt down from his horse, leaving Danni still mounted, and knelt in the snow at its feet. "My lady!" his voice rang out, "A hundred sorrows pierce my heart, that I have offended you, a maid of Guinevere!" He bowed his head. Danni stared down at him. Then she looked up to Gil, approaching cautiously on Lionheart, and raised her hands in a baffled shrug.

One by one, the others joined them, until their ponies made a half-circle around Danni and the kneeling knight. He looked up dazedly and seeing himself surrounded, proclaimed, "My lady, I dare not ask your forgiveness. But if these be your liegemen, commit me, I beg you, to the mercy of their swords. I deserve no more."

Arnkel's eyes lit up but Gil caught his borrowed horse's bridle, holding the animal back. "He's either crazy, or we're missing something," he said to Ismail.

"Her hands," Ismail murmured. "He sees her hands. Sets free."

"The ring!" Rachel cried. "'A maid of Guinevere.' He saw Guinevere's ring!" She slipped from her pony and ran forward. Kneeling in front of the knight, she extended her arm, revealing the bracelet given her by the Lady Griselle. "Do you know this, too?"

The knight's eyes widened. He took her hand in his own, bent his head over it, and kissed it tenderly. Then he rose to his feet and, looking up to Danni, gently took her hand and kissed it, too. "Alas!" he mourned, "I truly have laid hands upon a maiden of my queen. May Heaven strike me dead a hundred times."

"Then stand back," growled an angry voice, "And let a Northman save Heaven the trouble." Mounted absurdly on the little black pack-pony, Lucy, Floki Magnusson rode into their midst. Sword in hand, he cantered up to the knight and held the tip in front of his face.

"No!" Danni cried. "He didn't mean it." Floki hesitated, but only for a second.

"Then whatever 'it' is," he said sharply, "He should not have done it," and he flicked the sword, cutting a curl from the knight's red beard.

"He's not an enemy!" Rachel said quickly. "He serves Queen Guinevere."

"Then why does he attack my ship?"

The knight looked up at Floki. The sword tip, yet set to his throat, seemed not to worry him at all. "Slay me, if you wish, but if it please you, I would first speak."

"Speak!" Floki cried. "Why not? It is but the sixth hour, and I have only to drag my keel a fair Norse mile of river marsh before nightfall! But speak! Let us chatter like women to pass the time!"

Still facing the sword, the stranger bowed warily. "I am a knight of King Arthur," he began, "Owain by name."

"Another of those," Floki groaned. "And does he not sound like our own noble fool, Palamedes?"

"Sir Palamedes?" The knight's face lit joyfully. "Does he ride with you?"

"At this fine moment, he does," Floki answered, "though more often he but weighs down our ships with his armor and his monstrous horse."

"Oh, sweet it is to hear his name!" the knight declared. "For once we shared a table. But, alas, as any could see, I have fallen from those days. Reduced by Lady Poverty to lurking embushed in the forest like a beast of prey. Falling upon hapless travelers. Stealing women to sell to the Northmen, for my bread."

"I am a Northman," growled Floki. "Do I look in need of buying a wife?"

"He doesn't mean you," Danni said quickly.

"Oh, does he not?" Floki snapped. "Well, that is good then. For, should he sell you to me, there would be no coin small enough to pay the price." He waved the sword dramatically and sheathed it. "But since you defend him, so, then, have him." He turned to the knight, "Have her." He spun Lucy about and turned back to the forest. "I have a ship to free."

"Then let us help you!" cried the knight. And before Floki could move to stop him, he reached down to his side, not for his sword, but for a cow horn, slung by a ribbon from his belt. Lifting it, he blew one pure, sweet note.

"Curse you!" Floki shouted and he kicked Lucy hard, driving her at Sir Owain and again drew his sword.

Danni shrieked. "No, Floki! He's on our side! He's calling his friends!"

"He calls for swords," said Floki. "Sharp steel beneath sweet words."

Suddenly the knight lunged forward and grasped Floki's sword arm by the wrist. Gil gasped at his speed and his betrayal and reached for his own blade, while Ismail charged to Floki's defense. But Sir Owain only turned the sword toward himself, laying the edge again against his own throat.

"See!" he said softly. "You may take my head from my body if one of them offers you harm." He paused, then released the sword.

"Let them come," Floki said, with something like respect.

A sound rose, then, in the forest, a high, keening music, both beautiful and strange. Gradually, it drew closer. Lionheart snorted and stamped because it was new. Floki and Arnkel turned, weapons ready. Then, out of the snow-bent trees came a tall, white-haired man playing an instrument made from the puffed-up skin of an animal, stuck with hollowed out pieces of wood. Into one, he blew with a steady breath and on another, he fingered a melody.

From all sides came men and boys, armed with shields and swords, bows or spears, some mere sharpened stakes. But old men came, too, hobbling in the snow, and women and small, frightened children. The men were dressed, in rough grey shirts and long wrapped cloaks of many-colored wool. The women wore ragged dresses of the same grey cloth and draped their cloaks over their heads. One had a baby wrapped tightly in hers. Others enfolded their shivering children. All were barefoot and thin, their faces lined with weariness.

When two dozen had gathered, the old man ceased to play, and rested his bagpipes under his arm. Sir Owain smiled sadly and turned to Floki. "These are my people," he said. "Once they were knights and esquires, ladies and their maidens, the joy and delight of Arthur's court. And to this," he gestured with a mournful look, "They are reduced, vassals of hunger and thralls of winter, so the Usurper may deck himself in gold."

Rachel looked stricken. "Can't we help them?" she asked Floki.

Sir Owain shook his head. "We have grieved you too much, already. But ahead lie the marshes where neither sail nor oar will serve you. We have horses and strong backs. Let the debt we owe you be repaid."

"And when your warriors ride from the hills, these wretches will be already among us," Floki said. "Each with a knife at our ribs."

Sir Owain's face darkened. "Sir," he said. "I owe you much, but not the right to besmirch my honor. By what cause do you make so ignoble a charge?"

"By good cause!" Floki grinned cheerfully. "For it is what I would do myself. That is why I still live, and others are the sport of ravens."

Sir Owain met Floki's mocking grin with a look of grave alarm. "I pray you but jest, good sir, for you grieve my heart with your discourteous words."

"And you grieve mine with your foolishness," Floki answered. "It is my custom to grant my enemies wisdom equal to my own. In your case, I am mistaken. But look! Here comes one at least your equal. Welcome, noble Palamedes!"

He bowed dramatically from the little pony's back as Palamedes cantered out of the forest, mounted on mighty Doombearer. His eyes fell on Sir Owain and he gave a great shout of joyful welcome. Flinging himself from his horse, he wrapped the red-haired knight in his enormous embrace. "Well met! Well met! Sir Owain!" he declared, and then, standing back, he said with lowered voice, "Ah, good sir, our king would scarce know us, today."

"Nor would you know him," said Floki, "With his bare bones gleaming through his grave clothes."

A murmur of shock swept round the gathering and in the midst of the unhappy crowd a little girl with a smudged face said innocently, "But our king still lives!"

Floki looked down at the child and gave her a small smile. "Then I am wrong," he said. "Forgive me. I am but a Northman." He raised his eyes to the adults. "Enough. I have work to do." He turned the little pony in a circle, and then looked back to Danni. "Do you ride with him?" he said sharply. "Or with me?"

Danni looked hard at him and then suddenly she jumped down from the knight's horse, caught Frosti's loose reins and leapt on his back. "I ride with my friends," she said. She swept past Floki without a glance. Rachel turned Freya and followed and Ismail reined Chocolate around. Teeth bared and ears flattened, Lionheart edged past Lucy, and Gil, too, cantered back through the snowy forest to the river and the ships.

Men and ponies were loaded again, oars lowered, and the re-floated *Silver Dragon* slipped free of the riverbank and the tangle of sunken logs that had held her fast. Behind, *Storm Serpent*, too, surged out into the river's flow. Looking back, Gil saw no sign of all that had happened but a trampled patch of snow at the water's edge. But then, in the forest, the strange music arose again, joined by women's voices wailing in wordless grief for the dead boy and the knight Palamedes had slain.

Over his shoulder he heard Ismail's soft voice. "Do you still seek justice, my friend?" Fiercely, Gil shook his head. Then he turned his face to the dragon prow as the powerful oars of the Northmen bore them away.

CHAPTER FIVE

The sun was below the hills when they reached the marshes. The land opened out between wooded ridges and before them stretched a broad, rough grassland buried in snow. Hummocks of marsh grass and heather glistened pink in the fading light. The river, which had tumbled over rocks and rapids, slowed and shallowed. Oar blades came up muddy and strewn with weeds. A flock of grey geese took wing in front of their prow, circled, and set out in a lengthening vee, calling hauntingly into the dusk. Gil looked down at the ice-rimmed channel of the river, winding through impenetrable marshland. "Now what?"

Erling laughed. "Now," he said, "we work." He shipped his oar and rose to his feet, stretching weary arms. All around him, the Northmen raised their oars and stacked them out of the way. Hakon's crew carefully poled *Storm Serpent* through the shallow waters until she and *Silver Dragon* rested side by side.

Wrapped in furs against the cold, Hakon stepped from his ship to Floki's, and the two young cousins stood looking out over the snowbound landscape and talking quietly in their own tongue. Floki turned away. "Now," he said to Danni, "we will see what price your noble warrior's diversion."

"He's not my warrior," she cried indignantly. "He was stealing me, remember?"

Floki grinned. "I thought women of honor died by the sword before they'd be sold to the Northmen." Danni reddened with fury, but he only shrugged. "Whatever. He has cost us a day. We cannot cross the marsh in darkness."

"He did offer to help," Danni snapped. "You refused."

"I did not trust him," Floki said. "A traitor once many prove a traitor again."

Hakon nodded. "A wise judgement, cousin. Better a few sore backs than treachery in our midst."

But Arnkel, who had been watching and listening intently, laughed. "Aye," he said. "When it's our backs, not yours. I saw no treachery. Nor did you." His eyes flicked from Floki to Danni. "It was your lady you did not trust."

The look on Floki's face sent Arnkel scrabbling for his sword, but his hand never came close. Floki was already upon him. Grasping Arnkel's tunic with one hand and his trousers with another, he lifted him off his feet and flung him like a grain sack over the side. The enormous splash of his landing won the attention of every man on the ship. There was a slow in-drawing of breaths as Arnkel spluttered to the surface and looked up in terror. But Floki just turned back, then, to Hakon as if nothing had happened.

Relief and bafflement exploded in laughter as Arnkel, helped by his shipmates, clambered warily back on board. Throwing Arnkel overboard seemed to have cheered Floki's mood. He turned from the darkening landscape with a resigned shrug. "Beyond this marsh," he said, "Lies open water, and a far better place to spend the night. But night has found us here, with trees over our mast and marsh grass beneath our keel. So Odin wills." He looked up at the forested ridges on either side. "I need runners."

A dozen men stepped forward. "We must see," he said soberly, "if our friends of the forest hold these hills. Thorfinn!" He greeted a lean, extraordinarily tall man among the volunteers. He laid a hand on Thorfinn's shoulder and turned him to the right-hand ridge. "Seek out the view from that fine hill." With a silent nod, Thorfinn leapt from *Silver Dragon* to *Storm Serpent*, moored beside her, and down to the shallows of the marsh. Splashing through the water at a run, he set out for the ridge.

Floki's eyes swept his crew for a second man, then dropped abruptly to Arnkel, shivering under his woolen cloak. "Hail, Arnkel Fish-Tail!" he called cheerily. "Do you run like you swim?" Arnkel grinned and nodded and climbed sheepishly to his feet. Floki cuffed his wet head with a friendly hand and pointed to the ridge on the left. "Warm yourself mounting that hill before dusk."

Shouts of "Hail!" and "Fish-Tail!" went round the ship. Arnkel grinned and jumped down from the rail, at exactly the place where Floki had thrown him, waded through the water to further shouts of encouragement, and set off for his ridge at a run. Gil watched the runners until he lost sight of both in the dimming light. Behind him, he heard Hakon's quiet voice. "They run fast, but they will see little. The sun is long gone, and there will be no moon this night."

"They will see fires," Floki said.

"Men intent on plunder do not light fires."

Floki grimaced wearily. "You are full of joy, Hakon Sea-Friend. What other course would you have me sail?"

"No course," Hakon smiled. "If it were me," he reminded his cousin, "I would not be here at all."

"If it were you, we would be in our beds beneath our fathers' roofs," Floki said. "I think it is you I should throw in the sea."

"You will not do it twice," said Hakon, with an untroubled smile.

Then Rachel spoke, so suddenly that both Floki and Hakon broke off their confrontation in surprise. "I have a course," she said. And when she had their bemused attention, she added calmly, "I will go."

"You?" Hakon looked simply confounded.

But Floki grinned, delighted. "You will outpace Thorfinn Lang-Stride?" He measured her height mockingly with outstretched arms. "From head to toe, you do not make the length of his leg!"

"True," Rachel smiled, "But I will see both hill tops before he sees one, because I will fly."

Hakon breathed in slowly. "Of course," he said to his cousin, "She is one like you."

But Floki shook his head. "If my arrow can pluck a hawk from the sky, so can another man's. She is young. I will not risk her. Nor," he added, "is she like me. What I am, I was born. She has but the gift of a sorcerer. Such gifts can fail."

Gil stared at Floki. Was that true? Who, but a true Change-Thing, would know? A vision of Rachel plummeting, half-human, half-bird, from the darkening sky flashed through his mind. "No!" he said. "The runners can do it."

But Danni cried vehemently, "Aidan's not a sorcerer!"

"It is not Aidan's gift," Rachel's voice remained sweet and reasonable. "He only gave his blessing."

"Ah, forgive me," Floki bowed dramatically, "I am but a humble oarsman, unused to subtleties."

"No matter," Hakon said quickly. "Gift or blessing, it will serve our need." He looked up at the sky. "And the longer we argue, the faster the light fails."

But Floki shook his head again.

"You are both right!" Rachel gave the cousins her sweetest smile. "Floki seeks to guard my safety; Hakon, to guard our ships. But I am not safe without the ships, nor the ships safe, without me. So if I fly now, I do the will of both."

Hakon and Floki gave each other a long, wary look. Abruptly, Floki turned back to Rachel. "Then do this now, or not at all. No hawk flies at night."

Hakon cast a glance at the watching crew. "Not here. A holy man's gift, to one, is a sorcerer's witchcraft to another. Do not let them see." This time, Floki did not argue.

"The forest," he said.

Together, Rachel and Danni jumped from *Silver Dragon* to Hakon's ship, then ran down *Storm Serpent*'s gangplank to the shore. Gil followed, with Ismail. Hakon and Floki took places at either side, and both drew their swords as they entered the shadowy forest. Rachel pressed on through the drifts of snow until a cluster of black, moss-coated trunks stood between them and the ships. There, she stopped and looked up at the sky, a pale white patch between the bare, rustling branches. With a bright smile, she unsheathed her sword, and drew a circle in the snow with its tip.

"Ace!" Danni cried, and raising her skirt above her boots, jumped neatly within. Rachel raised her eyes from sheathing her sword and blinked in surprise.

Danni grinned sheepishly. "Sorry. Your circle. You go first."

She stepped carefully out again. Rachel turned uncertainly to Gil.

"One is enough," Gil said.

"Why?" Danni demanded. "There are two hills."

Gil met her eyes honestly. "Last time you didn't come back," he said.

"So, you think I'd fly off now and, like, abandon you here?"

Gil shrugged. "We're different when we're Other. If I turned Cat right now, I'd probably just curl up in a heap of furs and go to sleep." He cast a desperate glance at his companions. Ismail was crouched by the sword-drawn circle, studying a blade of frosted grass. Floki looked at the sky. Hakon smiled quietly and suddenly spoke.

"Two men on the steering board make a crooked course."

"What has that got to do with anything?" Danni snapped.

"Gil is your leader. Obey him." He cast Floki a grim look. "As I obey mine."

Floki laughed with glee. "Behold! The Merlin of the North! Praise Odin for the wisdom of Hakon Sea-Friend!"

Hakon laid his hand on his sword hilt, and then let it drop. "Praise Odin for the patience of Hakon Sea-Friend," he said wearily. Then he looked up at the sky and back to Rachel. "Come," he said more cheerfully. "Let this Change-Thing fly."

Rachel stepped with solemn grace into her circle in the snow. She folded her arms, her lips moving as if reminding herself of the words. Then, touching the talisman at her throat, she began to recite the blessing. Gil shut his eyes until in the darkness he heard a whirr of feathered flight and opened them in time to see a flash of brown wings mounting the air.

"Yesu spare us," Hakon whispered, his face pale. Floki laughed, watching the hawk circle, already high above their heads. Then, all fell silent and in the hush of the snowy forest, they waited for Rachel's return. The light faded. Night gathered itself among the dark trees and doubts rose again in Gil's heart.

"You should have let me go," Danni said. She looked worried now, rather than angry. "Rachel's really new at it." Gil knew that didn't matter. No one taught him how to be Cat.

"Maybe she's hunting," he said, remembering his own easy distraction.

"Or she roosts for the night." Hakon sounded as uneasy as Gil felt. "No hawk will fly where she cannot see." But Floki still looked calmly up at the sky. And then, suddenly, he placed his fingers to his mouth and whistled a high, piercing note. Slipping his fur mantle from his shoulder, he wrapped it, skin side out, around his forearm. The light flickered, and a swift shape swept out of the dusk. Darting through the darkening trees, the hawk dove like an arrow into their midst. Wings outstretched, grey-banded tail spread, she alighted with a slap of fierce claws on Floki's outstretched arm.

He laughed with delight. "Now here is a prize worth winning," he said. He bowed his head to the fierce creature on his arm and said, "I would keep you like this a little longer, but night falls. Come." With his free hand he unbuckled his sword belt and held it up with the loose ends clasped in his fist, making a loop. "Fly, pretty one," he whispered. "Fly home."

The hawk spread her wings, leapt free of his arm, and flashed through the circle. Floki dropped the sword belt and reached out both arms, and suddenly Rachel was in them. Her cheeks were pink and her red hair tumbled free, half-hiding her face. Her eyes sparkled and she looked up into his exactly as she had as Hawk. "Wonderful!" she cried breathlessly. "Oh, wonderful!" Then she became at once dutiful. "No one," she said. "No one on either hill, no one in the valleys beyond. Nothing. No one moves. No tracks. No fires. I saw a herd of stags, two mountain hares and three wolves. A fox. A wildcat and her kittens. Nothing more." She paused dreamily, oblivious in her excitement of Floki's encircling arms.

Danni watched with the befuddled expression of somebody woken from sleep. "I didn't want to come back," Rachel said suddenly. Then, looking around, she seemed to come awake herself. "Excuse me," she said politely, and with a gentle smile, Floki lifted his hands and released her. "I flew on and on, much further than I needed." Rachel turned and looked right at Danni. "I'm sorry. I really didn't understand."

Danni shrugged. "It's okay," she said. But she looked at Floki as she said it and she didn't smile. She turned and started back, alone, through the forest.

Gil walked quickly after. It was so dark now that he had to follow footprints in the snow. Danni walked on ahead, her back stiff and straight. "Is she still mad at me?" Gil whispered to Ismail.

Ismail smiled. "She is mad," he said. "But, be glad! It is nothing about you." He nodded wisely toward Floki, walking side by side with Rachel. They stopped while Rachel described something she'd seen, and Hakon overtook them impatiently. When he joined Gil and Ismail, he laughed.

"Women are like longships," he said. "Should you wish to go there," he gestured left, "you turn the steering oar there," and he mimicked thrusting the rudder hard to the right. Then he pointed back to Floki and Rachel, and ahead to Danni. "Now she thinks he sails away from her. Now she would have him sail back!"

Gil peered into the darkness and at last something clicked in his brain. "She's jealous!" he cried. Ismail laughed softly and Hakon slapped Gil's back.

"Reef your sail, my friend. I think Odin sends storm."

Back at the marshy shore, they found the crews of both ships still peering up at the dim hills, seeking the returning runners. Floki said nothing of what he had learned from Rachel, but took his place among them, watching, too.

Thorfinn Lang-Stride was the first back, smiling broadly, his clothes, hair, and beard covered in snow. Floki listened to his report and clapped his hand on his shoulder, thanking him. When Arnkel, too, returned, to welcoming shouts of "Fish-Tail!" he listened as carefully. Then, holding Arnkel's arm up, like that of a conquering hero, he called out two quick orders that brought a cheer from every man: "Fire," and "Ale."

As Arnkel swaggered off to claim the ale cask, Floki laid his fur mantle aside and began humbly gathering firewood. He was joined at once by a dozen eager followers, each vying with the others to collect the biggest hoard. First among them was Arnkel, the man he had thrown into the marsh.

"Warrior!" Gil looked up. Erling stood on an open patch of

shore, scraping snow from the sand with the broad side of an axe. "Dream less! Work more!" he pointed at the snow-cleared spot before him. "No hearth, no fire." Ismail was already staggering toward Erling, weighed down by an enormous river stone. Gil ran to help. When they had collected enough flat rocks to make a dry platform, Erling knelt in the snow to lay his fire.

Patiently he set out a selection of kindling, graded from clusters of pinecones and tiny dry twigs, to thin, dead branches and sturdy chunks of driftwood. Last, he unwrapped a hank of oily wool, kept dry in a covering of leather, and laid it in the center. Gil watched eagerly for the final step: the freeing of the fire itself, which Erling carried, trapped like a genie in a little metal box. Just as at Cille Aidan, where the evening's embers were re-kindled for each morning's fire, so, from the first night on the Pentland shore, all down the wild coast, the campfire was lit with a glowing coal from the night before. Thus, Magnus Redbeard's hearth fire had warmed them all the way to Hy.

But the magical box in its nest of leather-wrapped straw did not appear. Instead, Erling untied a leather pouch from his belt and took from it a rectangle of rough, grey metal and three small dark stones, and laid them on the stone hearth. "Two days pass," he said. "Fire dies."

Gil puffed breath onto cold hands. At least there would be no flame from the hearths of Hy to remind him of the crueler fires that had burned there. Erling teased out a piece of the wool, and then, with two sharp cracks, he struck the metal bar against the stone and sparks showered over the wool. One caught and smoldered and Erling deftly teased more wool over the glowing point until smoke curled upward. He added pine needles, two cones, and then twigs, and in moments a small heart of flame flickered brightly, lighting the night. "That is, like, amazing!" Gil cried.

"You have no fire-striker in Tir nan Og?" Erling's bright blue eyes widened.

"No." Gil paused. "We have...." Things. Small things. He could almost see them; they were so close to the surface of his memory. But when he tried to focus on them, they faded from the picture like a dream at dawn. "We have no fire-striker," he said.

Erling had replaced the metal rectangle and the dark stones in his leather pouch, while Ismail and Rachel built a frame of sticks around the flame. He thrust the pouch into Gil's hands. "Take," he said. "Make own fire." He nodded toward the dark forest. "In Caledon."

Gil shook his head. "I can't take this! What will you do?"

Erling shrugged. "I warm myself by Bjorn's fire. Or Thorfinn's." He pointed to Thorfinn's belt where he wore a similar leather pouch. "Fire-striker is like sword. Each man carries." Again, he handed the leather pouch to Gil. "Take."

Gil let his eager fingers close around the gift. Fire; anytime he wanted fire. It seemed a luxury beyond price. "I'll give it back to you," he said fervently. "As soon as we get back."

Erling regarded him silently, his vivid eyes unusually sober. "Yes," he said. "That will be good." Tugging solemnly on his bristly, half-grown beard, he turned away, and Gil realized Erling did not expect any of them ever to return. He saw Danni, Rachel, and Ismail all watching him uncertainly.

"I'll bring it back to you," he said again, calmly and clearly, for all to hear.

The fire and the cask of ale so cheered the company that the evening's meal, their first hot food since Christmas, seemed like a longhouse feast. A black, battered cauldron hung from a greenwood tripod over the flames, bubbling with a soup of dried fish and cabbage. Rachel and Danni kneaded barley meal into bannocks and spread them to bake on the hot stone hearth.

But with the dark, brooding forest all around, the songs were gentler, the stories less bold. One was even a love song, chanted innocently by huge, fierce Bjorn. And, when Floki stood up to recite, his story was gentle, too. He told of a young Northman, ship-wrecked on an Irish shore, who sought shelter with a kinsman, an old, settled Viking wed to the beautiful young daughter of a king. "When she smiled," Floki declared, "The sun itself shone brighter. And when she laughed, the small birds sang in the trees."

"They'll fall in love," Rachel whispered in Gil's ear. "Wait for it!" And, in Floki's story, they did, and the Northman found a new ship, and begged the Irish princess to sail with him to the Northlands. But she refused, lest the betrayal of her husband cause war with her father. And so, the Northman sailed away, as she stood watching from her husband's tower.

"The sun set," Floki recited, "and still she watched, until the tip of his masthead vanished from her sight at the rim of the twilit sea. And then, eluding her serving maids, who loved her, she climbed to the highest battlement of the tower. And with a last, sweet look toward the empty sea, she flung herself to the white surf below." He bowed his head and then looked up again solemnly. "And there is peace in that land to this day," he said. "But to this day, no bird sings."

"Surely, there was no other course!" Palamedes declared stoutly. "Honor demanded nothing less."

Floki whirled on the Saracen knight and his eyes blazed with real anger. "Honor?" he said. "Is it more honorable to be bones in the sand than warm flesh in a lover's arms?"

"But it is only a tale," Palamedes protested.

"Yes. Only a tale." Floki kicked snow into the fire and it hissed like an angry snake. He wrapped his fur cloak tighter and stared into the lowering flames. "And now we sleep."

"What happened to the man?" Danni asked.

Floki smiled distantly. "He found another to love," he said, "as men do."

As the weary seamen settled on the snowy shore, Gil and Ismail rolled themselves in their sheepskins. Exhausted and aching Gil slept at once, but at the edge of morning he dreamt the awful bone dream once more. The bones were not in the Indian Kettle, now, but in the sea, and they were not his father's bones. They were light and delicate and they fell like gentle rain to the sand. Yet each landed with a thud that shook the ground. He jerked awake, gasping for breath as if he, too, was drowning in the sea. Then he heard the thud again and sat up in terror.

It was dawn, but all around his shipmates were on their feet. Palamedes had gathered the ponies and was harnessing Doombearer. Bjorn and Floki wrestled a heavy band of twisted rope around the stern of *Silver Dragon*. The ship itself looked odd and bare with her mast lowered. Aboard Hakon's ship, four crewmen brought their mast down, too.

Rachel and Danni were already saddling their ponies. Then a booted foot prodded his back and Erling's cheerful voice shouted, "Dream less! Work more!" Gil scrambled out of his sheepskins, glad not to dream at all. The heavy thudding continued, but he knew it now: the sound of axes. Within the snowy forest, the Northmen were felling trees.

Arnkel and Ragnvald appeared, carrying a long, heavy log on their shoulders. They tossed it down on the marshy ground and went back for more. Ismail emerged, dragging a log of his own and Gil ran to help. Ismail dug out two bannocks from his tunic. "Here, I save you breakfast."

Gil munched the bannocks as he followed Ismail back into the trees. They found Thorfinn and two others, lopping branches from a felled trunk. Thorfinn divested the tree of its crown and then turned it over to the boys. With the heavy trunk on their shoulders, they staggered back to the shore. When they came out of the forest, the first cut logs rested on the ground in front of *Silver Dragon*'s bow. As the combined strength of men and horses dragged the ship ashore, the rumbling of keel on wood drowned out even the thud of axes. "See!" Erling slapped Gil's back. "Floki Magnusson sails seas of wood!"

Floki rode precariously, clinging to the dragon head and calling orders to one side and then the other to pull on, or slacken, their ropes. Spotting Gil and Ismail, he pointed at their new log, then at the snowy ground before the *Silver Dragon*. "There! Now!" The bow of the moving ship was passing the foremost log. Gil and Ismail stumbled across the rough ground and pitched their tree trunk down just in time. Floki grinned and waved as the bow rode forward and then, twisting around, pointed at the stern.

"Another!" he shouted.

Two crewmen lifted the last log from the flattened ground and waved. Ismail grabbed Gil's arm. "Quick!" They ran together to the stern and took the offered log. It was slippery and snow-covered, and they struggled to keep it aloft as they ran back to the bow.

"Good!" Floki grinned, as they flung it down and the ship moved forward. Gil felt a flush of pride at the praise. Then Floki waved them again to the stern and Gil's pleasure vanished under the weight of a dawning realization.

"We keep doing this?" he whispered to Ismail. "How long?"

Ismail pointed to the far side of the marsh, where, in the growing light of the day, clear water sparkled. "That long?" he said.

Gil looked up at Floki riding the dragon prow. "I'm seriously going to kill him," he said, as he ran with Ismail back to the stern.

Hauled by rope teams of men and ponies, the two hulls surged over the rolling logs and out into open land. Ducking beneath the stern and grasping the next log, Gil thought how strange their passage would look from the hills above; two longships sailing the snowy marshlands like a still, white sea.

The snow was both friend and enemy, slick and smooth beneath sliding keels, but a churned quagmire for the feet of ponies and men. Once moving, the ships were never allowed to stop, and when men dropped out to rest and others took over, they rumbled steadily onward. Floki and Erling swapped places without a pause, Erling scrambling aloft the moving dragon prow, and Floki wrapping Erling's rope around his own shoulder as he leapt to the ground.

Bjorn began a work song and the Northmen took it up, chanting short vigorous verses that drilled their way into Gil's brain. Sweat poured down his back and glued his tunic to his shoulders. On each return, he glimpsed the red, sweaty faces and straining muscles of his shipmates, bowed beneath their rough jute ropes. He passed Floki, striding ahead as if the rope over his shoulder was a girl's hair ribbon. Their eyes met and Floki grinned. "Hey! Warrior! Do they not run in Tir nan Og?"

Something within Gil cheerfully snapped. *Bjorn's axe!* he thought gleefully. *Why mess up my sword? One quick swing. All men die.* To the rhythm of his own stumbling feet he sang a mental chant of his own to Bjorn's tune: *Axe! Sword! Floki dies! Axe! Sword! Floki dies!* He did the next two relays at a hearty trot. Then, as the burst of malevolent energy wore off, and he struggled to lift yet another log, two powerful hands suddenly whipped it from his grasp. "Rest!" Floki grinned as he and Thorfinn took over the miserable task.

"He is good leader," Ismail panted, as they slowed to a walk, falling behind the thundering ship. "He does all men's work."

Gil nodded. "But I'm still going to murder him," he said. They took their place amid a half dozen men trotting beside the longships. Unburdened, Gil's legs strode easily through marsh grass and snow. His shoulder felt light and detached, like it might float away. Beside him, Danni rode a wet and muddy Frosti, pulling on a rope, bound around her saddle pommel. When Floki ordered him to take her place, Gil found that struggling to keep the animal steady on the rough ground and the rope taut against the saddle, was almost as hard as carrying logs. Later, he took his turn hauling a rope of his own, and by the end of that, he was ready to fall into the snow and quietly die. Even murdering Floki seemed too much like hard work.

But then he heard a joyful shout and raising sweat-blurred eyes saw the white-splashed blue of a river, and sunlight sparkling on the dark waters of a loch, beyond. Around him, men broke into a run, and somehow Gil was running too. The speed of the dragged ship quickened until the river was before them. With a last sprint, they reached the shore, flung their lines aside, and leapt to safety as the hull rumbled past and swept with a mighty roar into the water below. Half a ship's length behind, Hakon's *Storm Serpent* followed, raising a splash that drenched Gil from head to toe.

Bjorn and Erling scrambled aboard *Silver Dragon* to raise the mast, as men and ponies were loaded. Last aboard was Floki, and barely was the gangplank free of the shore, when oars dipped deep and the ship surged into her native element once more. Gil flopped against a rower's kist, grinning at Ismail. Above, the sky was blue, and behind them rose a stout south wind. They slipped out into the open loch and Floki called for sail, and as the battered cloth rode up the mast, all seemed right with the world.

Running before the south wind, they made fine speed and at the sixth hour they reached the head of the second loch.

Again, they portaged the ships across land. Men and ponies worked familiarly now, and well before dusk, the crossing was complete. With the ships safe in open water, they found a sand beach and made camp, though this night even the Northmen were too weary for songs and wanted only to sleep.

The next day was grey and stormy, but the south wind held true, and a half day's sail brought them to the last portage. Gil felt the muscles hardening in his arms and he hoisted the first log to his shoulder with a twinge of pride. At None, they were in sight of the next river, and though dusk was falling as they raised their mast, they pressed on. And so, at nightfall on the fourth day from Hy, they came to the last great loch. Almost at once, the wind fell light and Floki and Hakon ordered their sails lowered. The ships seemed suddenly small and alone in a silent, brooding fearsome place. As oars dipped softly into silken black water, no man spoke.

Gil looked around warily, in the last fading light. The loch was huge, filling all the great cleft of Glen Alban with its water and stretching away into blackness, north and east. Great hills rose on either side, their tops gleaming with ice and snow, their flanks dark with forest. Above, the clearing sky was a high, pale crystalline blue in which shone one cold star. But lower down, just above the water, mist was already gathering, like the sea-mist the morning they left Hy. It swirled in moving wisps right up to the rails of the ship, wrapping like a living thing around the Northmen's dripping oars.

Floki looked grimly across the still waters to the dark land beyond. "Here, we set no foot ashore," he said. No one argued. The boldest of the Northmen seemed more than willing to sleep beside their ready oars, that night.

Floki signaled to Hakon and the oarsmen brought both longships into the shelter of a curving bay. Bjorn stowed his oar, climbed up to the bow, lifted the rusted anchor from its resting place, and pitched it, with a great splash, overboard. A second splash broke the eerie silence as Hakon's anchor followed theirs into the loch. Though they were only yards from the shore, the lines ran out nearly to their ends before they tugged, at last, to rest. Watching the tethered longships twisting and turning like

snared prey, Gil shivered at the thought of so much black water
beneath them. But, raising his eyes to the mist-cloaked shore, he
saw no better refuge there.

They ate their meal of bannocks and dried meat in silence,
and then Gil, like the others, curled wearily into his sheepskins.
But, despite the brutal work of the day, he struggled to sleep, his
senses so heightened that on the edge of dreaming he imagined
for an instant he had slipped into Cat unaware. Each breath of
the cold air assaulted him with the reek of ponies and unwashed
men. His ears were filled with the creaking of ship timbers and
the velvety splash of waves on the shore. But then he awoke
fully and every blister and bruise of his aching limbs defined
his human form. Turning over painfully, he looked around.

His eyes picked out the figures of dozing men on both ships.
He saw the great bulk of Palamedes, sitting stiffly upright in
Storm Serpent's stern, and a smaller figure that might have been
Hakon, at the bow. On their own deck, Bjorn watched by the
stern and Floki by the dragon head. Gil rose, wrapped himself
in the sheepskins and picked his way over kists and sleeping
figures, to the prow.

"Hail, Warrior." Floki did not take his eyes from the misty
water, but his voice was cheerful.

"I can watch now," Gil said, "if you want."

Floki looked up briefly, but he did not move. "Thirty men
sleep on this ship, Warrior, with no care in their empty heads
but Irish gold. Let them watch."

Gil smiled. "At least they can sleep." He crouched on the
deck, wrapping the sheepskin closer around him. Floki turned
and looked straight into his eyes. "Are you afraid?"

"Yes," Gil said, not seeing much point in lying.

"Good. You would be very stupid if you were not." Floki
turned and stretched one arm toward the distant mountainous
shore. "Look, Warrior," he said. Gil peered into the darkness,
where the hills, rising above the low-lying mist, gleamed
sullenly beneath a starry sky. "See there? That notch like the
cleft of a Northman's axe?" Gil nodded, his eyes on the great
cut in the dim horizon. "There lies a valley, steep and rugged,
and through it flows a river no longship will ever sail. Twice it

breaks over rocks and tumbles down the mountain side, and in the lower of those places lie the Falls of the Fugitive. There, tomorrow, I set you ashore. It is but two days ride, then, to that place men once called Camelot. Though it is the fiercest road any man can ride, haunted both by this world and the next." He looked back at Gil. "And there," he said, "You ride alone."

Gil thought of the first time he saw Floki Magnusson and his ship full of Viking warriors, on the shore of Cille Aidan. How could he have imagined a day when parting from them might be the scariest thing he could do?

"Are you afraid?" Floki repeated.

"Terrified," Gil said. He tried, and failed, to grin. Floki watched him solemnly. In the starlight he looked uncannily like his selkie mother.

"You do not have to do this thing," he said. He sounded almost kind.

Gil was silent. Then he answered quietly, "What would you think of me if I didn't?"

"I would think you were a coward," Floki said. "But I would think you were wise."

Gil laughed weakly. "That's such a great choice."

"Better than no choice."

Gil nodded again, thinking, actually, he'd prefer no choice. He saw himself balancing on the edge of the Lookout Rocks, at home in Greene Mountain Falls, struggling to make himself jump into the awful waters of the Indian Kettle Pool. "I would never have known any of this," he murmured softly. Floki shook his head, puzzled. Then Gil said clearly, "Tomorrow, I ride to Camelot."

Floki laughed. "Then you are very stupid," he said.

"Okay," Gil refused to be riled. "But probably not too stupid to watch this ship."

Floki leaned back against the carved wood of the dragon's long neck. He smiled then, suddenly. "No. Probably not. But you are young and the young need sleep. Go," he ordered. As Gil turned away, Floki called, "Warrior!" Gil looked back over his shoulder. Floki nodded. "You do well, this voyage, Warrior," he said.

CHAPTER SIX

Gil woke to the sound of the anchor thudding on board and the subtle lightening of the un-tethered ship. The dawn was swathed in grey, bereft of landmarks beyond the faint shadow of *Storm Serpent* raising her anchor beside them. The wind had fallen so light that, as oars dipped softly into glassy water, he could hear each ripple resounding from the hidden shore. He berated himself for not taking a compass bearing last night. But, untroubled by the enveloping mist, Floki set a sure hand on his steering oar and turned the longship's prow to their unseen goal. Under steady oars, they rode out into the loch.

It was an eerie passage, like their sailing from Hy, but without *muinntir* bell or crashing surf to guide them, nor barking seals, nor mewing gulls for company. Danni climbed up onto her perch on the bars of the pony pen, as if that small height would overcome the blanketing mist. Gil peered into the greyness, but saw only small, swimming spots before his eyes. He lost all sense of time and grew irrationally certain that they had escaped the walls of mountains hemming in the loch and sailed out of the world of men and beasts entirely.

Suddenly a small wave raised the longship's bow and rippled with a murmuring whisper beneath its keel. Floki called, "Raise oars," and *Silver Dragon* settled gently into her wash. Beside them, Hakon's ship did the same. Floki left the steering oar with Erling and walked softly up the deck and stood, his hand on the dragon prow, peering into nothingness. Then he shrugged and clapped his hands and the rowers on both ships bent again to their task, as he walked slowly back to the stern, listening and watching.

But just as he laid his hand on the steering oar again, Danni suddenly shouted, "Look!" She waved an excited arm, "A ship! Another ship!" Gil stared into the swirling mists, and then he, too, saw: grey against grey, the graceful outline of a longship's dragon prow. Here, where they had seemed alone in the universe, a stranger sailed, too.

They watched in wary silence as the ghostly prow grew nearer. Gil's hand dropped to his sword hilt. He fixed his gaze on the bold figurehead, trying to still his ragged breathing, and in that moment, the whole figurehead turned. The head pivoted at right angles on its graceful neck, and Gil saw, looking back at him, a gleaming, living eye.

He grasped a shroud to keep from falling. "It's alive!" Rachel swayed against him and clutched his arm for support. Gil's gaze stayed fastened helplessly on the glistening swaying head and the glowing eye that held his with a cobra's stare.

"What is it?" he whispered at last.

"Dragon," Svein murmured, as calmly as he might have said "otter" or "fish." He stood still, his hand frozen to his sword hilt. Then Floki, standing like a statue on the steering board, said in the same calm voice. "Do not move. It hunts by sight."

It was so close now that Gil could see the glittering scaly skin of its arched neck, and the dark clarity of its enormous eyes. It shook its head, splashing droplets of water, and he saw shining tendrils of translucent hair tumbling like a horse's mane from the arch of its neck. It turned its quick head, showing the flutter of a stubby webbed ear. And then it snorted and he cringed back from its rank, fishy breath, and his hand slipped an inch on the shroud.

Instantly, the head snapped back and the eye shuttered closed and opened again. Gil caught his breath in his throat and froze himself still, as the long neck reached out and the wet snout hovered a yard from his face. Then, like a bored cat, it yawned and he saw twin rows of gleaming scimitar teeth. He clung to his shroud and closed his eyes.

And then he heard a quiet, collective sigh from his shipmates and when he forced himself to look again, the beast had turned away. Swiveling its alert, intelligent head, it looked from *Silver*

Dragon to *Storm Serpent* as if recognizing a facsimile of itself in each of their figureheads. Then, arching its neck, it bowed down to the silky loch water and with a rippling undulation of its long dark back, plunged beneath the surface.

Gil caught the flick of a webbed fish-fin, and glimpsed a supple tail, and then it was gone. The loch bubbled and smoothed and then nothing was left but silently spreading rings. Rachel said in a small girl's voice, "Is it gone?"

"Do not move," Floki answered. "And do not speak." And so they stood, silent in the mist, for a time Gil could not measure.

At last, Hakon called softly across the water, "What say, cousin?"

"I feel it near," Floki answered. But then he turned cautiously on the steering board and looked all around.

"Perhaps it sleeps," Hakon called. "We cannot wait forever, cousin."

Floki nodded. "Then let us go," he said, but for the first and only time, Gil heard uncertainty in his voice. Still, he signaled his oarsmen, and as the oars bit deep and the ship surged forward, relief swept the crew like a breath of south wind. And then, with a crack like rock against their keel, the beast struck. Its mighty back rose beneath their bow, thrusting it into the air. *Silver Dragon* lurched hard to her load board, burying her rail in black water, and pitching Floki from the steering board into a tangled heap of his stunned crew.

Gil lost his hold on the shroud and landed on top of Bjorn who brushed him off like a dead fly. Scrambling to his feet on the slanting deck, he saw Danni clinging to the tilting pony pen as the beasts within stumbled and careered against each other. Gripping a sliding kist, and then the mast, Gil staggered through a rush of water to reach her. Then he heard Svein's warning shout, looked up, and cried out in terror.

Above the bow, the great sinuous neck of the beast rose once more. Teeth flashing, it twined around the figurehead and locked itself in mortal combat with its wooden foe. Again, every man on board froze, clinging to whatever handhold they could find. Gil heard a pony squeal and saw Freya rear high, then crash down against the railings of her pen. The wood splintered and gave way and Danni fell to the tilting deck and tumbled toward the black water of the loch. The beast's head snapped around, and in an instant, it abandoned its wooden adversary for living prey.

"Danni!" Gil shouted, as the long neck snaked towards her. "I'm coming!" Drawing his sword, he flung himself down the sloping deck with no thought but getting himself between her and the worst death he could imagine.

But Floki was there before him. Sword in hand, he clambered over the backs of his stunned crew and up to the splintered figurehead. Gripping it with his free hand, he swung himself over the dark water, slashing at the beast's mighty neck. The razor-sharp steel scraped across shining scales and barely left a mark. Then the beast whipped its fearsome head around, drew back and snapped forward so fast Gil saw nothing but a blur. Its jaws fastened on Floki's sword arm and shoulder, wrenched him from his hold, and flung him like a bloody rag onto the deck. His sword fell beside him with a ringing clash and then there was utter silence.

Every man of his crew stood staring with disbelief at their captain, sprawled face down on the blood-soaked deck; the unearthly animal swaying above him. Then the dragon flattened its webbed ears, shook its glittering mane, and raised its snake-head high for the kill.

"No!" Danni cried. She scrambled to her feet and crossed the deck before anyone could move. Crouching, she took up Floki's great sword, and struggling even to lift its weight, rose and stood over him. "No!" she cried again, and looking straight into the eyes of the dragon, she raised the blade with mighty effort and swung it over her head.

The beast swayed to left and right. But Danni mirrored each move, turning as it turned, swaying as it swayed, meeting each darting lunge with the point of the sword. The dragon snorted and yawned, blinking its huge eyes at the small, baffling irritant between it and its prey.

But Danni held her ground, and at last, with an angry shake of its mane, the beast turned away. Its scaly head shot out and its jaws closed again on the battered figurehead, venting its frustration on the splintered wood. With a final petulant snap at its painted foe, it arched its great neck and slipped beneath the waters of the loch and was gone. The circling ripples died away and again silence fell on the stricken ship.

Then, to his amazement, Gil heard a low familiar laugh. Floki raised himself on his uninjured arm and turned his head, just enough that he could see Danni standing above him. "Now there is a woman to die for," he whispered. He dropped his head again, to the bloody deck, and a pained sigh swept over the watching men. Then he rolled over with a gasp of agony and raised his fist to his crew, or the beast, or the sky itself, and shouted, "I am Floki Magnusson and *I do not die this day!*" He closed his eyes and drew a deep breath and then called out, "Hakon! Hakon Sea-Friend! Now!"

Storm Serpent drew alongside, and Hakon leapt black water before his ship was even moored. The wet deck planks rang with the urgent thudding of his boots as he ran forward and pushed his way through the cluster of Northmen surrounding Floki. He looked gravely down, then slowly shook his head. "You are wrong, cousin," he said. He smiled sadly, "Say your prayers, now, my friend, to whichever god you choose."

Floki clutched his bloody shoulder and squinted up at Hakon. "If I had known you were so holy," he whispered, "I'd have left you on Hy. Cease preaching, Sea-Friend! I need your help!" The two cousins locked eyes in what Gil guessed might be the last battle of their lives, but Hakon abruptly gave way. He shouted to his ship and a crewman appeared with the leather bag of ointments he had used on the boy Danni had wounded with her sword.

Floki watched with grim approval and murmured, "Odin save me from the piety of Northmen." Then, gritting his teeth, he sat up with an effort that took the last color from his face and braced himself against two of his crew. As his cousin stripped away his shredded tunic and bathed and bound the terrible wounds of the dragon's teeth, he sat in silence, so calm and still that Gil thought he was in a kind of trance. But then he suddenly spoke. "Water laps our topmost strake, Erling," he said, quite gently, "Would it not be wise to bail?"

Erling leapt to his feet, shaking off his fear and his shock. Shouting orders, he took charge of the ship and its crew. Gil and Ismail were sent to haul up deck planks, climb down onto the bare ribs of the ship with leather buckets, and scoop out the icy water that had breached the rail.

Gil was glad of the work, something to take his mind from what Floki was enduring and from the beast that had caused it. Still, images rose before his eyes, of the savagery of the dragon and how quickly it had wrought such awful damage. He turned to Ismail, as he dipped his bucket into the lowering pool of water. "Can he really stay alive?" he whispered. Ismail looked guarded. "I mean, just by saying so?" Gil said. "Just by, like, refusing to die?"

Ismail thought and nodded. "Some men can." And Gil imagined that if anyone could survive by sheer stubbornness, it was probably Floki.

Gradually, the ship righted herself, and when there was nothing left between the curved ribs of the *Silver Dragon*'s hull but shallow puddles, they straightened up and re-laid the deck planks. The sky was clearing overhead, revealing brief patches of blue. Over the splintered figurehead, Gil saw the faint outline of the mountainous shore they sought. It seemed startlingly close, with not many more oar-strokes they might have escaped the assault of the dragon entirely. *Odin's will*, he thought suddenly.

Hakon put his medicines away, and Floki sat now with his back to a sea-kist, wrapped in furs and shaking with cold, but alert. He looked around at his crew, all still watching him fearfully, and shook his head in exasperation. "Have you forgotten how to row?" They jumped to their places then, and setting his eyes on the clearing sky, and then the trembling of a stay in the rising wind, he called, "Raise sail."

They made landfall on a silver beach at the foot of a wooded bluff. High above, the ice-bound Falls of the Fugitive glittered in the morning light, and through the dark pines beside them ran the road to Camelot. Gil stared up at it in the faint winter sun, barely believing they were here.

Floki ordered his crew to set their passengers and their mounts ashore and turn the longships at once back the way they had come. But Hakon quietly shook his head. "Every man here needs warmth and food and sleep. You most of all." He commanded the ships unloaded, a guard mounted, and wood gathered for a fire.

No one moved. The Northmen stood shuffling their feet and looking warily from Floki to Hakon, weighing up the dangers of a change of allegiance. Hakon waited, keeping his calm quiet for an impossibly long time. Then suddenly his brows lowered, his face darkened ominously, and his black eyes lit with fury. He drew his sword and waved it in a flashing arc around his head. "Go!" he shouted. "Go! Go! Go!"

There was a thundering stampede of feet in all directions as men fell over each other to obey his orders. Hakon lowered the sword then and turned and pointed it at Floki. "And if I hear one word of retribution from you, I will finish myself what that sensible beast began. I have tholed you all my life, cousin, and today I have had enough!" He sheathed the sword and stalked off the ship, and nobody spoke a word.

Gil and Ismail crept past Floki and joined the girls leading the ponies from their shattered pen. Lionheart followed meekly, nose to ground. *What's wrong?* Gil said as the pony's shod hooves plodded softly over the sand. He saw a picture of the dragon, rearing from the loch in all its ferocity. *It's gone,* he said. *The dragon's gone.* The picture faded a little, but Lionheart still had no words. Gil patted him sadly. *Poor little pony. I wish you were still at Cille Aidan.*

That day's camp was like none they'd made before. Hakon mounted not two guards, but a ring of warriors with swords and shields, holding the beach and the high ground around it. When Gil and his friends went into the forest for firewood, they were aware, all the time, of watching eyes on every side, and were glad.

The fire burned brightly already, when they got back to the strand, and the two cousins were together by the flames. Hakon sat on a driftwood log and poked at the fire with his sword. Beside him, Floki lay shivering under a heap of furs. The effort of leaving the ship had taken a toll and he rested now with half-closed eyes and the same remote stillness as when Hakon had dressed his wounds. Hakon watched him in silence, though whether it was a concerned or a threatening silence, Gil wasn't sure. They approached as quietly as they could and laid their wood on the flames. But just as he had done on the ship, Floki suddenly spoke. "Warrior," he said, "Come here." Cautiously, Gil stepped closer.

Floki opened his eyes properly and studied him. For all his bravado, he looked weary and beaten. "Can I do something?" Gil said, trying to sound cheerful.

But then Bjorn Break-Neck suddenly appeared, solemnly carrying Floki's sword down from the ship. He knelt with it, almost reverently, and laid the weapon down on the furs, its hilt beside Floki's good hand. Then he stood and stepped back in silence, with the same solemnity. Gil guessed his purpose at once: were they to be attacked, Floki could die fighting like the rest of them. He imagined the grimness of Bjorn's expression meant he knew what little quarter would be given a wounded man. But Floki looked down at the weapon and then up at Bjorn and suddenly he laughed. He winced sharply and waved his hand as if waving Bjorn away.

Then, ignoring the huge Northman, he turned to Gil, his eyes full of laughter still. He laid his fingers lightly on the weapon's beautiful hilt and said, "Bjorn gives me this, so I may die with my sword in my hand. That way, I enter that place Bjorn calls Heaven." He looked up at Bjorn and then back at Gil. "Now why," he said, "Would I choose to spend eternity looking at that mournful face?" He shook his head, trying not to laugh again. "Go away, Bjorn. You're gloomier than my cousin. I see my burial cairn in your eyes."

Bjorn took no offense, but he nodded, still gravely. "The teeth of a dragon are enchanted. They carry a poison few men can bear."

Floki closed his eyes and said gently, "There is no poison and no enchantment. It is but an animal, like a wolf or a bear. Besides, your own father fought one and lived."

"He was thrice your size."

"And a third my intelligence. I but defended my ship. He chose to hunt the thing."

Bjorn nodded sage agreement. "He thought it would provision a longhouse all of a winter."

"Anyhow," Floki murmured tiredly. "It meant no harm."

"Meant no harm?" Hakon raised incredulous eyebrows. "It sought to tear you limb from limb, and it made a fair start." A muttering swept around the crowd of Northmen who had gathered by the fire.

"It must eat," Floki said, "Like any living thing." And he refused to be angry with the dragon, regardless of what anyone said. "Enough," he finished. "We have more important matters." And he called Gil back to his side. He struggled upright for a moment and twisted around so he could see the hill behind them. "The day is good and the road lies open. You must go." He stared up at the hill for several moments, then rested painfully back on the sheepskins and furs. "Before this fire of Hakon's draws companions we do not seek."

"Good sir!" Palamedes cried out, "That cannot be. You are in need. Courtesy forbids we leave you here."

Floki shot Palamedes a look of fury. "Did I speak to you?"

But Gil, too, shook his head in dismay. All he could think of was Hy and the brutal price paid for sheltering them. He turned back to Floki and shook his head more firmly, "No."

Floki's eyes narrowed as much in amazement as anger. "You say what?"

"I say 'No,'" Gil repeated.

"To me?" Floki's incredulity brought a smile, unbidden, to Gil's face. "And you laugh?"

"I'm not laughing." Gil shook his head and turned away in frustration and then caught a flash of movement out of the corner of his eye, and a flash of steel in front of his face. The sword that Bjorn had laid at Floki's side was in his left hand, and the tip beneath Gil's chin.

"I am not dead yet," Floki said. "And I am almost as good with this hand as the other." Then he dropped the sword and clutched the blood-soaked linen bandaging his shoulder and rested back against the furs. His eyes swept the circle around the fire and settled suddenly on Danni. "I make a bargain," he said softly. "You stay this night. And when you go," he reached his hand out to Danni, "you let this one stay with me."

Danni stared. "I can't, Floki," she said sadly. "You know I can't."

He leaned forward. "What is it to you who rules this land?" he whispered. "You do not live in dreams of lost kings." His voice fell so low that Danni stepped closer to hear. "You live now," he said. "You are one like me."

"It's not true," she protested. "And even if it was, I have to go with my friends. I have to find my brother."

Floki dropped his hand to his side again, his fingers just brushing the sword hilt. "What is a brother?" he said. "I will give you sons."

Danni was silent, blinking back tears. "I'll come back," she said at last.

"Boldly spoken by one who has seen little. And if you do," he said, "What makes you think you will find me meekly waiting?"

She shook her head and said honestly, "I don't know. But I know I will."

Floki laughed delightedly and winced again. "As bold before my face as before the dragon!" he cried. "Well, you are right. I will not find better." And then he was suddenly serious. "Go, then," he said. "And I will pray to both my mother's gods, that you return." He shivered and closed his eyes and said quietly, "I think now I sleep," and leaned back against the heap of furs. Hakon watched him for several minutes, then rose and leant over, and closed his cousin's hand around the hilt of his sword. Gil left the fireside to prepare for his journey, not at all certain who would say farewell first.

But when he woke, at dawn the next day, Floki was on his feet, leaning on his patient cousin's arm and calling orders to his men. As startled as Gil by his recovery, they fell over themselves to obey. "See now!" Hakon smiled innocently, "What man can boast a more loyal crew?"

"Loyal as snakes," Floki growled. "But for the threat of your sword, cousin, I'd leave them all on this unkind shore."

Hakon only smiled. "Then you would have a long walk home."

"That," Floki answered vehemently, "I do not desire." Tiredness overcame him abruptly, and he knelt down by the lowering fire while the work continued around him. "Though, I would like nothing more this moment," he said, "Than to sleep beneath Magnus Redbeard's roof."

Ismail tugged Gil's arm. "Come, we must work, too." At the edge of the forest the girls were watering the ponies at the stream that ran from the falls above. Gil followed, looking back over his shoulder at Floki and Hakon, and thinking of the long, grueling journey down Glen Alban that lay before the Northmen.

Quickly they loaded the pack pony, Lucy, with their bedrolls, a generous portion of the provisions from Hy, and Gil and Ismail's quivers and bows. The girls slung their own over their shoulders, while the boys would rely on their lances and swords. Then, having armored his trembling pony, Gil pulled on his padded undercoat and trousers and his chain chausses and hauberk. The chain felt cold, and stained his hands with rust but warmed by his body, grew supple. Following Palamedes' lead, he added the heavy helm to Lucy's burdens, strapped his sword belt around his waist and slung his shield around his neck.

His fingers closed around the compass in his pocket; the gift from his father that once he had hidden in shame; a gift without price in this dangerous world. "There's something I have to do," he said to Ismail. He returned, then to the dying fire of the Northmen's camp, with the compass held tight in his hand.

He found Hakon and Floki lying on the sand beneath the bow of the beached *Silver Dragon*, examining the oak keel and curving strakes for damage. Floki looked up from the hull and smiled. "Look, Sea-Friend, my *Dragon* defeats even the dragon of the loch!" He slapped Hakon's shoulder in triumph, tried to sit up, and then lay back on the sand again and briefly closed his eyes. Hakon stood and reached out a hand and, grasping it, Floki climbed painfully to his feet.

Resting against his cousin's shoulder, he turned to Gil. "You are ready, Warrior?" he said. Gil nodded. "Then go. You have no time for elaborate farewells, even were it my nature to make them. Your road awaits and so does mine." He turned again to his ship.

"Wait," Gil said. Floki looked back tiredly. "I have something for you." Gil held out the compass.

Floki brusquely shook his head. "A forest is like a sea-mist, Warrior," he said. "You will need that." He turned again, and when Gil again called him back, the look of tiredness had turned to one of impatience.

With a wary shrug, Gil said, "I have two who can fly."

"And when you are separated from them?" Floki shot back. He inclined his head wearily. "You have travelled from Orkney, to Hy, to here, under my protection. You have seen one battle, with idiots, and a rather small dragon. You are untried and untested and now you are on your own. I promise you, you will need every help you can get. Take that," he thrust Gil's hand away, "And may it be your salvation, for I do not see what else will be." He grimaced with pain and frustration. "And be done with noble gestures," he said.

Gil stepped back, hurt, and then suddenly, hurt turned to a treacherous tide of anger. He closed his fist around the compass and the idea of throwing it at Floki flashed through his mind. But some last remnant of good sense saved him. He lowered his fist and said quietly, "You offend me."

"Oh do I?" Floki said coldly. Hakon gripped his arm to pull him away and Floki shoved his cousin aside with his good hand and stood, swaying slightly, alone. He smiled without humor, "So you have become a true knight! Ready to defend your offended honor, like Sir Palamedes. Well, draw your sword, Warrior, and let us get on with it."

"Cousin," Hakon whispered softly, shaking his head.

Floki whirled on him, "Have done!" he shouted, and staggered and almost fell.

Gil held his ground and met Floki's furious gaze. "No," he said. "Because you'll kill me. But that still would not make you right to refuse my gift." He opened his fist and the compass shown on his palm like a little lost star. "My father gave this to me on the Feast of Christ's Mass, the last time we shared that feast together. It was his and his father's before him. I give it to you, and you refuse it. You offend me. Not my honor." He clutched the compass in his fist against his chest. "Me. You offend me."

Floki stared at him. Something passed like a shadow across his face and he shook his head slightly. The small gesture almost unbalanced him. Gil turned to Hakon, but Hakon had stepped back with folded arms and looked more than willing now to let him fall.

"Your father," Floki said softly. His eyes seemed fixed on something far away and when Gil nodded, he said dreamily, "Magnus Redbeard – my father – said once to me that I am like a great wave on the open sea. I need a rock cliff to break me and I do not find one." He looked long and hard at Gil and said, "I think, perhaps he is right." He held out his hand. "I will take your gift, if you still give it."

Gil nodded. "I still give it." He handed the compass to Floki who took it with great care.

"I am sorry, Warrior," he said. He flashed a smile of rare honesty. Then, without turning, he held out his arm toward Hakon, who was beside him at once. "Sea-Friend, I am humble as a monk of Hy, and I dearly need your help. Turn this ship of mine to the West that we may sail."

Then he nodded to Gil. "Come, Warrior." He released his hold on Hakon's arm and laid his own across Gil's shoulders. "Let this captain do his work. I will rest a while, like a true earl, with servants to do my bidding." He gave Hakon a sly grin and, leaning on Gil, returned to his rough bed by the embers of the fire.

Stretched out there, he played at royalty, accepting the farewells of each of his guests with noble grace. He listened raptly to Palamedes' courtly speech, then clasped Ismail's hand with real affection. Bowing his head, like the knight in the forest, he kissed the girls' hands with only a hint of laughter in his eyes. But when they rose to go, he called Danni back.

"Come sit by me," he said. "Let me look on you a while." Danni sat cross-legged on the edge of the furs. She looked up and then ducked her head, unnerved by the intensity of his gaze. Seeing it, Gil remembered the sea-mist breaking as they sailed away from Hy, and the Northman standing on the rail of his ship, measuring mountains with his hands.

"What do you want, Floki?" Danni asked. He shook his head without answering, and Gil knew he was drawing her face in his memory, the way he drew mountain and headland to guide his ship.

Floki looked up then, and saw Hakon waiting by the gangplank. He released Danni with a smile, and summoned Gil to take him back to the ship. At the foot of the gangplank, he cuffed Gil's head, just hard enough to hurt. "Godspeed, Warrior," he said. "I pray for you, too."

Then, with his cousin again by his side, he boarded *Silver Dragon* and Gil mounted his pony and turned to the forest and the road to Camelot. As the ponies picked their way up the hill, with the knight Palamedes and Doombearer in the lead, Gil twisted in his saddle to look back, once, over his shoulder.

The longships lay, just offshore, their prows to the West, but their oars raised and their sails yet shrouding their spars. He saw Floki, leaning against his mast and looking up. Gil thought of his story of the Irish princess. But now it was Danni who was riding away, her eyes set on the road ahead, and he who watched. And Gil knew, all at once, that she was the rock that would break Floki Magnusson.

CHAPTER SEVEN

At the first turning of the road, they met the first breath of rising wind. Dead oak leaves shivered and dried grass trembled above the frozen snow. A black line of storm clouds rode above the hills and a stray snowflake fell, and then another. Below, the water was dark grey and splashed already with white horses. The longships were hidden from sight by the hillside and another turn in the rocky path hid the loch, as well.

The road was too narrow for two to ride abreast, and so steep that only a hill pony could easily climb it. Thawing snow had run in streams, and frozen again into ice, while spray from the tumbling river coated each stone with rime until the road itself became a frozen waterfall. Twice, Palamedes dismounted and led his warhorse, whose mighty, feathered feet slipped and skidded in the track's tight confines. But Lionheart scrambled contentedly upward. His ears flicked forward for the first time since the encounter with the dragon, and when Lucy balked suddenly in front of him, he gave her black hocks two sharp nips. She shimmied backward, one hoof straying over the icy edge. "Gil!" Rachel shouted, struggling with Lucy's lead, "Can you never control that foul pony?"

Gil jerked his reins tight and leaned forward, grabbing Lionheart's fuzzy ear. *I see you've recovered.*

At the top of a rise, amid a stand of gnarled dark pines, the road turned and left the tumbling river behind. The oak woods were below them, and the pines thinned as the land rose higher. There, the wind roared down from the mountains, bending trees and flattening heather. It tore at loose clothing and rattled arrows in quivers. Ponies' tails and manes streamed out like hero's flags, and upraised lances bowed like sails. It clawed at Gil's hair, whipping it around his throat. He pulled the cloak over his head and wrapped it around his face. Squinting against a blast of icy snow, he peered into the distance. The outlines of the mountains were already lost.

He could barely make out Palamedes, riding in the lead, hunched on his warhorse, the tip of his lance swaying and trembling in the gale. The snow had turned Doombearer half white, and the windward side of the knight's chain hauberk, it crusted white, too. Dry and fine as ice-dust, it flowed across the battered land like water. Drifts built in seconds against rock, and heather and withered tree. When Palamedes stopped to lower his wildly swaying lance, snow-ridges engulfed Doombearer's feet. The knight turned the lance backwards, twisting the leather fewter, until the point trailed behind, leaving a thin track in the snow.

Gil drew on his reins. Stamping and whinnying, Lionheart stood watching the others move away, while Gil, too, dropped his lance down out of the wind. Swinging his leg over it and regaining his stirrup, he caught up his reins. But then, in the moment's relative quiet, with hooves and harness stilled, he heard the sounds.

At first, he thought they were a trick of the wind, a faint murmuring and muttering, beneath the roar of the gale. But they had a cadence of no natural thing, a rhythm of human speech. He twisted in his saddle, staring wildly all around, but he saw nothing but drifted heather, wind-bent trees, and half buried rock. Beyond, mist and blown snow hid the landscape, but from that distance, not even a shout could possibly be heard. Much less, the soft whisperings that seemed as close as if another rider passed at arm's length on the track.

And there! He whirled. The voices came, too, on his other side. And with them, other sounds: creaking of leather and jingling of harness, the clank of armor and the sharp ring of shod hoof against stone. Not one rider, but many. An army surrounded him, invisible, but alive with murmured anger and threat, and something deeper: enormous, terrible fear. It swept over him, a wave of cold terror that met his own terror, reaching out to it, from within...*the hardest road a man can ride, haunted by this world and the next....* Gil cried out, but no sound came. He was caught in the worst of all dreams, alone in this desolate place, trapped by an army of ghosts.

Alone! Alone! Lionheart's small voice came from somewhere within the fear, jarring him into awareness. The pony shook his snowy head; nostril's flaring, wild eyes staring to where the hunched back of the laden pack beast, Lucy, was vanishing into the blizzard. The others were already gone, swallowed in whiteness.

"Go!" Gil cried, kicking the frantic animal, who leapt forward with desperate relief, stumbling through growing drifts. It took an impossibly long time to catch up, with Lionheart vainly trying to trot in snow too deep to walk, while at every step, the short lead of the others kept them on the fatal edge of visibility. *If I lose them, I die,* Gil thought numbly. He shouted out, "Danni! Ismail!" but although the ghosts had freed his tongue, the sound was lost in the wind.

At last, only three strides separated Lionheart's nose from Lucy's windblown tail, and the snow plastered shapes of the others were all in sight. They plodded on, as oblivious of Gil's return as of his absence and of the eerie battle he had fought, alone, with an unseen foe. Gil turned and looked behind. Whiteness had swallowed the path; their ponies' hoof prints covering over as fast as they made them. Were it not for the road, they would be, already, hopelessly lost. But then, looking forward, he saw no sign of a road at all, only a bewildering landscape of drifts and hollows, veiled by sheets of blown snow.

A dark hill emerged, momentarily, from the curtaining snow and Gil reached by instinct for his father's compass. Then his numb fingers stopped halfway to his empty pocket and he groaned aloud, confronted with the foolishness of his own noble gesture. *A forest is like a sea-mist.* "And so is a blizzard," Gil whispered through stiff, frozen lips.

His mind flashed to Floki, and he felt a surge of irrational anger toward the Northman and his arrogant wisdom. But all at once, his anger was swallowed in shame. He twisted in his saddle again and looked back over the tail of his struggling pony toward the one place worse to be than here: the wind-torn waters of Glen Alban. Channeled boldly between its walls of hills, the wind would rage there like a dragon of the air, the Northmen's fine ships hapless prey in its merciless jaws. A wave of anguish, as dark as the engulfing waters of the loch, swept over Gil at the trail of destruction that marked their journey.

Anger arose, deeper and fiercer than that he'd felt even for the burnt village or the brothers of Hy. But this anger had no human target. He looked up at the sky, a swirling maze of grey and white, as if he could see black wings above him. *You*, he addressed the black bird, Feannag, in his heart, *You brought me here. I hate you and I hate your quest. There is nothing in the world that can be worth all this.*

The wind slapped his face like a brutal hand, blinding him with needles of ice. His cloak tore free, flapping wildly and threatening to drag him from his pony's back. He wrapped it tighter and twined his frozen fingers in Lionheart's mane. Lionheart stumbled, colliding with something that bulked suddenly out of the storm: Lucy, standing motionless with head low. Gil glimpsed, through the snow, the dim shapes of Frosti, Freya, and Chocolate, standing still, too, and Doombearer, turned toward them, his breath clouding the freezing air and his mighty nostrils coated in rime.

Palamedes heaved himself down from the saddle and gathered the reins of all five ponies, drawing them near. "We can go no further in this devil's storm," he shouted, "We must find shelter, here, or die."

Gil saw the others look around with the same disbelief he felt himself. The land was bare and open, a high, wild plateau between higher, wilder hills, now hidden from their sight. In every direction, he saw nothing but snow and low, black rock. They had left the forest below, all but for a few bent trees and clusters of dark, half-buried gorse that would shelter not even a rabbit. Nothing moved and nothing lived, but for themselves.

Black memories crept into his mind of stories of travelers lost in blizzards, crawling in circles, slowly freezing. Or, he thought wildly, driven to slaughter their ponies, scoop out their entrails and crawl within their warm carcasses to survive! Lionheart tossed his head and rolled his eyes back. His neck trembled and he shimmied beneath Gil. *Will I be dead?*

What?

When you scoop….

Gil jumped down quickly and ran forward, grabbing his bridle and pulling his furry face close. *I'm not going to scoop you out! It was just an idea. A bad idea.*

Can I be dead first?

No! Yes! Gil clutched at his snow caked hair. *What does it take to get you to believe me?*

I want my tree.

So do we all! Gil leaned against the pony's trembling neck, trying to wipe his brain clean of thoughts. A tree. Any tree.

Palamedes peered over their heads into the blinding fury of the storm. Suddenly, he smiled, cracking the ice coating his moustache and beard, "Take heart! Not half a league from here, there lies an ancient chapel, where Arthur and his knights oft stopped to pray. Once, I knew it well." He peered again into the blizzard as if seeing it still. "It is a ruin, now, and its gentle priest lies buried beneath his altar. But its walls yet stand. So also, its humble byre. If we but find those ruins now, we are saved."

Rachel pulled her fluttering cloak closer. "Half a league…a mile and more. And which way?"

The knight raised one huge hand and pointed toward the land to the right of the road. "There is a small river this road must cross. It would take us there, for the chapel stands on its very banks. Indeed, it could be beneath our feet, even now. Frozen and drifted over; who would know?"

Gil looked around at the bewildering sameness of snow and rock. To seek the chapel without road or river would be simply to seek a new place to die. Stay here and death would come to them. So that was the choice: die waiting, or die, like Northmen, fighting, if only a phantom of snow. He thought of Floki with sad respect. "Come," he said. "Let's ride."

He put his hand to his pommel to mount his pony again, but Danni suddenly jumped down from Frosti and beckoned the others to join her, on foot. "Join hands," she commanded. "Make a circle." She grabbed Gil's wrist and joined his hand to

Rachel's. Then, suddenly, he understood.

"No!" he cried. "You can't fly in this!"

"I can!" Danni shouted. "I know I can."

But Palamedes laid his great hand on her shoulder. "No," he said firmly. "A Change-Thing has every strength and skill of the creature it becomes. But it has no more. No bird takes wing in such a storm. You would be dashed to your death on the rocks, or hurled into the great loch itself. I cannot allow it."

"But you're wrong!" Danni cried. "I flew from Tir nan Og to the Land of Ice and Fire, through wind and snow and storm. I can fly here."

She stepped closer and looked boldly up into his face. "Look!" she said. Then she drew her sword and thrust it deep into the snow. It stood, half-buried, and the dry crystals began at once to drift around it. "I will fly," she said, "and if I have not returned when the snow covers the hilt, ride for the chapel, whichever way seems best. The worst that happens is I die a little quicker than you. And the best, I find the chapel and lead you there, and all are safe." Her eyes met Gil's, fierce and imploring until, yet holding Rachel's hand, he reached the other to Ismail. Then, with great reluctance, the Saracen knight took his place, too, and as they closed the last link, Danni ducked under Gil's arm and stepped within the ring.

She placed her fingers on the talisman at her throat, but her soft words were lost in the wind. A fierce gust slapped sleet into Gil's eyes and squinting against it, he glimpsed a wild dark eye and ruffled feathers, and then, with a frantic beating of gale battered wings, a blurred bird shape leapt from their circle of arms into the howling sky. At once, it dived and seemed to skim the white drifts, but rising again, it gained height, circled wildly, and then struck out with steady wing beats into the full force of the gale.

They drew their ponies tighter together and huddled beside them for warmth. Palamedes stood stalwart, placing himself and his warhorse between the children and the wind. Gil stamped his freezing feet and slapped hands against arms and stared into the sky for Danni while the snow crept ever higher up her wind shaken sword.

Then, just as it topped the crosspiece of the hilt, the clouds above them suddenly broke apart, and though neither wind nor snow relented, he saw a swathe of blue and a flash of tormented sunlight. He shaded his eyes and peered into the distance as light and shadow raced each other across the snow veiled land, sweeping it with extraordinary beauty. And then a wild careering speck came, driven toward them on the gale, just as the drift whispered over the last bare inch of Danni's sword.

Gil thrust his hand triumphantly into the snow and drew out the ice-cold blade. Waving it around his head, he shouted, "Danni! Danni! Here!" as she homed to them out of the sky. Whirling above their heads, she dipped low, and then rose and circled back, beating against the storm once more. With Danni's sword in his hand, Gil leapt into his saddle and quickly gathered Lionheart's and then Frosti's, reins. Looking around to see all were together, he dug his heels into his pony's snow-caked flanks, bending low over Lionheart's wind-whipped mane, as the pony plunged bravely out into the drifts.

It was a hard and bitter mile, the snow swept bare in places to treacherous ice, at others piled belly deep before the struggling beasts. But the sight of Danni ever circling and the certainty of shelter at the end drove them on. They came to a thicket of tightly woven thorny bushes and dismounted to lead the ponies through. Then, emerging on the other side, they saw, across a smooth dip in the snow, a cluster of buildings, some whole, others just broken walls of tumbled stone. "It's like Cille Aidan!" Rachel cried.

Gil nodded grimly, as they mounted again. Cille Aidan, indeed, as he had imagined it on the dark day before Danni's return: ravaged and roofless, its walls blackened by fire and its dim sanctuary open to the sky. But half the thatched roof yet remained, bowed down by the snow. And beside the church, two small round buildings still stood, the larger with its thick thatch intact.

Palamedes pointed from one to the other. "There is the byre and there the hermit's cell, in which the snow now falls. But no matter. There, in his holy church, he rests his bones beneath the earth and needs no other roof. And there, we too will find shelter." Danni's bird shape rode the back of the gale in a last circle above the little church. Then, sweeping down with outstretched wings, she vanished into the hermit's round, roofless cell and, moments later, emerged from the empty doorway, wrapping her cloak around her like folded wings.

Gil nudged Lionheart into a stumbling trot, and they plunged down from the thorny thicket to the snow filled hollow below. And then, barely a dozen feet from safety, the pony stopped short. Stiff-legged and trembling, he turned his head left and right in response to Gil's urging but refused to move. Gil kicked him sharply with impatient heels, and he sat back on his haunches and dug in all four feet. *There's a noise.*

Gil shook his head. The wind was howling, louder than ever. Cloaks flapped, arrows rattled, harnesses jingled. *Which noise?*

"Gil, move!" Rachel shouted, behind him. She barged on past, tugging Lucy's lead rein, and Freya and Lucy trotted together onto the smooth inviting snow of the hollow. "Have a nice night," she laughed over her shoulder. Then her laugh was cut short by a shriek from Danni, waiting beyond. A black, jagged hole had appeared in front of Freya's feet. Rachel pulled sharply on her reins, turning Freya back the way they'd come. Then a second hole opened behind Lucy. "It's a snow bridge!" Rachel cried. "I'm on the river!" Then, with an ominous cracking thud, the whole white surface collapsed and ponies and rider disappeared in a cloud of disintegrating snow.

Gil leapt from his rearing mount and ran to the edge of the treacherous hollow. What had appeared a patch of drifted grassland had been a snowy roof over a dark course of water. Freed of its muffling shelter, the river thundered and roared over glistening rocks, disappearing into a black tunnel at either end. In its raging midst, swept by foaming rapids on either side, were Freya, Lucy, and Rachel.

Unseated in the fall, Rachel found refuge on a projecting boulder, while Freya scrambled for the crumbling bank. Lucy floundered on her knees, her saddle packs twisted lopsided, the water washing over her back. She lurched to her feet, snorting and dripping, and shook herself like a dog. Her sodden burden broke free, tumbling into the rushing water, as the pony scuttled up out of the river and mounted the snowy bank.

The lost saddle packs jammed between two rocks and burst open, spilling two meal sacks into the torrent. At once, they were swept into the black tunnel beneath the snow. "Stay where you are!" Gil shouted to Rachel. "Don't move!" Balanced precariously on her slippery rock, her frightened eyes on the tunnel's hungry mouth, she nodded without speaking. Side by side, Gil and Ismail eased themselves over the edge of broken snow, and bracing with their boot heels, slid to the bottom. Rachel turned around to see them and her foot slipped into the water. Instantly, the current clutched her leg and wrapped itself around her soaking skirt. Flailing wildly, she fought to keep her balance, while they frantically searched the rock-strewn torrent for a way to reach her.

But then a great shadow swept over their heads, as Palamedes, jousting lance in hand, jumped his mighty warhorse across the river's width. Landing beside Danni, he swung himself from his mount and plunged down the steep bank. "My lady!" he shouted and stretched the lance out across the water till it lay within Rachel's grasp. "Step careful, my lady," he called then, "and hold firm." With fingers white from cold, she gripped the smooth shank of the lance and stepped out across the torrent. She won a slippery foothold, and then another, until Palamedes huge arm swept out, swinging her to safety at last.

Gil and Ismail climbed back up the bank, stamping a path in the wind-packed snow, Gil using his sword to cut steps. Then, while Ismail, riding Chocolate and leading Frosti, picked his way down the snow staircase, Gil stepped warily out to Rachel's rock, with one hand secure on Palamedes' lance. Hauling the wedged saddle packs from the water, he heaved them up to Ismail and sent ponies and rider safely on their way. Then he returned over the treacherous stones, to the bank, and Lionheart.

He found the pony whickering nervously, alone in the snow. His whole body trembled with eagerness to be with the others, but when Gil took his jousting lance in his hand and rode him to Ismail's carefully wrought path, Lionheart froze. *Come,* Gil urged. *It's the only way.*

Lionheart tossed his head, flaring his nostrils and rolling his eyes. *There's a noise.*

Gil rolled his own eyes. *This is where I came in. The noise is water, Lionheart.*

I want the ship.

You hate the ship. Gil pounded his saddle pommel in frustration, but Lionheart stood rooted to the spot. Gil got down and caught the pony's bridle. Lionheart went back on his haunches and made himself heavy as lead. Gil took off his cloak, folded it, and covered the pony's head. *Hey! Here's night! Remember? You like night.*

The noise is bigger.

Gil sighed and removed the cloak. *Chocolate went through it.*

Doombearer went over it.

Doombearer is three ponies high! His legs are higher than your ears!

And then, suddenly, above the howl and bluster of the wind, Gil heard a thud of hoof beats where no hooves fell. Murmuring voices rose on either side. Harnesses creaked and armor clanked and a sword scraped from its scabbard as the ghost army closed around him again. Shaking his head free of the treacherous web of sounds, he jumped up again to the saddle and kicked Lionheart so hard that the pony reared in astonishment. "Go!" he shouted and slapped Lionheart's snow-covered rump. Lionheart leapt forward and hit the trampled snow at a gallop. "Jump! Jump! Jump!"

The little pony launched himself two strides early, soared over the broken snow bridge, and alighted three full strides safe of the edge. Skidding wildly, he slipped to his knees. Gil flew over his head, landed in a snow drift, and lay flat on his back, laughing giddily. Then he climbed to his feet, picked up his fallen lance and grinned. "You cannot believe how glad I am to be out of there," he said.

Ismail nodded solemnly and put his hand on Gil's arm. "We must go back."

"No way! Nothing on earth would make me –"

"Firewood," said Ismail. He looked soberly around their refuge. "There is none here. Much there," he pointed at the thorny thicket through which they'd led the ponies. "We build fire now, big fire, or all freeze."

Gil surveyed his companions. Their clothes were soaked, their bedding drenched, most of their food was gone. Rachel trembled with cold, despite being wrapped in Palamedes fur-trimmed cloak. The walls and broken roof of the chapel would provide shelter from the wind, but nothing more. He tightened his grip on the lance and turned back to the river. "Let's go," he said to Ismail, "Before it's dark."

Ismail pointed up-river, to the unbroken roof of snow still covering the hidden torrent. "We use the snow bridge. On foot, we are light. Walk fast." Gil nodded, but he took the lance, anyhow, and when they crossed, walking as softly and swiftly as they could, he held it out, balancing like a tightrope walker, to save himself if he went through. They climbed hurriedly up to the thicket, laid their cloaks on the snow, and filled them with dry, dead wood. "Enough," Ismail said. "It grows dark." Gil collected his burden and his lance and turned back. The ghosts remained silent; perhaps, he thought, they only came when you were alone.

But suddenly Ismail stopped; his hand dropping to his sword belt. "Who goes?" he whispered to Gil. Then Gil, too, saw a shadowy figure, a man on a horse, tall, like Palamedes, but lean, and wrapped in a formless cloak. And beside him, another appeared, and another. Gil tightened his grip on his lance as the mounted figures gathered, side by side, blocking their path home, yet strangely oblivious of them. "Go around them," he whispered.

But Ismail shook his head. "Keep walking," he said. "Do not turn."

"They'll see us."

"Turn and we'll be driven on and on, up to the wild places, until we die."

"What?"

"They are ghosts, my friend," Ismail answered. "I know. I have met them before. There has been war here. They are ghosts of war."

Then Gil heard the sounds again beneath the endless keening

of the wind, the murmur and clatter of an army preparing for battle. "What do they want?" he whispered.

"Us. They are lonely for the world. Keep walking."

Ismail walked so calmly, so straight and slim and fearless, never turning his head or averting his eyes, that Gil was compelled to follow. Then they were yards away, and then feet, and then the apparition was all around, the sounds in their ears and the mounted figures right before their eyes. But they passed through them as through shadows, untouched and unhindered, and as they did, the figures broke up into small pieces that faded at once into the dusk.

Gil looked at Ismail and Ismail looked back. "Go for it," he whispered, and they bolted and ran. Racing recklessly across the snow bridge, they kept running, past the round byre where Palamedes was tethering the ponies, and on until they crashed wildly through the empty doorway of the chapel. Rachel and Danni, huddled out of the wind, jumped up in surprise.

Gil and Ismail exchanged a wary glance and said nothing. Gil dropped his load of firewood and looked around their refuge. Nothing remained of the church but bare, blackened walls and the sagging remnant of the thatch still sheltering the stone altar at one end. Snow drifted in the two high narrow windows and lay deep between the walls where the broken roof ended and the building lay open to the sky.

But under the stubborn, unburnt thatch, the stone floor was dry. Danni and Rachel had emptied Lucy's drenched saddle packs and their meagre goods were spread neatly along the inmost wall. Gil was relieved to see their helms and bows had survived, since they would be far harder to replace than food. He crouched down and examined the small heap of provisions that had escaped the river: a sack of battered apples, another of sodden barley meal, a string of dried fish and a dark hunk of cheese. It looked like one lean meal for the five of them, but it would probably have to do for several.

Ismail arranged neat stacks of twigs and branches on the stone floor, just at the edge of the sheltering thatch. Gil untied the leather pouch that held the fire-striker and the roll of oiled wool. When all was prepared, he struck flint to steel, showering his tinder with sparks. The wind yet howled over the open walls, but, within them, the shelter of Ismail's hand was enough to guard the tiny flame.

Gil teased the wool over it, as Erling had done, and Ismail added the smallest, driest twigs. The flame flared and crackled, and piling on more kindling, Gil rejoiced at the warmth and the light of his fire. Despite the storm and the ghosts, they were alive and in shelter. He felt a flicker of pride, smaller and more humble than his fire. *Thank you, Erling*, he thought, slipping the fire-striker into its pouch. *And I will return it.* Then he thought of the storm driven loch and wondered who was alive to return it to. He turned to Danni. "Did you fly high?" he asked. "Could you see the great loch?" She nodded. "Did you see the ships?" he asked, searching her guarded face.

Slowly, she shook her head. "They must have been in the river. Beneath the trees."

He turned away. Looking into the growing flames, he imagined beating against that wind, or dropping sail and fighting on, under oars, trying to reach the river mouth. It would take all day.

"They'll be okay," Danni said. "Floki's sailed everywhere."

"Right." He stared unblinking into his fire. He heard a creak of armor as Palamedes stepped within the ruined chapel. His dark face lit with a broad white smile. "The good beasts have foraged beneath the snow for their supper, and now, forgetting every difference; share their humble shelter in affection and courtesy. As, indeed, we will share ours, shielded by this holy place." Gil smiled, too, glad the animals at least were safe that night. For, unlike themselves or the Northmen, the poor beasts had set out on this journey without any choice.

Danni settled cross-legged and spread her damp skirt out to dry in the growing heat of the fire. "I saw something else," she said. Struggling with sorrow, Gil was only half listening. "I saw Camelot," she said. Gil snapped to amazed attention. "I was circling," she said. "The wind drove me higher and higher. And then the clouds broke and for a moment the sun shone over everything! And then I saw the great loch beyond the hills." She gestured the way they had come. "And there," again she pointed, now the opposite way, "There were more hills, much higher."

"The Grey Mountains," said Palamedes. "They would lie in sight of here, but for this storm."

"And beyond, there were valleys and lochs and a great dark forest, covered in snow. So, at first I thought what I saw was snow, so white in the green forest. Then I saw it was towers and great walls, all standing high above the trees. And then the clouds came back and it disappeared in the mist. But I did see it!"

"By truth, you did see it, my lady. For just as you described it, I have seen it many times. How often I have ridden there, a summer dawn or a winter dusk, and joyously glimpsed, just as you did, that blessed citadel where our king held his noble court!" He fell into sober reverie while Rachel and Danni divided a portion of their provisions into smaller portions still, to share among them. Gil and Ismail piled the fire high and spread out bedding and clothing to dry. Between the walls of the ruin, the heat of the fire grew fierce and they basked in its very fierceness.

Palamedes suddenly inclined his head to the wind which had grown stronger still and growled across the mountains like a living thing. "That is the very sound," he said. "So like the voice of the Questing Beast that even I, who know it well, could be beguiled. And, indeed, it was but a day's ride from here that first I heard the fearsome thing, and last, too, above the Linn of the Rainbow Bridge.

"Three times have I heard it, now! Three times it has crossed my path. Three times, too, my father's. And three times, his father's before him. And once, he not only heard it but saw a dark, uncanny shape, like a serpent with blackened wings, arising above the forest with glittering eye, and shining claws, and a breath of fire! And on that very day, he made the vow! For neither hawk nor hound would ever stir a nobler quarry, and so he could not rest until it was won. Alas, death overcame him first, and thus my father took up the quest. And on his death, imparted it to me. Thus, I set out that sorrowing morning, and even as you see me, so yet I ride in fated pursuit."

Awed silence fell on the gathering around the fire. But then Danni balled her hands into fists and cried, "Why do that? What if you never find it? Your father didn't. Your grandfather didn't. You'll spend your whole life looking for it! And then you'll die and you'll still never have found it!"

"But I will have sought it, my lady!" he said. And, rising to his feet, he bowed to her and to Rachel and kissed both their hands. Then he stepped away from the fire and spread out his fur bedroll at the edge of the snow, so no intruder could enter without encountering him first. Taking his sword from its scabbard, and laying it ready to hand, he stretched out to sleep.

Gil and Ismail unsheathed their swords, too, before wrapping themselves in their nearly dried sheepskins, leaving the girls the space closest to the fire. Lulled by the flickering light and the endless sweep of the wind Gil drifted toward sleep. Danni reached out and poked a finger in his ribs. "Do you believe him?" she whispered. It felt strange, now, having her lying just a couple of feet away, like they were still little kids, camping behind his house. He rolled a little away and then bumped into Rachel and rolled hastily back.

"I believe he's chasing it," he said.

"But do you think it's real?"

Rachel prodded his back. "It's probably just make-believe," she murmured sleepily. "You know. Like dragons."

Breakfast was half an apple each and sour-tasting bannocks made from damp barley meal. They all wolfed their portions down, except Ismail, who broke his bannock in half and put the uneaten half in his pocket. Beyond the crumbling edge of the thatch, the snow still blew in rippling sheets and low clouds yet wrapped the hills; Gil knew they would not travel that day. His eyes strayed unwillingly to their dwindling stack of firewood. The thought of gathering more, with nothing more to eat, first, was daunting. But without it they would freeze, before they even had time to starve.

The storm blew for four more days. Sometimes the sky cleared and the wind dropped, only to return with greater fury, from a new direction. The snow turned to rain, then froze, and turned back to snow. The ponies foraged bravely, breaking the hard crust with their hooves, then retreated willingly to their byre.

Rachel flew as Hawk three times, and returned with fat white mountain birds, twice her size. She struggled to carry them and flopped exhausted into their shelter, with each. But stripped of their fluffy feathers and roasted on spits, the birds were delicious. When the sky cleared for all one afternoon, Ismail and Danni took their bows onto the hill and came back with three mountain hares. That night, Gil slept by the embers with contented hands resting on a stomach that was, at last, full.

In the morning, the fire had burned to cold ash. Defying the ghosts, Gil and Ismail crossed the river one last time to the thicket. But every dead branch had already been stripped for the hungry flames. They returned over the snow bridge with a pathetic bundle of straggly twigs. "We go further," Ismail pointed to the sky. "Look, we can see even the hills."

By the time they had saddled their ponies and armed themselves, the weather had already closed in. They rode out, regardless, leading Lucy and leaving Palamedes behind to guard their camp in the ruined chapel. The going was slow, with the animals stumbling over the crusted drifts and Gil regretted the weight of his armor, the steamy restriction of his helm, and the awkward, swaying lance. But Palamedes had insisted that they ride prepared for battle.

"No sensible knight would be out in this," Gil grumbled.

"War is not sensible," said Ismail.

Still, they saw no trace of any living thing, much less any person, as they crested one ridge and then another, leaving their refuge far behind. The wind had lessened and the snow fell softly and thickly, covering everything. Not trusting to find their tracks, they sought landmarks for their return among the tiny scrubby trees. Gil counted paces and tried to hold an image in his mind, to draw mind-maps as Floki had done. But he had not Floki's skill, and the pictures fell apart, leaving him adrift in white nothingness.

Then, Ismail shouted, "Look! There!" Peering through the falling flakes, Gil glimpsed a dip in the drifts, like the river by the chapel, but smaller. And surrounding it, a cluster of the white birch trees that grew above Cille Aidan, their branches swaying gently in the wind. They tethered their ponies to the first tree, and gathered mossy dead branches, loading them onto Lucy until she bristled with sticks like a hedgehog. "Good!" Ismail grinned. "We go now. Come back again tomorrow." Gil looked up from tying the last bundle to Lucy's patient back and felt a chill of alarm. The mist had rolled in, soft as a hunting cat, and the land had vanished.

"Whiteout," he whispered in dismay.

"Quick," Ismail said. "We follow tracks."

They freed their ponies and mounted, and Gil caught up Lucy's rein. "There," he said, finding the line of hoof prints disappearing into nothingness, and he pulled Lionheart up, so Ismail could lead. Returning single file, as they had come, the ponies plunged eagerly into their old broken trail. But the further they went, the more snow had fallen since they'd passed and the fainter the trail grew. On the first windblown ridge, they lost it entirely, until Ismail, riding back and forth, picked up a faint broken line, descending through the drifts.

Gil followed, keeping Lionheart's nose just inches from Chocolate's snow-covered tail. The mist was so thick that Gil's landmark trees had all vanished. A rock outcrop loomed out of nowhere and disappeared the moment they passed, leaving nothing but whiteness. Ismail reined Chocolate in and sat blinking and shaking his head. "It is like ship," he said. And he spun his finger in a small, dizzy circle.

Weird as it was to be sea-sick in the middle of the mountains, Gil understood. With no landmarks, there was no horizon. Direction and distance vanished and he could tell up and down only by the tilt of his pony's back. They sailed a moving sea of cloud on solid ground. "I'll lead," he said, and he rode forward so Ismail would have something on which to rest his eyes.

Gil realized he had reached the top of another ridge only when Lionheart's back flattened. Struggling to regain his mind-map, he said, "This should be the last." But before him was only more whiteness, and not one, but two faint lines of tracks. "Did we separate? Make two trails?" he whispered.

Ismail shook his head. "Look," he said. "They go different ways."

The two dark lines led off to left and right, in a widening angle that would set their destinations far apart. Thinking where a wrong choice might take them, Gil said warily, "Which are ours?"

Ismail shook his head again, then spoke an even greater concern. "Who else rides?"

For a moment, Gil thought of the ghosts. But though he had heard them, and even seen them, he knew that no horseman he could walk through could leave real tracks. Whoever had ridden here was flesh and blood. "I don't think we want to know who," he said.

Ismail jumped down and walked from one set of tracks to the other, crouching to study each. But they were already only faded indentations in the snow, drifting over as they watched. "We've just got to choose," he said, "And hope we're right."

Ismail stared into the impenetrable whiteness. Then, suddenly, he handed Gil Chocolate's reins. "I follow one. We must be near chapel now. If I do not find, I come back. We take other."

He stepped away from the ponies, and Gil said, "What? Walking? It'll be dark before you...." But Ismail grinned and held up his hand against Gil's protest.

"I cannot fly," he said. "But I can run." He began carefully tramping a circle in the snow. When he had finished and stepped within, he said, "Keep circle clear. Too much snow, I cannot come back."

Gil nodded vigorously. "Take care!" he shouted. He tried to make himself watch, but as soon as Ismail's face lengthened into the deer's long snout, and his forehead sprouted growing antlers, he turned away and shut his eyes. When he opened them again, the brown stag was trotting back and forth from track to track, just as Ismail had done before. It raised one foreleg, flared its nostrils, and twitched its ears. Then, shaking its great rack of antlers, it bounded away, soaring over the drifts, and disappeared into the mist.

Chocolate stared after and shook his mane in puzzlement.

Gil patted his shaggy neck, then sat back in his saddle and wrapped his cloak close. Solitude enfolded him, silent as the mist, and fear sifted down, like snow. He imagined Ismail falling into a river, like Rachel and Freya, or losing the track, or losing interest, the way he did, as Cat. Or finding other deer and running with them, as Danni had flown with the wild geese.

He looked down at the snow and saw the circle was almost gone. Jumping from his saddle, he tramped it clear again. But the snow filled it in, behind him. The two diverging tracks were themselves barely visible any longer. And then, looking up, he saw at last a shape, thickening out of the whiteout, like a ghost growing flesh. "Ismail," he whispered joyfully, but the name froze on his lips.

Moving toward him through the falling snow was no stag, but a mist grey rider, mounted on a mist grey horse. A knight, with helm and shield and bow and lance, like he'd seen in the thicket by the chapel. But this knight had living substance, even in the insubstantial light.

The grey was the dulled silver of chain mail, and his enveloping cloak was dark green plaid, as Sir Owain had worn in the forest. The device on his shield was green too, a spreading, green-branched tree. The only ghost-like thing about him was his remote, oblivious gaze. But Gil saw then that he held his bow at the ready and his eyes, shadowed by his helm, were utterly focused on something hidden in the mist. He was hunting, and not for sport; a hungry man, hunting for food.

The knight reached back for an arrow from his quiver, and set it to his bow, never taking his gaze from his unseen quarry. He half-drew the bowstring, and waited, still as a statue on his obedient horse. And then, antlered head held high, the Ismail-Stag stepped out of the mist. The knight-hunter raised his bow and took slow, careful aim. "No!" Gil whispered. And he did the only thing he could. Whipping his own bow from his back, he set arrow to bowstring and took aim at the knight's right arm. "Friend or foe, forgive me," he murmured, and let the arrow fly.

The man cried out and his bow fell to the ground. He clasped his wrist and flung the arrow free. Then he turned and saw Gil. He stared, shaking his wrist, more in annoyance than pain.

Gil felt a surge of relief that he'd done no real harm, but it was drowned, then, in a wave of panic. With a final irritated flick of his hand, the knight lowered his fewtered lance, and charged. Once again, there was nothing to do but act. Gil lowered his own lance, raised his shield, and spun Lionheart around to meet the foe.

The ground was rough and thick with snow. The knight was charging uphill, and himself and Lionheart, down. His helm, rimed with his frozen breath, blocked half his vision and the swirling mist blocked the rest. The warhorse reared and plunged wildly, as they passed, and Lionheart skidded sideways in the snow. Both lances missed and both riders struggled to keep their seats. Gil whirled Lionheart on the spot, blessing his hill pony agility. Then the warhorse thundered back, with the slope in his favor. Lionheart spun around again and ran. Gil hauled on the reins. *Turn!* he commanded desperately. The thundering grew louder as the knight closed the distance. At the last moment, Lionheart spun again. Lance cracked against lance, and both animals slipped to their knees, clambered up, and galloped on.

Silence fell and Gil peered around. The knight had vanished into the mist. Then the muffled sound of hooves on snowy ground signaled his return. "If I could just see!" Gil cried. He grabbed the helm and yanked it off, tossing it into the snow. He knew it was crazy and he'd probably get his skull split, but he gulped fresh air with relief. This time, he saw his adversary in time to raise his shield and line up his lance. *Go,* he told Lionheart. *In and close. We've got the hill.*

The warhorse grew out of the mist, puffing and blowing, mounting the steep slope, and Lionheart flew down, snorting with excitement. Hair flying in the wind, eyes grimly intent on the swaying figure of the knight, Gil tightened his grip on the fewtered lance and charged. Then, just as he braced for the crack of the other's weapon against his upraised shield, the knight suddenly swerved. He flung his lance to one side, dropped his shield, and ducked. Gil's lance swept over his head as they passed, and Lionheart galloped on.

"What?" Gil cried. He turned his pony and looked back. He

remembered Floki, teasing Palamedes with Northmen's games, but the knight was not playing. He turned his horse and drew it to a halt and then slowly trotted forward until he was close enough for Gil to see the glint of his eyes behind his helm. He reined in his horse, lowered his lance to the ground, and bowed his head. Then he turned and galloped away. In moments, he was gone, into the shroud of white.

Gil stared after, until a sound behind him shocked him into awareness. Lance raised, he whirled his pony. But it was only Ismail, transformed into boy again, stepping cautiously out of the circle in the snow. Gil sighed with relief. "What was that about?" he said, nodding towards the vanished knight.

"You won," said Ismail.

Gil laughed. "No. I promise you. I did not win."

"He surrenders. You win." Gil shook his head vigorously. Ismail shrugged. "So why did he run? I find chapel," he added then, with a grin.

They were still arguing about it when they reached the ruined church. While the girls laid the fire with their freshly gathered wood, Palamedes listened with grave attention to the story of the knight. "He dressed in green?" he questioned and Gil repeated what he'd said. Palamedes raised his eyes to the unseen hill. "And what device did he bear upon his shield?"

"A tree," Gil said quickly, "a green tree."

"The Green Tree of Caledon." The Saracen's eyes were darkly somber as he studied Gil's face. "Surely Allah protects you, that you still live." He looked again to the hill. "That was Lance'lot."

CHAPTER EIGHT

The next morning, the sky was clear and the wind still. The walls of the chapel glittered white with hoarfrost, the girls wore sparkling snow maiden tresses, and Palamedes arose from his bed as silver-bearded as the Ab of Hy. Gil peered hungrily at the snowbound horizon. "Today," he said, "we ride."

In the grey light of dawn, they ate a breakfast of cold bannocks and the last of the apples and cheese, while the ponies, released from the byre, pawed through the snow for tufts of grass. Only a last bundle of Danni's barley bread remained, to be packed with the bedrolls and arms. Ismail filled leather water-sacks from the river and added them to Lucy's much lightened burden. The land was a cold desert, with its burns and rivers locked beneath the snow.

Palamedes and Gil hauled the saddles from the dry interior of the chapel. Outside, the mountains stood bright and clear against the brightening sky. Gil thought of the day the sea-mist broke, on the way from Hy. He saw the ridges he had crossed with Ismail in the whiteout and even fancied he glimpsed the site of his joust with Lance'lot. Palamedes touched his shoulder, "There, where the hills part. There beneath the crescent moon! There lies the road to Camelot." A shadowy, forested pass wound between two of the great, round-shouldered mountains. Above, a thin slice of moon shone beside the morning star. They faded, together, as the tops of the hills turned pink.

"A day for adventure," Palamedes cried. "Doombearer!" he called and the big warhorse raised his head from his grazing by the chapel and whickered eagerly. "A day to set foot to stirrup and string to bow!" he slapped Gil's back, knocking him half off his feet. "Come, mount up, and away!"

Following the subtle dip of the snowbound river, they set out toward their waiting road. Doombearer trampled a path through the wind-packed drifts and the others followed, plunging through the thick crust and struggling out again. At last, the animals clambered up onto the track that they had left so desperately five days before. Gil strove to imagine it as the same place they had huddled, watching the snow drift over Danni's sword.

Rachel pointed back to a distant dark smudge of gable wall, rising above the white moorland. "Look!" she said. "You can even see the chapel! We were so close." The road stretched ahead and behind, safe and tame as the hill of Einar's Holm. The blizzard seemed now as unreal as the ghosts. And yet both, Gil knew, could yet return. "Let's go," he said, "while we can."

The road ran high, keeping to the windswept ridges and was often nearly bare of snow. With shod hooves ringing on frozen ground, the ponies pressed on happily and six miles passed in the time taken by the first. Soon they descended to the dark forest below. The winter sun had reached its highest point above the southern hills, when they reached the edge of the trees. Palamedes halted Doombearer in the shelter of an ancient, fallen pine and swung down from the saddle. "Fortune favors us upon this splendid day!" he declared. "It is but the sixth hour, and yet, only a mile lies between us and the Linn of the Rainbow Bridge. We shall see Camelot by dusk."

Dismounting, they turned the ponies free to graze, while Rachel divided up their final rations. Gil accepted his allotted two bannocks and sat, shielded from the wind, with his back against the soft red bark of the tree. The sun was warm on his face, and at his feet, green moss poked out of the thawing snow. He devoured one bannock and then the other, rolling each crumb over his tongue. But eventually both were gone, and he was still hungry. He hauled Lionheart, still munching a clump of marsh grass, out of a snowy thicket. The pony took reluctantly to the road, while Gil, on his back, tried not to wonder where his own next meal would be found.

Within the forest, the ground lay brown and bare; what snow had fallen caught in the thick fir branches high above. The road descended into a deepening gorge, leaving the storm-swept hill behind. Far below, a river glinted mysteriously in the dim light. In the shadows, the air was as cold as night. Their ponies' hooves thudded softly on deep layers of fallen pine needles, making their passage almost silent. Only the distant river disturbed the hush. And then, Gil grew gradually aware of another sound. At first it was so faint that he thought nervously of the ghost-knights of the chapel. But then it grew louder and Palamedes raised his hand, and drew Doombearer to a halt.

"List!" he cried. "We approach the great linn." Soon, the distant thunder of the waterfall filled all the air. Then they rounded a buttress of rock and the cataract was revealed before them. Tumbling over a jagged rock ledge, it fell like a silver ribbon, an unbroken hundred feet to the black pool below. There, two further cataracts burst forth, crossing each other like crossed swords as they arced into a second pool beneath the first.

Just where they met, there hung one frail, pretty tree. Its branches, bare but for small clusters of lacy stems the ghosts of last autumn's berries were white with rime. The same rime coated every surface, glazing the rock face and the edges of each pool with glistening, treacherous ice. "Behold!" Even Palamedes huge voice was almost drowned by the water's roar. "The Linn of the Rainbow Bridge! Here, I heard above me, the voice of the Questing Beast. Here I fought the Usurper, and here I saw him ride to Tir nan Og!" He pointed again. "And there is the tree that saved me from the Evil One as surely as the Tree of Life shields Adam's sons!"

Gil saw in his mind Palamedes grasping the holy branch, his last desperate defense against the Golden Knight; and then the great rainbow rising from the pool to the tree-shrouded sky and the Knight himself, glittering in his golden armor, riding into another world. Their world. He stared hungrily at the pool. At no moment since the day they left Cille Aidan had he been so close to home.

Then suddenly Danni grabbed his arm, pulling him half off

his frightened pony. "Gil!" she cried, her mouth right at his ear. "What's that?"

He heard a sound, so low and deep it seemed to come from the earth itself and so powerful that even the thunder of the cataract could not vanquish it. Lionheart reared and backed away and suddenly his mane streamed out as it had in the great storm on the hill. But this wind came in an instant, born in their midst, within the shelter of the forest, though the sky was clear above and all around the forest trees stood calmly still.

The sound grew louder and louder, shaking the air itself with its eerie shrieking roar. And yet, the closer it grew, the more weirdly familiar it became. Gil shook his head, struggling to hold his frantic pony, and looking up, his eyes met Ismail's and in them he saw the same bewilderment he felt himself. *I know this.*

Then he saw, framed against the thunderous linn, the Saracen knight Palamedes sitting still as stone on his fearless warhorse, his black eyes fixed on the sky and a look of joy transfixing his dark-bearded face. Raising one long arm, he pointed upward, as if to the indefinable source of the sound. "It comes! It comes! At last, it comes!" Around man and beast, waterfall and forest, light rippled and froze. Gil's eyes, fixed on the Saracen knight, saw each hair of Doombearer's wind-streamed mane stand motionless in the air. Then, in an instant, it was over and everything was again sound and furious movement. Palamedes whirled his charger and drew his sword, and holding firm to the pawing animal's reins, looked fondly on them all. "May Allah protect you!" he cried. "May fortune favor your cause! And may we meet again!"

Danni stared at him. "You're leaving us?" she cried.

"Alas, my lady," he smiled down on her sadly. "I am. For it is the Questing Beast! Hear its great voice shaking the hills! By the pledge I made my father, I cannot stay. Farewell!" He flicked his reins once, and the great horse leapt over the flowing stream that ran from the pool to the river far below. Turning his mount one final time, the Master of Lances raised his sword in salute to them all and then galloped headlong into the forest in pursuit of his invisible foe.

Quite suddenly, all fell still. The howling ceased and with it the whirlwind and all that remained was the roar of the haunted cataract. Gil looked from it to his companions. One by one they tore their eyes from the spot where Palamedes had disappeared and turned to him. "Well," he said, with as bold a grin as he could muster, "I guess it wasn't make-believe."

Rachel brushed the freezing spray of the waterfall from her skirt. "Okay," she said and smiled gamely, "what now?"

Gil returned the smile. He set his wary eyes on the road ahead, "Now, we become warriors." With a last look at the Linn of the Rainbow Bridge, he turned his pony's head to Camelot.

The track beyond the linn ran steeply downward, rocky and poorly marked. The ponies picked their way warily, and Gil struggled to keep the trail. Too soon, dusk was falling. He turned to check his companions, following in line beneath the great shadowy trees; then faced forward, adjusting his balance instinctively, as at home on Lionheart's sloping back as on his own feet.

A sudden, small sound caught his attention, a sharp crackling, as of a small snapping branch. He whirled and looked back. Ismail gazed warily around. Still, the sound did not come again, and at last Gil shrugged and they went on, more cautiously, listening all the while. The forest, in its vastness, had beguiled him, exactly as had the mist on the Great Loch. The feeling of being alone in all the world was a lie. The loch had held the dragon. The whiteout on the hill concealed the knight, Lance'lot. And these endless walls of trees might hide an army.

Without Palamedes' guidance, the time gained in the bright morning was rapidly lost. The ache of his muscles beneath the weight of armor, the stiffness in his neck from the shield hanging at his back, and most of all, the emptiness of his stomach, told Gil the day was nearly done. Wearily, he searched ahead for a place to camp. And then, to his alarm, he saw a thing Palamedes had not described: a Y-shaped parting in the road. Each track graded downward, though one more gently than the other. For all they knew of where they were going, either could lead to Camelot. "I'll fly," Rachel said.

Danni echoed, "I will."

Gil shook his head. "It's too late," he said. "It'll be dark before you could get back. We have to choose."

He got down from his pony and Ismail joined him and they walked a little way on each road. "To the left is fainter," Ismail said. "Though both are faint."

Gil nodded. Few travelled either road now. Like the chapel on the hill, both had fallen to ruin and decay. He paced carefully along the right-hand track, scouring the frozen surface for some sign of its more recent use. His eyes fell on a single dark indentation on a remaining patch of deeper snow. He ran to it, then knelt down, running his fingers across the outline, and finding the sharp edge cut by an iron shoe. He jumped up and walked around the print in a widening spiral until, several feet away, he found another, on another snow patch. And then, winding back into the forest, a whole line of prints in the softer snow within. "Ismail!" he shouted. "Here! Someone's ridden here."

"Good!" Ismail said. "Good tracker! Better than me!" He knelt beside the trail. "Today. No hoarfrost in print. A man rides from forest, seeks shelter before night falls, takes road home. Road to Camelot." He pointed down the right-hand trail.

Gil raised his eyes and looked warily ahead. "Do we follow?" he said. "He's not going to be a friend."

Ismail, too, looked down the road. "Yes," he said. "Follow. But far back." He dropped his soft voice lower. "Not heard. Not seen."

Cautiously, they set out, not speaking and wincing each time a pony's hoof struck stone. Once again, Gil thought he heard a sound, this time far ahead, but now he doubted his senses. Every shadow held an ambushing raider; every creak of a branch signaled a passing horseman. He heard his own tense breathing and fancied he heard the others' as well.

Then he rounded the first bend after the dividing roads and fanciful fear took solid form. Directly before him loomed the dusk-shrouded figure of a mounted knight. Green-clad, wrapped in a cloak of green plaid, he sat with his back to them, still as a ghost on his tall grey horse. Lionheart's ears flicked back and forth and his nostrils flared at the sight of the stranger's mount. Gil tightened his hand on the reins. Then his eyes settled on the shield slung across the knight's back and his breath caught in his throat.

Back, he said to Lionheart. *No sound*. And the pony carefully stepped backward until the bend in the road again hid from sight the knight, his horse, and the Green Tree of Caledon on his shield. Gil turned Lionheart and held up his hand to Danni who rode just behind. "Back," he mouthed and she turned Frosti and the others followed. A hundred yards up the road, Gil urged Lionheart forward and, overtaking his friends, stopped and turned to face them. "It was him," he said to Ismail. "It was Lance'lot."

"You are sure?"

"Positive. I saw the shield."

"He didn't see you?"

"He was facing the other way. Not moving. Just sitting there. Sort of waiting."

"For us?" Danni asked, wide-eyed.

"I didn't ask, Danni," Gil said, with a weak grin. "I'm the idiot who shot an arrow at the best knight in Camelot. I so don't want to meet him again."

"Take other road," said Ismail. The left-hand track was gentler than the right, and a little wider, as well, though here and there a shrubby tree had taken root in it, showing how little it was travelled. Ismail rode up beside Gil and Danni brought Frosti side-by-side with Freya, with Lucy trailing on her lead. When they had gone far enough that sound could not possibly carry to where Gil had encountered the knight, Ismail suddenly spoke. "He is great warrior, this Lance'lot?"

"The best," Danni said from behind.

Ismail paused and then said, "Great warrior always sees behind him."

Danni said quickly, "Well, maybe he wasn't Lance'lot."

"He was," Gil said, over his shoulder., "The last time I saw that shield, it was coming straight at me, with him right behind it. I definitely remember it."

"Well," Rachel put in logically, "maybe he's just not that great."

"Or, maybe," Ismail said, "We go now the way he chooses?"

"Like, it's a trap?" Danni said.

"Perhaps." Ismail inclined his head thoughtfully. "But why does great warrior set trap for children?"

Danni leaned forward then, over Frosti's neck and said urgently, "The Lady Griselle said the Golden Knight and Lance'lot are enemies. So maybe he's on our side. Arthur's side."

Gil shook his head. "He fought Arthur. He's the reason all this happened." He waved a disconsolate hand at the deserted road, encompassing in his own mind the chapel, too, and Sir Owain's defeated knights, and Hy, and even the burning village: every bad thing that he'd seen and heard of since he'd arrived. "Whoever's side he's on, it can't be ours." He thought and said then, "Lance'lot's an outlaw. He has lots of enemies. He didn't see me now because his mind was on other things. Anyhow, whatever his problems are, we've got our own. It's getting dark. We have to get off this road and make ourselves some kind of shelter. Now."

He turned Lionheart's head toward the forest and, by happy fortune, glimpsed exactly what he'd been looking for: a clearing among the trees. He rode quietly into the open space. Here, the snow lay deeper, but it was soft and the moment he dismounted and dropped his reins on Lionheart's neck, the pony began to paw for grass.

The clearing was a little lost meadow, with juniper and bracken growing where once sheep or cattle had grazed. It had, like all the land, a feeling of sad abandonment. But it was lighter, out of the shadowy forest, and the pressing urgency of nightfall receded. Time enough to cut branches and make a lean-to, like he and Danni used to do, in the woods. Time to light a fire, if he dared. Gil looked around at his waiting companions and loneliness descended upon him. It was his decision, the first to be made on his own.

He missed Palamedes badly and he missed Floki even more. He racked his brains, trying to decide what Floki would do. *A fire's a beacon and smoke a flag.* But then he imagined a night in this cold and snow and knew they could not survive it. "Make a hearth," he said to Ismail and Rachel. Then, leaving his pony grazing, he set off across the meadow, with Danni, searching for firewood. They found a dead pine, at one end, and right in the center, an ancient apple tree. A few small, yellow apples clung yet, high above their heads. Vowing to climb for them in the morning, Gil broke off dead branches for Danni to carry to Ismail.

Nearby, stiff, thorny stalks rose out of the snow, bent with the dried remnants of ungathered berries. The lost harvest reminded him again of Arthur's lost kingdom, and he wistfully imagined the meadow in summer, laden with fruit. And then he saw it, as he had seen it before, through the circle of white stone. "Danni!" he cried, so sharply that she looked up in alarm. "We're here! It's the meadow of the raspberries! It's the place I saw Janetta. Where the Knight's raiders caught her and the lady found her veil." He looked down at the ground as if he could see it there, yet, white in the white snow.

Then Rachel suddenly shouted. "Listen!"

Gil tore his gaze from the empty place in the snow and raised his head. The light wind had shifted, carrying to them the barest whisper of sound, the ringing of a church bell, dreamy and far away, like the bell of Hy from the shore of the Western Sea. "It's the convent," Danni said softly. "The Convent of the Grey Sisters."

"Quick!" Rachel cried, "Get the ponies and follow the sound. They'll have a guest house." She was already gathering Freya's reins, leaving their half-built hearth abandoned. "We can sleep there."

But Gil shook his head fiercely. Danni gave him a cautious look. "It'll be a lot warmer and drier than here."

"Sure," he said. "And for the sake of a warmer bed, we bring to them what we brought to Hy?"

"Not here, Gil," Rachel smiled solemnly. "This is the safest place in Caledon. The Golden Knight can't touch it. Guinevere's here. And," she added, "there's nowhere we'd be safer, either."

"Nor, indeed, more welcome, child," said a sweet, low voice, behind Gil's back.

Gil spun around. At the edge of the forest, half in its shadow, stood a slender figure beside a laden horse. Shame swamped him that he'd allowed himself to be caught unaware. He saw the same humiliation on Ismail's face. Even he had failed to hear the stranger approach. *We could all be dead*, Gil thought dully. Nor was he relieved when the figure, stepping clear of the trees, was revealed as a woman, in the grey habit of a nun. Shony was a woman. If not exactly a nun. "Who are you?" he muttered stupidly.

"A wood gatherer, as are you. Though I have more." She turned slightly and he saw her long back was bowed under a great burden of sticks. The horse behind her was heavily laden, too. Despite the weight she carried, she smiled cheerfully and though she was slender, she looked strong. Greying blond hair showed at the front of her veil, and her eyes were soft blue-green and set in a beautiful, fine-boned face.

"Let me help you!" Rachel cried. She ran forward, reaching out for the burden. The woman caught her wrist, holding her back.

"It is no concern. I have often carried more and carried it farther." She smiled again, still holding Rachel's wrist, and turning it with a gentle hand. "Welcome, child," she said solemnly, "We have waited long for you."

Rachel shook her head uncertainly. "You know who we are?"

The woman nodded. "I do know," she said. "And I would have known by your gentle heart alone, had I never seen my bracelet on your arm."

"Your bracelet?" Rachel's eyes darkened, almost in fear, and she pulled back. "Are you Queen Guinevere?"

The woman released her at once. She touched her nun's veil and shook her head, laughing gently. "No," she said. "We have but one queen here, that good Lady, Mother of Our Lord." Her smile softened. "But I am Guinevere." The wind shifted again, and again they heard the far-off bell. "Come," she said quickly, extending her arms as if to embrace them. "We must go now." She turned away to gather up the reins of her packhorse. Quickly, they caught the bridles of their own ponies, and walked behind her into the forest.

They emerged from the trees into an open space with

vegetable gardens and orchards, covered in snow. In their midst, a tall stone wall shielded the convent buildings from view. Only their turfed roofs poked out above, and from one, a curl of sweet blue smoke rose into the sky. A wooden door, wide enough for two ponies to pass through abreast, was set into the wall. Guinevere led them to it and knocked firmly on the weathered planks. They stood waiting while footsteps came closer, and Gil imagined the same door on a beautiful summer day and Janetta and the Lady Griselle riding out, side by side. The door swung open and a young nun stared out in startled silence. Then she stood back with bowed head as Guinevere led them all inside, and then closed the door on the night and the forest.

They found themselves in a cobbled courtyard. At one side was a stable and on the other, the guest house. Before them stood the chapel, hardly any bigger than the church at Cille Aidan. The nun who had opened the gate hurried to its waiting door as the bell chimed a last time. "Come," Guinevere said, "We must set your animals at their ease, and then, sing praises for the ending of the day."

After prayers, while the girls disappeared into the convent, Gil and Ismail brought their bedrolls into the guest house. In the flickering light of an oil lamp, they chose two of the four simple mattresses and sprawled on them, wrapped in their sheepskins, savoring the luxury of a sturdy roof over their head. A quick, light tap sounded at the door. Gil got up to open it and found Rachel and Danni, each holding a basket laden with food. Behind them, Guinevere smiled gently.

They ate ravenously, sitting in a ring on the floor with the food on a cloth between them: boiled hens' eggs, cheese and apples, a mound of hazelnuts, barley bread, butter, and honey. Guinevere sat cross-legged beside them, her eyes shining with pleasure. When they'd all had seconds, and even thirds, she unwrapped a small white cloth filled with little honey cakes. "These were my favorites when I was a girl," she said, and she would not take any herself but smiled with delight as the children wolfed them down. Then she tidied the cloth and the baskets away and called them all to sit close by her.

"I shall speak with you this night," she said, "Because come morning, I again must keep silence, and when you have heard holy mass, you will be, at once, on your way. Here is the route you must follow." She leant forward, and spreading the cloth that had held the cakes, she began to draw a simple map in the crumbs. First, she showed the road they had travelled to Camelot, and the juncture where they had first gone one way, and then retreated from Lance'lot, to the other. That branch she drew so it came past the convent, below the fields, and Gil realized they had taken a shortcut through the meadow and the forest.

"There," she said, "This road, too, winds down to Camelot. But here, beyond it," she touched the cloth, "A steep, lost path descends, and this, un-travelled by all but ourselves, will take you to the edge of the Forest of Pentecost. And there," she drew a soft circle, "Lies the Forest Mews where shelter the Lady Janetta and the Holy Fool. It lies within a garden and the garden within a wall that has but one entrance gate. The Usurper holds the key, and carries it upon his person, and sleeps with it close to his hand." Her eyes softened and she smiled gently. "I know this place well. Before Holy Church gave her blessing, my love and I stole precious moments there." She lowered her head and her veil slipped forward, shielding her face. "Even a king can grow impatient for his bride."

She straightened, and continued urgently, "But here, you must tread with care, for twice a day, at the third hour and the ninth, the Usurper rides this way, to and from the hunt. And returning, unlocks the forbidden door, and rides the garden's avenues to the tower. There, beneath her window, he sits upon his gold-trapped charger and seeks to win her friendship with sweet words. For in his pride, he would have her as a lover, before a slave. Though, in the end," she said solemnly, "he will have her either way."

"But if the Knight always holds the key," Gil said, "How can we get in?"

Guinevere smiled for the first time in the telling of her story. "Within the walls, there is an older key. For, though the gate stood open in our innocent days, we would lock it firm behind us, to guard our tryst. We hid our key with youthful boldness, high up in the ivy of the wall, in a crevice in the stones, where only the young might dare to climb. And that key yet remains, I know," she said dreamily. "For I placed it there myself, on the eve of my wedding day. I set it for safe keeping in a little golden box, and the box itself in the crevice in the wall. Three stones from the gatepost," she recited, remembering, "and three from the coping stone. I kissed its silver tassels and locked it away forever. For on the night to come, we would share the marriage bed, and leave unlawful trysts behind."

She paused and said sadly, "Or so I truly thought, as Lord Yesu is my witness, and so I pledged before Him, on that day." She shook her head and leant closer. "One of you must climb the wall, tomorrow, and drop down the other side, then claim the key and release the gate for all. But I warn you; it is high and smooth and has defeated many." She stood up, brushing crumbs from her skirt, folded the cloth, and gathered her baskets. "And now I must go."

Rachel slipped the bracelet the Lady Griselle had given her, from her wrist. "This is yours," she said hastily, offering it back.

"And this!" Danni tugged her ring off and held it out, too.

But Guinevere only smiled. "No." She stretched out a long, graceful arm, pulling back her sleeve. A plain black cord, knotted again and again, was wrapped around her sun-tanned wrist. "By this I count the psalms," she said. "It is all the adornment I will ever need." She replaced the ring on Danni's finger and the bracelet on Rachel's arm. "Wear these with my blessing." She turned to go and then turned back and smiled again, sadly. "And if ever your hearts call you to what Heaven says is wrong, then look on these. And remember Guinevere, for whom Heaven's own kingdom fell." Shepherding the girls before her, she went out into the night.

Gil and Ismail doused their oil lamp and curled in their sheepskins again. Gil lay quietly in the dark, thinking of the Lady Janetta in a mix of joy and trepidation. For, by tomorrow's end, all might be won, but all might also be lost. He heard a sound outside, a frightened pony snorting, and started awake. Quickly, he got up and felt his way through the blackness to the door and slipped outside. Above, the sky was clear and starry and wrapped amidst the stars were dancing streamers of white. The Northern Lights. He'd seen them once on a winter night at home, but never like this. He stared in wonder, and then ran to the stable under the dancing sky.

Inside, it was warm with the comforting smell of horses and faintly lit by the stars and the aurora through slits in the walls. A cluster of pony shapes formed a lumpy huddle. Hooves clunked sleepily and a beast blew gently through its nose.

Is that you? he said to Lionheart.

I'm over here. Gil peered into the dimness and saw a dark shadow alone in a corner. *He's outside.*

What? Gil snapped instantly alert. *Who's outside?*

The horse from the snow.

The snow… the joust! Lance'lot's horse?

The horse that chased me.

Because you ran away, he reminded Lionheart. Then he got suspicious. *You're in a stable. And that's inside a wall. How do you know there's a horse out there at all? Never mind whose.*

I smell him, said Lionheart. He flicked his ears with authority.

Gil stared at the pony in the faint, pulsing light. *Okay*, he said. *I'll check this out.* Out in the courtyard, he surveyed the wall. It was blank and twice his height, the door firmly closed. Quickly, he sought somewhere to climb. His eyes settled on the guest house roof, its turf peak clearing the wall by a foot. He was reaching up to the eaves, seeking a low point to which he might scramble, when he belatedly remembered who he was. Stepping back from the guest house, he drew a circle in the thin layer of snow, stepped within, and became Cat.

The Northern Lights flared into a flickering veil of brilliance, lighting the whole of the convent grounds. At once he was assaulted by sound. Ponies snorting and stirring and snuffling in the stable, hens clucking in a coop somewhere, Ismail's soft breathing within the guest house and from the convent, a single voice chanting a prayer. He stretched quickly and glorying in his supple strength bounded to the turf of the eaves, and then to the roof tree. He sat down to wash a paw, then remembered what he was there for, stood up, ran along the roof tree, and bounded again to the gable. From there, it was a kitten jump to the top of the convent wall.

Looking down, Gil froze still, then settled on his haunches and with a sharp flick, wrapped his tail close. On the edge of the forest, half hidden in its shadow, sat a man in armor on a tall grey horse. In the eerie light from the sky, even Gil's human eyes would have seen the Green Tree of Caledon on the shield slung over his back. The knight's attention was fixed on the building, and when Gil swiveled his head and looked straight behind himself, he saw a small, darkened window, directly in the line of Lance'lot's gaze.

He felt a remote, feline sorrow, as if some place of great comfort, with warmth and food, and solace, was forever beyond his reach. His human self struggled to translate and suddenly the image of Guinevere feeding them honey cakes arose in his mind. Then boy and cat found agreement. If you loved such a person, wouldn't you love them forever, no matter what?

He stood and stretched in the soft flickering light, then leapt back to the roof and down to his circle in the snow.

CHAPTER NINE

Raising a warning hand, Gil reined Lionheart in hard. Ahead the steep, narrow path from the convent twisted out of the trees onto a precipitous ledge, before snaking its way downward again. As the others jostled to a nervous halt behind him, he let Lionheart pick his way to the edge of the exposed rock and stared out in silence. Rising above the dark forest, a crenelated wall shielded the remnants of a great castle and *muinntir*, both now roofless and blackened by fire. Around the ruined citadel were open fields with cattle and sheep and small huddled buildings of stone and turf. A soft haze of blue smoke hung over all and the fields themselves were wrapped yet in the morning's mist. "Camelot," Gil whispered, as Danni brought her pony in close.

"It was so beautiful from the sky," she said sadly. But then she pointed down and cried, "Look! The mews!"

Directly below them, a high stone wall, well-tended and undamaged, surrounded a square of green trees and hedges, fresh-tilled earth, and neat, snow-filled pathways; a walled garden, and in its center, a small grey tower, smoke curling gently above its roof. Beyond the Mews Garden, another wall, taller, and of grim grey stone, extended far into the distance. Before it was a wide expanse of open ground through which ran a beaten track, the snow churned to black mud by the passage of horses. Where the track met the wall, great double gates stood, locked and barred. "The Forest of Pentecost," Gil said warily.

Suddenly the pure sweet note of a hunting horn, like that Sir Owain blew to summon his ragged knights, sounded in the winter air, and then, from far behind, the bells of the convent rang the third hour. "Quick!" Gil jumped down from Lionheart. "Hide in the trees."

They had barely backed their nervous ponies into shelter, when a tall, slender boy clad in gleaming chain mail beneath a cape of rich brown velvet; appeared. His horse, which he rode with lordly ease, was dapple grey and decked in gold trappings. Over his shoulder was slung a great bow and he carried a pole bearing a golden banner that rippled and flowed behind him as his horse pranced and shied. Behind the boy with the banner came seven men on foot, each leashing a pair of great, grey dogs, lean and bony and shaggy as wild goats.

"Deerhounds," Rachel whispered. "That's a wolfhound," she pointed at a huge animal, tall as a pony, which trotted into view. Behind it came seven mounted knights, their richly trapped horses trotting shoulder to shoulder. Like the boy, they wore chain hauberks and chausses and flowing velvet cloaks, each of a jewel color: red, green, violet, and blue.

A single rider followed upon a mighty horse, creamy white against the snow, and draped in Cloth of Gold. His cloak, too, was Cloth of Gold, and over his steel mail, a lighter layer of fine gold links glittered in the morning light. Unlike the others, he wore a steel helm, and that, too, was decorated with gold and a golden plume. "The Knight," said Gil.

"He rides to the hunt armed for war," Ismail whispered softly. "He trusts no one." The knight, whose stolen gold proclaimed his power, yet rode ready for battle on a day of play. A tiny flicker of hope stirred in Gil's mind. Surely, a man who so feared defeat could be defeated.

The boy drew his horse up and sat with his banner to one side of the gate. The seven knights wheeled their mounts and took up a place at the other. The Golden Knight rode alone to the door in the wall and waited as the rest of the hunting party followed. Gil counted two dozen mounted, armed men, the hooves of their horses churning and splashing in the thawing snow. Another twenty, at least, followed on foot. All were surrounded by a yapping pack of skinny white dogs and one man struggled to control a leashed pair of huge mournful-faced hounds. At the rear came a heavily laden cart, drawn by two buff ponies, hill garrons with bristly manes and tails.

The ranks of the hunting party parted to allow the cart passage and as its driver pulled up in front of the mews, the Golden Knight dismounted his white warhorse and strode to the gate. He withdrew from beneath his hauberk a necklace of golden links from which hung a great dark key. Without removing the necklace, the knight reached up and fitted the key into the heavy iron lock. The gates parted and swung inward. The Knight mounted his horse again and waited while the cart passed within.

The white dogs yapped and the deerhounds strained at their leashes and the knights struggled to control their restless mounts. But the wolfhound lay down beside his master, crossed his huge paws, and rested his chin on them in silence. At last, the cart trundled out again, empty. The gates were closed by two men on foot, but the Knight himself rode close and leaned down from his saddle to lock them with his key.

The deerhounds leapt forward, their leash men struggling now to keep up. The white dogs snarled and snapped at each other in their eagerness for the hunt. Only the great wolfhound kept his solemn dignity, rising to his feet, and padding behind the gold trapped charger's heels, as all set out through the muddied snow to the Forest of Pentecost. But the cart, pulled by its humble garrons, turned back the way it had come, to the ruins of the castle of Camelot.

Outside the distant wall, the hunters halted again. Two of the seven knights dismounted, and with their leader approached the entrance; but whatever key the Knight used to unlock its tall, grim gates was hidden from Gil's sight. With a great howling, the dogs poured through. Dog handlers and mounted men followed, whooping and shouting. Then the Knight himself entered with his youthful standard bearer at his side, and the gates creaked closed once more.

Gil led Lionheart from his shelter and mounted. He looked from the Mews Garden, below, to the barred entrance of the mysterious forest. "We turn back to the hill when the bells of the convent ring for Saxt. No matter what." He shook Lionheart's reins and began the descent.

Close up, the walls of the Mews Garden were high and
forbidding. Gil trotted Lionheart cautiously across the muddy
snow where the hunting party had passed. Casting a wary
glance to the forest gate, he swung down quickly to the slushy
ground. He scanned the smooth stone wall for several yards
in each direction but found nowhere even a cat could climb.
Then his instinct told him to be Cat before he made decisions
that only a cat could make, and crouching down, he drew a
circle in the melting snow, with the tip of his sword. His last
human thought as he pronounced the blessing was how he
would make his return, once the wall stood between himself
and his friends. But before he could worry about it, he was Cat,
who never worried about anything. Leaping from the ring in
the snow, he trotted a few feet, and then sat down and began
carefully to wash.

"Gil, go!" Rachel hissed. "We're sitting ducks out here!"
Gil ignored her. Then he heard a sound that flattened his ears
against his skull and brought an involuntary growl from his
throat: a faint yelping troubled the morning air. Dogs. Hunting
dogs in the Forest of Pentecost. His ears unfolded and his tail
ceased to swish, and, dismissing the baying of the hounds, he
rose and trotted along the base of the enclosure, sniffing the air
as he went.

He smelled the vine before he saw it. An ancient ivy, its
wood as grey and thick as a tree trunk rose up against the wall,
its tendrils penetrating mortar and stone. High up, it had been
hacked back, so only new growth reached the top of the wall,
too frail and thin to hold a climbing man. For a climbing cat,
though, it was a green ladder up which he leapt with ease. He
trotted back along the coping stone toward the gate, his nose
twitching with the excitement of rich, new smells. Hens, doves,
wood smoke, horses. Dogs. His ears flicked down. But the dog
smell was old. And all the smells were far away. Below him, in
the wintry gardens, nothing moved.

He swished his tail and bunched himself on his haunches
and looked down over the edge. *Three stones from the gate post,
three from the coping stone.* Guinevere's words came back to him,
but he struggled now to envision what they meant. *Three.* He

looked at his front paws. Two paws and another paw. He lifted one forepaw and then the other and then a hind paw. He peered from the gate post to the first stone, to the next, and the next, lifting paws in succession. *There. The third stone.* Then he did the same, vertically, and found the third stone down. With a small chirrup of relief, he crouched on his haunches again and then leapt into the heart of the ivy.

It was a four-paw landing and required every claw to hold on. But, hanging spread-eagled there, he spotted a gleam in the green darkness and a quick batting of leaves revealed its source. Just the corner of the little box remained in sight, so thickly had the ivy grown around the crevice that concealed it. But, being gold, it had lost none of its luster, and as an exploratory paw drew it into the light, it glistened bright as the sun. "I've got it!" he meowed, and he heard Danni shout from beyond the wall, "Is that you, Gil?"

No. Just one of the two dozen other cats up here, he purred wearily. With a deft paw-swipe, he scooped the little box from its hiding place and watched in triumph as it tumbled to the ground. Leaping and scrambling down the precarious ivy, he descended after it and, with a final wild jump, landed in the snow and pounced upon it with eager-clawed paws. When claws didn't work, he tried teeth and was gnawing fruitlessly at a golden corner when he remembered he could have hands. He growled at himself in disgust and looked for a circle.

The garden, with its formal hedges and snow-filled avenues, comprised nothing but straight lines. Beside the gate, a stone watering trough was filled from a spring, but the pool of the spring was long and narrow and the trough itself was square. A stone shed was set at the opposite side of the gate. It had neither smoke hole, nor chimney, but its rectangular door stood slightly ajar. He wormed his way in through the small gap and found among a heap of dusty, broken tools, a discarded cooking pot. Rusted through at the bottom, it was yet perfectly circular. Gil rubbed his forehead possessively against it and jumped within. The light tickle of his whiskers warned him it was narrow, but there was no fear-inducing bending of their sensitive length. *I fit here,* they told him, even as the "I" of him was ceasing to be cat. And then he was Gil, within the gates of his lady's prison, at last.

He turned eagerly to the door, strode toward the light and tripped, wildly, over a foot grown ungainly and huge. With a clang like a great ringing bell, he sprawled on the stone floor, staring at the iron cooking pot jammed solid on his right boot. He gave the boot a savage shake. The pot stuck firm, defying any attempt to kick it off. "Thanks so much, Cat!" He staggered upright and hobbled quickly from the shed, his foot clanging with each step.

"You do battle?" Ismail called, alarmed.

Gil sat down again, placed both hands on the iron vessel and struggled valiantly. Far off in the garden, he heard the whinny of an excited horse. "Not now!" he groaned, "Don't let her come now!" He gave a last, frantic tug and the pot flew free, thudding viciously into his forehead as it did. With a cry of pain and fury, he flung the miserable thing into a tall green hedge and ran back to the golden box.

Human hands made easy work of its simple latch. Within, lay a weathered iron key, a hand's breadth in length. Gil lifted it from its long shelter, stepped quickly to the gate and slipped the key into the battered keyhole. The latch released, as if Guinevere had locked it only the day before, and the gates parted under his hand. Danni's glowing face appeared in the opening. She leapt onto Frosti's back, and tugging Lionheart by his bridle, rode into the garden. Rachel and Ismail followed, with Lucy on her lead, the ponies' shod hooves ringing on the stones beneath the snow. Ismail helped Gil swing the gates closed and watched as he turned the key in the lock and then replaced it within its golden box. "Put it in your pocket," Danni urged, but Gil shook his head.

"This is a big place. We could get separated. We all have to be able to open the gate." He retrieved the iron cooking pot from the hedge, laid the box within its broken curve and replaced the pot among the dust-coated tools.

Danni twisted around in her saddle, surveying her surroundings. Rachel studied the elaborate design of trees, paths, and hedges, and then smiled. "It's a summer hunting lodge! Look, that little shed was a gatehouse. The hunters would ride here from the castle and gather for breakfast, to plan the hunt. They'd come back after, to feast. Hunts could go on for days. Sometimes they just had tents outside the forest, with wine and food and even beds. Here, they had the tower."

Seeking a glimpse of the thatched roof with its curls of smoke, they searched the close grown hedges, the many avenues, now half-closed by tangles of briar, and the stands of birch and oak beyond, "So many paths," Danni murmured.

"It's a maze," Rachel said. "That would have been part of the fun."

With the sun rapidly climbing toward Saxt, it was fun Gil could do without. "We all saw the tower, from above," he said. "Can anybody remember where?"

Rachel grinned. "No," she said, dismounting. "But I can see it again, right now." She tossed her sword belt into the snow and jumped within, chanting the blessing as she did. Swept into her Other, she soared from the circle, and rose above their heads. Clustering together on their ponies, they watched her darting progress through the treetops and into the open sky. She circled, and then appeared to turn back in triumph, but then something else shot into the sky from the hidden ground below. Swift as an arrow, it swept past her and spread out wings, soaring briefly, before plunging down with outstretched pinions.

"Another hawk!" Danni cried. The two birds met in a clash of wing and claw that scattered feathers like brown snowfall. Rachel whirled and defended herself, but the other creature was bigger and faster and stronger. The birds closed again and clashed, and she fluttered and flapped, tumbling as if she would fall. Catching air again, she turned valiantly, but the other's third pass harried her downward, toward the ground.

Ismail whispered. "It drives her from the sky."

Gil's eyes swept the maze of hedge and thorn. "That way!" He galloped into the narrow gap between dark walls of green. Behind him, the muffled hoofbeats of the cantering ponies fell back, as the others struggled to follow his trail. But he drove Lionheart on through the twisting maze to where Rachel fought her uneven battle. Then suddenly he burst into a clearing, a perfect square of once-tended lawn, now wild with fallen meadow grass. At his pony's feet lay a scattering of brown feathers in blood spattered snow. He looked up, but the sky was empty.

Remembering Floki calling the hawk in Glen Alban, he wrapped his cloak twice around his arm, and whistled. But no proud, sweeping wing cut the air. Then, as his eyes dropped lower, he saw her at last, a small, hunched shape, cowering in the glittering depths of a holly tree. Red blood splashed her feathers, bright as the berries amid the leaves. "Rachel," he whispered. He turned to dismount, but some growing instinct murmured caution, and he looked carefully all around. And then, as his eyes swept the clearing, he saw the knight.

At the far edge of the square meadow, majestic in sky-blue trappings, stood an iron-grey horse, as big as Doombearer; so big that his armored rider seemed small on his back. But the knight's upraised lance was stout and tipped with glistening steel, and his armor gleamed as if new-made that morning. On his helm was a plume of sky-blue feathers and his tunic, beneath his chain hauberk, was blue as well. On his shield pranced a snow-white beast, like a horse with a single horn; a unicorn, set on a sky-blue field.

A lean grey deerhound lay waiting silently at the grey horse's feet, and on the knight's chain clad arm sat the great brown hawk. Obedient now to its master, it turned its head and fixed Gil with its merciless golden eye. He felt a wave of outrage. No wild thing had savaged Rachel, but this knight's well-trained hunting hawk. Then the knight ducked his plumed helmet and lowered his lance. Gil had seconds only to do the same before the grey horse charged.

Lionheart snorted in terror, but bravely obeyed Gil's urging heels and the two animals thundered through the snowy meadow at a gallop. Gil lined the tip of his fewtered lance with the eye of the beast on the sky-blue shield and braced himself for the clash. But then the brown hawk swept like a whirlwind between them and descended in feathered fury on Gil's helmed head. "Get off!" he shouted. His lance veered wildly and Lionheart stumbled. Then his own shield shook with the force of the other's blow. His arm jerked back, wrenching at his shoulder, and he lost both stirrups, and almost his seat. Recovering, he drove Lionheart on to safety and whirled him angrily for the second charge.

"Okay," he murmured, jamming the lance into its fewter and regaining his stirrups. "Let's play rough." With the lance firm beneath his right hand, he drew his sword clumsily with his left. If the hawk came at him again, he'd slice it out of the sky. Again, the two mounts closed, and again Gil lined up his lance. But, with only yards between them, a grey shadow suddenly sprang from behind the grey horse's galloping hooves and leapt savagely at Lionheart's throat. Lionheart skidded to a halt, rearing up to save himself from the deerhound, and then Gil, struggling to stay aboard, saw a flash of equine teeth and felt something pinch hard against his mailed left elbow.

Jerking his arm free of the grey horse's teeth and barely holding on to his sword, he tightened his reins and hung on as his pony skittered sideways like a kitten. Then the hawk struck from behind, batting at his helm and the blue-plumed knight lined up for a third charge. Lionheart balked and reared, rolling his eyes at the deerhound. *Kick him*, Gil said malevolently. *And then bite the horse.*

Gil charged, swinging his bright blade in a circle around his head. "Get into this, hawk, and you're feathered lunch." With an angry screech, the hawk veered away. Lionheart's steel shod hoof sent the snapping deerhound cowering, and before the big horse's teeth could reach Gil, Lionheart's were nipping at its angry ears.

Swerving to escape, the grey horse lost its footing, skidded sideways in the hoof-churned slush, and thudded to the ground, flinging its armored rider head over heels. Meadow grass cushioned both falls and the horse was on its feet in seconds. But before its rider could rise, Gil was beside him, his hand on the knight's helm and his sword against his throat. Heart pounding, breathing in gasps, he held the blade firm and hissed fiercely, "Surrender or die!"

The knight made a small, whimpering gasp. His shoulders shuddered and two trails of water dribbled from beneath the eye-pieces of his helm. Gil stepped back, astounded, and lowered his sword. Then he grasped the knight's blue plume firmly and wrenched the helm from his head. Tear-filled blue eyes squinted up at him from a round, terrified face. "Percy?" Gil whispered.

Suddenly, Lionheart whinnied in alarm and the weeping knight shrieked. Swift, light footsteps crossed the snowy ground behind Gil. He flung himself desperately sideways as a weight, slight but determined, struck his shoulder blades and a slim arm wrapped itself around his throat. Rolling over, he tore the arm free, but his face was enveloped in a cascading black veil of shining hair. Blindly, he grasped two silken hanks and clawed the glossy curtain apart. He looked up into a girl's face, so white with fury that the freckles stood bold on the bridge of her nose and her brows made two fierce lines of charcoal above her brilliant green eyes. "Release me!" she cried in a voice trembling between fear and outrage. "And release my innocent knight!"

Gil dropped the hanks of her hair as if they were red hot. He scuttled sideways and sat up, slowly, so as not to frighten her. She sprang to a wary crouch, her red velvet dress pooling around her, her black hair tumbling down her back. Her eyes, narrowed by thick black lashes, followed his every move. "It's you!" he whispered wonderingly. He held out empty hands, but she flinched away. "My green-eyed girl!" He stared with such intense amazement that she gave him a little puzzled smile.

"I am Janetta de Troye," she said. She climbed warily to her feet, her eyes never leaving his. "Daughter of a lord and betrothed to a lord. Both of whom I deny. If I am not theirs," she looked him up and down, and again gave him the puzzled smile, "by what chance am I yours?"

Gil thought of the Golden Knight and his followers, riding in splendor to the hunt, and saw himself as she must see him: a rough Viking from the North, smelling of wood fires, ponies, and fish. He took a deep breath, marshalling his courage. Then he undid his chain face-guard, lifted his helm from his head and looked up into her face; the face he had seen through a stone in a time and a place a thousand years yet to come. "Do you deny me, too?" he said.

She gave a small cry of astonishment and her white hands flew to cover her mouth. Behind them, her cheeks reddened girlishly as she meekly shook her head. Then she lowered her hands and regained a little of her composure. "No," she said with a radiant, still disbelieving smile. "Nor shall I ever deny you," she whispered, "Though time denies us both." Solemnly, she reached out her hand. Gil stepped forward to take it, but suddenly fear flashed in her eyes as a thunder of hoof beats sounded suddenly from the maze behind them. Gil dove for his sword. Snatching it from the snow, he grabbed Lionheart's reins and leapt into the saddle, ready for battle.

Then, into the square meadow burst Frosti with Danni, red-cheeked and wild-eyed, on his back. "We've found her! We've found Rachel!" she cried. She galloped straight at Gil and had almost reached him, before she saw Janetta, and then Percy, behind her. She pulled Frosti to a skidding halt and stared. Then with a scream of joyful recognition, she flung herself from the pony's back and ran, slipping and stumbling, to embrace her brother. Percy shrank back. Then suddenly he shrieked and his moon face broadened into its widest smile, and then crumpled again into tears, as she wrapped him in her arms, her flowing cloak enfolding them both.

Danni looked from the boy in his unlikely armor, to the great warhorse that grazed quietly behind him, with the brown hawk perched on the cantle of its saddle and the deerhound lying with chin on paws, at its feet. Janetta smiled in answer to the unspoken question in her eyes. "They befriended him, and he, them, in the mean stable that was our grim prison. By his loyalty, they were transported here, and now that loyalty is returned, three-fold. Never was a knight served better by hound, hawk, and steed!"

Percy grinned, basking in the pleasure of her approval and Gil felt an absurd flicker of jealousy. Then Percy's eyes suddenly widened and he raised his gloved hand and pointed over Gil's shoulder. "It's the brown boy!" It's Lara Croft!" Gil spun around and saw Ismail, his arm supporting Rachel, walking carefully into the meadow with their ponies trailing behind. Rachel's face was streaked with blood from two gashes on her forehead, and above them, her thick hair was stained a darker red. One of her hands was bloodied, too, and she bent and, wincing, rubbed one ankle.

"My lady!" Janetta cried, "What has happened? What evil soul has so mistreated you?"

Danni pointed furiously at Percy's hawk. Rachel shook her head sharply and her dark eyes flashed a warning. "No one has mistreated me," she said and she managed a small, pained smile. "I fell stupidly from my pony into a holly tree."

Danni blinked. "You didn't fall. You weren't even riding…it was that creature," she said, pointing again at the hawk.

"I saw my Percy's hawk fight with a hawk," Janetta whispered. "One that bore no jesses." She gestured to the trailing ties that hung from the brown hawk's legs. "A wild bird. But only a bird." She looked fearfully at Rachel. "Are you a witch that you bear the wounds of your familiar?"

"Of course not," Danni said indignantly. "She's just a Change-Thing!"

Janetta's face went white and she backed away. "But that is worse!" she cried. "Even a witch is human."

Rachel gave her a hard look. "So is a Change-Thing," she said firmly. "Most of the time." And when Janetta still edged backward, she suddenly lost patience. "Stop being such a baby!" she shouted. "I only did it so we could rescue you!"

Janetta lowered her head in remorse. "I am so sorry," she said. "Forgive me. You are a very brave and a very beautiful Change-Thing. I do not deserve to have so noble a champion." She rode forward then and bravely held out her hand. Though, when her fingers touched Rachel's, a shadow of fear crossed her face. Rachel smiled kindly and gave her name, and then Gil introduced Danni and Ismail and then himself. "Gil Lake." she said after him, and he saw in her eyes as she spoke his name, the same pleasure he felt in speaking hers.

"Listen!" Rachel looked at Gil in alarm. Far away, from beyond the garden walls, came a faint chiming.

"'Tis but the convent bell, ringing Saxt," Janetta said, puzzled. "Why do you fear it?"

Gil caught Lionheart's reins. "Come on," he said. "We have to go."

Janetta watched him with confusion and dismay. "Go?" she said. "But where?"

"Back to the gate and safe up in the forest before the hunt returns. Come on, Percy," he said with a grin. "Show your sister how you can ride." But Percy was watching Janetta, and she was looking at Gil in disbelief.

"The forest?" she cried. "The forest safe? But surely there is no more dangerous place for you in all of Christendom! Since word came that the Warriors of Tir nan Og were in Glen Alban, the Raiders have searched the Forest of Caledon day and night!"

"Who brings this word?" Ismail said warily. "We travel with friends and meet only friends."

Janetta shook her head sadly. "Then a friend has betrayed you. For all here know it. Indeed, my foster-mother, Grania, who shelters with me here, learnt it from the humblest of the servants. They who drive the cart that brings our food. And more! That you sailed Glen Alban with the Viking, Floki Magnusson, and did battle with Sir Owain the Red and sorely defeated him."

"But who would betray us?" Danni cried. "Sir Owain is loyal to Arthur."

Janetta's face was calm and sad as she studied them. She said softly, "I trust that is so. And all who follow him. But hunger is a harsh test of loyalty." She shrugged, tossing back her green cloak. "It matters little," she said. "For it is done. And now the Raiders prowl Caledon to the Grey Mountains, seeking you." She smiled gently then at Percy. "For should this sweet child claim the holy relic and escape to Tir nan Og, all the Knight's power, all his cunning, and all his wealth will not save him."

Gil looked at Percy watching them as if everything was a big, safe game, and suddenly he caught Janetta's hand and led her aside. Leaning over so his face was close to hers, he whispered, "Why doesn't he just kill him?"

She stared at him in surprise. "For the same reason he will not kill you until you have accomplished his purpose," she said. "When you have met the enchantments of the chapel, faced its fierce guardian, and claimed the treasure for which you have come – all of which are beyond the evil Knight's power – then he would kill you all. And so, the relic will be his. That is his purpose for imprisoning the Fool and waiting, like a spider in a web, for you to come."

"Then it's hopeless!" Gil whispered back. "We've played right into his hands."

She shook her head and her smile was radiant. "In the center of this web, there is a place the spider will not see." Then she lifted a little horn that hung from a ribbon at her waist, raised it to her lips, and blew a beautiful note. From the far side of the meadow, a man appeared, leading a grey palfrey and carrying a woodsman's axe. His hair and beard were white, and his legs bent with age. Yet, seeing Janetta surrounded by Gil and his companions, he broke into a shambling run. Raising the wood axe, he stumbled forward to defend her. "Sir Alisander!" Janetta called. "Put up your brave axe. These are our friends, for whom we longed and waited!"

The old man staggered to a halt, peering with misty blue eyes at Janetta. "These? These are the Warriors?" He looked as doubtful as Hakon Sea-Friend had, on the shore of Einar's Holm.

"Who but these!" she cried joyfully. "This brave Saracen, and this beautiful Change-Thing." She bowed toward Ismail and Rachel, "And my Percy's noble sister, and here," her face lit, "my Knight of the River who I saw in a vision upon Our Lady's Day! And is he not just as I have told you, so many times? Now all will surely be well."

She mounted her grey palfrey, and with the old man at her side, shepherded them deeper into the garden. They came upon the muddy tracks of the cart, and then the hoof prints of the Usurper's warhorse, in the snow. Ahead, a break in the trees revealed the grey mews, standing alone in a snow-filled field. Built of dark stone, tall and narrow as a fortress, it had no windows at ground level, and a heavy studded door guarded the entrance. But, above, open shutters still bore faded blue paint and smoke rose from the sagging thatch. Janetta reined in her palfrey at the edge of the open field and turned to face them with a small, sweet smile. "Welcome," she said, "To my prison and my refuge. And may it be for you always the second, and never the first."

An old woman appeared at the corner of the tower, wrapped in a multi-colored cloak, and holding a basket of grain. Her face was tanned and weathered and at her feet, hens scurried and clucked. But she walked with a sure, regal gait, like the Lady Griselle on Hy. Janetta waved gaily and called out, "Good Foster-Mother! Come!"

She slipped down from her palfrey and took the woman's hand. "This is Grania, to whose care I was entrusted when I was small, before my widowed father found a wife. So, though I've had two mothers, and am daughter to both, to Grania I am always fosterling. And that," she said, kissing the old woman's cheek, "as all men know, is dearest; the tie of love beyond blood." One by one, they were introduced, and then, placing her hand on Percy's shoulder, Janetta said, "Come, good knight. Will you not show your sister and her companions where we go to play?"

"The secret place?" Percy's eyes crinkled with joy. He grasped Danni's hand, and pulling her eagerly with him, set out across the rough field to the dark yew hedge beyond. When he reached the hedge, he stopped suddenly and turned to them, his face still and solemn. "Never, ever tell anybody. Swear and hope to die," he said. And he would go no further until each had placed hand on heart and sworn. Then with slow, careful steps, Percy walked right up to the yew hedge, and stepped within. His hand reached from the dark foliage and pulled Danni in, too. Following, Gil slipped through the feathery branches into a secret avenue, screened by a veil of greenery. Beyond, down a green-arched corridor, he saw the white of untouched snow; a small square of lawn turned meadow, walled on all sides by the dark yew. In its center was a wooden building, as pretty and cheerful as the tower was dark.

It had not four, but eight sides, and was set high on wooden pillars enclosed by slats of wood. The upper half beneath the peaked thatch, had shuttered windows, one for each side. Gil thought of the little study of the Ab of Hy. "Did a monk live here?" he asked. Janetta tossed back her head, so that her black hair tumbled free of her hood and laughed with glee.

"Oh, a whole *muinntir!*" she cried. "But fearsome monks whose chant was like the howling of wolves!"

Rachel and Ismail, emerging with her from the yew hedge, looked bewildered. Janetta bowed her head, "Forgive me. How could you know? I am sure, in Tir nan Og, they have many strange things I would be lost to name. This, good Knight of the River, for all its prettiness, is but a kennel."

Danni stared at the ornate, eight-sided structure, "A doghouse?"

"Maybe not an ordinary doghouse," Gil whispered at her side.

"Indeed no!" Janetta cried. "These were King Arthur's kennels! Where once dwelt the finest hounds in Christendom! Hounds that would shame the Usurper's ill-bred curs. Hounds collared in jewels and leashed on ribbons of silk! And couched at night on beds of wickerwork," she said, as they stepped through the open door, into the dusky lower room. "Even a fire, for winter nights, below." She pointed to a blackened hearth. "Though that you must not use, lest smoke betray your presence here."

"This is where we stay?" said Danni as she looked around happily.

"Oh, no, my noble lady, but above, where there is light, and bedding, and much of simple charm." Janetta lowered her head again. "Forgive me that I offer you no better couch, but even Our Lord slept in a stable once. Come," she said, and she led them up a wooden staircase and through a trap door into a dusty, light-filled space. The eight walls were lined with eight low wicker beds, as she had described, but in the center of the room were scattered rugs and furs, and on them, toys; dolls made of straw and cloth, and wooden cups and plates laid out for a make-believe meal. She scooped up the furs from the floor and spread them over the wicker beds. "I will bring more; so many that you will not miss the fire at all!"

"This is fine," Gil insisted. "We have our own bedrolls. And it's not even cold!"

"But many a frost and snowfall may lie 'twixt this day and Candlemas."

"Candlemas!" Danni cried. "That's weeks away. And the chapel is so close, now. We should be at Cille Aidan, by Candlemas."

Janetta turned in alarm to Gil. "Surely, you do not enter the Guarded Forest before Candlemas! It would be death! Every day, from first light until the last, the Knight hunts the bonnie roe. And when he locks the gates, night already falls, and no living soul dare enter. For no place is more haunted than the Forest of Pentecost. Nor, on those darkened paths, could even an angel find its way."

She clasped Danni's hand and Gil's, in her own. "But keep faith and patience, and both shall be rewarded!" she cried. "On Candlemas, the hunting of the roe comes to its end, and a great tournament is held! Every knight makes certain to compete. And thus, on that one day, all Caledon is deserted, and no man moves within the walls of Pentecost. Then, the chapel and its treasure wait, watchful as a bride, for he who comes. And then," she tightened her grip on their hands and looked up into Gil's eyes, "we keep our tryst with fate!"

CHAPTER TEN

Backing Lionheart into a cul-de-sac in the Yew Maze, Gil leaned his lance against the greenery and stretched weary arms. The sun was warm, the churned snow at the pony's feet melting to slush. Birds sang, like spring. He closed his eyes and rested his head dozily against the lance. Pony Chess was the best game he'd ever played, but today even it couldn't keep him awake. *That's what happens when you sleep for four hours a night and spend the rest of it prowling the Forest of Pentecost as a cat.* If he could only wake up, they'd probably win again. His red team, himself, Danni, and Percy, were three ransoms ahead of Ismail, Janetta and Rachel, playing blue. After two weeks practice, he was getting pretty good.

They'd ridden the Yew Maze each day since the morning Janetta's foster father, Sir Alisander, showed them its purpose. A training ground for knights, the labyrinth, with its twisting corridors and sudden turns, schooled horse and rider for tournament and melee. Avenues, squares, and baffling spirals became a field of war on which teams of mounted champions advanced upon citadels of yew. Bloodless battles raged for silken scarves, "favors" bound as flags to the tips of lances; a lost favor was a lost life and "dead" knights exited the maze. The capture of the "king's" favor ended the game with knightly courtesy.

But as soon as the old man had left them, they made up their own rules, and as the days passed, ever more inventive ways of breaking them: Kings, like chess kings, couldn't leave their citadels. Captured knights were not dead, but hostages, forced to switch sides and change flags to prove it. (Only nobody did, so you never knew who was a friend and who an enemy.) The tall wooden ward towers from which the flags could be seen advancing through the maze, could be used only three times in each game. (But everybody cheated.) Pony-theft was rife. Mounting a ward tower practically ensured a long walk out of the maze.

Often, they played right through Saxt and missed lunch and only stopped at the last possible moment, when the hunting horns signaled the Golden Knight's return. Yesterday, as Janetta fled to her tower and they slipped through the hedge to the safety of the kennel, the white charger's hooves were sounding on the path. But no matter how hard they played in the day, Gil played even harder at night. With only one short day to seek out the chapel, he knew they must find the way there long before Candlemas dawned. And finding it was up to him. Only at night could the Forest of Pentecost be entered, and only one creature among them could see in the dark.

Barely had the mews gate closed behind the Knight each evening, than Gil was streaking through the maze on four swift paws. By the time dusk turned to dark, he was in the great forest, alone. On the very first night he discovered a fallen tree, cloaked in disguising ivy, that had breached the great wall just enough to give their ponies entrance. After that, he bent his feline efforts to finding the elusive chapel. On the fourth night, he discovered the first of the two inner walls, and on the sixth night, the second wall. Yesterday, he'd reached the edge of the mysterious briar wood. So late had he stayed, that the grey light of the winter's late dawn shone in the sky when he slipped, in human form, into his bed.

Gil's head slipped off the propped lance. He flailed with both arms, grasped Lionheart's mane, and regained his balance, blinking into wakefulness. In the distance, galloping hoof beats told of a pursuit through the maze. Lionheart snored. *Wake up.* Gil shook his loose rein. Lionheart shifted his feet and snored again. Gil looked around at the circular green walls. Playing "king," confined in the citadel, was easier than riding the avenues as "knight," but it was no use at all for staying awake.

He peered blearily at his lance with its fluttering flag of faded red silk, and suddenly grinned. Reaching into his tunic, he pulled out the long blue scarf he'd taken off Ismail, yesterday. Then he untied the red silk and replaced it with blue. *Palamedes would hate Pony Chess*, he thought guiltily. But then his grin broadened. *Floki would have loved it.* Raising his deceitful blue banner, he galloped illegally out of his citadel, in pursuit of Ismail's "king."

A quick climb up a ward tower showed him three blue flags, one in pursuit of a red, another circling a distant spiral, and the third, Ismail, honorably in his citadel. *And to do this to my best friend*, he thought gleefully, scrambling down the tower and slipping onto Lionheart's back. In his head he fixed the positions of his two opponents, slotting them into his mind-map of the maze. Setting a course that should elude both, he passed through the tall dividing hedge that marked red territory from blue and was halfway across enemy ground when Lionheart skidded to a halt.

Ahead, their path was blocked by a mass of greenery, a wall where he was sure was an open corridor. Hastily, he reviewed his mind-map; three turns past the open square, a left beyond the snail spiral...it had to be here. He prodded the greenery with his lance and it collapsed in a heap of cut branches. Gil drove Lionheart forward through the wrecked barrier, but then a loop of blue silk fluttered down over the pony's head and drew tight. Lionheart halted as if snared by a butterfly's wing. A slim little hand swept over the hedge and snatched the blue pennant from Gil's lance. Janetta's grinning face appeared above the yew. "You are hostage," she declared, "and a most discourteous king!"

He stared up into her sparkling eyes. "What are you doing up there?"

"Standing on my palfrey's back." She grinned again over the hedge. "Stand up on your pony and see." Warily, Gil drew his legs up, placed one foot on the jousting saddle, the other on Lionheart's furry rump, and stood. His eyes met Janetta's across the hedge. She reached out and took his hand, steadying him. "Now come," she said. And, balancing perfectly on the grey palfrey's back, she walked the animal along her corridor, parallel to him in his, until they reached an opening between the two paths.

Releasing him, she slipped down to her saddle, and jumped lightly into the wet snow, waiting for him to do the same. But the instant his feet touched the ground she caught his hand again and then bound his wrist firmly to hers with the silk from his lance. "Run!" she cried, and leaving her pony pawing for grass with Lionheart, she led Gil, stumbling beside her, from the maze.

They came out in front of the tower. She stopped in the hedge's shadow, scanning the lawn and the stable yard. Grania emerged, carrying a basket, and disappeared around the corner of the building. "She's gone to the garden for cabbages," Janetta whispered, "Quick!" And dragging him after, she bolted for the door. Inside, in the cool darkness of the stone tower, she giggled and untied his hand. Then, beckoning quickly, she darted to the foot of a narrow, curving stone staircase. He followed, his heart pounding from the run, his breath noisy in the silence of the tower. At the top of the spiral stair stood an iron-bound door. "Should I be here?" Gil whispered.

"Who will know?" She raised her hand and placed two fingers against his lips, "If we never tell?" The door hinges groaned as the door swung open, and they stepped within.

The tower room was as tall and imposing as the Feasting Hall of Einar's Holm. Grey stone walls rose to black roof beams high above the polished wooden floor. A great table, like Magnus Redbeard's, filled one end of the room and wooden kists lined the walls. But all here was grander by far. The table was smooth and polished and the great chairs at either end, padded with studded leather. The long benches bore cushions of rich fabrics and brilliant colors. And the windows even held glass. The stone hearth was set, not in the room's center, but against one wall, with a real chimney above.

Velvet and satin cushions were scattered on the floor in front of the hearth. A little harp sat by a window; a basket of embroidery linens, on a kist, with a book of Latin psalms beside it. A chessboard waited, set ready for play, before the fire. But what held Gil's wondering eyes were the tapestries that curtained the grim stone walls, their silken threads glistening in every bar of sunlight. The same characters appeared in each of seven pictures, knights on beautiful horses, ladies riding beside them, leash-men and hounds, and always in the center, a beast like a small white horse with one long spiral horn.

"'Tis the Hunt of the Unicorn," Janetta said. "See," she pointed from tapestry to tapestry, "it tells the story. They stir it from its rest and pursue it through the forest; it seeks refuge in water; they drive it out; it stands at bay; they slay it most savagely, and bear it homewards, dead." Despite being woven of mere thread, the pictures were almost too life-like. Red skeins of blood ran from the animal's wounds; its mouth gasped for final breaths; its eyes, gleaming with agony, looked heavenward for help. Dead, it sagged across the pack pony that bore it home, as lifeless as, a panel before, it had been too painfully alive.

"But look," he said, pointing to the seventh panel that hung alone above the hearth. In it the one-horned beast was again alive, no longer in the forest, but in a pen of wooden fencing. Above it was a pretty tree, around it, a thousand flowers, and yet, red thread marked its wounds, as before. "It was dead in the last picture and here it's alive. So, is this the beginning of the story or the end?"

"It is both," Janetta said. "The story is of love that lives forever and has no beginning, nor any end. Some say the love of a knight for his lady. Others say the love of Our Lord for the world. Either way, it is of love. And so, though it is savage, I do not fear it." She smiled quietly and looked away. Then suddenly she pounced on the chessboard in front of the fire and swept up one figure. "Here are you!" she cried, "my hostage king!"

Gil smiled, too. He went to the chessboard and found a companion figure dressed in long robes and wearing a crown. "Then this must be you," he said.

But she shook her head abruptly and turned from him. "I am not queen," she said. "Nor would I be." She leant over the board and took a third figure. "Here," she said, "This is me. A pawn who can move but a little way and waits always on the moves of others. For that is what I am."

"No," Gil whispered sadly.

"Yes," she said, meeting his eyes. "Look," she pointed to a low bed made up at one end of the great hearth. "This, my bedchamber, is also my prison, for the door is barred at night and my good foster-parents sleep below." Sudden anger flashed in her eyes. "Here I sleep like a nun, so my unkind husband can pluck an untouched flower." She toyed with the chess king in her fingers, and then set it down. "You are wise to be a man. I would not be a woman, if I could choose."

But then she laughed gaily and cried, "Forgive me. I waste our brief time with mourning my state. Come, enjoy the splendor of my captivity! Was ever a nun more grandly habited?" she touched her velvet skirts, "or granted more gracious hermitage?" She settled on a cushion by the chessboard and held out her hand. "Come sit by me and we will play the game a little while together."

Gil sat beside her, at a little distance. Firelight flickered over the board, making the small ivory figures shadowy and alive. "Make first move," she said softly. "They are but rude, carved liegemen, but they seek to do your will." Hesitantly, Gil moved out his knight. But already the warmth of the fire was muddling his sleepy mind. He stared at the board, struggling to keep the moves in his head and yawned with weariness.

She looked stricken. "Forgive me," she whispered. "I am a dull companion. I see no one but my aged fosterers and I do not learn the ways of lovers."

"No!" he cried. "It's not you! It's me. It's just that I haven't slept very much."

She bowed her head. "The beds are poor. Forgive me."

"The beds are fine! It's not the beds." He paused. "Look, I do something at night."

"Do?" she said then. "What is this thing you do?"

Gil clasped his head in his hands. "Okay," he said cautiously. "Do you remember the day we came?"

"How could I forget first meeting my knight?"

"Yeah," Gil said hurriedly, "but it's Rachel I'm talking about."

Her eyes grew huge and sad. "You pay court to her."

"No!" he cried. "I don't pay court to her. I don't do anything with her. It's just that I'm like her." He took a deep breath. "I'm a Change-Thing, too." He expected her to shrink back, terrified, like she had from Rachel, but she just looked sadder than ever.

"So," she said carefully. "You fly with her, too?"

"No!" he shouted exasperated. "I don't fly. I'm different. I'm a different kind of Change-Thing."

She tilted her head sideways and curiosity brightened her face. Relieved that she'd finally believed him about Rachel, he smiled. "I would see your Change-Thing," she said.

He shook his head sharply. "No. You really don't want to."

"I've seen Rachel's," she said.

He shook his head again. "Mine is different. It's really scary," he said grimly.

Instead of looking scared, she smiled a dazzling smile. "I care not! I will know it is you. I will be brave."

"It's too scary. Really."

To his huge relief, he heard, through the open window, the ringing of the convent bell. He jumped up, but she caught his hand by the wrist and pulled him back down. "Oh, stay," she said, sadly. "The day lingers long now, after the bell of None." Gil nodded. The Dark Time was receding, as swiftly as it had come upon them, the last days at Cille Aidan. He settled again on the cushion. She moved her hand a little, so the fingers were like a little cup, waiting to hold his. He slipped his hand into hers.

"I am glad you do not court Rachel," she said. He grinned happily, finding it hard to speak. "Of course, I suppose then you do court Danni." She watched him intently.

"Danni?" He stared at her. She dropped her gaze and the black lashes cast fire lit shadows on her cheeks. "I don't court Danni! She's...she's like my sister."

"Is there no courtship among you?" Janetta asked. She sounded genuinely amazed.

Gil shook his head again, "I guess we're all kind of young."

"But surely...." she studied his face. "Surely you have known as many years as I?"

"How many years is that?" he said uncertainly.

"It will be fourteen years, upon Lady Day in Lentron. And you?"

"I'll be fifteen on the 25 of April." It was true here, whatever happened at home.

"The Feast of Saint Mark," she whispered, her eyes sparkling. "I shall love Saint Mark ever after." She swung their joined hands back and forth. "I would think you were old enough for courtship," she said. "As indeed," she added, "am I." She turned her head away. "Have you kissed?"

"What? A girl?" he said with such a gulp of amazement that she giggled again. "Uh, no."

"We are both useless!" she cried. "Soon we will be grown entirely and unless we join the gentle Sisters or the good Brethren, we are doomed to fail miserably at this great art." She looked so alarmed that he himself felt a twinge of panic. "Unless," she said, "we practice."

"Practice?"

"To learn the art. Like I practice upon the harp, and at my embroidery. And you, no doubt, practice the arts of war, of sword and lance!"

"Yeah, sure," Gil said. But somehow this didn't feel like sword-fighting with Shony or jousting with Palamedes. Janetta moved closer and placed one of her hands on each of his shoulders, so they were face to face.

"Will you be my adversary, good sir? That we may practice?"

"Should we?" he whispered, his mouth gone dry.

"Is it not our duty?" she said. "To prepare ourselves for the Lists?"

He thought he wouldn't know what to do, but the moment her lips touched his, he did. It was like something he'd always known, that his mouth had a memory of, the rightness of it as sweet and certain as the moment he rode the great longship out into Pentland. Here was where he was meant to be. All kinds of wonderful feelings, some of which he didn't want to think about, came to join the sweetness of his mouth against hers. She snuggled in close and seemed as happy as he was, and the room and the flickering fire, and the darkening evening outside all drifted away into some place beyond time. *Let this last forever*, he thought. *Let time stop.* And then suddenly she pulled away. He reached for her and she shook her head, her eyes wild. Then he, too, heard the sound of the hunting horn, and the ringing clash of steel-shod hooves on stone.

"Oh, sweet Yesu," she gasped. "He is here." Gil jumped to his feet and grabbed his sword belt which he had left by the door. Janetta put her fingers to her lips and crept along the wall to the edge of the window. She glanced quickly out and shrank back. "He is right at the door! And not alone!" She waved to Gil to retreat. "You cannot leave. The tower has but one entrance and they and their chargers stand ready guard!"

"My lady!" The Knight's greeting rang as sharply as the hunting horn. "Come to the window that I might feast my hungry eyes."

"Hide," Janetta whispered.

"My lady, you tarry long. I have ridden hard, this day, and I thirst for the refreshment of your beauty!"

"I come! I come!" Janetta cried. "Hide," she whispered again to Gil. He dashed around the room, seeking shelter. The kists beneath the windows were too small to hold him. The table was without concealing cloth, the windows without draperies. Even Janetta's bed was but a humble low platform, like in the guesthouse at Hy.

Gil heard laughter, from below, and another voice, rougher and cruder. "She has gone to ground! Summon the terriers!"

When the Knight spoke next, there was a new, sharp edge to his voice. "I bring two liegemen, knights of my realm, who desire to see your lovely face. Now," he added sharply.

"I come!" she cried.

"So you do say." A chill entered the gracious tone and the Knight said then, "'Tis a small room. Who would imagine it so difficult to cross? Perhaps I must mount my lady's stair and come to her aid."

"No!" she cried. "I need no help. I but arrange my costume, the best to please you."

"He would be pleased," the second voice cried, "like any husband, with no costume at all!" Rough laughter greeted that. Janetta's eyes met Gil's, dark with fear.

"Don't watch," he whispered, and swiftly laid his sword belt on the floor, and stepped within. "Turn away." She did, warily, and returned her attention to the window.

"There. But one more ribbon!"

"To devil with ribbons," the Knight shouted, without humor. "To whom do you speak?"

But Janetta leapt then, to the window and swung it wide. "See! I am here! Naked of ribbons!" she cried, with a low, flirtatious laugh. The companions' raucous response gave Gil the chance he needed. In as soft a voice as he could manage, he recited the blessing, and with a sigh of relief that blended midway into a meow, he became Cat. Janetta whirled at the sound. Her eyes widened and she let out a shriek so loud that Gil leapt sideways from the sword belt, scrabbled across the room in claw-slipping terror, and collided with their abandoned chessboard. Chess pieces clattered across the floor.

"My lady!" the Knight shouted.

"'Tis nothing!" she cried. "'Tis but...'tis but my Fool!" She whirled wildly back to the window. "In his clumsiness he has scattered our chess pieces over the floor!" She turned into the room, her eyes fixed with utter amazement on Gil, who had taken a moment out to smooth his ruffled fur with an embarrassed tongue. "Oh, silly Fool!" she cried. "How can you be so awkward?"

"How indeed?" The Knight's voice was smooth as silk, "Since he rides his cursed beast across the green, as I speak. It seems his clumsiness knows no bounds." Gil saw Janetta's shoulders sag in terrified defeat. "Do you lie to me, my beauty? Surely it is a grievous sin for a wife to lie to her husband."

Janetta's voice quavered in her reply. "I do not lie."

"Very good," said the Knight. "Then with whom, I would ask, do you play chess?"

"Grania," she whispered, her voice shaking.

"Who is within my sight, tilling her garden, her own good husband at her side."

Janetta slowly shook her head. "'Tis true. I lie," she said. Gil's ears flattened in alarm and his tail sank low. She looked over her shoulder but her eyes were calm. "I do not play with Grania or my Fool. Or any other. I but mimic the moves, like a child," she said ashamedly, "so as to improve and please you, when we are wed."

"A lofty ambition," the Knight answered. His voice

suddenly dropped low, "But the defense of your honor is yet loftier. Marriage is like chess, my lady. A queen, once taken, is worthless. I move checkmate."

Gil heard the creak of leather and saw by the panic in her eyes that the Knight had dismounted his horse. "Stay!" she cried. "Good Sir, I play indeed a foolish game. I must be truthful. I am not alone. There is another with me as I speak."

Deep inside Gil's Cat self, a human shock reverberated. But Cat saw no threat in her eyes, and when she crouched beside him, he stretched out his nose to sniff her hand. She jerked it back. Out of kindness, he drew back, too. He bent the tip of his tail into a friendly hook, blinked twice, and made his paws all innocent pads and plush. Then suddenly, she clasped her arms around his furry middle and whisked him off the ground. Mortification overflowed into a yowl of despair.

"Oh, poor Pusskins," she murmured. "I will not harm you." And then, clutching him to her chest, she gently kissed his ear and to his total confusion, he began to purr. *Cat? What are you thinking?!* He struggled vainly to still his vibrating throat. "Be brave, Pusskins," she cried, and staggering under his hefty weight, she returned to the window and swung him aloft. "See, my good husband?" she cried. "Here is my suitor! Do you now burn with jealousy over your faithless wife?"

Peals of laughter rose from below. Gil twisted his head over his shoulder and stared down at the Knight, standing beside his charger. His two mounted companions made rude gestures with their fists and pointed gleefully up at the window. The Knight stayed very calm. Gil saw a long, thin nose beneath the gleaming metal of his helm, narrow lips, a golden beard trimmed short. And though the helm shadowed his eyes, they glinted yet deep blue, in an unwavering gaze that assaulted feline propriety. Gil glared back, daring the man to look away. He stopped purring and his hackles rose.

"Dear Pusskins," Janetta whispered. She held him close and he felt his Cat self go all soft and melty, his paws hanging limp with delight. She raised her voice and addressed the Knight. "I feared to try your patience, good husband, with yet another beast. But this is mine and not my Fool's. Indeed, it came to me, most wondrously gentle, and gives me comfort in my solitude. Please, do not bid me send it away." She sniffed and Gil was startled to feel a real tear splash on his head. Cat flicked a wet ear with distaste.

"Look, sir," the Knight's bold companion spoke again. "She weeps with loneliness and comforts herself with a cat. No lady of mine has such cause for sorrow!"

"I know enough of women's tears to judge those false," the Knight said coldly. Gil felt Janetta flinch. The Knight's hidden eyes sought his own and for an awful moment he was sure the man saw through to his human self.

The second companion laughed. "Be glad that she has something to warm her bed, and preserve her chastity these winter nights, from other prowlers."

The Knight turned his cold blue gaze to his liegeman who suddenly sobered. But then the Knight himself laughed. He looked up at Janetta. "You may keep him and he may do you that service," he said, and he smiled charmingly. "I will grant him a fine sheepskin upon our wedding day for keeping my place for me!"

Gil growled, but the three men all laughed uproariously, punching each other in glee. Then the Knight turned once more to Janetta and when he spoke all laughter had vanished from his voice. "Play no more games with me, lady," he said.

She lowered her head and held Gil tighter. "Yes, my husband." He nodded gravely, then mounted his horse, and with a sharp shout and a flick of his reins, sent it cantering away.

As soon as the sound of hoof beats faded into the night, Janetta bent and gently set Gil on the floor. Then she stretched up to the window, and drew the shutters closed, and the casement after it, as if frail wood and glass could protect her from the Knight. She turned and looked down at Gil washing vigorously. He stopped, mid-way down his forepaw, and looked up. Tears streaked her face, real enough now. "Forgive me, noble Change-Thing," she whispered. "I treat you with little dignity. But there was no other way." She held out her hand and, deciding to accept her apology, he rubbed his head against it. But when she started to tickle his ears, a treacherous rumble started up in his throat and he forced himself to growl. He'd had enough of Cat and for once was more than ready to reclaim his human form.

With a quick flick of his ears, he stood up, and with slow, stiff steps he crossed the room to where his sword belt lay on the floor. Then, looking back over his shoulder, he meowed sharply. She hesitated, then stepped closer, but jumped back when he hissed. His tail swished angrily and he felt his eyes widen with glittering challenge. She looked frightened and then suddenly she understood. Cautiously, she raised her hands and held them over her eyes. With a last, satisfied tail-swish, Gil jumped into the circle of the belt.

She did not lower her hands until he stood before her. Then, slipping her fingers from her eyes, she cried out in delight. "Oh, my knight, you were wonderful!"

"Oh, fabulous," he said. Her smile faded.

"You are angry?" He shrugged. "But why?" she cried. "You were a magnificent brave cat and you boldly growled in the very face of the Usurper!"

"Well that really scared him, didn't it? Your noble husband."

She winced. "I displease you," she said quietly. "And I do not know how."

"'Good husband! I come! Naked of ribbons! I fear to try your patience! See, my good husband! See my useless suitor, only a cat!'"

"But you know I made sport with him to save us both!"

"Good sport, too. You sounded like you liked him. Like you flirt with him. Like he really is your husband. And he's not! And you're not his 'faithless wife,' either. You're not married to him!"

"No. I am betrothed." She paused. "Is this different in Tir nan Og?"

"We call it being engaged," he said. "There's a ring. And if the girl changes her mind about the man, she gives it back."

"Oh," she said softly. "What a wondrous thing." She bowed her head, and then suddenly she sank down on the cushion by the fire and turned her face away. Gazing into the lowering flames, she said, "I am betrothed to him. My father has pledged me and he has accepted the pledge. Hence, he has every right over me as a husband but one, for which he must wait upon the witness of Holy Church. But he is an evil man, with no respect for the Brethren whose *muinntirs* he burns, nor for my foolish father. If I cause him insult or mockery, or fail to please, he may forego these courtesies.

"And so, I play chess. And make my moves with care. I tempt him, but not so much that he forgets my youth. I am obedient, but not so much as to bore him. I guard my chastity, for without it I have no worth and my life is forfeit. And he circles me and seeks checkmate. And, of course, I cannot win." She said simply, "My only hope is you."

Gil stared at her, stunned. He reached out his hand. "So come!" he cried. "Now! Come with me. We'll ride out of here. We'll get through Caledon, somehow. Back to Cille Aidan. Back to Tir nan Og, even. I'll take you so far from him, he'll never find you."

Slowly, she shook her head. "He'll find me if you take me to the ends of the earth. And beyond! To the end of time itself. He has powers you cannot imagine."

"He's just a man."

"He's more than a man. And he is evil. No." She shook her head again. "You are my hope because you are the hope of our kingdom. When our king returns to set right every wrong, then I will be free. I only pray he comes soon."

Gil's anger and reckless courage both faded. But something quiet and firm slipped softly into their place. "Then that will happen," he said. And he understood, at last, why he was here. "I will make it happen. Not for the guardians or for Aidan, or Hy, or the friends I've lost. For you. Because I love you. I always have, since I saw you at the river. I always will." He bent and picked up his sword belt and strapped it around his waist. Tonight, he would find the chapel.

He was already planning his route through the Forest of Pentecost when he slipped into the kennels. Eagerly, he climbed the stairs to the eight-sided room and thrust one hand up to open the trap door. It didn't budge. He shoved harder and felt himself pressing against an immoveable weight. Annoyed, he made his hand into a fist and rapped three times on the underside of the door. "Who's there?" Danni's scared voice whispered in response.

"Me!" he answered, irritated by the delay. "Who else?"

The trap door was jerked open and he found himself looking up into Danni's furious face. "Who else? Just about anybody else, for all we knew. Like, starting with the Golden Knight..."

"What?" he spluttered, forcing his way past her into the room.

"... after he'd tortured you into telling about us!"

"We thought you'd been captured," Rachel said quietly. "You didn't come back from the Maze. We found Lionheart abandoned. Then we heard the Knight arrive. We thought he'd caught you."

"We block door," Ismail said unhappily. "We think he comes for us, next."

"Meanwhile, we work out how we get to the stables, get our ponies, and somehow get out of here, first," Danni said. Her eyes bored into his own. "Where were you?"

Gil turned slightly. "I was with Janetta," he said, not looking at any of them. "In the Tower. We were...talking. I forgot the time."

"You forgot?" Danni's outrage narrowed her eyes into black slits.

"It doesn't matter," Gil said quickly. "The Knight didn't see me."

Danni shook her head very slowly. "Gil, this isn't some kind of game for you and Janetta, you know."

Gil thought bleakly of Janetta's chess moves with the knight. "Oh, I do know."

"Then act like you know," Danni shouted. "You forgot the time? Why? Because your brain is in your pants when you're around her? You risked everything!" She spun away, too angry even to look at him, then turned back. "This has been about her, for you, from the start," she said fiercely.

"Yes," he said, returning her look of challenge with one of his own. "And it still is. And that's why I'm going to succeed." He held her cold gaze a moment longer, then looked away, made a circle of Lucy's lead rein, and dropped it on the floor.

He shrugged and muttered, "Sorry. I have to go." He was aware
of her eyes upon him as he stepped into the circle, and even as
he made the terrifying transformation into his Other. But then
he was Cat and he didn't care. He stepped out of the circle of
the rein with swishing tail, leapt to a window sill, nudged the
shutter aside with his forehead, and jumped to the ground.

His route, over the wall and into the Forest of Pentecost, was
practiced and swift. He loped easily along the path that led to
the second wall, grabbing shortcuts through the trees that he
knew by heart. The ground, familiar to his paws, the dim sights
and rich scents; all marked the way. He passed the great oak
where he'd foolishly pursued a big, dark weasel-thing, until it
turned on him. Beyond, was the sandy stream bank rich with
the tang of rabbit. He shut his nostrils to it, his keen eyes already
seeking the new gate.

He found it readily, sagging and overgrown with ivy, with a
gap beneath the broken latch so wide that not a whisker brushed
wood as he entered. He knew that human hands and feet would
make easy work of it, and his human self was dimly troubled.
It was as if what lay beyond needed no defense, so fierce were
the fabled spells that bound it. But Cat was running already, a
low, buff streak, nose thrusting toward what lay ahead. Hunger
troubled his lean stomach and heightened his senses: Gil had
learned by now that as alien as an Other was, it carried the same
needs and weaknesses as its human counterpart. He had eaten
no supper and slept little, and Cat was as hungry and tired as
he was.

The third wall had no gate at all, and with an uneasy chill
that raised a peak of fur down the length of his spine, he slipped
through into the third circle, wherein lay the briarwood. He
found the tangled edge of the thorny thicket, gave a chirrup of
triumph, and plunged within. But as he threaded his way, like
a small furry needle, back and forth through the twisted rose-
trees, triumph faded. He crossed and crisscrossed, winding his
way through every nook and cranny of the ancient roots, but
still the chapel eluded him.

Eventually, weirdly certain he had paced every inch of the
baffling maze; he stretched out on his stomach, panting with

frustration. Dimly he remembered somewhere like this and realized then that it was the Turnip-head Tomb, where, in the darkness, he had hunted vainly for the Wandering Pool. Eerie despair threatened even Cat's unruffled confidence. Had the chapel vanished, slipped from the briarwood, like the Pool from the tomb? Did he search for nothing?

He stretched out an irritated paw, claws unsheathed, and yawned wearily. Then he dropped the paw and his toes closed on something smooth and cold. Instantly, his second paw joined the first and pinned the cold thing to the ground. Starlight picked out its outlines, long and curving and white. He sniffed and a faint, remaining scent confirmed it: bone. Rising smoothly to his feet, he sniffed again, then walked the length of the bone, stepped over it, and walked back. It was a leg bone and at one end were the bones of a foot. Broken free from it, he found another foot, more leg bones, and then, scattered at a distance, ribs, arms and hands, and a skull. His cat self recognized the scavenging work of foxes; his human self, the bones of his own kind.

From deep inside himself, Gil heard a whisper of horror. A skeleton. The skeleton of a man. But Cat only sniffed one bone and then another, undisturbed. There was no flesh. No smell of death. The bones were old and of no interest. Turning away, he explored further and found the bones of a horse and then the rusted remains of a lance and shield. A sword lay just beyond the skeletal fingers of the hand. As if the man had died holding it, Gil thought, and some borrowed Northman's sensibility was glad for the dead warrior.

A helm lay at a distance, flung off in the knight's last fall. *What did he do battle with here?* Gil thought, deep in his troubled heart. But Cat sniffed at the battered helm and his ears pricked forward with pleasure. Mouse! Mice! A whole nest full, cowering in the grass-lined curve of the metal. Joyously, he pounced, crunching up the first while it still squeaked with life. There were seven; a mother and her six, small hairless young. He ate them all. Then, stomach full, he washed blood from his whiskers, stretched and yawned, and sought a place to rest. Velvet-pawed, he stepped silently through the deathbed of the fallen knight, slipped within the whitened ribcage, and curled himself tight. Purring gently, he went to sleep beneath a roof of bones and stars.

Gil woke to the pleasant sensation of sun-warmed fur. He twitched an ear and stretched out his hind legs so luxuriantly that they crossed his forepaws. He felt each toe re-curl and purred contentedly. Then suddenly he remembered where he was and snapped alert. Eyes wide, he scrambled out of his bone-lair and into the open, staring around himself in astonishment. It was morning. Weary boy and weary animal; he had slept the night through. The bells of the convent, far away, had not disturbed him, nor the rising of the weak winter sun. Then he heard again the sound that had wakened him: the pure silver notes of the hunter's horn.

Terce, he thought. *I've slept until Terce.* Another sound broke through the morning stillness, and for once Cat was more terrified than he was himself. The new sound was the baying of hounds. He was running before he even thought about where. He streaked out of the briarwood, despite its thorny shelter. Cat instinct told him that the high yapping amidst the howls of the hounds meant ground dogs, digging dogs, terriers. Terriers that would root him out and devour him as he had devoured the mice.

Retracing his way through the inner circle, he sought the open gate and escape. Walled in, the hounds would tree him, and hold him until their masters arrived. And, if among those masters was the Golden Knight, it was over for them all and for Janetta, too. Instead of rescue, he would have brought her disaster. He wondered, even as he wormed through the broken second gate, what happened when a Change-Thing died? Would the body ripped apart on the forest floor be cat or boy? Cat seemed pretty certain it would be cat, and he kept running.

Emerging into the great outer forest, he paused; one paw raised, and sniffed the air. Dogs, horses, men, leather, metal. He heard another flurry of yapping and baying. But the sounds and smells were still distant, as far as the great first gate. Gil's human mind pictured the hunt at the start of the day: milling hounds and restless horses, dismounted men seeking tracks and droppings on the forest floor. Relief smoothed his fur and his ears resumed their confident points. He was not the hunter's prey, after all, but the red-brown roe deer, grazing in the forest glades.

He began to trot, less urgently, toward the wall and his fallen tree, ignoring the canine clamor and smell. But then a high, sharp yelping cut the air. Gruff shouts answered it, but the yelping continued, broke from the distant group, and grew louder and sharper and rapidly nearer. No one had told the terriers they weren't hunting cats.

Gil set off like an arrow through the forest, nose low, tail stretched, his whole feline being focused on the distant wall. Behind him the yelping turned to snarls, drowning the curses of the distant men. A corner-of-the-eye glance showed Gil flashes of white among the dark trees. He leapt, twisted in mid-air and plunged into a hazel thicket. The snarling followed and the scruff of his neck prickled as if terrier teeth were already closing. Panting, exhausted, paws scraped and claws torn, he ran on. Somewhere deep in his feline brain, a faint murmuring whisper arose and grew and became a fatal chant: *Turn. Turn. Turn and fight.*

No! his human self cried. *There's too many! There must be a dozen!*

But Cat chanted again, *Turn. Turn. Turn,* because cats, like Northmen, died fighting. And besides, Cat couldn't count.

And then suddenly, he burst out of the thicket into a bare forest track and there, lying quietly facing him, was the end. Grey, shaggy, and as big as a pony, it held the path like a canine citadel. The rank smell of dog hit Gil like a whip and he froze. Before him crouched the Knight's own beast, the great shadow that padded behind the white charger; the wolfhound. Only the dragon had had bigger teeth.

And yet, it lay silent and peaceful, its enormous forepaws genteelly crossed, its great head held upright. As he stood, back arched high, each hair on end, pathetically striving to look big; he stared directly into its eyes. But the wolfhound made no move. Over-riding every clamoring instinct, Gil turned his back and ran. Even as he fled, a strange thought flitted through his human mind. *It turned me the way Lance'lot turned us in the forest. It's on our side.* But Cat just kept running, glad to be alive and happily aware that the terriers were no longer with him.

Intent yet on the wall, he circled to reclaim the course denied him by the wolfhound. A stream blocked his way. He splashed in, with distaste; yet instinct forced him to endure it further by running a dozen cat-lengths downstream, before he emerged on the opposite bank. But then, in the forest, the yelping resumed. The terriers had got past the wolfhound and found his scent. Still, he was in sight of the wall and his tree, when they caught him.

Suddenly, they were all around him. One snapped at his left hind leg, the teeth grazing the fur. He leapt and tumbled, rolled over, and came up running, swerving back and forth, with snapping jaws on either side. And then, directly ahead, he saw something as inexplicable and welcome as a gift from Heaven: a thin circle of cord, hanging from a tree. A circle. A circle. Gathering himself, he leapt with all his failing strength and passed through the hanging loop. It snapped shut with the force of a whiplash, but the mind that cried "snare!" was human and the leg in the cord's savage grip, was the leg of a boy.

The terriers fell back in confusion. Crouching and growling, they nosed at him, then jumped back, barking frantically. Upside down, one leg aloft in the snare, Gil stayed utterly still. "Nice dog," he croaked, and got a vicious growl in response. Then they all barked and whined and turned away, as a great crashing of booted feet in the undergrowth signaled their masters' arrival. Relief swept over Gil, followed instantly by confusion and despair. He was saved. But by whom, and for what worse fate? As gruff voices sounded their astonishment, he had one fleeting moment of joy. None but the dogs had seen him as Cat. Janetta's secret was safe.

Hanging upside down, Gil craned his neck to see. Still holding their paired deerhounds, six leash-men gathered around him. Pointing and shouting, they stared at Gil, and lavished praise now on the terriers they'd earlier cursed. One man slapped the bony sides of a white beast, rolling it playfully onto its back. "Well run and well caught! We'll gut him and feed you his liver!" A roar of laughter drowned the snapping and snarling of the dogs. But suddenly the forest floor rang with steel-shod hooves.

"Silence!" shouted a voice Gil knew too well. "Is this the welcome my kingdom offers strangers?" Gil twisted around and glimpsed the great feathered feet of the white charger and a flutter of gold trappings came into his truncated view. "Cut him down," said the voice and the sobered leash-men moved toward Gil. A knife blade flashed by his leg and he felt the snare hacked free. Then he fell and rolled onto his back and looked up into the helm-shadowed eyes of the Golden Knight. They studied him with great care, and just as when he faced those eyes as Cat, he felt them probe inside and know things they couldn't know.

But then the Knight swung down from his charger and offered Gil his hand. The contrast with the savagery of the dogs and their handlers was so great that the gesture appeared a kind of refuge. Gil took the hand and the Knight lifted him to his feet with masterful ease. He turned to the leash-man who had wanted to gut Gil, and said, "Bind him. But gently. Do no harm."

Chastened and obedient, the other gathered the remnants of the snare and tied Gil's arms behind his back. A pony was led forward and the Knight himself helped Gil to mount, checking, as he did so, that the cords around his wrists were not too tight. Again, Gil had the eerie feeling that the man was his friend and protector amidst the rowdy huntsmen. "Take him to my Hall and make him secure," the Knight ordered, stepping back. But to Gil he said, courteously, "These are dangerous times. I would not have ill befall you. My protection may seem harsh, but it is much to your benefit."

Then he looked up at his followers and said, "Merlin's Tower." Gil saw a shadow of fear pass over each man's face. The Knight laughed softly. "Come, come. You will not need to tarry there. Only enter, bind him, and be gone. With body and soul intact." A chill ran down Gil's sweat-soaked back, as each man muttered obedience and turned away. "But give him meat and ale, that he might eat and drink, as befits my guest!" the

Knight declared jovially. Then he turned and faced Gil. "I will come to him," he said softly, "upon the Vespers bell. By then he will have thought of much to tell me." He smiled and his eyes glinted beneath his helm with strange merriment.

Then he reined his white charger in a circle and rode off to the forest and the hunt.

CHAPTER ELEVEN

Nothing, Gil thought fiercely. *I'll have nothing to tell you, whatever you do to me.* But doubt and despair overwhelmed him as, hands bound and flanked by six armed guards, he rode past the gate of the Mews Garden. He had failed his friends. He had failed his cause. He had failed Janetta. The scorn with which the Knight abandoned him to minions told Gil escape was hopeless. He was in the heart of the Usurper's kingdom, utterly at his mercy. They had not even bothered to take his sword.

They left the mews behind, and the bare back of his pony sloped sharply as the beast mounted the steepening track to the walls of Camelot. Gil clamped his knees around the animal's warm sides and, twisting his bound arms awkwardly, turned over his shoulder for a last, wistful look. The back of a rough hand smacked across his face. "Seek not your past," growled the man riding at his left. "It is finished." Gil jerked his head forward. His cheek stung, but his powerlessness stung more. He thought of Percy, the way he saw him through the stone, riding the donkey through Camelot. All Gil had done, after all this, was manage to take his place.

Grimly, he set his eyes on the approaching citadel walls. A golden banner flew over the highest point of the roofless ruins. The lift and flutter of it in the morning breeze stirred something deep in Gil's memory. He puzzled briefly over the image, alive and moving, that flitted through his mind, an image beyond the skill of artist or scribe…of castles, and pennants, and knights. "Camelot," he whispered, captivated, for all his fears, to find himself in this place, whose fabled splendor was remembered even in Tir nan Og.

There was little of splendor to be seen now. In the bare, brown winter fields, men with horses labored to till the land. Some stopped to watch then shrugged wearily and turned away. Small, turf-roofed houses huddled beneath the imposing walls of the castle. Some stood beside the ruins of older, finer dwellings. One boasted a door fashioned from faded wall panels of painted wood on which knights and ladies rode yet like ghosts in a ghostly forest. What vanished household had dined beneath them, to the music of the harp? And did they now ride as beggars in the Forest of Caledon?

The grandest houses stood abandoned entirely, but for stray hens and, once, two black goats perched high on a fire-blackened wall. Sheep were penned in a lordly hall, and a shaggy brown cow stood tied to a doorpost while two small children milked it. They looked up and stared at Gil. He smiled, as jauntily as he could, but their dirty faces were solemn. His pony's steel shoes rang suddenly on stone. On either side, stone walls rose high against the pale, winter sky. A hand slapped his shoulder in mocking camaraderie. "Welcome to Camelot, my friend, noble seat of your sovereign lord."

They came first to the great *muinntir*, just within the citadel walls. Ravaged by fire and worn by wind and rain, its crumbling church stood open to the sky. Yellowed grasses swayed amid the fallen roof beams and charred choir stalls. Dried thistles sprang from niches in the tumbling walls and a rose-tree had taken brave root in the altar's fire-cracked stone. A small brown sheep mounted an empty windowsill with a clatter of hooves, looked out with yellow sheep eyes and gave a loud baa. "See, the holy cleric sings his psalms!" laughed the guard on Gil's left. He gave Gil's head another hard shove, turning him forward.

But the man on Gil's right, a sturdy knight with a thick, bushy beard, like Erling's, suddenly laid his hand on his sword hilt and growled, "Enough. Risk your own soul if it pleases you, but not mine. And leave the boy alone." He gave the ruined *muinntir* a wary glance as if the tumbled stone held power yet and hurried his horse on its way.

The Great Hall stood beside the *muinntir* and it, too, lay abandoned. That the Usurper had no use for a church was known to all. But no symbol of Arthur's sovereignty was more powerful than his feasting hall with its storied table. Still the few quick sideways glances his captors allowed showed Gil only a shadowy cavernous ruin. Goats grazed, undisturbed and doves fluttered like the souls of vanquished knights. An eerie light fell through the blackened beams of the roof. His captors led him quickly away, as if Arthur's Hall was too haunted even for them.

The road mounted higher up the hill, and a new wall appeared. Within, stood a new citadel, square and solid, with a roof of sturdy thatch, a fortress within a fortress. The Knight's golden pennants flew from its highest point. Gil braced himself to enter the blank, impregnable walls, knowing he was unlikely ever to leave. Imagining some dark dungeon waiting, he looked up at the sky to say goodbye. A sharp blow rattled his teeth. "What? You look to Heaven for help?" Then a hand closed on his head and turned it roughly to the left. "Look there, instead," his laughing jailer said. "That's where you're going."

There was nothing in view but a grassy hill, and on it, another roofless ruin like so many he'd seen. "There?" Gil whispered.

"Heaven holds no keys to Merlin's Tower," crowed the laughing knight.

The quieter man on his right turned to his companion and said, "Be still." And with his eyes on the ruined tower, he murmured, "To send a boy to such a place. The devil curse him."

The other laughed again. "The devil does not curse his own." Then he dropped his voice and said, "And if I were you, I would hold my tongue. The tower has room for many."

Gil stared straight ahead as the ponies mounted the grassy hill. The words of the gentler man were scarier than the bully's because he meant no harm. It was clear he served the Knight from fear, not love. Men like that would switch sides if they could. Gil felt a small flame of future hope take light, if only for his friends. He wasn't expecting much future, himself.

Thirty feet from the tower, they stopped. It looked smaller than it had from below, blank-walled at ground level, like Janetta's tower in the Mews Garden, with arched windows above, one in each of the two walls he could see. Like the *muinntir* and the Great Hall, it bore the black marks of the fire that had destroyed its roof. The bully turned his horse and pointed to two of the four knights who had followed, in silence. Gil stole a glance over his shoulder. The four were young, as young as the youngest of Floki's crew. Their faces blanched at the bully's order and one nervously shook his head. Then the others did the same.

Outraged, the older man burst into an impotent rage, shouting and cursing and demanding obedience. But the boy-knights bunched their horses into a rebellious clump and the impasse only ended when the quiet man beside Gil drew his sword. Silence fell on all and the bushy-bearded knight growled, "I will do it. One is enough." He gave his companion a mocking smile, "You stay bravely here and guard the door." Then he turned to Gil, "Come lad. I will take you," he said.

He leaned over and took the reins of Gil's pony from the other and led the beast to the foot of Merlin's Tower. There, he dismounted and reached up to help as Gil, with his hands yet bound, slid clumsily from his pony's back. Unbuckling Gil's sword belt and loosening the strap of his shield, he laid both on the ground and turned to the entrance of the tower. A simple door barred their way. Its key rested in clear view, in its lock, so Gil guessed the tower was empty. But when the knight swung the heavy door inward, the first thing he saw was the figure of a man, seated, secured to a wall.

The prisoner wore a faded cloak of the many-colored plaid of Sir Owain's followers and he appeared asleep, his drooping head covered by the hood of his cloak. Then, as Gil's eyes adjusted to the light drifting down through the sooty roof beams, he saw the man's hand. Adorned yet, about the wrist, with a bracelet of silver, it hung from the sleeve of his cloak, fleshless, white bone. Gil cried out in horror. His jailer laid both hands on his shoulders and whispered in a voice of great sadness, "His troubles are over. No man can harm him now, and he can harm no man."

Gently, the knight steered him toward the wall, to where two black rings were embedded in the stone, a foot from the floor, and but an arm's length from the skeletal figure. "Sit, lad. I must bind you," he said. Gil looked at the rings and the awful thing beside them and realized he was to be tied there, within reach of it, unable to flee. Every fear he had ever known rose in a wave of unbearable panic.

"No!" he cried. "No! Please, please. Don't do it to me. Let me go, please. I'll do...." and then he stopped, overwhelmed with shame. Before his trial had even begun, he had abandoned every bold pledge and was more than ready to surrender.

Numb with despair, he allowed his jailer to press him down to the floor and secure his aching arms, behind him, to the rings in the stone. The man leaned very close, as he did, and in a voice almost too soft to hear, whispered, "Have courage. They can take your life and probably will, but even in this awful place, your soul belongs to God."

Then he was gone, and the door creaked closed behind him and the key grated as it turned in the lock, and rattled as it was drawn out and taken away. Gil closed his eyes and wept, shoulders shaking, breath catching in sobs, like a little boy. Eventually, the sobbing stopped and he sat rigid, remembering a story he'd heard about men trapped with dead bodies and how they went insane with fear.

He opened his eyes and stared vigorously ahead, but he could still see the cloaked shape from the corner of his eye. Still, he thought, he was just a man; some poor enemy of the Golden Knight, maybe even a boy, like the boy Ismail had to kill in the Forest of Caledon. If he himself died here, tied to this wall, and they brought someone else to the tower, would he fear Gil the way Gil feared this stranger?

"No," he murmured to the imagined newcomer. "Don't be afraid. I wouldn't hurt anyone." He forced himself, then, to look at the skeleton. Again, he saw only the hand and the bracelet. It glinted softly in the filtered light, a sturdy band of beaten silver decorated with a dragon's head and tail. A warrior's ornament, like the Northmen sometimes wore. It made him sad to think of the dead stranger dressing in his fine things, maybe to please a girl like Janetta.

Gil stared resolutely at the hand until his fear faded a little, and he saw it as he might see animal bones, on the hill at Cille Aidan. Then he remembered Cat, sleeping contentedly beneath the ribs of the dead knight. *If I could be Cat*, he thought eagerly. But it was impossible. There was no circle he could reach. Besides, if Jocelyn Guidbairn ever linked Gil with the cat in Janetta's arms, her fate would be worse than his. And, looking with calmer eyes around his prison, he saw at once that not even a cat could escape.

The walls were high and featureless, without ledge or crevice to climb. They soared, twice a man's height, to the base of the windows, and even the door was flat and smooth, set into the wall without handle or lintel. Gil's eyes rose instinctively to the open space where the roof had been, but it was so high above that he might as well have been at the bottom of a deep, square well. A dry well, he thought, realizing he was thirsty. There was no water, and no food; no sustenance at all. He looked grimly at his silent companion. Was that how he died? Of starvation? Or worse, of thirst? He thrust the thought from his mind and looked up again at the open roof. At least it wasn't a dungeon. At least he could see the sky.

The air grew cold and it began to snow; small, light, dry flakes. Gil shivered and rubbed his freezing cramped hands back and forth, the bare inch his bonds allowed. He would freeze, surely, before thirst or hunger took their toll. And they said that was easy, like going to sleep. Though, thinking of the blizzard and the nights in the chapel on the hill, he wasn't sure it was true.

He dropped his eyes from the darkening sky and studied the windows below. He could see three within his view, and he remembered seeing a fourth, in the wall behind his head. They were tall and narrow and arched at the top, like church windows, framed in stone and open to the air. But there was something odd about them, some trick of light, as if they held glass, though he could see flakes of snow blowing through their empty frames. The more he looked, the more he seemed to see things in them, like in a faint, pearly mirror, or the reflection in the moving water of a stream. Suddenly, they frightened him and he looked quickly down at the floor.

The dark stone slabs beneath him were hard to see, now. The sky above was nearly dark. *I'll be alone here. In the night.* He looked away from the skeleton, not sure it was worse to see it clearly in the light, or just to know it was there in the dark. But then he thought of whoever it had been, when alive, with such sorrow for the man's lonely death, that he was almost glad to keep company with his bones. He dropped his head wearily on his knees, aware that his posture mimicked that of his dead companion, but too exhausted to care.

Then, something caught his attention, and he slowly raised his head again, and then it was there once more: a sound, so faint that he strained his ears in the silence that followed and wondered if he'd imagined it. But it came again, faraway but real, drifting and fading with each sigh of the snow-filled wind. A bell. The ghost of a bell, like the bell of Cille Aidan from the Turnip Head Tomb. The convent bell! It had to be; no bell rang in Camelot's desolate *muinntir*. He thought of Janetta, hearing it too, and his friends in their eight-sided room, and was filled with joy, just to be joined to them by its thin ribbon of sound.

But it was dark. Time had passed unnoticed. The bell rang, not for None, but for Vespers. And before its last chime died, the key rattled in the door of Merlin's Tower. Gil shrank back against the stone wall as the door creaked inward, revealing his two jailers in the juddering light of a windblown torch. They hovered in the doorway, each holding something against his chest, until a loud curse and the shove of an unseen hand propelled them into the room.

Gil's bullying tormentor stumbled to a halt in front of him, clutching a basket from which rose a wonderful smell of roasted meat. But better than that was the pottery jug carried by the other. Gil had never realized you could smell water, or that it could smell so sweet. Then, behind the two, strode a taller figure, holding high the lighted torch, the flames casting the shadow of his golden helm over cheeks and beard. He nodded courteously to Gil, and then addressed the others. "Put those down and be gone," he growled. "And be glad not to find yourselves in the place of this poor lad, whose punishment you more richly deserve than he."

They set their burdens down and scurried out, and the Golden Knight drew the door closed and locked it from within. "So that we are not disturbed," he said. He stretched up and fitted the base of the torch into a socket in the stone, above Gil's head. The light flickered wildly in the snowy wind, setting Gil's shadow, and that of the corpse, leaping and dancing on the floor. "I offer my most humble apology," said the Knight. "My serving men, for some childish reason, fear this place – it is the nature of their tribes to find fear everywhere – and so they neglected to provide the sustenance I so clearly ordered."

Gil had forgotten the Knight's promise of food. And, for all the horror of his surroundings, his stomach lurched with hunger as the Knight laid out a cloth on the floor and set a platter of still sizzling venison upon it. Still, he hesitated. Did accepting the Knight's food make him somehow his friend? And was it right to eat beside the chained bones of his victim?

The Knight seemed to read his mind. He nodded to the corpse. "Your companion would not begrudge you that for which he has no need." His voice was soft and remote, as if the death of the man was nothing to do with him. Gil's head sided with his stomach. Food might not come again. He needed strength. He needed to live. He moved to reach for the platter of meat, and his wrists jerked fruitlessly against his bonds.

"What? They have tied you?" The Knight's protest of regret rang with such sincerity that a wild thought passed through Gil's mind. As his captor reached gently behind him and untied his hands, he wondered, was it possible that the Knight was not the monster everyone said he was? He gratefully rubbed his aching hands together and nodded as the other again offered the meat. But, as good as it looked, the jug, with its cool contents, looked better. "Could I have the water first?" he said.

"Eat first," the Knight said. "And wash it down. It is better that way." He made it sound so right that Gil nodded again. But somewhere, far back in his mind, a memory stirred. *His voice,* he thought. *When he talks like that. Sort of kind and scary at once....* But the memory came no closer and in his eagerness for the food and then the water, he thrust it aside. The venison was wonderful, rich, tangy, and salty. He stuffed as much down as he could before the dryness in his throat begged that he stop. "Could I...?" he gestured to the jug.

"There is little remaining. Finish. And then drink."

Reluctantly, Gil gulped the rest down. He was so thirsty now that it was hard to swallow. The Knight looked at the plate and smiled, like an approving father. "Well done," he said, in the same soft voice. He stepped sideways and lifted the jug and then somehow, just as he extended his arm toward Gil, it slipped from his hands and fell to the stone floor.

The pottery shattered and the water spilled in every direction, soaking at once into the cracks between the slabs. Gil stared in dismay and the Knight said in his softest voice, "Alas. And you thirst so. A pity." Gil lunged forward to wet his fingers in the last trickle, or even to lick the dampness of the stone. But the Knight caught his hands and held him back. "Do not demean yourself," he said mildly. "I will send for more." He smiled and Gil compulsively licked his dry lips as his hope rose. "But first," said the Golden Knight, "We will talk."

He smiled again, and Gil sank back on his haunches, struggling to swallow the desperation that stuck in his throat like a lump of the meat. *Thirst won't kill you that fast*, he told himself, and he heard again the quiet jailer's whisper, *Have courage.* "Okay," he croaked and he met the Knight's smile with one of his own, feeling his dry lips catch on his teeth, as he did.

"Very good. But I would be comfortable, first," said the Knight. And, still standing in front of Gil, he reached both hands up and lifted the golden helm from his head. Gil took one look, then rocked on his haunches and fell back against the wall, his own head swirling. His stunned eyes on the face before him, he opened his parched mouth to speak. But the Knight shook his head. "No," he said. "You are wrong. You do not know me."

"But I do," Gil cried. "You're...."

"Jocelyn Guidbairn, Knight of this realm and of realms greater and darker than your imagining." The voice grated, like steel on ice.

Gil shook his head, unable to dismiss what his eyes were seeing. "But I do know you. From home. From Tir nan Og! You're him. You're Dr. Fairchild," he cried. "I know you are." Looking up into the face above him, he was certain of every feature, but most of all, the brilliant blue eyes. So often hidden, yes, but he had still seen them. He tried to picture the dark things they were hidden by but could not. "You wear…shields…over your eyes, in Tir nan Og. But I've seen them and I know them. I know you!"

The Knight gave him a brief, pitying smile. "So certain we are of everything, when we are young."

"But I am certain," Gil cried, forgetting even his thirst, in his protest.

The Knight sighed and explained, as to a little child. "I am the eldest of many brothers. The family resemblance is strong."

"Dr. Fairchild is your brother?" Gil stammered.

"In a manner of speaking," the Knight said, with another faint smile. He sighed again. "There are few things more wearisome than the details of another's kin. I will not tire you with them. Besides, I would far rather know you here, than in that place." He waved a dismissive hand. "Your world bores me. Men there are as full of courtesies as those who held this ruined court. But they lack that humble thing that gave these fools their strength."

"What humble thing?" Gil whispered, still staring, dumbfounded, at the Knight.

"The knowledge that more exists in the world than their eyes can see. A knowledge forgotten in Tir nan Og. There, men see only themselves, reflected ever larger in a fattened mirror." He gestured suddenly toward the chained skeleton. "They were worth battling. You, in your pride, are too easy prey." He smiled coldly and then shrugged. "Still, when the hart is out of season, I hunt the roe. And when even he cannot be sought, the trembling hare."

He crouched down and laid his hand on Gil's shoulder and even as Gil fought to still the quivering of terror, he felt the Knight's cold soul seep into his, seeking every crevice, to lodge and freeze and shatter, like frost in stone. "Come," he took Gil's hand and lifted him effortlessly to his feet. "Let me show you the splendors of your new abode."

Still holding Gil's hand, as if in a bond of friendship, he led him to the very center of the square room. Gil struggled against the instinct to pull away, feeling all the while the same cold flowing through the other's fingers and into his own. "Look up!" commanded the Knight, and he raised both of his arms, at last freeing Gil from his unwelcome grasp. Gil looked to where the Knight boldly gestured and saw one of the four great windows; the one set in the wall to the right of the door. It seemed almost opaque now, with pearly light, and he was sure he could see things moving within it, though all the while, the snow blew right through them.

"Behold!" said his captor. "The Window of Time Past!" He turned Gil, with his hands brushing his shoulders like the winter wind. Gil found himself facing the wall to which he had been chained. "There, the Window of Time Present." Then he turned him another quarter circle. "The Window of Time Yet to Come." The cold hands turned Gil a last quarter. "And there! The treasure of them all. The Window of Time Out of Time."

The Knight laid a companionable hand on Gil's shoulder again. It didn't feel quite as cold. Gil guessed he was getting used to it and that thought filled him with a new foreboding: that he was somehow slipping into his captor's power. "Rare treasure indeed," the Knight said. "And you are privileged, for these are the Wisdom of Merlin. Few men have seen them, fewer still have seen them, and lived."

"What are they?" Gil whispered.

"They are what you see. Windows. Windows into Time. Here, Merlin read all that had been, all that was, all that would be. And, greatest of all, all that men's hearts desire. With such knowledge, even a fool could rule the world." He laughed softly and leaned over Gil's shoulder. "What do you see?"

Gil shrugged, fascinated in spite of himself. "Something," he said slowly. "Swirls, like mist, or water...like pictures except they keep vanishing." He heard the frustration in his own voice and felt, growing within him, an eerie desire for the elusive images.

"That," said the Knight, "Is because you do not have this."

He reached within his hauberk and drew out a pouch of worn leather on a leather thong. It seemed rough and ordinary, compared to the splendor of his garments, but he held it with great care. Opening a leather drawstring, he drew out something white and laid it on his hand. It glowed softly in the torchlight, a small, white circle of stone, pierced by a smooth round hole.

"A seeing stone!" Gil blurted in surprised recognition.

The Knight nodded, his eyes boring into Gil's. "There are, indeed, others," he said. "Fallen into the hands of guileful men. It would be good for you, and for all, if they were returned." He smiled graciously. Gil groaned inside. Stupidly, he had betrayed himself, and Aidan, as well. But his captor abruptly turned away. He held the stone up and, smiling slightly to himself, looked through it at the window called Time Past. Gil wet his lips and felt the thirst parch his throat and drag his attention away. Then suddenly the Knight grasped his shoulder, pulled him to his side, and held up the stone before him. "What do you see?"

With an eagerness he tried not to show, Gil took the stone and raised it to his right eye. A gasp of astonishment escaped his lips. In the circle of white stone, he watched a story come to life: Sir Palomides' story of his joust at the Linn of the Rainbow Bridge. Palamedes, Doombearer, their fierce opponent, the thundering linn itself, were as uncannily real as if it all was happening in this instant, directly in front of his eyes.

"What do you see?" the Knight repeated.

Gil remembered his mistake about Aidan and jerked the stone away. "Nothing," he said. "I didn't see anything."

The Knight hit him so hard that he careened into the wall, cracking his head against stone. Flashes of moving light filled his vision and vomit rose in his throat, adding its bitter taste to the misery of thirst. "Do not lie," the Knight hissed. "You see the Saracen, Palamedes. You know him well." Then he caught Gil's elbow and dragged him onto his feet. His voice returned to its soft tones and he said, "And myself, who, one day, you may know even better." And he gave Gil a weird, courteous smile, as if they were friends and someone else entirely had just thrown Gil against the wall.

"And now," he continued, "I will show you more." He leaned over and picked up the seeing stone from where it had fallen to the floor. Gil flinched as the stone was again placed in his reluctant fingers. "Look there." The Knight touched his bruised chin, gently tipped his head back and pointed up to the window again. Cautiously, Gil raised the stone to his eye, afraid to make any move or sound that might enrage his captor. But again, the vision through the circle came as a shock, though this time the sound that escaped him was only a murmur of sorrow. "What do you see?"

Gil shrugged. He dared not lie, and there was no point, anyway. The man he saw was beyond his betrayal. "It's Floki," he said. "Floki Magnusson."

"Ah, your Viking friend. And what does he do?"

Gil stared back through the window in time, into the past. Though he recognized Floki, he did not recognize the scene. "He's holding his sword up," he said. "In both hands. This way." He lowered his own hand and held both out, as if he held a sword across his open palms. "Like this," he said. Without the stone, he saw only a swirl of pearly light in the window, and he shook his head sadly.

"Look again," said the Knight, and fearing to refuse, Gil raised the stone again. "What else do you see?"

This time, Gil realized he was seeing another figure, too, just a portion of a dark-cloaked shoulder and the back of a head. "There's another man. I'm looking over his shoulder." He kept his gaze on Floki's calm, handsome face, seeing the focus of his grey eyes intent on the shadowy man.

"The Viking offers his sword to him, am I right?"

"I guess so," Gil muttered.

"Am I right?" the Knight hissed, and Gil shrank away, expecting another blow. He nodded his head again, quickly.

"Yes. Yes. You're right. He's offering it."

"Who is the other?" the Knight pursued.

Gil shook his head. "I don't know. I can't see him." He shrugged suddenly and took the stone away from his eye. "What does it matter?" he said. "It's all in the past. It's all over," he said quietly.

"If I had been betrayed," the Knight said with an air of studied thoughtfulness, "I think I would desire to know to whom."

"What?" Gil cried. He turned instinctively back to the window, and then scrunched the hand that held the stone into a fist. "Betrayed by Floki?" he cried disbelieving.

The Knight's voice dropped to a smooth whisper. "Long before you set foot beneath the Falls of the Fugitive, I knew you sailed Glen Alban. I knew your every move. Your every landfall. Someone betrayed you."

"Sir Owain!" Gil cried.

"It is not Sir Owain the Red you see through the stone. But Floki Magnusson, offering his sword, his loyalty, to another."

"No!" Gil cried. All his instincts rebelled. "Floki wouldn't serve anybody. For any cause. Good or bad."

"Not for a cause, young friend. For gold." The Knight leaned closer. "A man who has won lands from the earls might wish to build a longhouse," he suggested mildly. "But that requires gold."

"No," Gil insisted. But an image appeared in his mind, rivalling the image in the window. *Floki, on the shore of Pentland...a longhouse...thrice the size of Einar's Holm. Fit for a king's son....*

"Land, and a longhouse, and ships. Gold is power, my friend. Perhaps he would be earl."

Floki seeks power. Aidan had said it. "No!" Gil cried. "Floki wouldn't betray us!" But his mind was racing. The battle in the Forest of Caledon. Floki riding on his own, on Lucy the packhorse. Time enough to meet someone...but Danni! Danni! He wouldn't betray Danni. *Go then. Leave this one with me.* Of course. Gil's heart warred with his head, but to no avail. He saw himself in the blizzard, mourning his friends on the loch, and felt a kind of second mourning overcome him. "I don't believe it," he said a last time, without conviction.

The Knight smiled. "Look through the stone. The windows cannot lie." But Gil shook his head. He didn't need to see it again. His shoulders slumped and hopelessness descended on him and when the Knight turned him to the next window, the one above the chained corpse, he did nothing to resist. "Time Present!" announced the Knight, raising the stone with a satisfied smile. "Behold, we find again your Saracen friend." He handed Gil the stone with a brief, graceful bow.

Gil raised it and looked through. The scene before him was so innocently pleasing that he smiled, in spite of himself. "Sir Palamedes, sharing a longhouse feast! I have seen that before."

"But with whom does the noble knight dine?"

Gil looked again, hungry for another glimpse of his friend. But then, peering closer, he saw something else, something that chilled his blood. Behind Palamedes and his companions was a huge hearth upon which a mighty fire of whole logs burned. Above rose a stone wall, and on it hung a rippling pennant of gold. Then, looking to Palamedes' right, he saw two faces he knew, and among the boisterous crowd on his left, another. Three young knights; three of the four who had ridden with him to Merlin's Tower and rebelliously refused to step within. As he watched, all three turned together to the golden pennant and raised their drinking vessels on high. The Saracen knight bowed his head in respect.

Guidbairn suddenly took the stone from Gil's fingers, looked through it, and handed it back. "I am charmed," he said. "Such gracious guests! They cheer my health around my humble hearth."

"Your hearth...." Gil whispered stupidly.

"You see my colors upon the wall?"

"Your guests...but Palamedes...he's your worst enemy! Why...?"

"Ah, yes. My noble Palamedes. But for a little while deluded into the cause of some foolish rebels. But his delusion is over and I have welcomed him back to the new table of Camelot. A worthy knight, seeking a worthy master."

"Impossible!" Gil shouted. "He is loyal to Arthur. Loyal to Camelot!"

"But this is Camelot. If only one sees it so." The Knight laid his hand on Gil's shoulder. "I believe he left you," he said mildly.

"To follow his Questing Beast! That was fair. He always said...."

"A pretty story," said the Knight.

"More than a story," Gil shot back, forgetting himself in his anger. "It's real."

"Have you seen it?"

"I heard it!" Gil answered vehemently.

"But you did not see it." And when Gil turned to argue, the same hand closed gently on his shoulder and then tightened until he winced in pain. "The tribes here have an instrument of war – a kind of horn – shaped like a dragon's head. It makes a fearsome noise."

Gil shook his head, uncertainly. "But it was so loud. It shook the forest."

"The windows cannot lie," said the Knight. He smiled pityingly at Gil's confusion and then said, "Enough of the Present. Let us see the Future. That faithless lady all men seek." Again, the Knight touched Gil's shoulder, and shrinking from the touch, Gil turned. "Behold. Time Yet to Come."

Gil saw to his surprise that his captor seemed to struggle to hold the upraised stone, and the sweat of fierce concentration dampened his forehead as he peered through it. *It's hard*, Gil thought. *He made it look easy, to scare me, but it's not.* And he realized with a flash of hope that Jocelyn Guidbairn was not all powerful. Nor was he full master of Merlin's Tower.

"Ah," the Knight said at last. "Your friend comes to me, but not willingly. Look there." Triumphantly, he handed Gil the stone.

Gil raised it to his own eye and cried out, happily, "Ismail!" But his pleasure faded into confusion and then growing horror. "What's he doing?" he murmured.

"And what does he do?" said Jocelyn Guidbairn innocently. "Tell me. Perhaps I will find sense where you do not."

Gil shrugged, sinking back into hopelessness. What did it matter? The Knight knew everything about him, already. His betrayers had seen to that. He looked up into the brilliant blue eyes. "Well, if it's the future, then Ismail gets home somehow. Because this isn't here. It's Africa."

The Knight nodded wisely. "Africa! A far land indeed. But not beyond the reach of ship and sail. What does he, in this far place?"

Gil looked again, his eyes narrowing in shock. "It can't be Ismail!"

"You can see it is."

"But why would...?" He stared, against his will, into the circle in the stone. Ismail, in his army trousers, his tee-shirt, his red headband. Some kind of leather straps crossed over the tee-shirt, like sword belts without swords. And in his hand, a kind of sword, broad-bladed and short. And in front of him, hands bound, a dark, kneeling man who looked up with patient gentle eyes, even as the blade swooped downwards. "No!" Gil threw the stone to the floor. "It's not true! Ismail wouldn't!"

"The windows cannot lie."

"I know him. He's my friend. He'd never kill someone tied up like that!"

"He would and he has done. The place you see is Tir nan Og. Which you and I both know lies not across the Western Sea, but far ahead in time. What you see in your friend's future is already in his past. The blood he sheds, already dry. Do you wish to see whose blood it is?"

"No!" Gil cried. "No! No! No!" But even as he shouted it, he heard Ismail's words on the strand of Hy. *You know this...you are never my friend again.* And suddenly Gil was sobbing, crying, a broken child.

The Knight laid a gentle hand on his head. "I would loathe to have such a man for a friend. Indeed, you appear unfortunate in friends. Perhaps, now you will choose better." And he leant over and scooped up the hateful stone and turned Gil a final time. But now, he did not look at the fourth window at all. His eyes on Gil's face, he said, "If time itself should stop, young knight, where would you choose to be?"

Gil froze. Without seeing stone or time window, did Guidbairn yet read his mind? Striving to blank out his thoughts only made it worse: clearer and clearer arose a picture of himself, wrapped in Janetta's slender arms, his mouth on hers. *Let time stop.* "Nowhere!" he cried stupidly. "I mean, I don't know."

The Knight regarded him mildly, and if he saw through Gil's frantic lie, he did not show it. "You don't know. This is wise. So many men are certain they know and so many men are wrong. Few, few indeed, are those who can read their own hearts. Even Merlin in his famed wisdom doubted he could do that. And so, he built this tower." Guidbairn turned around with a grand sweep of his arm. "This was the citadel of his soul. Here, the wisest man in Camelot came to seek that wisdom that lies within. And here, he failed."

"He did?" said Gil. The cold hand rested on his shoulder as Guidbairn continued his story.

"Merlin was old and wise, and one day there came to him a maiden, almost as wise as he. A joy to an old man's heart, a scholar both exalted in knowledge and winsome in face and form. And she sought him out, from a far, far land, to share their common delight. And all was well. But Merlin, as all knew, had turned time upon its head, and where all men age, he grew but younger, day by day. And, as youth returned, his blood warmed to the ways of younger men. And, knowing that, he came each day to the tower he had built, to see, himself, his true desire.

"For that is what is seen in the Window of Time Out of Time: where a man would choose to be, if time stood still. And, seeing himself always with the maiden, among his books, he went safely on his way to visit her. Not by ship, or horseback, but across a particularly marvelous bridge that lies but a few leagues from here." He paused and studied Gil. "Perhaps you have heard it named the Rainbow Bridge."

Gil said nothing.

"It has another name," said the Knight, then. "The Bridge to Heaven and Hell. For on it, one man finds the one, another man, the other. It is a door, as this is a window." He raised the stone at last to the fourth arched opening in the tower walls. "Through this, a man can see the place of his heart's desire. Through that, he may journey there. And so, Merlin did, knowing always the truth of his own heart. But then the day came when the window told him a new truth, and instead of books and scrolls, he saw himself in the maiden's bed. And he knew he must see her no more."

"What did he do?" Gil said, thinking sadly of Janetta.

The Knight laughed. "You are young indeed." He held the stone up to his eye and looked, not at the window, but at the black sky above. "He lied, of course."

"To the maiden?"

The Knight laughed again. "To the maiden, indeed. To the

sun and the moon and the stars. To Arthur the King. But most of all, and all that mattered, to himself. He declared the tower faulty, the window a fraud, indeed would have declared night to be day, to have her. And so, he crossed the bridge and fell into her thrall. For the maiden awaiting on the other side wanted not his wizened body, but the power his knowledge would bring. And so, she tricked and enslaved him and imprisoned him, where he will remain 'til time itself ends." He looked up at the sky again. Then, he turned to Gil and said in the softest of whispers, "Now. Will you see your heart's desire?"

"No!" said Gil, too vehemently. The Knight inclined his head graciously.

"And why not? It is knowledge of great value, as I have told you."

"I don't believe it. It's just stories."

"Then look!" The Knight held out the stone. "If it is but stories, it can do no harm."

"I don't want to," Gil said. The stone was thrust towards his fingers.

"Look."

"No."

The Knight's hand cracked across his face. Gil reeled and stumbled and crashed to the floor and into the skeleton, by the wall. The rotted, disguising cloth shredded and the bones clattered free. Gil rolled through them and over them and ended lying on the stone floor, face to face with the grinning naked skull. "No!" he screamed, covering his face and his head with his arms. "Please, please. Someone help me," he sobbed. "Get me out of here."

There was no answer and then he felt the Knight's hand on his shoulder, with all its dreaded gentleness. "Come. On your feet." Numbed by terror, Gil stood. Again, the stone was placed in his fingers, and, facing the fourth window, he silently raised the white circle to his eye. Through the tiny frame, a vista opened marvelously, so he seemed to see all the wild Western Sea stretching from horizon to horizon. On it was a ship, and he knew the ship well. *Silver Dragon*, sailing fine and free, her striped sail bent to the wind, sunlight sparkling on her fierce dragon prow, miraculously whole again.

At the helm stood a slim, young man, and beside him a girl, leaning on his arm. Floki and Danni, he thought. But there was no splash of sunlit yellow hair, and the girl's head was black as a raven's wing. He made himself look closer and closer until he saw for sure what his mind couldn't grasp. *It's me,* he thought. *And Janetta. It's* Silver Dragon *and I'm at the helm.* He could smell the salt and feel the wind and wet spray on his face, as the ship ploughed her beautiful course. *This is where I am meant to be.*

"What do you see?" whispered the Knight, at his ear.

Gil stared through the stone and a slow horror enveloped him. *If I lie, and he knows, he'll probably kill me. But if I tell him this….* His eyes fell longingly on Janetta's beautiful, spray-drenched face. She looked so joyous. So free. Gil drew a deep breath. "Home," he said. "I see my home."

He waited for the blow. But it did not come. The Knight was silent and he made no attempt to take the stone to see the vision Gil saw. Gil felt a surge of hope, as he realized that not even the Golden Knight could read another's desires in the Window of Time Out of Time. Nor, for all his power, could he do what Aidan and the Ab of Hy both did; he could not read Gil's heart.

Finally, Guidbairn spoke. "Very good," he said. "Indeed, a noble objective. Many a hero has honorably sought home." He reached and took the stone away. Then, with a firm but gentle hand, he backed Gil toward the wall. There, by the scattered bones of the ruined skeleton, he forced him again to the floor. "A great sorrow to live in troubled times," he said. "That oblige a man to so mistreat a guest. But it is for your own best interests, as always." Then he leaned over and again bound Gil's hands firmly to the iron rings in the wall. Gil shuddered as the bonds drew tight and panic rose, heightening his aching thirst.

"I must depart," said the Knight. "The duties of kingship are ever present. But first, water." Gil nodded eagerly, in his relief. "Of course," said the Knight soothingly. "Did you fear I might forget?" He went to the door of the tower, unlocked it and called a sharp order. At once, a shadowy figure appeared and as he came into the flickering torchlight, Gil recognized the kind jailer. He carried a fresh pottery jug into the square room and stood waiting fearfully. Gil smelled the water, cold and sweet, and his dry throat gulped helplessly. But the Knight stood back and looked around at each of the four windows, before he spoke.

"When Merlin vanished," he said, taking up his story unexpectedly, "Arthur took back the stone and locked it away from all, in this, Merlin's Tower. Safe in the heart of Camelot. Until Camelot fell. Of all Arthur's treasures, this," he held up the seeing stone, "is the most precious, but one. And with this within my hand, I will win the other, too." He leaned forward and stroked Gil's face with the smooth white edge of the stone. "Indeed, you may help me!" He smiled as if he had offered Gil a wonderful gift. Gil looked up into his brilliant eyes and knew at once what all this strange meeting had been about. The misery of his friends' betrayals; the temptation of the beautiful vision of the sea. They were all for this.

"Never," he whispered defiantly and braced himself for the Knight's savage hand.

But Guidbairn only smiled. He took the water jug from the jailer and set it down with great care and for all his defiance Gil could not stop himself from straining toward it, against his bonds. But writhe and struggle as he might, no part of his body, shoulder, head, or foot, could be made to reach it. The Knight dipped his fingers into the water and let it run, pure as a mountain stream, onto the floor.

"Oh, yes," he said. "You may." He stood straight and shoved the jailer aside, and as the man scurried out into the darkness, the Golden Knight said, "He waits just beyond, mounting the guard. A single word will bring him, and the water jug, to your side. And," he nodded up at the fourth window, "the sweet vision of Time Out of Time, within your grasp." Then he reached up, took down the flaring torch, and went out, closing and locking the door.

Gil was left alone in the blackest darkness of his life. At first, it helped that he couldn't see the jug, but only smell the water. And the scattered bones of the corpse existed only in his mind. But, as his eyes adjusted, his vision returned, and with it, the white skull grinning up from the floor and the dark curve of the water jug.

He tried again, fruitlessly, to reach it, twisting and turning until his wrists were rubbed raw by his bonds and the joints of his shoulders and elbows burned with pain. He could barely swallow any longer and panic beat at the base of his throat. One word and he'd have water. One word. He shook his head fiercely, shutting his mind to the thought and to the wonderful vision of Janetta and the ship. At last, aching in every muscle, exhausted and freezing, he somehow slept.

And then he was awake again, and the room was filled with light. For a moment, he thought he had survived the night and it was dawn. But it was not morning, nor was it starlight or moonlight. Eerie, white, flickering, fading and growing, it filled the sky with such brilliance that he could see the shadow of the water jug on the floor. Above, veils of white and green, blue and red, flowed across the heavens. The Aurora! The Northern Lights, just as he'd seen them the night at the convent, but a dozen times brighter. Brighter than he ever knew they could be. For a few seconds, he was caught up in their beauty, in spite of his terrible prison. But then his eyes fell to the floor and he saw a second shadow, a shadow that could not be there, at all.

Heart pounding, Gil raised his eyes to the shadow's source, and saw, just beside the dim outline of the door, the tall, lean figure of a man. Wrapped in a cloak, his face, hidden by its hood, a hollow darkness within darkness, but Gil still knew him. Bones re-gathered and freed of their chains, his grim companion stood before him. "Get up," said the figure in the softest of voices. "I have come for you. We must go."

CHAPTER TWELVE

"No," Gil moaned. "No. Get away." He shrank back against the wall and turned his head aside, willing the apparition to vanish.

"Get up," the voice said again. The figure reached out a long arm and the loose cloak fell back, the hood slipping from the head. Gil shut his eyes, then forced himself to open them, bracing for the grinning skull. But then he shook his head in terrified disbelief.

Even in the eerie light, the lean face and the rough mane of bright hair were unmistakable. "Floki?" Gil whispered, his voice a dry, tremulous croak. The cloaked figure strode quickly from the shadows. "Get back!" Gil cried. He kicked out at the apparition. "Leave me alone!"

The figure halted. Gil peered at it in the ever-shifting shadows and caught a glimpse of its pale eyes, surveying him with care. It stepped forward and again Gil shrank back. His gaze swept the impregnable tower. "How did you get in?"

"Through the door."

"It was locked!" Gil pressed himself against the wall.

"The key is in my hand."

"But the guard!" Gil protested. "There was a guard!"

The apparition fell silent and kept its distance. Then the voice answered quietly, "He is with his fathers."

As the meaning of the words sank in, Gil whispered, "I didn't hear anything."

"Nor did he." There was another silence and a quiet sigh. "Warrior, I have but one good arm. I do not make courtesies."

Gil peered, wonderingly, at the apparition before him and

saw that the sword belt around the figure's lean waist was worn reversed, scabbard to the right, as by a left-handed man. "Floki? Are you alive?" he whispered.

He heard a soft, low laugh as the figure stepped forward. "That is the stupidest...." But the voice cut off short, as Gil flinched away. Floki crouched down before him then and threw back his cloak. When he spoke next, his voice was a gentle whisper. "Warrior? Come. Look at me. Come." The dancing light of the aurora lit up the clear grey eyes and shining hair. "Do I look dead?"

Gil shook his head. A hand reached out and touched his face. He flinched, again, at its coldness, but it was only the cold of the winter air. He felt something wet against his cheek, and looking down, saw the fingers that had touched him were smeared yet with the blood of the jailor. "You must be real;" he mumbled crazily. "Ghosts can't kill people."

Floki jerked the hand away, seeing what Gil had seen, and wiped the fingers quickly on his tunic. "I am sorry," he murmured, and for a moment he dropped his head, looking down at his hands, both blood-stained in the silvery light. "This is a terrible place, Warrior," he said softly. "Come. Let us go."

Then Gil realized, all at once, that he was free: free of the power of the Golden Knight, and free of the horrors of Merlin's Tower. His gaze fell on the water jug and he strained forward. "Floki, please. The water." He jerked his chin helplessly toward it. "I can't reach."

The Northman's eyes flashed to the jug, then back to Gil, taking in everything: the bonds, the tantalizing closeness of the water, the desperation. He swept up the heavy jug and held its rough lip to Gil's mouth, tipping it gently. "Drink! Drink!" Gil gulped frantically at the blessed, cold stream washing over his lips and down his chin. "Slowly, Warrior, slowly." Floki pulled the jug back.

Gil coughed and spluttered and begged for more until he was allowed a few more swallows. Then, setting the jug down, the Northman drew his sword, and severed the rope binding Gil to the iron rings. Gil flung himself on the jug, clutching it with his numb fingers and pouring its contents over his face.

"A little. Only a little," Floki murmured. But Gil couldn't stop himself from swallowing enormous quenching gulps until his abused stomach finally rebelled.

A cold lump rose in his throat and then his guts heaved and he barely struggled to his feet before he was puking the Golden Knight's venison all over the stone floor. "I'm sorry," he gasped, wiping his mouth with the back of his hand. "He gave me food. But it was so salty. And then he wouldn't give me water." His body trembled all over in a horrible cold sweat and his stomach heaved again.

Floki laid one hand on Gil's back and with the other, held Gil's long hair away from his face while he vomited. "Thirst is such an easy weapon to use against a man," he said quietly. "None can resist it." More quietly still, he added, "And he uses it against a boy."

Gil straightened up. "I think I'm done," he said weakly.

Floki offered him the water again. "A little. Slowly."

Gil drank a few sips, obediently. Feeling more normal, he looked around, remembering where he was. "We better go."

"Wait. And then take a little more."

"The Knight might come back," Gil said, coming fully to his senses, at last.

Floki laughed. "May Odin grant me the pleasure," he said. And he would not leave until he was satisfied Gil had had all the water he needed.

It was only when he reached the door that the questions crowded into Gil's mind. "Floki, how are you here?" he whispered. "And the storm, the ships, we thought…and how did you find me? How did you know…? I can't believe it!" he cried in a burst of wild relief. "I thought I'd be here forever!"

Floki held up a hand, shaking his head. Gil could see his familiar teasing smile. "Warrior, if we do not leave this place, quietly and quickly, we may both be here for the rest of our very short lives. Stories are for the longhouse. Here, and now, we ride."

"You've got horses?" Gil said eagerly.

"Horse," said Floki.

"Just one?"

"One. But he is big enough to carry Bjorn and his father. You and I, he will not know are there. Come." He slid the key into the lock, and turned it, somehow silently, to release the door and Gil followed him hurriedly into the soft, snow-sifting air of freedom. Floki stopped and bent over something dark and bulky, and then Gil recognized his jailor, the kind man who had tried to give him hope, lying soaked in dark blood. He watched silently as the Northman lifted the man's body, under its shoulders. "I beg forgiveness," Floki addressed the jailor solemnly, "that I mistreat your corpse. But its silence speaks against me." Then he dragged the body through the doorway, into the tower.

Gil waited numbly until Floki returned, locked the door with the key, and bent to wash his hands in the snow-wet grass. In his heart, Gil wished it had been the other man, the bully, who had met Floki's sword. But then a strange confusion overcame him: who was he to judge who should die? And which was better, anyhow, for a good man to die, or a bad?

His hands clean of blood, Floki caught up Gil's sword and shield, gave them to him, and then strode down the grassy hill. Gil ran after, buckling the sword belt around his waist. At the foot of the hill, Floki turned to him and handed him the heavy, iron door key. "I give you the key to the Golden Knight's prison," he said. "Throw it into the deepest pool we pass. And may he drown himself, seeking it."

Gil took the key and slid it into his pocket, determined to find the deepest, most unpleasant pool imaginable. "A pool with a dragon in it!" he said.

Floki smiled. "Even better." He looked up at the sky, which was brighter than ever, turning all of Camelot to silver. Gil looked around, too awed by its beauty to feel properly afraid. Floki smiled again, "Odin's maidens dance tonight. They hang their shields on the stars."

"What?" said Gil, uncertainly.

"Look! There is the light of his fire, glinting off them. Shields of silver and gold!"

Gil stared at the heavens. The Northern Lights. He knew what caused them, once. And even if he couldn't remember, he knew it wasn't maidens' shields. He stole a quick glance at Floki, wondering how much of what he said, he really believed. "Okay," he said warily. Floki's eyes narrowed, assessing him.

"You question my word?"

"No!" Gil said.

Floki laughed and slapped his back with bone-crunching cheer. "Very good. Behold!" He pointed. "Our noble charger." Gil looked, and at first saw only a big stone wall, with something pale and hazy appearing above it. Then he realized the pale shape was the rump and back and shaggy mane of an enormous horse, poking up above the coping stones. "I hide him, but not very well." Floki ducked around the end of the wall and untied the reins of the huge horse from the tree to which it was tethered. "It is like hiding a mountain."

Gil stared in awe at the beast they were to ride. It was so tall that its shoulders were above Floki's head. Yet its bridle was but a rope halter, the reins another loop of hemp. For a saddle it boasted only a sheepskin, fastened with a leather girth, before which a bedroll had been slung, over the animal's neck. Stirrupless, Floki leapt onto its back with an agility that Gil didn't hope to emulate. Climbing quickly onto the wall, he jumped across to the beast's huge rump and sprawled over it, half on and half off. Floki laughed, pulled him upright, and murmured, "Hold fast, Warrior. Hold fast!" Then he did something swift and subtle with his hands and his heels and the enormous animal leapt from standing to a gallop in three short strides. Gil had barely time to fling his arms around the Northman's waist before they were careering down the hill through the silence of Camelot.

It was the wildest ride of his life, worse than his ride from Einar's Holm, his first time ever astride a pony. Only his horror of the Golden Knight's revenge kept him aboard the monstrous beast. Remembering the bareback acrobatics of Floki's joust with Palamedes, he realized ruefully that that was simply how Floki expected a man to ride. Three times, Gil nearly bounced off as the animal jumped ditches, and a sharp turn beneath the walls of Camelot sent him sliding so far sideways that one foot brushed the ground. Floki twisted quickly and hauled him back up, laughing gaily, and as they plunged into the dark of the forest he shouted over his shoulder, "Now comes danger, Warrior. Hold fast!"

Suddenly they were amid a pinewood as thick and as baffling as the rose briar maze of Pentecost. If Floki knew where they were going, Gil could not reckon how. The canopy of the forest blotted out even the wondrous aurora. There was neither road, nor track, only a featureless wall of trees into which the Northman drove their horse at the same wild gallop. Again and again, at the very last moment, he steered the snorting beast left and right around one great trunk and then another, ducking as huge branches whipped over their heads.

Gil hunched as low as he could, buried his face in the rough fur of Floki's wind-whipped cloak, and closed his eyes. At least, he thought, the Northman was taller than him; the first head to be knocked off by a branch, would be his. Then, just when Gil felt he had no more strength in arms or legs to hold on, Floki slowed the galloping animal to a canter, then a trot, then brought him to a halt. "You are well, Warrior?"

"Fine," Gil lied, panting for breath.

"I beg your patience. We must rest this beast a while. But soon enough, more play."

"Great," said Gil. "Can't wait."

"Hey," Floki turned and cuffed his head appreciatively, "you are real warrior!"

No, Floki, I am real liar, Gil thought, but he decided it was safer not to say it.

Floki tapped the horse's flanks lightly with his heels and obediently it set off at a smooth walk, passing silently through the forest. Gil relaxed on its back, and as the tension left his body, he felt tiredness creeping into his bones and he struggled to keep awake. "This is a good horse," Floki said suddenly, and Gil jumped, realizing he had been dozing. "He is but a plough horse, and a monkish one at that," Floki continued, "But I think when he works before the plough, he dreams of war. And well he suits it." He leaned forward and patted the animal's powerful neck.

The beast's ears swiveled back and then ahead, and Gil sensed equine satisfaction, though the horse was silent. "A monkish horse?" he asked, mystified.

"Ah. A story. I will tell. But first we run." And again, with a swift light shake of the reins, Floki set the great beast galloping. Gil gritted his teeth and hung on for dear life. Galloping, and then trotting, and then galloping again, they rode for what felt like hours. They climbed higher and the trees grew farther apart, making the way easier, lit once more by the Northern Lights, still dancing over their heads. Gil looked up through the passing branches and was filled with weary joy, as if the sky itself celebrated his escape.

But he saw no landmarks he knew and he felt instinctively that they had set off to a different part of the forest than any he had travelled. Only when the curtains of light began at last to fade, retreating northward, could he judge direction, and he realized they had ridden south, miles and miles, into the heart of the mountains. Then, suddenly, Floki drew their mount to a halt. "Enough," he said. "This good beast has worked hard. We are far now. He can rest."

Gil hoped that meant they could rest, too, and as he slid stiffly down from the great height of the horse's back, he was looking around longingly for shelter. Though the thin snow had stopped falling, it was bitterly cold, and his hands, bruised by the Golden Knight's bonds, ached painfully.

Floki slipped down from the horse's back, also, and for a moment leaned against the animal as if he too had had enough. But then he straightened and looped the reins around his arm and set off on foot, southward, again. Wearily, Gil followed on feet still numb from the long, cold ride. And then, as they walked, Floki began his story. "That day on the Great Loch," he said suddenly, "Scarce do we set our sail, beneath the Falls of the Fugitive, than the storm strikes us. Never have I seen a wind rise so swiftly, as that wind, in that place."

Gil nodded. "We were on the hill. It was awful."

"I know, and I fear for you. But soon we have our own fears. The loch is long, but it is narrow. The wind crowds down it. Our course is set full against it. We beat one way, then the other, but we make no headway. We take on water. Three men bail. Then four. We need landfall, but there is none. I say to Erling, we turn her back to the Falls. But it is not easy, to turn before such a gale, and I take the steering oar, because no one can helm her as I do. But it takes strength, and I have little. We signal Hakon, reef our sails, together we turn and run down that wind. And then, Warrior," he laughed and slapped Gil's back, "You think this ride wild? Ah, would you were with us there! We ride the Great Loch as if on the dragon's back!

"We make for our landfall, again, but the wind drives us leeward, I cannot hold course against it, and we pass the Falls. But I am thinking then, there is a bay, I remember from when I sailed with Redbeard. A fortress guards it, but on a day like this, men keep to their own troubles. We make this bay, we are saved. So, with only the scrap of sail I need to keep her head up, we run down the wind again, for this bay.

"I am so weary that I call Erling to stand by me, and I rest against him while I hold the tiller and so we sail, like two old men leaning on each other on the steering board." He laughed, remembering. "And I see the headland, through the mist, and the fortress, and know the bay is beyond and we are winning. But then there is a gust, a mighty one, and she outruns the seas and buries her prow like a horse stumbling. And the force of the wind, still behind us, snaps our mast."

Gil stared up at Floki, wide-eyed, picturing the great pine mast of *Silver Dragon* splintering before him.

"I try to hold her, but she slews around and there is too much force in the water. The steering oar parts from the strake: we are rudderless. And we are done." He fell silent, remembering, and shrugged slightly. "I signal to Hakon to go on, but he will not leave us. So, we are both done. I bid the oarsmen row for the shore, and I steer her with a loose oar, which is impossible, and watching the shore, I think where I wreck her, so most survive. "And then, in all of that, I hear a bell." He shrugged again, as if amazed himself at what he said.

"A church bell?" Gil asked. He trotted a few steps beside the tall Northman, trying to keep up with his long strides.

"Like on Hy," Floki said. "I think I am dreaming, because of the fever, but Erling hears it, too. And then I remember what Redbeard tells me, that there is a house there, at a place called the Field of the Church, a *muinntir*, like Hy. Indeed, some among them are men of Hy. And suddenly, I have hope. There will be a landing, if not for a longship, for some kind of boat. And above, there will be barns that might shelter men, and if we make landfall without too much damage, there will be workshops, a forge, somewhere where we can fashion a mast, repair our ship. And then, Odin, at last, is kind, and the sky clears a moment, and Arnkel, with his good sharp eyes, sees the *muinntir* for that moment, and we bring her in.

"The landing is rock and gravel, and so narrow a strand that Hakon must lower his mast before he can creep in beside us, under the trees. And so, we shelter there, like foxes in a lair." Floki paused while he led the horse through a narrow gap between trees, then continued. "But we have solid ground beneath our keel, if only just, and we tie *Silver Dragon* to two stout oak trees and *Storm Serpent* beside her, up against the good brothers' pier.

"And so, drenched through, we wade ashore and climb the hill in the wind and snow. It is not good for any man and less good for me. Tomorrow will not be my concern. I know this. But I have thirty men; boys I have taken from their fathers' hearths. Erling is a good helmsman. Hakon will lead them home. But this night, I must find them shelter." Floki stopped walking, suddenly, and stood still, his hand on the huge horse's neck. Even though the aurora was gone, the stars shown so brightly that Gil could still see shadows on the ground. Furtively, he looked around the soft carpet of pine needles, hoping it was time to make camp. But Floki said only, "This is how men die, Warrior. Stupidly."

Startled, Gil studied the Northman's face in the starlight and then shook his head. "It doesn't sound stupid to me," he said. "It sounds pretty brave."

Floki leaned back against the horse with an exasperated sigh. "I do not say this to humble my soul, Warrior," he said, "but for you to learn from me."

Gil stepped back, annoyed at the rebuff, but a little proud, also, that Floki thought he was worth teaching. "Okay," he said, uncertainly.

"One mistake," Floki said. "And one piece of ill-fortune.

Either one, you survive. Both together, maybe you do not survive. That is why you must make no mistakes."

"What mistake?" Gil said. "The storm? You couldn't know...."

Floki shook his head sharply. "Not the storm. Hakon. I listen to Hakon when I know the dragon is near. You remember?" Gil nodded. "Hakon is cautious," Floki said. "I am bold. This time, I am cautious and he is bold. I should know this is wrong. I should not listen to my cousin. I know the dragon, and he does not. But I am proud, and I will not show fear when he does not." He looked up at the sky. "Without the storm, it would not matter. But then we have the storm. I deserve to die, that night, Warrior," he said quietly. "But I do not die." He shrugged. "Odin's will."

He turned toward the horse as if he would mount it again, but he stood still, then, just looking at it. "No," he said. "There is more than that. I will tell you. But first I decide which is more work; walking or getting back on this horse." Then he gripped the huge animal's mane and jumped and swung his leg over its back once more, but with none of his earlier grace. He leaned down and hauled Gil up after him and again they rode out through the starlit forest.

"We come to the *muinntir*," he said. "It is smaller than Hy, much smaller, but there is, as I hoped, a church, barns, cells for monks. We smell fires and hear the sounds of beasts and of men working, even on this foul day. We see a longhouse, with smoke above its roof. Hakon and I go to the door. We take off our sword belts and lay them down, so they will know we mean no harm. But still, behind us stand sixty armed men who could seize what we ask for in a moment.

"He opens the door, this man in monks' robes, their Ab, and sees all this. And he is not afraid. I see his eyes. Like calm water. He gives me his church and his barns to shelter my men. And he brings me into his own house." Floki fell silent, and then said slowly, "He gives up his bed by the fire, for me, and sleeps on the floor. He is not young. I am ashamed that this old man suffers hardship for me, but he will have it no other way, and I am too weary to argue.

"He is as kind to me as a father. I wake in the day, he is there. I wake in the night, he is there. And yet he knows who I am and what I am and well I may return come another spring and burn his *muinntir* and slaughter his monks." He paused and said then, "I do not burn churches. But he cannot know that. Nor is it from respect for him or his god, but for fear of my devilish mother." He laughed softly, but Gil did not laugh with him.

"Shony isn't devilish," he said firmly.

Floki turned and cast him a cold look. "It is a jest." He rode on then for a long while, without speaking, and Gil wondered if he would continue his story at all.

They came to an open, marshy place. There was a lochan, black under the night sky. It looked deep and mysterious and could well have held at least a little dragon. Gil reached in his pocket for the Golden Knight's key. Drawing it out, he leaned back on the horse and flung the key silently. It made a white splash, and a circle of starlit ripples. Floki whirled around, and then realizing what Gil had done, laughed quietly. "Well thrown, Warrior. And may that black place keep it from its black-hearted master." He smiled approvingly at Gil, his anger seemingly forgotten; and drew in the reins. The tired horse halted readily. Floki stretched his arms over his head and then nudged Gil. "Down."

Gil slid off the horse and landed on weary feet and Floki dismounted after him. "Do you think, maybe...." Gil began warily, but the Northman was already walking, with the reins over his arm, and he had to trot to catch up.

"We are there many days," Floki said. "I do not know how many. Hakon does well. A great tree is felled and, with the monks' tools, Svein and Ragnar, who are carpenters, shape a fine mast. At the forge, our broken steering oar is mended. When that is done, Hakon sends bowmen onto the hill for game for the *muinntir* larders, and axmen to fell trees for their hearths, that we be no more burden than necessary. I know none of this. I am more ill than I will ever be again and remain in this world. But this man has skill to match his kindness and though I deserve to die, I live."

He led the patient horse through a little stream and up the bank beyond and Gil plodded numbly through the water after them. Floki waited for him to catch up and continued. "One night, when I can think again, I lie watching him at his prayers, because I do not understand him, and he looks up and sees me. 'I have brought a wounded lion into my house,' he says, 'and now it grows stronger and remembers I am prey.' And he laughs! They are like Northmen. They laugh at death." He walked a little farther, with Gil stumbling to keep up, and then said suddenly, "I ask him; why does he do this? Why is he so kind to me? He answers, 'My Master walks the roads of the world. I shelter Him in you.'"

Floki stopped walking. He rested his hand gently on the horse's big muzzle, then looked directly at Gil. "I know who his Master is," he said. "And I know who is in me. So, I show him my hands. I show him my sword. I tell him, in these hands, this sword has killed thirty men. I have burned homesteads and robbed their silver and driven their people into the snow. I have lain with an old man's wife and brought her death as surely as by my sword." He paused quietly and then continued, "He listens, and he says, 'I shelter Him in you.'" Floki shrugged and set out again into the forest. "He is mad, Warrior," he said, over his shoulder. "Or I am."

They went on, and Gil lost all track of time in his exhaustion and all sense of anything but the ache in his feet, the freezing cold, and a seething resentment of Floki's relentless pace. Then he was struck suddenly with a shame as fierce as his illogical anger. Floki had rescued him from a very dangerous place and was doing all this to keep him safe. He stumbled on, with resentment and gratitude warring within him until, at last, and quite suddenly, the Northman stopped. "This is a very long day," he said calmly. "And I have had enough of it." He pointed ahead to a break in the forest. "We will go there. The good beast may graze and we may sleep."

He led the way, down toward the starlit clearing and Gil stumbled eagerly after. At the edge of the clearing grew a hazel thicket and Floki stopped there. He released the leather girth holding the sheepskin on the horse's back and untied the bedroll slung over its withers and piled both on the ground. Then he un-looped the hemp rope that had served as reins and sent Gil to tether the horse in the meadow, while he attacked the hazel thicket with the little axe he wore at his belt.

When Gil returned, Floki had already fashioned a lean-to frame of hazel saplings between two trees. He turned his attention to hacking off pine boughs to cover it, and Gil, thrilled with the prospect of shelter, joined him, tearing off branches with his hands. "He does not want me to leave," Floki took up his story again, as he worked. "He says it is too soon, and he is probably right. But there is more. This is a strange thing, Warrior. I like this old man. And he likes me. He calls me 'his Lion.' He shows me his books. He shows me the letters and what they mean." Floki paused, stripping feathery branches off a gnarled bough. "Do you do this thing?" he said abruptly.

"What? Read?" Gil heard the incredulity in his own voice, and said, more cautiously, "Most men read in Tir nan Og."

"A kingdom of scholars," Floki said, impressed. He laid some more branches on the roof of their lean-to. "I am not a scholar," he said, without emotion. "But I see this is maybe not difficult. They are patterns, these letters. I read the stars, and the winds, and the Northmen's runes. I see those patterns. I can see these." He stopped working a moment and said, suddenly excited, "Warrior, I see something else. I see that when he is with these books, he talks with men who are not there. Dead men. Men who are dead a thousand years. This is a wonder, Warrior." A shiver went down Gil's back, and he nodded hastily and busied himself piling branches onto the lean-to. Floki brought more pine boughs and began stripping those.

"One day, when I am stronger," he said, "We sit in the winter sun, outside his house, watching an eagle circling over the loch. This is another strange thing, this eagle. For I have seen it come to him, a wild bird, and alight, like a hawk on his arm. But these men have a way with animals. Aidan, too. So, I am not surprised. But this day, as I watch it, I can see across the loch to this place," he touched a tree as if it itself were Camelot, "And my eyes stray to it. 'Who is she, Lion?' he asks. And I am amazed he reads my thoughts. But he laughs. 'A young man in love has no secrets,' he says, 'Be he monk or Viking.'"

Floki smiled. "I did not know this happens to monks," he said. His smile faded slowly. "You know, Warrior," he said, puzzled, "I am happy there, with his kindness and his books. And even his prayers which soothe my mind." He shrugged. "But I have sixty Vikings, crowding his beasts from their barns and his monks from their choir. And all the while, their sword hands restless for Ireland. So, we make ready to leave. He makes me promise I will not sleep in the rain. And I will rest if I have fever." He laughed softly. "I think he does not know a Northman's life. But he is kind."

Floki went back, then, to where they had first stopped and collected the bedroll and the sheepskin. "So then, Warrior," he said when he returned, "there is a problem." Gil looked up, curiously, from within the shelter which he was hastily lining with pine boughs to sleep on. "I am a Northman," Floki said. "My promises are like snow in spring. And my honor shines as feebly as the stars on Saint John's Eve. But I pay my debts. And to this man, I owe the greatest of debts. I owe my life. Perhaps, too, the lives of some among my crew. I owe my ship. I owe everything." He stood, holding the sheepskin and bedroll still, his head bowed. "I offer him gold," he said solemnly. "He will not take it. I offer him the service of my sword."

Gil looked up, startled. "You what?"

"I offer my sword."

"How?" Gil said. Floki looked baffled. "How. Show me how."

Floki shook his head, but he dropped the bedding inside the shelter and quickly drew his sword and then extended it on his palms. "The way a man does, Warrior, when he offers protection," he said, and with another baffled shake of his head, he sheathed the sword.

Gil nodded dully and felt shame creep into his soul and with it a bitter anger toward the Golden Knight and his trickery, itself a sword to divide a friendship. "I see," he said quietly.

"I would lay my protection over his house as I lay it over Cille Aidan."

"You do?" Gil cried.

"Of course. And few men in the North would challenge it.

But he refuses. As would Aidan," he said, "if he knew. Which he does not." He grinned cheerfully and leaned against one of the trees supporting the shelter. "So, I am penniless before them. I have nothing else. And he sees how this troubles me. So, he says to me, there is one thing I can do for him. One thing I can bring him to repay the debt. But he warns me it is very dangerous, and I might die in the effort.

"This I do not mind, for this is exactly what I owe him. Besides, when he tells me what it is, I do not expect to die, for it is but a foolishness. A quest. Indeed, a quest as foolish as yours." He smiled wearily. "I tell you of the eagle. So now, the old man says to me, the eagle has a nest that it flies to, high on the cliffs beyond the loch. And it lines this nest with the down from beneath its feathers." He laughed, "As you line our nest here. This is what he wants. He will use it in his medicines. Very rare. Very dangerous to collect, high on the cliffs. That does not worry me. I climb the rock cliffs of the High Island. But, whatever. He wants this. And I agree. Though he is lying to me, Warrior."

"He is?"

"They do not make medicines like this. I know this. They grow their medicines in their garden. Herbs, bitter and sweet. Some they bring from far countries. The Holy Land, even. He reads their uses in his books, in Latin and Greek." He laughed. "I hear of these feathers and I hear Bjorn with his dragon charms. He lies to me."

"Why?"

Floki shrugged. "When I see where the eagle flies, I think maybe this is yet another gift from him, because it brings me closer to my lass. Or maybe he just wishes to make a fool of me. I do not mind. For this man, I am willing to be a fool. So," he said, turning to the meadow where the beast grazed like a great, earth-bound cloud, "he gives me that enormous animal to ride and we load it aboard *Silver Dragon*, and we sail again to the Falls of the Fugitive, and make again our landfall there.

"And I unload the great beast and set Erling at my helm and release my cousin from his promise and say to them, go, seek out Irish shores. But they stay. Indeed, they wish to accompany me, but the good man said, clearly, I must go alone. Still, they will not leave me. And so, the longships lie yet beneath the Falls of the Fugitive, awaiting my return."

Gil smiled. "Your loyal snakes," he said.

Floki was quiet. Then he repeated after Gil, in the quietest of voices, "My loyal snakes." Gil turned away and then suddenly there was a flash of movement in the dim light and something caught at the back of his neck like a hawk's talons, clutching his hair and jerking his head back so hard he felt his neck would snap. "That is twice you cross me, Warrior," Floki's voice growled beside his ear. "What? You fear my wraith and not me? That is very stupid." The iron fingers closed tighter and wrenched his head back again. "Do not grow too bold with me, Warrior. Never. Ever." Floki yanked his head back one more time, then thrust him forward so hard that he tripped and sprawled over their new laid bedding. He looked down at Gil in silence for a long moment, then turned his back and walked off into the night.

Gil got up on his knees and twisted his neck back and forth, to see if it still worked. Then he sat back against the side of the shelter, wrapped his cloak around himself, and shivered wearily. He peered into the night and wondered if the Northman would just take the horse and abandon him. But then Floki returned, with a bundle of dry wood in his arms. He dropped the wood at the entrance of the shelter and crawled in beside Gil. "Light a fire, Warrior," he said amiably. "I have had enough of this cold." Gil looked up, startled. "No, it is not wise," Floki said. "But we do it. And I deal with what comes."

Gil crept warily around him, arranged the kindling carefully and lit it with the fire striker Erling had given him. Ruddy brightness filled the lean-to and he stretched his bruised hands gratefully toward it, soaking up the heat. "Come," Floki said. "Eat." Gil looked over his shoulder and saw bannocks and cheese and apples spread out on a cloth on top of the sheepskin. "It is but monkish food," Floki said with a smile. "No venison, salted, or sweet."

Gil grinned weakly. "I never want to see venison again," he said. Cautiously, he reached out and took a small portion of bannock.

"No," Floki pushed the rest toward him. "This is yours. I eat better, this day, than you." Gil shook his head, but again he didn't dare argue. He wondered for a moment if Floki's generosity was a kind of apology. But then he realized it wasn't, because Floki wasn't the slightest bit sorry. Gil ate in silence, grimly determined not to break any rules again. Floki leaned against the other wall of the shelter, wrapped in the thick fur of his cloak. Gil saw in the light of the flames that his face was not just lean, but gaunt from illness.

"So, Warrior," he said, as if nothing had interrupted his story. "I ride up beyond the great falls and follow this eagle. And if the old man makes a fool of me, then the eagle determines to do so twice over, for it circles and flies, circles and flies, far beyond the cliffs. Ever southward, until I wonder, does it make its nest among the Saxons or indeed the Saracens? But I ride on, on this great mountain of a horse, my eyes always on the sky. And then, I see another bird. A bird I know. A hawk, a sparrow hawk, and as pretty a creature as one can find. So, I whistle and she stoops to me, out of the sky."

"Rachel!" Gil cried.

"Indeed." Floki smiled, "And the pretty thing alights upon my arm, most enchantingly. But since we would talk, I offer her the circle of my sword belt and she flies through it and takes her human form. And thus, she rides a while before me, upon the great horse. Which I enjoy very much," he said, smiling again.

"And so, I learn all that has become of you, and how that dunderhead Palamedes abandoned you, just as I said he would. And how you found refuge among the holy sisters, in the company of our less than holy queen. And more," Floki said, with a broader smile. "I hear you find a lady of your own. This is true?" Gil nodded warily. But Floki grinned and slapped his shoulder with a friendly hand. "And is she fair, Warrior? 'The fairest of the fair?' Or did the bard lie?"

Gil set down the bannock he was chewing and looked the Northman squarely in the eye. "The bard lied," he said.

Floki looked stricken. "Oh, Warrior," he whispered, "I am sorry." And so genuine seemed his regret that Gil burst out laughing.

"She is fair!" he said. "So fair that no bard could ever describe her!" He stopped awkwardly, feeling his face go red.

"Ah, Warrior," Floki smiled gently. "I tease you. Even the lovely Rachel says she is fair and thus I know she is good as well as fair, because women begrudge beauty if it does not reflect the soul." He leaned back against the wall, his eyes merry, but his voice became solemn. "And is it true, Warrior, that you stay so long in the lady's bedchamber that you barely escape her betrothed and your friends despair for your life?"

Gil hung his head. *Thanks a lot, Rachel.* "It's true."

But Floki only laughed with glee and cuffed his head with affection. "Oh, Warrior. If you could know, how many walls I have clambered down, from how many windows, made my exit! With, like as not, a husband on my heels!" He laughed again. "Had I ale, I would drink to your success!"

Gil grinned uncomfortably. *Please, please,* he thought. *Don't anybody ever tell him about Cat.*

"Then," Floki's expression changed, "She tells me how you go, as your Change-Thing, to the walled forest, and how you do not return. And this time, they all fear the worst. And then word comes from the Usurper's court that you are captured and held in Merlin's Tower. And so, she seeks that place, from the sky. And I send her back, lest her wings are clipped before they are fully grown, and I come for you, myself."

Gil nodded. "Thank you," he said. Floki looked startled, but he bowed his head graciously and accepted the courtesy.

"I am happy for you Warrior," he said. "There is no sweeter thing than love. It is what a man lives for. Sweeter even than battle." He leaned back and closed his eyes. "Men tire of battle," he said. "No man ever tires of love."

He laughed quietly. "When I lie sick in the good man's house, Bjorn comes again with my sword. He is the guardian of my Viking soul, Bjorn, and will not have me barred from the Hall of the Slain, the resting place of our fathers. But does he think to ask, do I want to go there? No. Nor does he think what this thing of swords says to my good Christian host, who already gives me his own rites. So, I lie between two Heavens, with Bjorn on one side and the good father on the other." He laughed again. "I would not think my soul worth the battle." He smiled without opening his eyes. "In that place of Bjorn's, each day is spent in furious fighting; each night, drinking in the ale house. And then, next day, all the slain warriors are alive again, and so it continues."

"Forever?" Gil asked, chewing heartily on a great hunk of monkish cheese, and thinking Bjorn's heaven sounded pretty much like anyone else's hell.

Floki nodded. "Fighting all day. Drinking all night. Waking every morning with a head that's been kicked by a horse and seeing Bjorn." He laughed softly. "Oh, Warrior. There's a fate. No. It does not last forever. In the end, even the gods die and there is a mighty battle when that happens, at the end of time. I might enjoy that. But not the waiting for it. I have no patience."

He smiled again, on the edge of sleep. "Bjorn is very stupid," he said, and, as if sensing Gil's objection, said, "Oh, he is, Warrior. When I have ten winters, I think better than Bjorn. But he is strong. Worth two men on the oar. Three in battle. He is loyal when none will be. But he is stupid." He was quiet for a while and then said, "Sometimes, I think it would be good if I were like Bjorn."

Gil finished the last apple and looked in amazement at Floki. "Why?"

"Because he suits this life, and already I tire of it. Life has seasons. For Bjorn, it is always summer. But I feel the seasons change. I weary of winter strands and making my bed amongst warriors." He paused and then said, "I want to wake beside a woman. I want to take sons to sea."

Gil looked up, surprised at the sad way he said it. "But you can do that," he said cautiously. "I mean, when you find a woman you want to marry."

"I have found the woman I will marry." Floki opened his eyes and looked straight at Gil. The wistful sadness had vanished, replaced by an unwavering conviction.

Gil thought very carefully before he spoke next. "If," he said, pretending to be busy gathering the last crumbs of his supper, "that woman came from far, far away, and if she married you, she'd never be able to go home again, never see her family, her friends...."

"Why would that be? Warrior, I have sailed every coast of these islands. I have sailed to Spain and the Great Pillars and I would have sailed beyond them if the men with me were not lamenting for their harvests and their women. I will take her to her kinsmen if she so wishes." Gil shook his head. Floki said bluntly, "I do not believe in this sea I cannot sail."

Defeated, Gil returned his attention to his meal, finishing the last bannock and a few crumbs of cheese. He paused while he rolled up the cloth and then said as casually as he could, "What if this woman doesn't want to marry you? What if she doesn't, you know, doesn't love you?"

"Why would she not love me?" Floki sounded utterly incredulous.

Gil looked quickly away but was still caught out by a treacherous giggle.

"Warrior," Floki said calmly. "I have killed men who laughed at me." Gil shook his head frantically. "I am young," Floki said. "I am strong. I am handsome. Women have enjoyed me." He smiled a small, quirky smile. "I have made my name known from the Northlands to Ireland, from Pentland to Northumbria! Through all the Kingdom of the Isles, and beyond." He paused to see Gil's reaction and then said almost angrily, "I am not a poor man, Warrior. I have gold and land." He paused again and then said with sudden intensity, "The day comes when I ride to an earl's hall, in the ermine cloak of an earl."

He stopped and shook his head and suddenly looked so confused that Gil leaned forward and touched his arm. "Are you okay?" he said.

"I am well," Floki said quietly. He looked past Gil's shoulder, into empty space. Then he said slowly, "Words come to me sometimes, words that I do not summon. Do you understand?" Gil didn't, but he nodded and then suddenly he remembered seeing that same look of confusion in Floki's eyes, the day he made his prophesy of Aidan's fate. Floki shrugged. "She would do well to marry me." He seemed content to take Gil's silence for agreement. He leaned back against the pine boughs and closed his eyes again. "Have you eaten enough, Warrior?" he said.

"I've eaten it all."

Floki laughed. Then he opened his eyes and shook off sleep like a dog shaking off rain. "Good. Rest now, Warrior. There is little left of this night. I will watch."

It was what Gil wanted to do more than anything on earth. Just the thought of lying flat was bliss. But it was also unfair and, forcing himself a little, he said, "You ate better, today than me. Well, I slept better. I slept in the Merlin's Tower while you were riding to rescue me. I'll watch first."

Floki started to argue; then abruptly surrendered. "Warrior, I doubt sleeping beside your unfortunate companion gave you much rest. But I thank you." He looked out past the embers of the fire, at the night, which was as black and star-filled as ever. "It cannot be far from dawn. Wake me when the sky greys. I will watch then." He stretched out gratefully on the ground and spread his fur cloak out over himself, then flipped an edge of it toward Gil. "Warm yourself," he said, adding sleepily, "though there is another from Tir nan Og I would far rather shared my bedding."

"Glad to hear it," Gil muttered, under his breath.

Floki grinned and then reached up and touched their pine bough roof. "See, old man," he murmured, "I do not sleep in the rain."

Gil sat up against the wall and pulled the fur cloak over his knees, luxuriating in its warmth. He stared into the black night, proud to be trusted and determined to be worthy of it. Alone in the darkness, he began to think about tomorrow and what they would do. Dared they go back to the mews? And what chance, now, of entering the Forest of Pentecost? Would the Knight now leave the chapel unguarded, even at Candlemas? What of Janetta, he thought wildly? How could he reach her, if the mews was closed to him? Worries crowded his mind so much that he was sure that had he tried to sleep, he would have failed.

Outside, the blackness slowly turned to deep blue and then grey, and when it was light enough to see the shape of the great horse grazing in the clearing, he knew it was time to wake Floki. But he was now so awake and Floki slept so soundly beside him, that it seemed pointless. He decided he'd wait until sunrise; another half hour would make no difference.

Then, somehow, the next thing he was aware of was not light, but sound; a voice saying quietly, "Get up." Gil started, jerking upright from his slouch against the lean-to wall. For an awful moment, he thought he had fallen asleep and was dreaming again his meeting with Floki in the tower. Then, in an even more awful moment, he realized he was not dreaming, but he had slept indeed.

Outside was no grey dawn, but full, sunlit morning. And the voice was not Floki's, but the voice of the armored man on horseback looking down on them both, steel-tipped lance in hand.

CHAPTER THIRTEEN

Gil stared up at the shadowy figure looming above him, mortified that he had made the same awful mistake, twice in a row. "Get up," the voice said again. Gil stiffened to rise.

"Do not move, Warrior."

Gil turned and saw that Floki, though lying utterly still beside him, was very awake, his eyes intent on the mounted man. Gil's shame doubled. "I'm sorry," he mumbled miserably. "I just...."

"You are young," Floki said, without looking at him. "The young need sleep." His voice was calm and without rancor.

"Do not touch the sword," the armored man said suddenly, and Gil realized Floki had been assessing the distance to his sword belt. The mounted knight thrust forward with his lance, hooked the belt with its tip, and flung it out of reach. "Get up," he said again, speaking not to Gil at all, but to Floki. "I have no quarrel with you, Viking. I have come for the boy. Get up and leave us."

Floki raised himself on one elbow and paused, as if the effort was more than he would manage. Then, very slowly, he sat up, and again paused, as if to rest. Gil looked at him with concern and the mounted man leaned forward on his horse, watching warily. The sunlight glinted on his helm, but his eyes were in shadow. Floki got to his knees, laying the fur cloak aside, and crawled out of the lean-to. "Go," the knight ordered. "Take your horse and go. I have no quarrel with you," he said again. Floki climbed stiffly to his feet, one hand on the lean-to for support. He stepped away from the shelter and staggered awkwardly. The knight leaned closer and then said sharply, "You are drunk early, Viking."

"He's not drunk," Gil said angrily, "He's sick. Leave him alone."

Stumbling clumsily, Floki turned his back to the intruder and rested both hands on the ridgepole of their shelter, as if he would fall without it. But then his eyes met Gil's and Gil saw they were sparkling with amusement, and suddenly he remembered the Northman's play-acting with the Viking boys, aboard *Silver Dragon*. Floki grinned and whispered, "Cover your head." Then his hands closed on the ridgepole and he spun around, wrenching the hazel sapling free. Gil ducked under a cascade of pine boughs and thrust them aside in time to see the sapling sweep the stunned knight's lance from his grasp.

The knight's grey charger reared and whinnied and before he regained control, Floki had crossed the distance between them. The man's gauntleted hand flew to his sword, but Floki was upon him. Gripping the cantle of his saddle, he jumped and swung himself up behind the knight, as once he had done with Palamedes. Then, suddenly, he was no longer playing. He wrapped his arm around the knight's neck as if to throttle him, and then flung himself backward off the rearing animal, dragging his half-strangled opponent with him. Both hit the ground with a bone-jarring thud, but Floki, unencumbered by armor, was on his feet before the other could move. Gil scrambled out of the shelter, seized the Northman's sword belt, and flung it to him.

"Stay clear, Warrior," Floki said quietly. He drew the sword with his left hand, then caught up his battered shield from beside the ruined shelter, not once taking his eyes from his opponent. The knight staggered to his feet and drew his own sword. Floki bowed his head formally and grinned. "You have a quarrel with me now."

The knight stepped to one side, studying the Northman warily, and then raised his own shield. Gil stared at its painted device in astonishment. "No, Floki!" he shouted. "Don't fight him!"

"And why would I deny myself that pleasure?" Floki's eyes never left the knight.

"Because it's Lance'lot!" Gil cried. He pointed frantically at the knight's shield, where the Green Tree of Caledon shone in the dappled forest sun. "He's on our side!"

Floki smiled. "Like Sir Owain," he said and suddenly he lunged forward. The knight flung up his shield and Floki's sword, flashing in a deadly arc, slashed deep into the painted tree.

Lance'lot staggered, but caught his balance and stepped back, still not raising his own weapon. "You wear no armor," he said. His voice was soft and sad and somehow dimly familiar to Gil, like a voice in a dream. "We are not fairly matched."

Floki shrugged. "I travel light. And that is my concern, not yours."

Lance'lot sighed, "So be it. I regret this, Viking. It was not my intention to kill you."

Floki lowered his sword until the tip of the blade brushed the ground and he looked heavenward. "Another like Palamedes!" He returned his gaze to the other's face. "If you will kill a man, do him the courtesy of enjoying it." Then he raised the sword again and said quietly, "But cease regretting. You will not kill me and you may be sorry you tried." He leapt forward again and swung the sword at Lance'lot's helm, but this time his blade, parried expertly by the knight, clashed on steel. Floki gave a happy nod of approval, as to a newly obedient child.

He backed away across the forest floor, ducking behind trees, circling his opponent, who turned to face him, just as the Northman danced back the other way. Lance'lot turned again. Floki dashed close, exchanged a quick flurry of sword strokes with the knight, and danced away. Lance'lot followed, always a little slower and always a little behind. The knight was skilled and strong, but he was fighting hard and the Northman was playing. The few hours' sleep were all the rest he had needed, and he was, again, as lithe and fiercely graceful as the lion the Ab had named him. And Lance'lot, the great knight of Camelot, was no longer young.

Hindered by his chainmail and burdened by his added years, he turned and turned again to face his opponent. Like a great hunted stag, Gil though sadly, noble and doomed. *Please,* he begged Floki silently, *Let him go. He's not our enemy.* But he knew it was hopeless. The knight's fate was sealed the moment he'd turned his lance on the Northman sleeping on the forest floor.

Floki began to close on him, pursuing him harder, exchanging longer flurries of blows and retreating less and less. The laughter was gone from his eyes and his concentration was absolute. A quick slash of Lance'lot's sword tore a rent in his tunic, reminding Gil how dangerous a game he played, fighting with his weaker hand, un-armored before bare steel.

Floki seemed to remember too. He ceased his playful dancing and stood still, eyeing his opponent in silence. Lance'lot paused as well, breathing hard, sword and shield ready. And then with insolent calm, Floki flung his own shield aside, joined both hands on the hilt of his sword and swung a single mighty blow that swept the other's weapon from his hands.

Lance'lot staggered and reeled back from the force of the clash, and Floki pounced. Forcing the knight down to his knees. His sword arm around his throat, he seized Lance'lot's helm, pulled it free, and tossed it aside. Then, knotting his fingers in the knight's hair, he jerked his head back, laid the gleaming steel of his sword once against his throat, then raised it to strike the last blow.

Gil's eyes fell on the face of the defeated knight, exhausted and yet quietly fearless, and the shock of what he saw hit him like a physical blow. His eyes glued to the face, he mouthed words that came out silent, like in a dream. The knight's eyes were blue and weary and accepting, as if death was a reasonable end to a winter morning. Then, his gaze met Gil's and he gave a small, sad shake of his head, cut short by the Northman's restraining hand.

"If you would die cleanly," Floki said, "do not move." He raised his blade higher, but then Gil at last found his voice.

"No! No!" he screamed, with such agonized desperation that the Northman stilled his hand. "Don't, Floki!" Gil cried. "Don't kill him!"

Floki turned and said gently, "Go, Warrior. Go by the horse. Do not watch."

Gil shook his head frantically. "You can't! You can't!" His

throat contorted weirdly and he felt darkness swirling around him. "Please. He's my grandfather," Gil whispered at last. He slipped to his knees and dropped his dizzy head into his hands, and then slowly raised his eyes to the Northman again.

"He is *what*?" Floki looked down at Gil as if he'd gone mad.

But then Lance'lot himself spoke, in a voice of infinite sadness. "God curse this place. It has taken half my life."

"Your grandfather?" said Floki.

Gil stared at the kneeling knight and then slowly shook his head. "No. He's not. He's...."

"Good." Floki lifted the sword again.

"My father!" Gil cried. "He's my father!"

Floki lowered the sword. "Warrior," he said bleakly, "you try my patience. First, he is Lance'lot. Then, your grandfather! And now, your father!" He shook his head. "Most men know the difference. Besides," he said suddenly, turning the sword so its point faced Gil, "you tell me your father is dead." His eyes took on a light of cold menace. "Do you lie to me, Warrior?"

Gil shook his head, helplessly. But then Lance'lot spoke again. "He does not lie. He is my son. And it is no doubt true he thought me dead."

Gil stared at the strange yet familiar face, closer indeed to his grandfather's than his father's. "You drowned," he said. "And we couldn't find you. I dreamt about your bones." He sobbed suddenly and, turning away from both men, buried his face in his hands.

A hand fell on his shoulder, heavy in its steel gauntlet, and he realized Floki had released the defeated knight, that he might comfort him. He looked up into the sad blue eyes set into a lined and weathered face. "Gil?" the man said gently.

Gil pulled away and the sad eyes looked even sadder. "Who are you?" he whispered. "You don't look like you did. You don't sound like you did."

"Twenty-two years," the knight said. He crouched down and then took off both gauntlets and reached out to Gil. Gil saw that the tip of his right forefinger was missing and the brown skin of both hands was crossed with white scars. "I have been in this world since before that man was born," he shrugged his shoulder toward Floki. "Two whole years before," he added. "And this is a world in which time is not kind."

He lowered his head as he said the last and Gil saw his hair was grey, where it once had been brown, and his shoulders, though powerful beneath his chain hauberk, were bowed. Then he saw one thing that united the man before him with the man he had known. On the ring finger of his left hand was a plain band of gold set into a band of silver; a wedding ring, a perfect match to the one on his mother's hand. "Mom's ring," he whispered. The knight looked down on it, and then up at Gil and smiled almost shyly.

"Does she still wear hers?" he said. Gil bit his lip, nodding vigorously and then flung his arms around the knight's neck and buried his face in his long, tangled hair.

When at last Gil looked up, he saw Floki watching him with a gentleness he would not have imagined he possessed. "This is my father," he said, his hand still on the knight's shoulder. Floki nodded and the knight looked carefully at him but neither of them looked in a hurry to be introduced. Gil turned back to his father, laughing in happiness and confusion. "Okay, the twenty years. I know about that. Time is different. But why," he asked, shaking his head, "Why are you pretending to be Lance'lot?" He laughed again, giddily, but his father did not laugh back and Floki turned his head carefully and looked away.

"I do not pretend."

"But the shield. The Green Tree of Caledon! And your horse." Gil pointed to the grey charger, grazing quietly, its green trappings fluttering as it moved. "You wear his colors!"

Gil's father nodded gravely, looking at the horse and the shield as if he had never seen them before. "I wear his colors," he repeated. Then he said, "I wear my colors, Gil." When he looked back at Gil his eyes were somber. "Lance-Laurent," he said.

"What?" Gil blinked.

"It is what I am called," his father said simply. "Lance-Laurent. Lance'lot." He turned and looked down at the forest floor where his fallen lance lay crossed with Floki's hazel sapling. "I was once famed for my skill with that weapon," he said. Then he looked up at Floki and added, "Perhaps I need a new name, now that this young heathen undoes my reputation." He smiled wryly and gave the Northman a small nod of respect.

Gil drew back and got quickly to his feet. As the meaning of what his father said sank in, he stepped abruptly away from him and closer to Floki. "Don't call him that," he said.

"Warrior," Floki said gently, "it is not far from the truth."

"I don't care!" Gil shouted. His eyes were fixed on his father's face and in his heart a black anger arose. "Don't call him that," he said again. "He's my friend."

"I know exactly who he is," the knight said quietly.

"And I know exactly who you are!" Gil shouted. "Lance'lot! Lance'lot who stole King Arthur's wife and ruined Camelot! It's all because of you. All the fighting and the misery and the poverty and the Golden Knight burning Hy and chaining people in towers...all of it. It's all your fault!" His father stared up at him sorrowfully but said nothing. Gil glared back in disgust and turned away, his whole body shaking with fury and shame. Then he looked back and said coldly, "And you know what? Maybe none of that matters because this is the past and everyone here is dead. But you betrayed my mother! While she was crying every night, you were with Guinevere." He took a deep breath and said bitterly, "And you still are." Lance'lot shook his head, but Gil shouted, "I saw you! At the convent! Staring up at her window!" He looked up at the sky and made a dumb romantic face and then laughed. "You bastard."

"Enough!" Floki suddenly strode between them, raised one hand, and gave Gil a quick, light slap that somehow still sent him sprawling.

"Leave my son alone!" Lance'lot shouted. He started to rise, but Floki whirled, drew his sword again and pointed the tip at his throat.

"Raise your hand to me and I finish you." He turned back to Gil. "Respect your father," he said.

Gil stared, astounded. "Me?" he said. "You were going to kill him!"

Lance'lot laughed softly. "He's a Viking, Gil. Don't expect logic."

Floki ignored him. "He's not *my* father," he said to Gil.

"No!" Gil said angrily, climbing to his feet and rubbing his stinging cheek. "He's my father and it's nothing to do...." he stopped.

Floki was standing very still with the point of his sword resting on the ground between Gil and Lance'lot, as if he couldn't decide who to use it on first. "Three times you cross me, Warrior?" Gil shook his head swiftly. "A man who does not respect his father is worthless," Floki said, and before Gil could argue, he raised his hand suddenly and whispered, "silence."

In the quiet that followed, Gil heard a sound that raised phantom Cat hackles, down his back. "Hounds," said Lance'lot.

"Our noble friend is hunting," Floki said. "And not the deer." Sheathing his sword, he turned back to Gil. "Bring the good beast, Warrior. We will debate the duties of sons at another time."

Gil ran and un-tethered the horse and held it while Floki saddled it again with the sheepskin, draped the bedroll over its neck, and looped the hemp rope into reins. Lance'lot's grey charger whickered a greeting as the knight returned his fallen lance to its fewter and pulled on his gauntlets and helm. "Come with me," he said. "I have shelter they will not find."

Floki wrapped his fur cloak around himself and slung his shield over his shoulder, assessing Lance'lot warily as he did. Then he said, abruptly, "Go with him, Warrior. He knows the forest. And I trust," he added, laying his hand on his sword hilt, "he will not betray his own kin. Whatever he has done before this."

Lance'lot's expression darkened, but he said nothing. Ignoring Floki, he extended his hand to Gil. Gil looked up uncertainly at the Northman. "What about you?"

Floki's eyes took on the sparkle they held before battle. "I will lead them a dance through these hills fit for a king's wedding," he said.

Lance'lot inclined his head gravely. "You would be safer with me."

"But I will have more fun with them."

Lance'lot nodded and gave him a slight smile. "Then do

not let them catch you," he said. "They might teach you some lessons in barbarity. Heathen though you are."

"They will not catch me." Floki jumped up onto the horse, and turned back to Gil. "Godspeed, Warrior," he said, spinning the animal around.

Gil watched for a moment, then ran forward and caught hold of the sheepskin saddle. "I'll go with you."

"Warrior ...."

"Why not? They won't catch you. So I'll have fun, too."

Floki grinned and looked suddenly to Lance'lot. "Do you see what a Viking I have made of your son?" He cuffed Gil's head. "Go with your father. He is your kin."

Gil shook his head solemnly. "My friends are my kin," he said.

Floki stared down at him in surprised silence. "Ah, Warrior," he said at last, "you cross me yet again. I think I must grow accustomed to insolence." He looked solemn, then suddenly smiled. "Come," he reached his hand down and hauled Gil up behind him. "Ride on," he said to Lance'lot. "I take your safety." And he kicked the horse into a gallop, behind the grey charger.

They rode until the sun was at its highest southern point, Lance'lot and his charger setting a course and a pace that even Floki struggled to follow. "They say he has a Change-Thing," the Northman said, over his shoulder, to Gil. "And that Change-Thing is itself a tree!" He laughed, "And it is so! No natural man can know a forest this well." He ducked his head under a screen of branches as the knight led them through another tortuous thicket.

The baying of the hounds had long ceased behind them, but Lance'lot rode on, intent on his secret refuge. At last, they came to a river, broad and shallow, and Gil looked up with relief to see unbroken blue sky overhead. Without pausing, Lance'lot drove his charger into the fast-flowing water, and then reined him about and trotted, splashing gaily, up the stream.

"And now he turns horse into longship," Floki laughed. "A magical man indeed." But there was admiration in his voice, and Gil felt a small, confused burst of pride. Watching his father on the prancing grey charger, he suddenly thought, *Where did he learn this? Where did he learn to ride a knight's horse and carry a knight's sword? How many years did it take to turn Laurent Lake into Lance'lot? More years than Gil had lived, more even than Floki had lived. What else could have happened in so many years?*

Gil's mind flitted disloyally to Guinevere, sitting cross-legged on the floor of the convent guest house, beautiful and motherly and kind. How many years did it take to fall in love? *Never*, he told himself. *Never*. If I was married to anybody, I'd never fall in love again. No matter how many years. He turned from the sight of the knight and his charger and hid his face in the Northman's cloak.

Abruptly, Lance'lot turned his horse in the river, and galloped for the shore, the beast scrambling eagerly up the bank, as if scenting home. The monkish plough horse followed, and as Lance'lot led them up a narrow steep path beside a tumbling burn, Gil tightened his grip around Floki's waist to keep from sliding off. He raised his gaze to the hillside, searching for some sign of shelter. But he saw none. Then the charger disappeared over a little summit in the rocky path, and when they, too, reached the spot, Gil saw a sudden, unexpected valley open out beneath a cliff-bound corrie. Grassy, with but a scattering of birch trees, it lay hidden from all below, as secret a place as the forest could provide.

Gil sat back on the big horse's rump, looking wonderingly around. They passed a cluster of four-horned sheep and came next to a small garden where a few cabbages yet grew, and then an open stone shelter, filled with hay. And yet, he saw no house, only a bare rock face with a vast dark holly tree growing beside it. But there Lance'lot reined in his charger with the satisfaction of a weary man returning home. He swung down from his saddle and facing Floki and Gil, held out a gracious arm. "Welcome," he said. Then he turned and stepped into the tree. Gil looked in astonishment at the point where he had vanished, and then turned back and looked at Floki. Floki was still staring at the tree.

"Warrior," he said, at last. "Your father is a fine knight and a very fine horseman. But he is also insane." Then he laughed cheerfully and gave Gil a friendly shove. "Down. I would see this tree."

Gil slid from the horse. Warily, he approached the huge tree and pushed aside a heavy, prickly bough. There, hidden behind the tangled grey branches, a small wooden door was set into a wall of turf and stone. The wall itself spanned the gap between two leaning slabs of rock, joining them into one. The door stood half ajar, and looking through it, he saw a dim room, with walls of stone, in which his father already knelt beside a smoldering turf fire. "A cave!" Gil cried. "A cave house!"

Lance'lot rose to his feet. "It was neither until I gave it a roof," he pointed up to the sooty beams and thatch above, "But now it is a little of both. Come in," he said and raised his eyes to Floki, standing yet beyond the door. "Come in, Viking. It is not the splendor of your father's longhouse, but it is all I can offer."

Floki bowed his head and said, "And far better than any longhouse of my own, since I am yet to lay a single stone." He smiled, almost a friendly smile. "But first I would tend my horse. Stay with your father," he said quietly to Gil. "He will have missed you sorely, as fathers do. I will care for both beasts."

Floki stepped back and closed the door, leaving him alone with Lance'lot. Gil looked with admiration around the room which was far more than a cave. Kists and benches lined the walls. Smoked game hung from the rafters. A black cooking pot stood ready to swing over the fire, and a bed covered in deerskins was built into one wall. "It's like a real house!"

Lance'lot smiled. "I have had time enough to make it so. It is many years since I slept under Arthur's roof. And more by far since I slept under my own. He paused and sighed softly. "I know you are grievously angered, and I will not trouble you further, but tell me this, is she well?"

"Mom?" Lance'lot nodded, his eyes filled with yearning. "She's okay," Gil said.

"And," Lance'lot paused and said, "like you...still young?"

"I guess so." He'd never thought about his mother being young. She was just Mom. "It was just a year ago."

"A year!" Lance'lot gasped. "But of course, you yourself... fourteen?" Gil nodded. "And she...oh, to see her," he said. Then he laughed and looked down at his hands. "And me. Rip van Winkle." He laughed again, bitterly

"What?" said Gil.

"A story. A man who sleeps and wakes in another time. Nothing true." He smiled and shook off the sadness. "Come. What's done is done. Let's have a feast for the sake of times past and the time we have now together." He got up and went to one of the kists and brought out wooden platters and piled them with cooked meat and cheese and bannocks from another. "Are you hungry?"

"Starving," Gil grinned. "I'll get Floki. He didn't even have supper last night."

Lance'lot turned from the roasted hare he was dividing and looked at Gil somberly. "You think well of him," he said.

Gil nodded. Lance'lot looked down and continued dismembering the hare. Then he said quickly, "I understand your loyalty. Loyalty is always good." He sighed and added softly, "But even a good thing can betray us."

Gil drew back. "So?" he said warily. "What does that mean?"

"He is a dangerous man, Gil."

Gil hooked his thumb in his sword belt and stepped back. "Really?" he said, shaking his head in mock amazement. Then he laughed and muttered, "Tell me something I don't know, Dad."

"Gil...." Lance'lot's sad blue eyes met his own.

"He's my friend," Gil said angrily. "You don't know him."

"I don't need to, Gil," Lance'lot said quietly. "He's written his name in blood from east to west, for every man to read." He turned away and looked at the fire. "He's a thief and a murderer."

Gil pushed away the plate of food his father had set before him and stood up. "Gil," Lance'lot said. "Listen to me." He reached out a gentle hand.

Gil ignored the hand and stepped away from the fire. "He brought us from Cille Aidan and risked his life for us, and almost lost it. And still came back and rescued me. From Merlin's Tower, Dad! That is not a nice place."

"I know. I've been there. And I was on my way there again, today."

"You were?" Gil stopped, stunned. "For me?" he said warily.

Lance'lot nodded. "As soon as I heard."

Gil fell silent again. Pride and love welled up inside him. But then he shrugged, "It was still Floki who rescued me."

"For which I am greatly in his debt. But it doesn't change who he is."

"No," Gil said. He looked at the soft glow of the fire and wished suddenly and fervently that he could be a real little kid, safe in his father's house. But he knew, now, he would never be that again. "You weren't there, Dad," he said. "I've had to make my own decisions and my own choices. And my own friends. Don't try to turn me against him," he said solemnly. "That's what the Golden Knight tried to do. I don't want it now from you."

He went out then and his father did not stop him. He found Floki inside a wood-fenced pen, spreading hay on the ground before both horses. The charger's saddle and armored trappings, and their sheepskin and bedroll lay outside on the ground. Gil poked at the saddle with his foot. "There's food," he said.

The Northman straightened up and looked at him carefully. "Then I suggest we eat it," he said. "Though I have rarely heard you less interested in your stomach." He climbed over the wooden fence, picked up the bedroll, and tossed it to Gil. "Carry that." Then he heaved the heavy jousting saddle onto his shoulder. "Nor do you sound," he added, "Like a son who has found a long-lost father."

He turned and strode back toward the holly tree. Gil shrugged and trotted after. "I think I've gotten used to not having one," he said.

"He does not please you."

"I don't know him anymore," Gil said. It came out sadder than he'd intended.

Floki laughed and stopped walking for a moment. Shifting the weight of the saddle, he looked down at Gil. "My sixteenth spring," he said, "I helm a longship, first, without Redbeard." He walked on and Gil followed, uncertainly. "I raid the Irish coast, as far as Dublin, and return with treasure to Einar's Holm, wanting nothing more than my father's praise. But he finds fault and quarrel with all I do. And I swear he is a foul-tempered fool and I am better without him." He stopped again and looked down at Gil. "He is not. And I am not."

Gil clutched the bedroll and stared at the ground. "He called you a murderer."

"With good reason. This morning, I am nearly his murderer." He smiled. "That is not what angers you, Warrior. What angers you is your mother."

"And the rest!" Gil cried. "How would you feel if your father brought down Camelot?"

"Very impressed with Redbeard," Floki grinned. "Warrior, do not judge a course you have not sailed." He walked on and said over his shoulder, "Come now. We dine with your father." Floki set the horse's harness down under the shelter of the holly tree. Then, at the door of the cave-house, he stopped suddenly and unbuckled his sword belt and laid down his shield. Gil watched, startled. The only places he'd ever seen the Northman go unarmed were his father's longhouse, or the sanctuary of the church.

"Is that, like, really smart?" he whispered. "I mean, if someone tried to behead me, I might feel kind of grumpy toward them."

Floki regarded him solemnly. "I have no choice, Warrior," he said. "I am his guest. And," he added, "since you are his son, I am your guest, as well." He bowed slightly and Gil wasn't sure he was joking.

"I don't think he likes you," he said carefully.

Floki grinned. "I am certain he does not. Warrior," he laid his hand on Gil's shoulder, "He could have killed me as I slept and saved himself much trouble. But he did not. He is another like Palamedes, with more honor than wisdom." He smiled gently, "Come, my young host, take me into your father's hall. I am perfectly safe."

Gil led the way then, still a little reluctantly. Inside, he found Lance'lot had spread a feast of meat, fish, and fowl, all the forest's bounty. They ate, sitting cross-legged on deerskins around the fire, and Gil found that not only could he face venison again, he was able to eat an awful lot of it. Lance'lot watched him with, at last, a light of happiness in his eyes.

Floki complimented his host on his skills as huntsman and the graciousness of his hospitality, and though the compliments were, Gil knew, a Northman's formality, they served to win a smile from his father. Lulled by the comfort of a warm room and a full stomach, Gil felt ready to sleep. But Floki said, again with formality as at Einar's Holm, "What story will you tell us, sir, of your life in Arthur's kingdom?"

Lance'lot looked startled, but then nodded, as if he was at least familiar with the Northmen's custom of storytelling. When he spoke, he sounded awkward, almost shy. "I guess," he said, "I should tell you how I got here."

Gil sat up, alert, studying his father's face. "It was the whirlpool, wasn't it? The Indian Kettle whirlpool." Lance'lot nodded, and Gil said, "That's how I got here. And that's where we found your kayak."

"What thing is that?" Floki asked and Lance'lot said quickly, "A canoe. A boat. A small boat. For one man."

"One man to row?"

"To paddle. Look." Lance'lot jumped up and went to a corner of his cave-house and brought from behind a stack of turfs, a familiar double-ended kayak paddle, worn by time. Gil stared at it, fascinated. "It came with me," Lance'lot said. "And somehow, in all my journeys, even when I was captured by those..." he looked at Floki and paused, "...by the Northmen," he finished, "even then, I kept it with me. It was my father's and somehow I felt, if I hung onto it, I might somehow still get home." He shrugged, and then handed the kayak paddle to Floki. Floki turned it carefully in his hands.

"This way," Lance'lot said. And taking it back, gave a brief demonstration of its use, which Floki instantly copied perfectly.

Floki grinned suddenly and turned to Gil. "Warrior," he laughed. "We make big one, like this, for Bjorn. Then he rows *Silver Dragon* by himself!" He handed the paddle back to Lance'lot. "I like this. You are clever." And, as Lance'lot returned the paddle to its place and began his story, Gil sensed a tiny flicker of friendship alight between the two men.

"For almost half a year," Lance'lot said, "I thought I was in Labrador. The angle of the sun told me I was somewhere far north. I'd seen paintings…" he paused with a dim confusion in his eyes, "…I'd seen paintings of Labrador."

"This is a land?" Floki said softly to Gil.

Gil nodded. "Like Tir nan Og."

Floki smiled wryly, "Another I cannot sail to?"

Lance'lot abruptly intervened. "Don't bother, Gil. They can't understand. I've tried."

But Floki said, with quiet dignity, "It is true, I am not a scholar; but I know the sea. There is no sea a man cannot sail."

Gil looked warily back at his father. Lance'lot leaned forward suddenly and looked into the Northman's eyes. "Can you sail to Valhöll?" he asked. "Can you sail to the Hall of the Slain?"

Floki shrugged. "If there is such a place, then, no, I cannot sail there." But before Lance'lot could speak again, he said, "What, then, do you tell me? That you come from a land beyond death? But how is it, then, that you live? For, surely, if you come from a land beyond death, it is not ourselves who are dead, but you."

Lance'lot looked at Floki with more respect and nodded gravely. "I could not understand it myself, if it had not happened to me. But it did." He turned his eyes to his son. "I was playing, in the whirlpool, the way we used to, Brian and Crazy Ivan and I. But then suddenly, it caught me. It caught the kayak. I couldn't escape." His eyes glowed with the intensity of the memory. "That silly little eddy. Suddenly it was so strong, and it was pulling me down. I fought to free the kayak, and then I capsized. I dropped out, thinking it would be easy to swim. As it should have been. But then I was under, going down and down, farther and farther, impossibly far. Then suddenly I was lying on the ground and it was dark. I thought I'd hit my head. My helm was gone, so that made sense. I still had the paddle, but my armor …" he paused, "…there was a kind of sea-armor I used to wear. Light, warm. It kept me dry. I've forgotten."

Floki suddenly laughed. "If you remember, tell me what it is. I would like that armor."

"I bet you would," Lance'lot said fervently. "I spent a year on a longship. I know what it's like." He smiled and resumed his story. "I thought I'd lost my memory and travelled north,

somehow. For a long time. Because it was June when it happened
and yet, in the place I woke up, even allowing for it being so far
north, it was clearly autumn." He paused, remembering. "And
it was a total wilderness. A total, barren wilderness.

"I had no clothing, except for my tee shirt and jeans. I was
freezing. The first two nights I slept in a ditch, covered with
branches...anything to keep warm. I knew I had to find help,
people, a town. I could see I was on the coast, with water
everywhere, both fresh and salt. I tried following the shore, but
I came upon a headland, with fierce cliffs, and had to turn back.
The nights were worst. In the day, there was some warmth in
the sun, still, but each day was colder than the last and I knew
it would be colder, still, if it really was Labrador. I had no food
either, of course. But I did have one thing, one precious thing,
without which I know I would have died."

Lance'lot looked at Gil with a fond smile. "I had a knife. A
hunting knife my son had given me at Christ's Mass, the year
before. On the third day, I found a deer carcass, torn apart by
foxes. It was rotten, foul. I dared not eat it. But I forced myself
to skin it with the knife and washed and dried the foul skin in
the sea and the sun, and made myself a kind of cloak. I found
some berries, bitter tasting, but I ate them, anyway, and was
lucky they weren't poisonous. Mushrooms, too, and I was lucky
again. Then I found a fish, trapped in a tide pool, and speared
it with the knife. Without these three things, I would be dead
now, many, many years." He turned briefly to Floki. "I was not
the huntsman I am today," he said simply.

"You learn fast," Floki said.

Lance'lot laughed. "I had to. Then, after a week, I had a
tremendous piece of good fortune. I was still sleeping in my
ditch and even with the deerskin, I knew I would die soon, of
the cold. Each morning, it was harder to wake. I decided, on that
last morning, to search inland. And almost immediately I came
upon the most extraordinary thing. I climbed over a little hill,
and suddenly, before me was a monument."

"The stones!" Gil cried. "The standing stones."

"I thought of Stonehenge," Lance'lot said. "But, of course, it
couldn't be. I would have had to have crossed the Atlantic." He

paused and said to Floki, "The ocean. You call it the Western Sea."

Floki laughed. "In that little boat," he pointed to the kayak paddle, "I think you do not cross the Western Sea."

Lance'lot smiled. "I think not, too." He drew his knees up and clasped his arms around them, leaning back. "Back then, I was so cold, so hungry, I just accepted them. And they led me to something that was, for me, more important. In a little, grassy hollow, just out of sight of the stone ring, I found a kind of dug out cave. Round, covered in grass, but built, constructed, of stone; made by human hands. I crawled inside and wept for joy, just to have shelter. And to touch something another man had touched."

"I set about making it my home," said. "I made a bed of dried ferns and bent all my energy to lighting a fire, now that I had a place out of the wind that blew there so incessantly, off the sea. It took me three days trying. Rubbing stick against stick, since I had no fire-striker. Charring grass, ferns, even sacrificing a corner of my shirt, trying to get something to burn. At last, I succeeded and for the first night in a dozen, slept without shaking with the cold." He closed his eyes, remembering. "Then," he said, "I realized I might actually live.

"I knew there were deer inland and fish in the streams, so I decided to make a spear, using the knife as its point. I cut a sapling, braided grass into a cord, and tied the knife to the wood." He smiled faintly. "Of course, it fell apart every time I used it and I never saw a deer that didn't see me first. But I did spear a fish. And even cooked it." He smiled again, looking around at the bounty of game hanging from his rafters. "The best meal of my life, Gil," he said. "And then," he added, his smile fading, "I found the sheep. It was small, like sheep here are. Brown. With four horns, which seemed very strange. It came to me. I realized it was tame. Lost. And I killed it." He sighed. "I hated killing it. And I did it so badly. It suffered and cried." He stopped in his story, the pain of the long-ago memory still with him.

"You must eat," Floki said gently. "Like any living thing."

Lance'lot was silent. At last he said, "Yes." And after another silence, he said, "That day was the beginning of the end of the man I once was. The man called Laurent Lake. I ate every scrap of that sheep. I scraped the skin, dried it, and made a kind of shirt. I even sewed it, with its sinews, like I'd read somewhere, making a needle from a sliver of bone. I made a bone dish out of its skull." He shivered. "Gruesome. But it worked. And by the time I'd used the last of the sheep, I'd changed. I'd stopped thinking about leaving the place and started thinking about living in it. I made a better spear. Searched for prints and droppings and at least tried to hunt the deer. And I stopped looking at the sky." He paused solemnly. "I wasn't expecting to be rescued anymore."

"But for rescue, surely you look at the sea," said Floki. "Or the land. But the sky?"

Lance'lot shrugged and then looked at Gil, as if for help. "There was something I looked for," he said slowly. "Birds. Great birds. And their tracks. They left tracks in the sky, these great birds." He stared desperately at Gil. "Don't you remember?"

Gil wanted to, because his father looked so sad, but he slowly shook his head. "Is that when you realized where you were?" he asked uncertainly.

Lance'lot smiled. "No. That came with Einar. Einar Hrolfson. Black Einar the Lame."

"Ah," Floki said very softly. He looked troubled. "That man was my grandfather. If you will speak of him, you will speak well. Or not at all."

Lance'lot's eyes met the Northman's and the room fell so quiet that Gil could hear the soft murmur of the flames. "I will speak well of him," Lance'lot said, "because he was a good and noble and courteous man. Whose grandson would do well to emulate him."

Gil looked warily at Floki, but Floki suddenly laughed. "Now, with that, I surely cannot argue," he said. "You are a good huntsman indeed, snaring your prey with words." He bowed, "Tell of my grandfather."

Lance'lot stared into the fire. "I was hunting, that day, near the stone circle. And there, at last, I saw a young hind grazing; and, creeping close, I cast my spear. It missed, as always, and splintered against one of the great stones. When I reached it, the spear head, my knife, was gone. Vanished. I could not find it anywhere. I searched until dusk, weeping like a child, to have lost not just my one, precious tool, but my last tie with home… with my son." Gil touched the knife at his belt wonderingly, as his father continued. "And then as I was about to give up in despair, I heard a voice. I peered into the darkness and saw, standing there, a giant of a man dressed in ancient clothes, carrying a shield and a sword."

He smiled. "Once, long after, when I had learned enough of his language to converse, I asked Einar what he thought that day he found me stumbling among the standing stones, in my rotten deerskin and shirt of ill-tanned sheep. He answered, 'If it smells that bad, living, what will it smell like dead?' He decided he must save me for the sake of his own nose. So, he took me with him to his great longhouse. We came over the hill and there it was, dark beside the starlit sea, the windows glowing with firelight. Just a few miles walk from where I'd felt myself the last man on earth." He fell silent, then laughed quietly. "Poor Einar, bringing me home, stinking like a dead whale, and all the while pouring out my story in a language of which he knew not a word! Sigrid, your grandmother, understood a little." Lance'lot nodded to Floki. "And there was a lovely young girl, Gunnhild, who understood even more."

"My father's sister. Sea-Friend's mother," Floki said to Gil. And to Lance'lot, "Her son, Hakon, my cousin and foster-brother, spent half his youth at Einar's Holm with me. And I, the other half, in Shetland with him." He leant forward, "Surely if you knew Gunnhild, you knew my father, too."

Lance'lot shook his head. "He was at sea, those winter months, and I was gone before he returned." He paused to lay fresh turf on the fire. "They thought me a sailor, shipwrecked. And I thought them?" He shook his head. "I guessed they came from some far land and kept some strange faith that made men dress in clothes from long ago. But they fed me and clothed me and warmed me by their fire. They could not have been kinder. I struggled to learn their language. I knew some German. It helped a little. And Chaucer. Chaucer helped too. I tried to explain where I'd come from. But they could not understand. They spoke of haunted pools and enchanted wells but those things made no sense to me. Then Sigrid cast the runes to read my fate, but that made no sense either."

"What about Aidan?" Gil asked suddenly.

"Aidan was not yet there," Floki said. "I have four winters when Aidan comes from Lindisfarne. Five, when he baptizes Black Einar and his kin."

Lance'lot leaned back on one elbow, studying the young Northman. "Then you are not a heathen," he said, surprised.

Floki laughed. "Not heathen enough to please Bjorn Break-Neck, nor Christian enough to please any other. I am but a Change-Thing in either world." He smiled at Lance'lot, "Tell your story."

Lance'lot stared into the fire. "One day, a longship sailed into the bay. I was alone on the strand. I'd been checking Black Einar's fish pool in a little skin boat, a curragh. It did not occur to me when I saw the dragon prow that I should run. Nor had it occurred to Einar to warn me of something so obvious!" He laughed. "So, I stood like a fool, holding that paddle," he nodded toward it, "watching. And all at once, I understood. I was not a thousand miles from home, but a thousand years. I was shipwrecked, indeed, but on a sea of time. The sea no man can sail."

He sighed, "I stood there, frozen in loneliness while they beached the great ship and leapt ashore. Only when two armed men came running did I realize that I was what they had come for. They grabbed me, tied me, and tossed me aboard. And put out again to sea. It took hardly longer than it has taken for me to tell it. And that was the end of my time at Einar's Holm. I never said goodbye," he smiled sadly. "It's haunted me all these years." He turned to Floki. "He is dead?"

"Drowned. In a storm off Mousa, on his way to a wedding. She died the year after, of grief."

Lance'lot bowed his head. "Were it not for them," he said, "I would have died before you were born. Do you see now, why I had no wish to fight you? Why I feared to do you harm? Though for that," he laughed, "I need not have worried."

Floki answered soberly. "Praise Odin that your son stays my arm! What bitter wrong to take the life my grandfather saved!" They eyed each other carefully, then reached across the fire and clasped each other's hands.

Lance'lot sat back again and continued his story. "I was to be sold as a slave in the Northlands," he said. "And we were headed there. But a great storm came up and two men were swept overboard and lost. They needed more hands on the oars then, and I proved useful." He paused. "I made a good oarsman. In time, they trusted me enough to provide me with a sword and teach me its use. After all, what danger was I against thirty? And where would I go without them?

"I was with them a year. Raiding in Ireland. They permitted me to stay aboard the ship. I had no taste for bloodshed. They presumed I was some kind of holy man, which they respected." He shrugged. "We summered on Bressay, where they had farms. And we crossed, then, to Norway, trading. And on our return, we were caught in another storm, off the coast of Moray, and wrecked. I was a stronger swimmer than any of them. Indeed, many could not swim at all. Only I reached land."

He fell silent, gazing again into the fire. "And so, once more, I was alone. But now, at least, better prepared. I knew the use of sword and bow. I could live off the land, even in winter. I was seven months wandering, and it was a hostile place. I crossed Druim Alban, into the Forest of Caledon. And there, one brilliant autumn day, I again found a rescuer. I met a knight. The first I'd ever seen. A knight of shining reputation and lordly manner, who took it upon himself to guide me and train me and teach me the arts of war. To make of me what he was himself, a knight of Camelot."

Gil stared at his father's face, lit by the flickering flames. "Who was he?" he asked, awed. "What was his name?"

"Jocelyn Guidbairn," said Lance'lot.

Gil felt a shock like cold water. His eyes met Floki's across the turf fire and even Floki looked stunned. "Jocelyn?" Gil whispered, drawing back. "The Golden Knight?"

Lance'lot nodded. "My rescuer, my mentor, my protector. And my betrayer."

"Your betrayer," Gil exploded. "You betrayed...."

"Warrior," Floki said. "We will hear your father." He cast Gil a look that said, *I do not need a sword to deal with you.*

"I trained with his esquires," Lance'lot continued quietly. "Rode with his guards, slept in his hall. I followed him to tournaments among the Saxons and as far as the Northmen's Francia. I became a master of the lance. And when he judged me ready, I rode at his side to Camelot. Seven years had passed since I set foot at Einar's Holm."

"Seven years," Gil whispered.

"Oh, yes." Lance'lot smiled his sad smile. "Ah, Gil," he said then softly, "if you could have seen Camelot then. The beauty of its towers, white against a summer sky. And, as if to enjoy them more, we stopped along the way and set up our pavilion outside the Forest Mews. And we rode to the hunt with the knights and ladies of the court. And there, in the forest, I met a young girl. Sir Jocelyn came riding to me, leading her palfrey beside his charger. Silver and gold, the trappings of the bonnie beast, and silver and gold, her habit, with a wreath of wild roses holding her white veil. Our forest queen." His expression flickered between joy and anguish. "I thought it was a game that they'd crowned her thus, and bowed to her, like subjects. She was a girl, as innocent to look upon as a young nun. But her laugh." he paused. "Her laugh was not a nun's laugh." His eyes slipped from Gil's face to Floki's and the two men both smiled. "I fell in love in an instant," said Lance'lot.

Gil's head jerked back as if he'd been slapped. And yet the image that flashed before his eyes was not the girl in the forest, but Janetta, through a circle of stone.

"Which was, of course," Lance'lot continued gravely, "exactly what Guidbairn wanted. For she was no May-crowned maid, but Guinevere of Camelot. King Arthur's wife. Our queen." He looked into the fire as into the past. "On any chessboard, the most valued piece. And I? Her loyal knight. And Guidbairn's pawn." He stared silently into the flames, then looked up at his guests. "Seven more years passed, before we fell into sin."

Floki smiled his quirky smile. "Then you, sir, are a far more patient man than I." He laughed softly, and even though

Lance'lot did not laugh back, Gil felt the hot blood of outrage in his veins.

Trembling, he got to his feet. "You were married!" he cried. "You were married to my mother." Tears of anger blurred his eyes, but through their mist, he saw Lance'lot slowly shake his head.

"She was widowed," he said. "And so was I."

"No!" Gil shouted. His hands tightened into fists.

"She was a widow for fourteen years. And you were a man. You were twenty-seven." He looked down at his scarred hands. "I had counted every passing day."

"One year," Gil said, his voice breaking. "One. And I wasn't a man. I was a boy trying to be a man. Trying to be you." He spat the words out and turned his back.

Lance'lot stood and reached his hand to Gil's shoulder. Gil jerked away. "Gil, Gil," his father whispered. "How could any man imagine time itself would stand still?"

Gil didn't answer and his father sat wearily down again by the fire. "All I knew was I was here in this place and everyone I had ever known was beyond my reach forever. I was a dead man to them, lost in a world of ghosts." He looked at Floki and shrugged. "Perhaps your pagan fathers were right. Perhaps this is Valhöll and we live among the slain."

Floki shook his head. "There is not enough fighting," he said.

"I hadn't noticed," said Lance'lot, with a trace of a smile. He looked up at Gil. "I knew I could never go home. That you would grow up without a father, and she, live on, without a husband. I hoped…." He paused. "I hoped she'd marry."

"She'd never do that," Gil said bitterly.

"Gil, in fourteen years, it would only be right."

"But it wasn't fourteen years!" Gil cried impotently. "It wasn't."

"I know," his father said. "But only now." He closed his eyes and spoke as softly as a man in a trance. "Just three weeks past," he said, "two days before Epiphany, I rode out to hunt. I followed a great stag, far into the hills. And then, in a snowstorm, I was set upon by a knight. He clipped my wrist with an arrow. And so, we fought. And then he flung his helm aside, and in the blowing snow, I saw him. My son. Not the man of thirty-five who lived in my mind. But the boy, the child, who lived in my heart. And so I turned away and fled, lest I do harm to my own kin." He breathed a soft sigh and opened his eyes and looked from Gil to Floki. "And I remembered Sigrid's prophecy, and at last I understood."

"What said the runes?" Floki asked, curiously.

"That I would be wounded by a son who would right his father's wrongs." He held up his left arm and showed them a small red scar on the outside of his wrist. "But I would never see home, again."

"But you can!" Gil cried. "You can go home. We can both go home. Together. There's a bridge...."

"Not for me," said Lance'lot. Gil stared at him in disbelief and he said, "I'm a dead man, Gil. When you go home, I will be only dust."

"No!" Gil cried. Floki stood suddenly and came beside him.

"Warrior, do you not see?" he said under his breath, "He is become like me between Bjorn and the good father. He is a Change-Thing between two worlds." Gil shook his head fiercely, blinking to hold back the tears. "You said yourself," Floki pursued, "she is young. And he, so old you thought him your grandfather." He smiled sadly. "Sigrid was wise. Wiser than she knew."

"If he loved my mother, he'd come back," Gil whispered.

"He does love her. That is why he will not."

Gil shook his head again and looked down at his father. "That's not the reason," he said aloud. "The reason is Guinevere. I saw you looking up at her window. You won't leave here because you won't leave her."

Lance'lot stared into the fire. "You did see me, but you did not understand what you saw. Will you believe," he said, "that I have not seen her face in seven years?"

Gil shook his head, less certainly. Floki laid a sudden hand on his shoulder. "Silence." The Northman listened and turned to Lance'lot. "Something disturbs the horses. I will see." Gil heard then a thin whinny, from beyond the closed door. He watched as Floki crossed the cave room and laid his hand on the latch. Then suddenly, he ran after. "Stay with your father," the Northman said, but Gil followed him out the door.

In the dusky shadow of the holly branches, Floki knelt to retrieve his sword belt. Strapping it around his waist, he said quietly, "There are worse men, Warrior." Still kneeling, he looked up into Gil's eyes. "He but slew a kingdom," he said. "I slew a lass."

Gil nodded solemnly. But then he said, tightening his own sword belt around his waist, "Let me tend the horses, please. Alone."

Floki got to his feet and regarded him gravely. His eyes troubled, he stepped back toward the door. "Take care, Warrior," he said. Then he went back within Lance'lot's house, and left Gil alone in the gathering night. His head spinning with confusion and anguish, Gil walked quickly to the wood-fenced pen where Floki had left the horses. Both animals trotted back and forth in the winter dusk, whinnying and tossing their heads in excitement. Gil listened within himself and heard an equine voice. *The herd! The herd!*

What herd? he asked. *There isn't any herd.*

But an answering whinny came from a shadowy shape by the hay barn. And in the same instant, a steel-clad arm caught Gil's shoulders in a mighty grip. "Let me go!" Gil cried. He fought wildly to free himself from the dark shape behind him, but then a second mailed arm closed around his body, crushing him in a ring of steel. "Floki!" Gil shouted. "Dad!" But his voice was drowned by a peel of thunderous laughter. Then four more horses appeared out of the darkness, and on their backs, four knights. The four young knights who had formed his guard on the road to Camelot. Gil saw a flicker of firelight through the branches of the holly tree, and then his father emerged with Floki by his side.

"Run!" Gil shouted as the huge arms lifted him off his feet and his captor laughed louder. "There's five of them! Run!"

But neither knight nor Northman ran. They stood calmly side by side while Gil fought for his freedom. Then Lance'lot smiled and held out both hands. "Welcome!" he called cheerfully. "Welcome! A hundred thousand welcomes, noble Sir Palamedes!"

CHAPTER FOURTEEN

Gil twisted frantically in the grip of his captor, and looked up, straight into the gleeful face of the black-bearded Saracen knight. His mind flashed to the vision in Merlin's Tower, and then to his father in the forest. *I have shelter they'll never find. No*, he thought despairingly. *Not unless you tell them the way.* "Run!" he shouted to Floki, as kicking and punching, he wrenched himself free.

"My noble friend...." Palamedes cried, but Gil was already running into the darkness. He ducked around the hay barn and stumbled past the horses' pen, sparking a frenzy of excited whinnying. Pursuing footsteps sounded behind him and he lengthened his stride, plunging insanely up the shadowy valley. Skidding on wet grass, he fell to one knee and scrambled up again. The footsteps grew closer, his pursuer as swift as a hound on his heels. Ahead, the valley ended abruptly in cliffs, looming against a starry sky. He dashed to left and right, hopelessly seeking escape from the closing trap. Then something slammed into the back of his knees and he was down, sprawling face-first in wet bracken. Rolling onto his back, he reached for his sword, but a powerful hand clamped over his own.

"Before you draw steel, know who you fight, Warrior."

"Floki?" Gil peered into the darkness.

"You say run. I run." Floki laughed, and then said gently, "The Saracen plays like a bear, but he means no harm."

Gil shook his head. "He's a traitor," he whispered. "He betrayed us."

"Impossible!" Floki replied instantly. "A blunderer, a blusterer, a songbird and a fool. But noble to the core."

"He's a traitor," Gil repeated. "And so is my father, for leading us here."

Floki drew back and stood up. "On your feet, Warrior," he said coolly. "Your tongue is as swift as your sword hand, this night. I bid you stay both." Not waiting for Gil's answer, he turned his back and walked away.

"He sits at the Golden Knight's table," Gil shouted after him. "I saw him. And the knights he rides with – they were my guards! I saw them all!"

Floki turned back. His eyes glinted in the dim light. "How do you see this?"

"In Merlin's Tower," Gil said. "It has windows. You see into time. Time Past, Time Present, Time Yet to Come." Floki said nothing. "And in Time Present, that's like, now, I saw Palamedes and three of those knights who took me to the tower, feasting and laughing and honoring the Golden Knight." Unnerved by the Northman's silence, he said, "It's real. I saw real things in all the windows. I know I did."

"What saw you in the others?" Floki asked. Gil could see his outline against the dim sky, hand hooked in sword belt, head cocked sideways in suspicion.

Uneasily, he said, "I saw you. I saw you in time past."

Floki laughed quietly. "I do not think I like this tower. There are moments of my life I would not share." He paused and added, "And what did you see?"

"I saw you offering your sword. In service. Like you showed me."

"As indeed I did, at the Field of the Church. And what did you think?" Gil hung his head. "What did you think?" Floki repeated

"That you betrayed us," Gil said miserably.

"And did I?"

"No," Gil whispered.

"Nor did Palamedes. If he sits at the Knight's table, he has good reason. Come, we will find what it is." He laid a friendly hand on Gil's shoulder, but still, Gil hesitated.

"What about the knights?" he asked. "They were my guards."

Floki fell silent. Then, still resting his hand on Gil's shoulder, he said, "Tell me this. Which should the herdsman fear most? The wolf on the hill? Or the wolf within his gates?"

Gil shrugged. "Within his gates, I guess."

"Or at his table. Or beneath his bed. The longhouse of a harsh earl is a whelping lair of wolves. Each ready, always, to bite the hand that feeds it."

"Even though they hunt with him and guard prisoners for him?"

Floki was quiet a long while. Then he said, "Men want to live, Warrior. They make bargains to live. But your father trusts them and I trust your father." He laughed softly, "Traitors do not sleep in forest caves, but on their master's fine linen. As for the others, between Jocelyn Guidbairn and your father, there are as many shades of men as colors of the sea. Some are weak, some are afraid. Some have a love or a child they cannot bear to leave. Some care for nothing but themselves. The world is not made of heroes, Warrior, but of Viking scoundrels, like you and I." He laughed again and tightened his grip on Gil's shoulder. "Now, will you stay on this cold hill? Or take your chances with me?"

"I'll take my chances," Gil smiled ruefully.

"Good," Floki said. "If they fall upon us and hack us to bloody pieces, I will apologize in Valhöll. Presuming the place exists."

"Great," said Gil. "Can't wait."

"Spoken like a true Northman. Now I ask you one other thing. Who showed you the window?"

"Who showed me? The Knight," Gil said. "He tricked me. I know. But what he showed me was real. The windows didn't lie."

"No. But half of the truth is more powerful than any lie." Floki turned Gil toward the distant cave house and then released his grip and strode off down the hill. Over his shoulder he called, "If you do not trust the rune-sayer, then do not trust the runes." A ruddy light flared suddenly ahead and Gil thought fearfully of the burning of Hy. But as they drew nearer, he saw only a single flaming torch, held aloft by one young knight. Dark figures surrounded it, all turned toward themselves, peering into the night. Hands dropped to sword belts as Gil and Floki approached, but Floki called, cheerfully, "A matter with the horses. It is resolved."

"That is well," Lance'lot said. "For we have need of them. Gil saw that he was dressed again in his chainmail and held his gauntlets and helm in his hands. "We ride at once," he finished somberly.

"Tonight?" Gil heard the weary dismay in his own voice.

Floki said, "It is late, sir, and the boy has slept little."

Lance'lot shook his head sadly. He looked old and worn in the flickering light, but oddly peaceful as well. "It would be sweet indeed to shelter him here," he said, "but I cannot. They have raided the Convent of the Grey Sisters. All is changed."

"The Convent!" Gil cried. And then, cautiously, he said, "What about Guinevere?"

"She is safe," Lance'lot answered. His face showed no emotion.

"They sought the Warriors of Tir nan Og," the young knight holding the torch said excitedly. "But, of course, they did not find them. Nor did they find any of our own." He grinned boldly at Palamedes, but the Saracen knight looked solemn.

"No. They were forewarned," he said. He turned to Gil. "Alas, my young friend, I am no longer what I was the day we parted in the forest. My honor is a tarnished breastplate, my knighthood, a splintered helm." He sighed, "You rode to your quest and I to mine, but another fate befell me. Headlong in pursuit of the elusive beast, I stumbled into a trap. Captured, I was taken to the very tower in which you later languished. The Usurper presented himself and my choices were two: resist him and know my death but increases his power. Or engage him on his own vile terms. And this shameful course, lamentably, I chose. I pledged my fealty with a lying tongue and re-joined his company. Thus, sitting at his cursed table, and sharing his cursed meat, I hear what none in the forest hears. And so, by this deception, I learn the aims of his evil heart."

"So, you knew he would raid the convent," Gil said. "And you warned them!"

Palamedes hung his head. "I am dishonored."

"But for a noble cause!" Gil insisted.

"For nothing!" said Palamedes. "The cause is lost! Your quest is done! All that remains is to save yourselves, if you can. To flee, to Glen Alban and the sea."

"But Candlemas! The tournament! It's just a few days."

"But too late," Lance'lot said quietly. "Tomorrow as the bell of Vespers rings, he raids the Forest Mews." Gil's heart lurched.

"By Candlemas Eve," Palamedes said mournfully, "All is lost. The Fool imprisoned in Merlin's Tower and the lady at her wedding feast. And on the holy day, the tournament will celebrate the bond." He sighed and shook his great bearded head. "Outwitted by the convent, he suspects now his own betrothed. And so, the trap is closed ere she escapes." He looked sadly at Gil. "Hers is but an old fate, come in haste. But for the rest, a new fate awaits. He has judged the Fool more danger than he's worth and the relic the same. None of your company is of use to him now. The child will die in Merlin's Tower. You will be hunted down. And the treasure will remain, locked in the Forest Chapel, beyond the reach of every hand."

"'And Arthur will sleep under Eildon, until time ends,'" Gil whispered. Palamedes, hearing his own past words, nodded gravely.

"We have tried, Gil, and we have failed," said Lance'lot gently. "But, truly, we have tried."

You are my only hope, Janetta's voice whispered from some place beyond time. "No!" Gil cried. "We have not failed. Not yet! There's still tomorrow. There's still a whole day!"

The young knight with the torch leaned closer, his eyes on Gil's face. "But to traverse the Forest of Pentecost at night is impossible," he said, "And by day the hunt rides until dusk. It cannot be."

"It will be. There'll be a way. I'll find a way." Gil's hand tightened on his sword hilt, and full of wild energy, he strode up and down in the firelight. His father stood with folded arms, and then stepped forward.

"There is time, and just enough, between tomorrow's Prime and the riding of the hunt, to save your friends and Percy from the tower. The lady must remain, or the Knight will know at Terce you have gone. If fortune favors, you will have crossed the Forest of Caledon by Vespers. A day's start will bring you safe to Glen Alban and the Northman's ships. From there, he and his warriors will win your way to the sea."

Gil stared at his father. "I will not leave her," he said. "If we flee, she comes with us. But we will not flee. There is a way, and I will find it."

"Gil." His father's face softened with a smile of pride, but he said, "It cannot be done."

"By you!" Gil shouted. "But I will!"

Again, his father smiled his proud smile. "No." He reached his hand out. "Come. We ride now and win at least the safety of some."

Gil pulled back from the offered embrace, and suddenly Floki stepped forward and turned Lance'lot's arm back, with his own. "Leave be," he said quietly. "Let the boy become the man." And to Gil he said, "Bring the good beast and we will ride."

Gil strode off into the night, so intent on his thoughts that he did not hear the footsteps behind him until a voice suddenly spoke at his ear. "I'm with you, if you try." He spun around and saw the young knight who had held the torch now trotting eagerly in the darkness at his side.

"But you said…."

"That it cannot be done. But you say it can. And I believe you."

Gil turned to face him. "You were my guards. And now you're, like, my friends?"

The young knight stood silent. And then he said, "There were four of us and two of them, and even though they were two of Guidbairn's best warriors, we could have taken them, and freed you."

"Yes," Gil said sharply.

"And then we, like you, would be fugitives in the forest, hunted down, as even now they hunt you. Will you believe that, though cowardice may have stayed our hands, so did good sense? I didn't fight for you," he added softly, "but I rode through the night, for Lance'lot." Impulsively, he drew his sword and held it out to Gil, flat across his hands. "I am Morians, son of Lianour. If you reject me," he said, looking down at the proffered weapon, "I hold no grievance. In your place, I might do the same."

"You were the one who was missing from the table," Gil murmured. And to the knight's puzzled silence, he said, "I saw Palamedes and three of you, through the window of Merlin's Tower."

"Three stayed, so one might not be missed," the knight said, and then added vehemently, "but the three are as willing as I to ride with you now."

Gil stood in the darkness weighing the choices as once he'd stood on the river rocks above the Indian Kettle pool. Then he stepped forward and reached his hand out and laid it on the knight's sword. "Then I accept," he said. "I accept all four." They clasped hands in the darkness, and strode eagerly, together, to collect the horses.

Mounted again behind Floki Magnusson, Gil rode from the hidden valley of his father's home. Turning back, he saw nothing but darkness, and were it not for the shadowy figures of Lance'lot and Palamedes leading the way, he might have dreamed it all. He studied the huge, familiar shape of the Saracen knight, uncertainly, and then leaned forward and whispered over the Northman's fur clad shoulder, "Floki?"

"Aye, Warrior?"

"Was Palamedes afraid? Did he make a bargain to live?"

Floki laughed. "That man has no more fear of death, than of the morning sun. He made a bargain that others may live." He paused and then said, "His honor is his dearest treasure. He bargained it away for the sake of other men." He fell quiet, and then said softly, "This is a noble thing."

Gil found that night that he had grown so accustomed to riding horses that he could do it in his sleep. Most of the long journey was a dreamy blur; the cool splashing as they rode back down the river, the piney smell of the high forest, the rustle of dead leaves in the oak wood. And then, suddenly, he was awake. The big horse had stopped. Gil raised his head, wondering if

Floki, too, had fallen asleep, but around him the others had stopped, too, and before them in the starlight was a shadowy wall. Blinking sleep from his eyes, he saw, beyond it, the turf roofs of the convent beneath a veil of thin smoke.

Releasing his hold around Floki's waist, he sat upright and heard again what had woken him: the creak of a bending war bow, at his side. The bowstring hummed softly, as Lance'lot's arrow flew into the night and thudded into the turf. Then, suddenly, a light appeared, a single, flickering flame, in the one small window of the convent that overlooked the forest. Guinevere's window, he had thought it, when he saw Lance'lot staring up at it, from the forest's edge. Now, Lance'lot waited, as silently, and then, from the distant building, a voice rose softly in chanted prayer.

"She sings Compline," the young knight's leader said.

"There," Lance'lot breathed. "Listen. She sings the canticle:
'Now let your servant go in peace
My eyes have seen your salvation...'"
It is the signal! All is well."

The gates of the convent swung open and a young monk stepped out and beckoned them within. The knights' leader whispered to Gil, "He is one of our own, hidden here, as many have been."

Palamedes leaned close from Doombearer's back and said, "The forest is threaded through with followers of Arthur, shining, each, like drops of dew on a silken web. Each strand knows the next. Touch one and you touch all. And at the center of the web, lighting it like the sun lights the dew is Guinevere, penitent in prayer for her husband's return. The candles in her window speak her silent presence and the psalms she sings, her secret words."

Gil nodded slowly, his eyes on his father. Lance'lot swung down from his charger and reached up to Gil, as Gil slid down from the great horse's back. "Come. Let me be near you one moment more."

"Dad?" Gil said, uncertainly, as his father closed his arms around him.

"You will be safe. Sir Palamedes and your noble Viking," he

laughed and nodded toward Floki, "are a worthy guard." To the two men, he said quietly, "Go, now. Enter. Before you are seen." He stepped back from Gil and gathered up his reins and laid his hand on his saddle, to mount.

"But you!" Gil cried. "What about you? Aren't you coming with us?"

Lance'lot turned to him again and slowly shook his head. "I cannot enter there. Both king and church forbid it. It is my penance for the past."

"Because of Guinevere? That's all over!" Gil stared up into his father's helm-shadowed eyes and suddenly he saw there all he needed to know. "But it's not," he said dully. Lance'lot turned his face away. "It's not the past, is it, Dad? It's not what you've done but what you might do. Right? *Right*?"

Lance'lot laid his hand again on the high pommel of his charger's saddle and then just stared at it, as if wondering suddenly what a jousting saddle was. Without taking his eyes from it, he said, "Gil, trust me. This is what is best. For you, for your mother, for everyone. Please. Just trust me. I'm your father and I love you more than life in any world."

Gil heard a sudden exclamation from Palamedes, behind him, and was aware of the young knights staring at him, but they all seemed far away. Slowly, he shook his head. "No. You don't," he said bleakly, as Lance'lot turned at last to face him. "It sounds great but it isn't true. And you're not true either. You're not my father. My father drowned in the Indian Kettle at Greene Mountain Falls. My father's dead."

Lance'lot slowly nodded. "This is true." Gil blinked back tears as he turned away.

Floki slipped down from the plough horse and came close by his side. "Make peace, Warrior," he pleaded. "Make peace. Do not speak harsh words in farewell."

"Leave me alone," Gil shouted. "It's nothing to do with you." Turning away from both men, he strode, with the four young knights around him, through the convent gates.

With Floki and the Saracen, they crowded into the guesthouse, where a young brother brought them food. After supper, when Gil made his bed on the floor, surrounded by his new young friends, Palamedes knelt respectfully beside him. "I could not but hear what was not for my ears, and my heart now forbids my tongue keep silence. Is it true?" he whispered, "Are you truly Lance'lot's son?"

Gil shook his head fiercely. "No."

"It is true," said Floki, without even turning to look at Gil. "Disown him though he may, that lonely man is indeed his father."

"He's not!" Gil shouted angrily. "And neither are you."

Floki looked up then and smiled. "That is well, since for that a holy miracle would be required. But I am a little older and a little wiser. And he is older and wiser than us both."

"Well, I'm sick of wise, older people telling me what to do."

Floki's eyes narrowed, and for once Gil didn't care if he'd crossed the invisible line. But then the Northman just laughed and stood up and stretched and then lay down on one of the low beds. "This wise old man would sleep," he said and covered his blond head with his cloak.

Palamedes leaned closer to Gil in the flickering light of the oil lamp. "But list, if he is your father, then surely it is of you that they speak in the rune. And that is a wondrous thing."

The youngest looking of the knights, a cheerful, black-haired boy the others called Gareth, whispered, "Arthur's rune?"

Palamedes recited solemnly:

"Of a father's sin, a son is shriven.
To the lamb, the lion's troth is given.
A white rose blooms in wintertide
The barefoot knight to the High King rides."

"What's that got to do with Arthur?" Gil said, curious in spite of himself.

"Nothing," Floki said, from beneath his cloak. "It is an old rune from the North. Sigrid taught me it."

"They say it is of Arthur, now," said Gareth uncertainly.

Floki looked up. "They say everything is of Arthur." He pulled the cloak back over his head.

"But surely Arthur is the High King," said Palamedes. "And Lance'lot, his penitent knight, for penitents often go barefoot. And the white rose in winter – is that not our hope in adversity, and, indeed, our Lady Guinevere, its guardian? And the lion; that might be…."

"Anything," said Floki. "Or nothing."

"It's like a riddle," Gil said slowly.

"It's all a riddle." Floki sat up and pushed the fur cloak aside. "A riddle and a rune-song, impossible to answer, meaning anything or nothing. And like as not it makes sense only when it happens, in which case, the answer is known to all, so what then is the point?" He got up from the bed and went to the little oil lamp and blew out the flame.

"It's like Sigrid's prophecy," said Gil, in the dark. He heard the rustle of the straw mattress as Floki lay down again.

"No," Floki sighed. "It is different. One makes right, the other makes penance. Not the same." His voice drifted into sleep and Gil fell quiet, thinking of the rune.

The white rose blooms in wintertide. The Lady Griselle had called Janetta a white rose. A white rose of Alba. A white rose blooming in winter….

"The lion!" exclaimed Palamedes out of the darkness. "Is not the lion fair Alba, herself?"

"Indeed!" Floki groaned from beneath his furs. "Or Camelot! Or the sun! Or the moon! Or that dragon in the loch! My noble friend, this night ends before it begins."

Silence fell then, but Gil lay awake bereft of rest in his fears for Janetta. He wished he could shake off the prophecy with the same ease as Floki, but he could not. The white rose suddenly had only one meaning: Janetta's dreaded marriage come too soon. In his mind, he traced the road from the convent to the Forest Mews, thinking of her in her tower room – the last night! Tomorrow, if he failed to rescue her, she would be in the Golden Knight's citadel, the fortress-heart of the usurper's Camelot. The night that was too short for Floki, was far too long for Gil. If only he could reach her. And then, all at once, he knew he could. He saw himself creeping from the guesthouse exactly as he had done, the night with Ismail, and just as on that night, stepping through a circle into his other self.

And then he was running on soft-furred paws, low and fast through the forest…he jerked awake. He'd dreamed…but it seemed so real. For one brief moment, he thought of acting out his dream. Would they miss him? Could he get there and back before the bell rang for Prime? Dare he risk it? And then, all at once, it didn't matter, because he had the answer. He sat bolt upright. "We can do it!" he cried. "We can do it! I've found the way!"

Palamedes and the boy-knights never moved. But a quiet voice from across the room said evenly, "I will kill the next man who speaks."

Gil nodded, still grinning, and curled himself silently to sleep. He woke at the first chime of the convent bell, filled with excitement. Beside him the young knights stirred sleepily and across the room, Floki quietly cursed. But Gil got to his feet, his mind racing. Thoughts crowded each other for his attention, but the first, and the sweetest, was Janetta.

"Come," said a voice out of the darkness. "The bell rings its last. We will be late for mass." The door was pushed open by the speaker, and Gil recognized Morians outlined against the starlight. "Surely before such a day, we must attend to our souls." The others all murmured agreement, and Gil, a little chastened, followed behind. He had been thinking more about breakfast. Outside the chapel, Palamedes took up his guardian's stance. But Floki entered quietly, behind Gil, though he stood just within the door, wrapped in his furs, like a wolf at the edge of a campfire.

Gil went forward and knelt with the knights before the wooden lattice that shielded the sisters' choir. The chapel reminded him so powerfully of Cille Aidan that, coming out into the dawn, he half hoped to feel the salt sea wind. And then suddenly a dark shape swept overhead as if his memories had summoned Feannag from the past. He looked up. High above the chapel roof a bird circled in the dim morning, its dark spread of wings too broad for hawk or crow. Beside him, Floki stared silently into the sky and the young knights, looking up also, pointed and gestured.

Gareth shaded his eyes and said to Floki, "What see you, sir?"

The Northman smiled; his gaze yet fixed on the bird. "An old man playing games with me," he said. He turned to Gil and

laid a hand on his shoulder. "It is my eagle," he said quietly.
"Come. Get the horse. We follow where it flies." Gil cast a
longing glance at the guesthouse where the young brother was
arriving with a laden basket. "Now, Warrior." Floki gave him
an urgent shove. Before the last star had faded from the sky, all
seven were mounted and gathered outside the convent gates.
The puzzled knights, wary of a Viking leader, turned hopefully
to Palamedes. But the Saracen bowed in deference to Floki,
though he himself looked perplexed. Then the first, distant cry
of a baying hound silenced all doubts.

"Ride!" Floki said. "They must not find us here." Gil knew
then it was the fate of the convent that rested on the haste of
their departure, as much as their own. And that Guidbairn's
raiders sought him still. He stared at the dark wall of trees with
a small, foolish hope that his father would suddenly appear and
join them, after all. But nothing stirred in the shadowy depths.
Above, the eagle spun out of its last circle and set off over the
treetops in a sure, straight course. Floki turned the horse and
followed, not by either road, but straight through the forest as
on their wild ride from Merlin's Tower.

But even as he mastered the big animal, he kept his eyes on
the sky and the eagle, glimpsed through the crowns of the trees.
The downward slope of the land told Gil that they were yet
descending to the mews, though not by any track. It was a steep
and dangerous ride, but the plough horse slid and stumbled
bravely on, skidding on its haunches, its long shaggy tail in the
dirt and the knights' chargers followed gamely behind. And
then, suddenly, they burst out onto the track again, at the very
point where Gil and his friends had first looked down on the
Forest Mews and the Golden Knight's hunt. The sky, bright with
sunrise, told Gil the third hour, Terce, was yet far off. They still
had time. "Quick," he said, "To the edge of the forest. And then
I'll get the key." Floki saluted him with a smile while high above
his eagle circled the Mews Garden on broad, lazy wings.

Snorting with relief, the six horses cantered easily down
the last of the track. Palamedes backed Doombearer into the
shelter of a great dark yew, and the others followed. Gil slid
down from the plough horse's back and unbuckled his sword

belt, buckling it again before laying it down on the ground. The young knights stared. "You disarm yourself? Here?" said Morians. Then Gil stepped within the belt, and as he recited the blessing their puzzlement turned to fear. And when, before their eyes, his body shrank and warped from boy to cat, they cried aloud in terror and backed their horses away. *Get used to it*, Gil meowed, and swishing his orange-striped tail, he leapt out of the sword belt and sat down to wash.

"He is possessed!" cried Morians, and Gareth hid his face behind his cloak and whispered, "He is the devil in disguise!"

"He is neither," said Floki drily. "He is a Change-Thing. And if he does not forsake his preening and get the key, I will throw him over that wall. Move!" he shouted down to the small furry animal at his horse's feet. Gil ignored him. In his own time, and when he was quite ready, he stood, stretched head up, and then head down, and sharpened his claws on a fallen branch. Then, just as Floki slid from the horse's back, he shot off, fast and low, to the Mews Garden wall.

He found his ivy vine and scrambled up it with ease and mounted the coping stone. Then, casting feline caution to the wind, he just leapt down the other side, landing on springy paws, his belly bouncing off the frosty ground. Shaking ice crystals from his fur, he streaked to the little square shed, and the key, hidden in the iron cooking pot. At the sight of the black metal vessel, he remembered his previous disaster, and backed off warily for a quick wash. Beyond the wall, he heard Floki's impatient shout, but he wasn't getting stuck in the miserable thing just to please a Northman. He contemplated having a sleep and seeing if the pot had improved when he woke up, but something human at the back of his mind told him it wasn't likely.

Then, fortune blessed him with a ray of dawn sunlight, which, probing the depths of the shed, lighted a broad wicker turf basket, roomy and round. *Deal*, he thought, and leapt within. "Warrior!" Floki shouted, "I skin you when I catch you and trim my cloak with your fur!" But Gil's hand was already closing on the key.

As soon as he opened the gate, the six horses and their riders cantered through. Floki, with Gil's sword belt slung over his shoulder, jumped down from the plough horse and helped Gil swing the gates closed. "Quick!" Gil shouted as he ran to hide the key, "we have to get clear of here before the hunt comes!"

He ran to the big beast, to mount, but Floki stayed by the gate. "Ah," he said, slipping the sword belt off his shoulder, "Now there is haste." His eyes narrowed ominously. Then suddenly he gave Gil a gracious smile. "But first, my pretty pet," he said sweetly, "are your whiskers now groomed? And your coat assured of its luster? Or shall we wait, in fear for our lives a little longer?"

"Floki, I couldn't help it!" Gil squeaked. "It wasn't me! It was Cat!"

Floki thrust the sword belt against Gil's chest with one hand and slapped the top of his head with the other. Then he leaned closer and whispered hoarsely, "I swim with my brethren of the sea, since I am a child. Do not hide behind your Change-Thing with me."

He jumped back up on the big horse and gathered up the reins. Gil buckled his sword belt and hauled himself aboard. "There!" he shouted over the Northman's shoulder. "Between the hedges. Slowly...." But Floki kicked the horse into his usual gallop and plunged headlong into the garden maze. Palamedes and the four young knights thundered behind while Gil frantically shouted, "Left, left!" and "Right, right!" and the plough horse wove back and forth, as nimble as a palfrey. The hedges were a high-speed blur, and the paths a muddy tangle and Gil dared not think what Floki would do to him if they galloped into six feet of yew by mistake. But then, ahead, he saw bright sky and tall trees, and the square lawn where he jousted with Percy. And beyond, the broad path leading to the tower. "There! There!" he cried triumphantly. Then suddenly he was filled with joy, because he was back, and she was waiting, and all things were possible now.

Before them lay the mews and its overgrown lawns, and then, as they burst into sight of the tower, Gil saw running figures scatter over the frosted grass, fleeing the sudden thunder of galloping hooves. Caught chopping firewood, Ismail turned to face them, hefting the wood axe in defense. At his side, Sir Alisander raised an ancient blade, almost as tall as himself. Danni and Rachel dropped their baskets of hen food and reached for their own swords, while Grania ran out in front, as if she could hide them, like little children, behind her skirts.

Floki shouted a warning to the others, and held up his hand, as he brought the plough horse to a skidding, apologetic halt. The beast reared and kicked in its eagerness to run, but he held it, turning and prancing, with a tight rein. Danni took her hand from her sword hilt and raised it to shade her eyes against the sun. With a glad little cry, she trotted forward and then broke into a run, racing toward them with outstretched arms. Floki laughed softly. Then suddenly he released his hold on the frantic horse, slapped its neck with the loop of the reins and shouted, "Hee-yah, beast! Run!" The animal leapt in the air and landed in a gallop. Gil clutched at the sheepskin, but Floki twisted around and grinned, "Godspeed, Warrior!" and with one long arm swept him backwards over the horse's rump.

With a cry of alarm, Gil turned a somersault mid-air, and landed on his butt on the frosty grass. Behind him, the four knights shouted with glee as Floki, leaning down from the running horse, swept Danni up before him on its back. He crossed the meadow at a gallop, then spun the horse around and galloped back. "Hey! Gil!" Ismail knelt beside him. "Is great! You are safe! And Floki is alive!"

Gil pulled one leg under himself and then the other and painfully got to his feet. "Great." He met Ismail's grin with a wince. "What a shame I'm going to kill him."

Floki drew the sweating plough horse to a halt before the tower door, dropped the reins on its neck and closed both his arms around Danni. She looked up at him wide-eyed. "We'd thought you were dead," she said, her voice trembling.

"I was dead, lass," he said. "But the maidens of Valhöll were not to my taste. So I have come back for my own." He slid his hands up under Danni's hair and knotted his fingers in it.

"What are you doing?" she asked in a small, puzzled voice.

"What I am meant to do." He leaned forward and kissed her, so long and so thoroughly that the four knights cheered and began thumping their shields. Floki turned and gave them a quick, sharp look, then flipped his cloak insolently over his head and Danni's and continued where he'd left off. When at last he released her and Danni emerged from under the cloak, blinking in astonishment, an elbow jabbed Gil's ribs. He looked up and met Rachel's eyes. She raised her chin and jerked it to his left.

Turning warily, Gil saw that Janetta had come quietly out from the tower door, with Percy at her side. Now she waited, wrapped in her green velvet cloak, looking off at the distant yew hedge with heroic nonchalance. Hesitantly, he touched her shoulder and reached out uncertain arms. She practically jumped into them, and he met her smiling mouth with his own for what felt like sweet eternity.

Percy giggled loudly and Gil raised his head. Floki was looking down on him, with Danni still clasped in his arms. "Ah, Warrior," he said softly, "the falling star that leads every man home." He smiled, but he seemed suddenly sad. Then he shook the plough horse's reins, as if shaking sorrow away, and spun the animal around and slapped its rump hard. "Hee-yah, beast!" he cried again, and as it thundered across the frosty grass he called back over his shoulder, "You may keep your quest, Warrior! I am away to the Northlands, with my lass!"

There was more laughter and shield-thumping, but suddenly it was silenced by a wild, grief-stricken howl. Gil whirled and saw Percy beside him; his arms rigid at his sides, his eyes squeezed shut and his mouth a round of despair. Danni shouted and Floki swung the horse around and came cantering remorsefully back. He lowered Danni quickly to the ground and as she ran to comfort her brother, got down himself and tossed Gil the reins. "Hey, Slanty-Eyes," Danni murmured, holding Percy close and kissing the top of his tousled head. "It's a joke." Floki came close and reached out a hand, but Percy shrieked and shoved it away. "Go," Danni whispered. "He gets like this. I'll look after him."

Floki wouldn't leave, but got down on his knees before the boy and reached out a hand again. Percy's eyes narrowed even more and, still clinging to Danni with one hand, he drew back the other and slapped the Northman's face. Floki jerked his head back, stunned. A gasp swept over the watching knights and even Palamedes whispered, "Oh, Fool."

Gil dashed forward and flung himself in front of Percy. "Floki, don't! He's...."

Floki's pale eyes turned to ice. "A child. I know. I am not an idiot, Warrior," he said and he angrily waved Gil aside. But when he looked back to Percy, the anger vanished. Again, he held out a hand.

"Go away!" Percy shouted. "You're a bad man." He stamped both feet.

Floki lowered his head, his yellow hair falling forward, screening his face. When he looked up, he was smiling and Gil could see he was ready to be slapped again. "I am," he said. "I am a very bad man. But I will not take your sister away from you. Never." Percy screwed up his face in concentration. "I play a game, Percy," Floki whispered.

"Stupid game!" said Percy, and Floki nodded.

"A very stupid game," he agreed. Once more he reached the hand to Percy and this time Percy took it. Suddenly the boy's huge smile lighted his face and he giggled. "Stupid!" He pointed at Floki and again the Northman nodded agreement.

"Right," said Danni sharply. "We've got the point." Percy grinned and then Floki allowed himself to be raised up to his feet by the boy's chubby hand, like a knight in service to his king. Danni stepped back and smiled at Gil in relief, but then her eyes fell upon Doombearer and the Saracen knight. As if seeing them for the first time, she cried, "Sir Palamedes! You've come back to us! And I haven't even...."

Palamedes swung down from his charger and bowed over her hand. "My lady," he said warmly, "All know that when lovers meet, there is no one else in the world."

Floki grinned and Danni looked quickly away in confusion. Then the sudden ringing of the convent bell brought all conversation to an end. "Terce!" Gil cried.

Janetta clutched his arm. "Quickly, take all to the hiding place. When the knight has gone, we meet again in my tower and share a merry feast." Her eyes sparkled and Gil felt a pang of loss for their days in the Mews Garden. He shook his head.

"No feast. And celebrations are going to have to wait. Pack food and a bedroll for each of you; Grania and Alisander, too. Be ready to travel the moment the Knight rides out." He paused, remembering the beautiful room and her small treasures. "Take whatever one thing is dearest to you. You won't come back here again."

"Never?" She looked terrified, but excited, too.

"Never before Arthur's return," said Palamedes solemnly.

"Where are we going?" Janetta's eyes swept the company and returned, trustingly, to Gil.

"To the Northlands." He grinned at Floki. "But first to the Forest of Pentecost. There's something in the chapel I promised to collect." He grinned again, boldly, as much to convince himself, as her. But this time she seemed only terrified.

"But the hunt! We cannot enter the forest while the Golden Knight hunts!"

"It's okay," Gil said, trying to sound like he rescued relics from haunted forests all the time. "We've got a plan." He nodded to Ismail and Rachel and Danni, but they all looked like he'd lost his head. "We have," he said, nodding more vigorously.

"Yes!" Ismail cried faithfully, "The plan! Very good plan."

In the distance, the first hunting horn sounded, and Gil hurriedly called Percy to his side. "I have a job for you." Percy's round face lit with pleasure. "Two jobs," Gil said. The happiness drained a little from Percy's expression and worry lines appeared between his brows. "Two jobs." He held up one finger of each hand. "First job: take all the horses to the stables." Gil beckoned quickly and the young knights dismounted, each casting Percy a wary glance as they handed over their chargers' reins.

"All the horses," Percy repeated, gathering two fistfuls of leads as Floki and Palamedes released their mounts, too.

"And when all the horses are in the stables, saddle every horse that doesn't have a saddle. My horse. Janetta's horse. Your horse. Alisander's horse. Grania's horse. Got it?" Percy blinked rapidly. His fingers clutching the reins turned white and his eyes squeezed shut with concentration.

"I don't think he can," Danni whispered.

"He has to," Gil said, because it was true.

Then the approaching sound of horses' hooves sent everyone running; Janetta and her foster parents into the mews, and the rest after Danni to the hidden gap in the yew hedge. Gil waited long enough to see the last equine tail disappear into the stable and then dashed through the sheltering branches to safety as the Knight cantered up to the tower.

There was barely space in the eight-sided room for all of them. Floki and the four knights perched on benches and kists around the walls. Palamedes stood like a great pillar in the center of the room, his mighty boots planted firmly on the trap door. Rachel and Danni sat on their beds among the scattered toys, while Gil and Ismail hastily donned their armor. When they had finished, all eyes turned to Gil, but the first to speak was Palamedes. Bowing his head he said, "With grave regret, I see no way of accomplishing this noble act."

"There is a way," Gil said. "We will cross the forest where the hunt will not go."

"Good sir," Morians said uneasily, "I ride with the hunt every day and I assure you, it knows no bounds but the walls of the forest. There is no route to the chapel that the hunt may not, of a sudden, cross."

Gil nodded respectfully. Then he asked, "Who leads the hunt?"

"Why, the hounds!" Morians replied, as if the question made no sense.

Gil smiled. "No," he said. "That is wrong. I will show you who will lead the hunt."

Morians looked taken aback, but he only bowed and said, a little sharply, "Show me indeed, sir, if you will."

Gil turned to Ismail and smiled again. Ismail's brown forehead wrinkled in brief puzzlement and then he nodded and flashed his white grin. "Right on," he said softly. Crouching on the floor, he laid out a circle, improvising with the scattered remnants of Janetta's childhood play. Blankets joined shawls, dolls were linked with hair ribbons, a boxful of gaming pieces were laid out, end to end. Palamedes watched with slowly raising eyebrows, as piece by piece, he was encircled.

"Ah!" he pronounced at last. "A worthy task!" And stepping carefully out of the ring, he removed his huge gauntlets and laid them down, end to end, to fill the final gap. "Good sir," he addressed Ismail, "proceed."

Ismail looked to Gil and, receiving a nod of approval, stepped into the circle. Touching the talisman at his throat with two brown fingers, he softly chanted,

"Bless to me my sister,
Bless to me my brother...."

With cries of alarm, the young knights scrambled back, retreating as far as they could in the little room. Gareth cast a fearful eye at Gil, clearly recalling Gil's transformation too well. He climbed up onto a kist, and two of his companions sought refuge on windowsills. Only Morians kept his composure. "It will be but a cat, after all," he reminded them. "And not very large."

Gil grinned. Then Ismail finished his chant, and Gil turned away until a shriek of boyish terror assured him the transformation was complete. Penned in the confines of the kennel, Ismail's stag loomed huge and menacing. With a clatter of hooves, he leapt from the circle and trotted back and forth, tossing his head and puffing clouds of steamy breath from his flaring nostrils. His eyes flashed challenge as he faced each of the cowering knights, his ears flicking back and forth and one foreleg pawing the polished floor.

With each toss of his head, his antlers scraped the wooden ceiling and when he rose on his hind legs and bucked and kicked, there seemed hardly a safe place in the room. But each fierce move stopped exactly short of doing harm and Gil realized that even as Other, Ismail was sure and certain and in control. Gil's eyes met Floki's and the Northman gestured gracefully toward the obedient beast, and grinned. *Let me see him do it with a cat*, Gil thought. *Let me see you do it with a cat, fish-breath!*

Ismail trotted once more around the room and then leapt back into his circle. The knights hid their faces behind their hands. Then Ismail was there again, standing, quietly apologetic, in the center of his ring of toys. "Forgive me if I trouble you. Wild animal is wild animal. Even if Change-Thing."

Morians smiled, reached out, and clasped Ismail's hand. "I have pursued the hart through many a forest glade. But never will I do so now without recalling this day! The lymer may discover him, the running hounds pursue him, the deerhounds bring him down. But 'tis true, the hart leads the hunt!" He turned back to Ismail. "You will lead us away from the chapel!" he cried excitedly. "I understand."

Gil knelt on the floor and using Ismail's circle as an impromptu map, said, "Look. Here is the Forest Gate." He moved two ribbons aside to make a gap. "And here," he moved a doll to make a second gap, "there's a fallen tree. Beneath it, the wall is broken down. Push the ivy away and you'll find a hole big enough to get a pony through. Or," he looked at Ismail, "a stag."

"I know the place!" Morians cried. "I will guide the huntsmen to it." He turned to Ismail. "When you hear the hounds take up your scent, run with all your power. They are fine beasts and rarely fail. And behind them come the deerhounds. Once they have sighted you, you have but little chance."

Gil stood up then, and placed his hand on Ismail's shoulder. Facing Morians, he said, "This is my closest friend. He is my brother. Can you keep him safe?"

Morians nodded gravely. Taking up a blue ribbon from a heap on the floor, he draped it across Ismail's circle, at a point beyond the second gap. "Here the river crosses the forest. He must elude the hounds in the water and retake his human form. I will carry a lymer's lead, and make of it a circle, ready, waiting! Elias," he pointed to the tallest and oldest-looking of the knights, "will turn the hunt at the river, pretending to yet follow the hart, and he and Gareth and Darras will lead them all the opposite way, as far from the chapel as is possible to go." He grinned, excitedly. "I, meanwhile, will take your brother on my horse and flee with him, into the forest," he finished, smiling proudly. But then his smile slowly faded. "But though this be done, and well done, what of you? If you enter by the tree, as will the hart, you will cross the path of the hunt. And, by the Forest Gate is impossible; for it is locked behind us, every day."

"Who locks it?" said Gil.

The fourth knight, the dark, quiet youth Morians had named as Darras, held up his hand. "It is myself," Darras said in a shy whisper. "My father was key-keeper to Arthur. At his death, the role fell to me, but for a lesser master," he said sadly. "Untrusting of all, he keeps the key upon his person, at night. But at the hunt, I carry it. Should a hound tarry behind or a buck elude us, I stay behind, and return the key upon my arrival at his hall."

Gil gave the quiet boy an encouraging smile. "Can you man a hawk?"

Darras looked startled. "Of course."

Gil realized it was like asking a huntsman if he could walk. "Good." He looked up at Rachel and smiled.

When she took her turn in the re-formed circle on the floor, the knights again shrank back against the walls, but with reddening faces, made redder still by Rachel's sweet smile as she, too, recited the chant. Gil closed his eyes until he heard a reassuring whir of wings and Morians cried, "Behold! So fine a hawk!"

"And so fine a woman," Floki murmured under his breath. "Who could ask for more?" Gil looked up and saw Rachel's hawk perched on Floki's cloak-wrapped arm. Danni folded her arms and stared out a window. Cautiously, Darras held out his own, gauntlet-shielded arm and Rachel flew to his fist. He smiled boyishly and turned to Gil.

"Lock the gate, as always," Gil said. "We'll send her to you from outside. Give her the key and release her back to us. And while you lead the hunt behind our stag, we will unlock the gate and ride to the chapel." He turned to Morians, "You and Ismail will meet us there."

The young knight hung his head. "If I could find it, truly we would," he said.

Gil blinked. "But you must be able to find it. You said the hunt rides everywhere."

"As it does," Morians answered miserably. "But few men follow the hounds to the briarwood. Willingly, I admit my cowardice, but I am not alone. Most draw rein before that fearsome gate." He faced Gil honestly. "I have never seen the chapel or its briarwood."

Gil shook his head in sudden despair, but Danni jumped to her feet. "It doesn't matter," she said, "I will know where it is. I will find them at the river, and they can follow me." And as Rachel swept through the sword belt, emerging in her own form, Danni stepped happily into the ring on the floor. This time, Morians and his companions remained in their places as she recited the blessing, as if, reassured by the hawk, they'd grown confident that as sweet and pretty a creature as Danni would have a Change-Thing of equal charm.

Gil grinned and closed his eyes, again, opening them at the first howl of horror. Hissing and beady-eyed, wings flapping aggressively, long neck outstretched, Danni emerged from the circle and bore down on the four terrified knights. Too confined to fly, she contented herself with a quick, hissing pursuit of the fleeing warriors, and returned through the circle to her human form. "See?" she said, suppressing a giggle, "I will be high above their heads, and above yours. Look up when you hear me call, and follow me to the chapel." She brushed her skirt, as if smoothing ruffled feathers, and sat down happily.

But Floki suddenly spoke from the windowsill where he sat quietly watching everything. "It is too dangerous," he said. "They will set their hawks on you for sport."

"I'll fly fast," she said. Then she laughed, "Besides, I am a big, fierce goose, too big for a little sparrow hawk." She flapped her arms and hissed suddenly at Rachel, a little fiercer than necessary. Then she turned and flapped and hissed playfully at Floki, but Floki still didn't smile.

"They will have peregrines," he said. "And bowmen. I forbid it." She flapped her pretend wings again and came right up to him, but he turned away. "I love you too much," he said. "I would not lose you in so awful a way."

Danni lowered her arms. She looked hard at the young Northman and seemed to teeter between fondness and rage. Then she said calmly, "Why? Why do you love me?"

He looked back and his face softened and he reached out one hand, the fingers just brushing her cheek. "Because you are bold and brave and as wild and lovely a thing as the earth holds."

"And to keep me, you forbid me to be the thing you love?"

He drew back as if she had slapped him. His eyes met hers and locked, but then he nodded. "Fly," he said quietly. "I do not hold you." And smiling his oddly sweet smile, he let her go.

The room fell silent then, and all turned their eyes again to Gil. He fidgeted, expecting somebody, Floki probably, to come up with some insurmountable obstacle that he'd missed. But the only person who spoke was curly-headed, round-faced young Gareth. "Please, good sir?" he said worriedly, "'Tis but the season of the roebuck. The hart," he pointed to Ismail, "Must not be sought 'til Holy Rood. Will not the Master of Game be displeased?" Gil stared, lost for words. Ismail was out of season?

Then Elias and Darras burst out laughing, slapping each other's backs. Morians laid his hand on Gareth's shoulder. "We are aiding the Golden Knight's enemies and stealing his most prized treasure. And his bride. I think we have bigger troubles than the rules of the hunt. Our days at Camelot are done, Gareth. We are men of the forest, now, 'til Arthur's return." He turned and smiled at Gil. "Like your noble…." he began, but Gil shook his head, cutting him off. There must be, one day, a time and place for telling Danni and the others about his father. But it wasn't here or now. Morians nodded. Then he said quickly, "All is agreed! At your word, sir, we ride."

A murmur of excitement swept the room but was cut short by a light rapping on the trap door. Then Janetta's sweet voice cried from below, "Make haste and come! He is gone and the way is clear!" They leapt up, as one, and hastily pulled up the door. Janetta was poised on the bottom step of the ladder, in her red dress and green velvet cape, with sturdy boots on her feet and a bow and quiver slung over her shoulder. Her cheeks were pink with cold and excitement, and she threw her arms around Gil as he scrambled down the ladder and kissed him boldly. "I am yours," she whispered. "Even should he capture us, I will die, now, rather than be his."

Gil caught her hand and held it tight, struggling to defeat the dark knot of fear within him. The stakes had risen higher than he ever imagined. Her life, all their lives, rested on the wisdom of his choices. *I can't do this*, the voice of the fear cried, *I'm just a boy.* But she was smiling into his eyes, and he knew the face she saw was the face of a man, armed for war. Hand in hand with Janetta, he ran for the yew hedge, his company of knights at his heels.

CHAPTER FIFTEEN

Thrusting the shielding branches aside, Gil burst out onto the Forest Mews lawn. Percy stood in its center, bristling with ponies, eleven leads clutched in his hands. The animals stamped and snorted. Gil spotted Lionheart in the midst of them; head down, neck snaked forward, nipping at the shaggy feet of the monkish plough horse. *It would be you, you misery.* Lionheart raised his head and seeing Gil, dropped his nose to the ground, hunching his back pathetically. *If you tell me Percy beat you, I'll cut your tail off behind your ears.*

He extracted Lionheart's reins from the clump in Percy's hand and swung up into the saddle, glad of the luxury of stirrups again. Seeing Janetta already astride her dappled palfrey, he trotted Lionheart to join her. Grania and Sir Alisander hurried out of the tower, clutching meager rolls of belongings. They hastened to their ponies, secured their little bedrolls, and, despite their years, mounted gamely and prepared to ride.

Morians brought his horse beside Lionheart as they trotted briskly through the maze. "We go ahead of you, now, to join the hunt. When the huntsman blows three long notes, know he calls up the hounds. Release the hart at once." He spoke as if Ismail was a real stag. "When you hear the baying of the hounds, know they have his scent and all are running. Only then, ride to the gate. The hawk," he glanced at Rachel, riding behind, "Must follow above our heads, for as soon as the gates are locked, the hunt begins, and she must bear the key away at once."

Morians galloped ahead then, and when Gil and Janetta reached the mews gate, he and Darras were waiting. "Hurry," the young knight called. "If Darras is late, the Knight may give the key to another, or unlock the gate himself. And all will be lost." Gil jumped down from Lionheart and ran to the shed for their own hidden key.

"Will he not question where you have been?" said Janetta, worriedly.

"He will," said Morians, "And I will tell him." Elias and Gareth laughed and a chill came over Gil as he clutched the key tightly in his hand. Floki put a thoughtful hand on his sword hilt. "I will tell him we have spent the night in the forest pursuing you." Morians gave Gil a happy grin. "As, in a way, we have. The best lies are the ones closest to the truth."

Slowly, Gil smiled in return. With a quick glance at Floki, who nodded very slightly, he fitted the key in the lock and released the gate.

Morians jumped down and helped him drag it open. "Close the gates behind us, that no stragglers see you," he instructed. Then he mounted again, kicking his horse into a gallop as he did, and the four young knights thundered out to re-join the hunt. Rachel had barely time to draw a circle on the ground, recite the blessing, and follow on swift wings.

Gil turned to drag the gates closed. Floki slid down from his plough horse, and on pretense of helping, came close beside him. His smile was gentle and wise. "If we are wrong about them, Warrior," he whispered, "no time remains even to think of it. All that is left is to die well." He slapped Gil's back. "Come! Let us have fun!" he said and leapt back onto the great horse and reined it around, his eyes sparkling with enjoyment.

The horses shuffled and snorted, puffing steamy breath onto the cold air. Harness and armor creaked. Ismail swung down to the ground and stood waiting within the circle from which Rachel had flown. Then, far off, Gil heard the hunting horn. One, two, three long silvery notes. He held his breath. Five notes was the call to retreat – the return to the hunting lodge that would seal their fate. But the horns fell silent. He turned to Ismail, his heart pounding in excitement. "Go!" Ismail laid his fingers on his talisman. Gil dragged one side of the gate open, and before it had cleared a yard, the stag leapt through the gap.

"Godspeed!" cried Palamedes, and Gil softly murmured

after him, "Godspeed." His mind leapt from fear to fear. Would Ismail find the fallen tree? Would Morians guide the hunt, as he must, toward the hart, but not too quickly? Or too slowly…there were so many ways it could all go wrong.

Gil's eyes swept his waiting friends and fell on Percy. Sitting on his grey charger, his hound at his feet, his hawk on his glove, he smiled happily back at Gil. The perfect knight: gentle and without fear. Then a whir of wings caught the attention of all. Floki reached to unbuckle his sword belt. But Danni jumped down from Frosti with her own looped belt held up in her hands and called the hawk from the sky. Gil saw a glint of shining metal in the bird's talons as she swept through the circle into her human self. Floki bowed to Danni. "See!" he announced to all. "I give her my ship and she steals my heart. I give her my heart, and she steals my hawk!" He bowed again. "I die a poor man for your sake, lady!"

Gil ran to Rachel and clasped the key, held out in her hand. And then, from the walled Forest of Pentecost, came a great clamor of canine voices, as the hounds took up the scent. The horns blew again, for the chase, and Gil felt sick with fear for his friend. "Now!" he cried. "Ride!" He shoved the gate wide and swung up on Lionheart's back. Reining his pony around, he took a last look at the Garden of the Forest Mews and galloped away.

Ahead, the horses threw up a cloud of sparkling rime and Percy's shaggy deer hound rolled and rubbed his muzzle in the snow. Janetta waved gaily back to Gil. The sun glistening on her black hair and, glowing on her emerald cloak; she rode as blithely as to a day of sport. And, with their chargers and palfreys and lead animals, their bows and their hound and hawk, they might indeed have ridden to the hunt. But no huntsmen stopped so silently, nor waited so warily, as they did outside the bleak stone walls of the Forest of Pentecost.

"I hear the hounds, still," Danni whispered.

Floki held up his hand and listened for a long while. Then he said, "They go further, the sound grows faint." He turned to Gil and nodded. Gil rode Lionheart up to the great gates and drew out the brass key from within his hauberk. Pulling its silken cord over his helm, he fitted it into the heavy lock. It turned with a satisfying clunk and the gates parted. Gil slipped the silken cord back over his head and tucked the key within his hauberk again. He had a place in mind for this one already, in a loch with a dragon, beyond the Forest of Caledon.

"I'll lead now," he called to Palamedes, taking up his reins. "I've been here before."

Palamedes smiled graciously. "And so, good friend, have I," he reminded Gil gently. "A hundred times in happier years. But still," he waved away Gil's embarrassed apology, "you have seen it more recently and no doubt much has changed."

But it was amazing how different a forest looked when you were a cat. And what places you could go where you might not take a pony. Or a monkish plough horse. He cast a wary eye back, but Floki rode the great animal through Gil's maze of thickets and low-hanging boughs without complaint, though at times lying flat on its bristly mane. Beside him, he guided Percy's charger, his hand never far from its bridle. Gil kept his eyes at cat height, where all his landmarks lay: There was the hole at the foot of the great oak, where he had fought the weasel-thing...*pine marten...you idiot, Cat...* and there the sandy stream bank, burrowed through by rabbits. And there, at last, the broad overgrown path that led to the second gate. Ducking beneath branches, his face scratched and torn by thorns, he cantered onward, until he reached the sagging barrier to the inner forest. Then suddenly Sir Alisander cried, "The horn! A single note. The hounds have lost the scent. He calls for the lymer – the leash hound – to find it again."

"The hart eludes them in the river!" Palamedes proclaimed triumphantly.

"It's time!" Gil cried, turning to Danni. "And we're not even at the chapel." He scanned the overgrown forest and the ivy-shrouded inner wall. "Can you find us here?"

She grinned and pointed to the gap in the canopy above. "If you can see the sky, I can see you." Jumping down from Frosti and drawing her sword, she marked a rough circle in the snow-covered leaves, closing it right around herself. She looked up to the sky again, to recite the blessing, and her eyes and Floki's met. "I'll be fine!" she said with a happy little smile. He returned the smile graciously, but Gil could see how little he wished to let her go.

"She'll be okay," he said as Danni whirled into the sky. "She's good at flying."

Floki turned and rested his cold gaze on Gil's face. "And so are they," he said. "Good at hawking and good at the bow."

Gil flinched away from the anger in his eyes. "Let's do this gate," he said quietly. It was tougher and solider than he had imagined when he wormed through it as Cat and, when he and Floki had finally reduced it to splinters, it was more than time for Danni's return. But the sky remained silent. Percy stared at the treetops, in innocent trust. Floki paced the forest floor, his eyes searching the emptiness above. Then, at last and far off, they heard her haunting call, as lovely on the winter air as the huntsman's silvery horn. Floki's face lit with joy and he grasped Gil's shoulders and hugged him in anguished relief. Gil grinned through the pain of crunching bones and looked eagerly back at the sky. The call continued and grew closer and he imagined Morians and Ismail, galloping through the forest, following her flight as he and Floki had followed the eagle. And then, suddenly, the sound was cut off short.

"She is silent," Floki whispered. Percy stared happily upward still. But she did not call again and the next sound that came to Gil's straining ears was the crashing of brushwood and thunder of hooves of a horse, ridden hard, through the forest. Then Morians' charger burst through the screening trees and into view, with the young knight and Ismail on its back.

"Where is my lass?" Floki cried.

"The hawk!" Morians shouted. "She flees the hawk!" He pointed at the sky and suddenly, high over their heads, Danni swept into sight, circling, flapping desperately for speed as the dark-feathered shape stooped from above. Floki dove past Gil and reached up to Rachel for her bow. Swift as her own hawk self, Rachel whipped bow and quiver from her shoulder and thrust them into his hands. Above, Danni spun half on her back as the hawk struck her a glancing blow. Feathers fluttered down and she flapped awkwardly. Regaining speed, she circled over their heads, and then swept downward.

Gil's hope surged, thinking she would escape, but the hawk had circled too. Climbing rapidly above her on its powerful wings, it stooped again. Floki strung the bow with swift, sure hands, and set an arrow ready to fly. Poised there, his eyes on the sky, he waited for longer than Gil would ever dare, as the hawk dove closer and closer, fierce talons outstretched. Then the bowstring sang and the arrow flashed skyward. A cloud of feathers burst around the stooping bird, turning its fearsome dive to a pinwheeling comedy. Flopping incongruously, its fine tail a straggling stump, it turned and struggled homeward.

"Hah!" cried Sir Alisander gleefully, "Away to the castle mews for an early molt!"

Floki smiled at the retreating peregrine. "Come after my lass again and I'll do more than shave your tail," he said softly. Then he held the unstrung bow up in both arms, forming a rough circle above his head. Orange feet reaching, wings outstretched, Danni soared through and landed, scratched and tousled, but safe at his side.

"Brilliant!" she laughed, looking up into his eyes. He shook his head.

"Not content to steal my heart," he said quietly, "You must strive to break it, too?" And without letting her answer, he enfolded her into his arms.

Ismail slid down from the charger's back and took Chocolate's reins from Rachel. Looking up at the young knight, he smiled. "You risk all for me. I do not forget. Should Allah grant we meet again, I am your friend forever."

Morians turned his big horse around. "And I, yours. We will ride to the hunt together, beside our rightful king!" He looked solemnly then at Gil. "I can help you no further. Already the hounds find a new quarry. I return, now, before our master grows mistrustful of my absence. Ride swift and true to the chapel. The sun is high. At None the hunt returns, and all will be discovered."

"What about you?" Danni cried. "If you're with the Knight?"

"I will obey his orders and ride to the forest in search of traitors." He grinned. "And indeed, I will find three: Elias,

Darras, and Gareth, and when I join them, we will be four. Our master shall bid us make our own escape!" He laughed. "Godspeed, friends, and bring home our king." With a last salute, he called up his charger and cantered away.

As the horse's hoof beats faded into silence, Gil said, "I was so wrong to doubt him."

"You were right to doubt him," Floki answered. "Doubt every man until he proves true. And some, even then."

"Good sir," Palamedes said mournfully, "That is no way to live."

Floki laughed. "But it is, friend. It is exactly the way to live. Come," he grasped the mane of the monkish plough horse and jumped up onto its back, gathering his hemp rope reins. "Let us not waste this brave man's good work."

Gil swung up onto Lionheart and gathered his own reins. Leading the way through the broken gate, he took up his trail again with renewed haste, trying to guess the distance remaining to the briarwood. As Cat he had homed to it, straight as an arrow through the tangled forest. Horses ran faster than cats, but detours and false starts and impassable thickets all slowed their progress. Gil glanced at the sky; his ears tuned fearfully for the huntsmen's horns and the notes of the retreat. But then he saw ahead a broad avenue that he remembered well, and at its shadowy end, the last stone wall, and the simple empty gap that was the final gate. "There!" he shouted back to Floki. "That's it! The briarwood!" He nudged Lionheart with his heels.

They reached the great wall at a gallop, and Gil swept on, through the open gateway. But then behind him, he heard a mighty voice cry, "Halt!" Reining Lionheart in, he turned the dancing pony and looked back. In the middle of the broad avenue, the whole party milled in confusion. Percy's deerhound ringed the jostling horses in joyous circles and his hawk flapped impatient wings. Only one beast was quiet. Doombearer stood, still as a black statue, and on his back, Palamedes sat with head bowed.

"This is it!" Gil said again, baffled. "This is right. I know it is."

Palamedes raised his head, and looking over those of his companions, answered, "Indeed. And a truer course could not have been ridden. You have done splendidly." He smiled sadly. "And so, I bid you farewell."

"What?" said Gil, "Now?"

Palamedes raised his gauntleted hand to the gap in the wall. "Through this gate, I may not enter, for on the hallowed ground beyond, I dare not tread. This is the gate of the briarwood, where lies the Chapel of Pentecost. See?" he raised his hand again. "No lock has ever barred the way, nor has any mortal man held a key. None are needed. Wise men look within their hearts for warrant. Men, less wise, ride on and meet their fate."

Gil pictured suddenly the scattered bones through which he had prowled as Cat. But Floki rode his horse beside Doombearer and laid one hand on the great knight's shoulder. "Am I to believe that the man I saw laugh at a hundred in battle, now quivers at phantoms?"

"More than phantoms," Palamedes whispered.

"Oh, much more!" Floki leaned close, over the knight's shoulder. "Shadows in the barley kist! Ghostly whisperings over the spindle. Old women's tales!" He slapped the Saracen's helm and turned his big horse about. "Come, my friend. Let us ride."

But Palamedes shook his great head and did not move. "Souls grown old like mine cannot enter here." He turned to Gil and the others. "Each man must search his own heart and should he find one trace of evil there, one trace of greed, or hate, or anger; turn away. As long ago I told you, this is the Guarded Forest. Here lies the holiest relic. Here only the innocent may ride. Enter in humility. Want nothing for yourselves. Armor yourselves with love. And, still, be prepared to die." Gil looked around at the others and saw each face grown still with uncertainty. "But know yourselves well," Palamedes urged. "Approach the relic's presence bearing one single evil thought, and that evil will rise up and burn you to the heart."

Alisander and Grania rode their horses close on either side of Janetta's palfrey. Each in turn kissed her and then both backed their mounts away. "We, too, must wait here, Foster-Daughter,"

Alisander said. "The chapel lies beyond our road as well."

"Never!" Janetta protested. "What darkness could ever lie in such sweet hearts?"

Grania smiled wisely. She pointed to an ancient oak tree, growing beside the wall. "It may be old," she said, "But its wood is hard as iron. Do not doubt the sins of old age, daughter. In the oldest hearts, the darkest thoughts may lie."

Floki threw up his hands in despair. "Then, I surrender. If I stay here, I will drown in a river of humility. Warrior!" he called to Gil, "Let us ride."

Palamedes turned to face the Northman, his face grown pale. "My dear friend," he said. "You face the briarwood?"

Floki dropped the rope reins on the monkish plough horse's neck and looked at the sky. "Gods of my fathers," he protested, "by what failing do I earn this penance?" Then he glared at Palamedes through eyes narrowed to slits. "Yes, I face the briarwood, black-hearted Viking reprobate that I am. And all the ghosts, ghouls, trolls, and goblins that reside there, I face, too." He grinned suddenly and slapped Palamedes' mailed arm. "Cheer yourself. I see another dragon, I run."

Palamedes shook his head gravely. "Were it only a dragon, I would not fear for you, my friend. A dragon can but savage your body. But the Guardian of the Chapel will claim your immortal soul."

Floki looked at the sky again. "Yet another would have the ill-kept thing?" He smiled wryly. "So be it. But it must wait its turn behind the rest." He tightened his hold on the plough horse's reins. Then he smiled again, with sudden sweetness. "Farewell, good friend!" he said gently and slapped the animal's neck and sent it cantering through the open gate, leading Percy's charger by his side.

Gil rode after and one by one, Janetta, Rachel, Ismail, and Danni all joined him at the edge of the briarwood. He reined Lionheart around, beside Floki's plough horse and Percy's grey charger, and looked back. The great knight leant toward them, yearningly, as if his heart yet followed where his soul feared to go. Bending close over Lionheart's neck, Gil spoke within himself to the wild-eyed animal. *You are safe. There are no evil ponies. Not even you.* Shaking his reins, he sent the nervous beast onward down an avenue of snow-bent briar.

At the beginning, the way was wide, and winding paths broke off to left and right, weaving in and out of the maze. Approaching the first, Ismail suddenly pushed Chocolate forward from his place at the rear and cantered past Floki and Percy, and Gil himself. Veering suddenly, he took the broad avenue to the right.

"Ismail!" Gil shouted after him. "It's this way." There was no answer. Gil turned to Floki who seemed as baffled as himself.

"Go," the Northman said. "I keep them here." Gil nudged Lionheart into a gallop, fearful of losing his friend in the overgrown pathways. But, rounding a sharp turn, he found Ismail sitting quietly on his still horse. Gil pulled Lionheart up beside him.

"Go back," Ismail said. "I go my way. I meet you there."

Gil shook his head. "What are you thinking of? How will you find it?"

"It will find me," Ismail said. "It is best I am alone."

"What?"

Ismail looked away, into the snow-covered thorn thicket. "Once," he said, "before war comes, I am herding my father's cattle. Five cows. And a storm comes, on open ground. Lightning strikes. Not all, but lead cow. But three die. She and two close beside. If lightning strikes, it is better I am alone."

"You think the Guardian is after you?" Gil said, amazed. When Ismail did not answer, Gil shrugged. "Floki doesn't believe any of this, and I'm not sure I do. But if Palamedes is right, there's a pretty obvious place for lightening to strike." He shrugged again, toward where the Northman waited with his friends.

Ismail suddenly smiled and shook his head, his wiry hair bouncing. "No," he laughed softly. "Floki is wild thing. Lion. Fierce. Not evil." And when he saw Gil was unconvinced, he said, "I will show you evil." And very lightly, he tapped his own chest.

Then, suddenly, Gil understood. He leaned over and gripped his friend's shoulder. "This is about the secret! The secret you wouldn't tell me on Hy, right?" Slowly, Ismail nodded. Gil shook his head. "You don't have to tell me," he said warmly. "I know. I saw the secret. In those weird windows in Merlin's Tower. I saw you kill that man. But I know about the windows, now. They tell only some of the truth. Which is worse than a lie. Like Palamedes at the Knight's table. And Floki offering his sword. I know whatever you did, you had a reason. It was the right thing."

Ismail smiled the saddest smile Gil had ever seen. "Do windows tell you name of man I kill?"

"No. But...."

"Only some of the truth. I tell the rest." He looked a last time at Gil, then turned away, as he spoke. "I tell you my father dies when Believers come to village. I do not tell you how." His voice was a whispered monotone. "I am nine when they take me from village. First, they are good to me. Give me food. Play football, like big brothers. Then they give me gun, machete, make me fight for them. Kill for them. First, they say, 'Kill that one, he is bad.' Then, 'Kill that one, who is not bad or we will kill some other, more innocent, a woman, a child.' They say, 'Burn that village, or we burn your village.' Then, 'Kill that one, or we kill your own mother.' And last, they come to my village. They take Maryam, Hassan, and say, 'Kill that one, or children die.' And that one, that one, he begs me, do it, do it, save Maryam, save Hassan.'" He swallowed, his lips trembling, "And I do it. And so, my father dies." He looked back at Gil with fathomless, empty eyes. "And now, I belong to Believers forever. They take my soul."

For a moment, Gil was unable to speak. Ismail lowered his head and looked down at his pony's thick mane. Then Gil nudged Lionheart forward until he stood side by side with Chocolate. Reaching across, he clasped both of Ismail's arms and shook him gently. "No!" he whispered, remembering his good jailor, lying dead in Merlin's Tower. "They can't do that. Even in that evil, evil place, they can't do that." He paused, then whispered, "I can't believe anyone can be so evil. You must hate them so much."

Ismail looked up, his eyes shining and wet. He shrugged.

"Mark, who is my master, he is with Believers eleven years, but he is younger than Floki. He comes, a captive, when he is five. When he is seven, they make him kill whole family. How can I hate him, when he is same as me?"

Gil stared at his friend, in stunned silence. Then he leaned over and grabbed Chocolate's bridle. Ismail reached to stop him, but he held fast, turning the pony, with Lionheart, back the way they'd come. "If the Guardian of the Chapel is good," he said quietly, "then it will understand. And if it's not good, then what does any of this matter? We'll ride together," he said, his hand still firm on Chocolate's bridle.

Ismail sighed, "Is okay. I come." And as Gil released the pony, he said, "You are brave."

Gil smiled ruefully. "No. I'm not brave. I just can't think of anywhere safer to be."

With Ismail at his side, Gil re-joined the others and hurried onward, seeking landmarks, knowing he was nearing the center of the briarwood. Knowing, also, that as Cat he had crossed it and crossed it, but found no chapel. Nor any guardian, though that gave little comfort. The Guardian would have no issue with cats. Around them, the thickets grew higher, screening out the sun. The air fell still and Gil felt a shapeless dread settle on his heart, like the frost on the briar. Quietness came over his companions, except for Percy who was giggling and playing a child's hand game with Floki, who rode blithely beside Percy's grey charger on his outlandish mount.

"Which way?" Ismail said. The path divided ahead of them. The way to the left was thinner and overgrown, but there lay a heap of tumbled stones, the cell, perhaps of the chapel's long vanished priest. And, just beyond, the white bones of horse and knight glistened, frost-covered, in the fading sun. The helm where Cat had feasted on baby mice lay yet over-turned, half-filled now, with snow.

"This way," Gil said confidently. He trotted a few feet ahead, separating for the first time, from Ismail. And, at once, the thing came, not for Ismail, not for Floki, but for him.

From the rose hedge, beyond the scattered bones, a figure suddenly appeared, a knight in tarnished mail, bearing a battered, unpainted shield. He rode his rangy brown horse as if he lived on its back and wore both sword and battle axe at his belt. With raised lance, he trotted a few paces into the open, and then turned and faced Gil, and with his helm shadowing his face, beckoned him with one gauntleted hand.

Warily, Gil sent Lionheart a pace forward, but Floki caught the pony's reins and held him back. "No, Warrior," he said under his breath.

"Let me talk to him," Gil whispered, "see what he wants."

"He wants battle," Floki answered. "I know this kind. He lends his sword to any man for gold. Nor does he go hungry. Leave this one to me." He grasped Gil's lance and lifted it from its fewter. Gil grabbed for the weapon, but Floki was already cantering out to meet the knight, with no mail, no fewter for his lance, and not even a proper saddle, just like at Einar's Holm. The knight smiled slightly, lowered his fewtered lance, and charged. The monkish plough horse broke into a thunderous gallop and Floki drove him on, so close to his armored opponent that Gil could hardly watch. At the last moment, he ducked low, driving the lance up at the knight beneath the battered shield.

But suddenly the shield was gone; the knight was gone, his tall brown charger gone, too. Floki caught the plough horse's mane, regaining his balance with ease, then spun the astonished animal in a ring of empty air. Gil stared, disbelieving, and then suddenly shouted with gleeful relief, "He's a ghost!" But Floki's eyes were on the rose hedge, where once again the knight had appeared, as suddenly and inexplicably as before. Again, the knight beckoned to Gil. "Ignore him!" Gil cried. "He can't hurt us."

Floki nodded to the white bones on the ground before him. "I think our friend would disagree." He lowered his lance again and charged. And, once again, the knight thundered toward him and vanished as they met. Floki cantered the baffled plough horse in a circle and turned to face the rose hedge. The knight was there, beckoning to Gil. Floki laughed quietly. "He plays my game. And he defeats me." He studied his opponent for a long while, then lowered his lance again and charged.

Again, the knight galloped to meet him. A stride away,

Floki swerved his horse and flung the lance aside. Drawing his sword, he swung it in a fearful arc across the other's throat. But only light spilled from the flashing blade, and for a third time, the knight was gone. Floki reined the plough horse to a halt, dismounted, retrieved the lance from the snow, and walked quietly back to Gil. "Warrior," he said solemnly, "I cannot help you. He seeks only you." With a sad shake of his head, he handed Gil his lance.

Gil set the lance in its fewter and turned Lionheart to the rose hedge to face the brown charger. The knight bowed then, and smiled, and then slowly lifted his helm and revealed his face.

"Gil!" Danni gasped beside him in the shock of recognition. "He's your...."

"No." Gil held up his hand, his eyes fixed on the face before him, weathered, bearded, aged and brutal, but uncannily like his own. "Not my father," he said calmly. "Me. He is me. He is me in Time Yet to Come. My future." He had entered the Guarded Forest with all his anger for his father yet in his heart, and now it stood before him, armed and ready. He reached up and settled his helm firmly and sent Lionheart forward.

"I do this!" Ismail shouted, barging ahead of him. "I, too, know this kind." But Gil caught Chocolate's bridle and held him back, as Floki had held Lionheart.

"He is the jackal," he said. "And I must kill him." He let the bridle go then and trotted out into the snowy list. Floki rode the plough horse up beside him for just a moment and lightly touched his shoulder with one hand.

"He is big," he whispered, "And you are small. Use it." Then he turned the big beast away and left Gil alone. The first charge caught Gil utterly by surprise. The knight was upon him before he'd fully lowered his lance or raised his shield. The steel point whisked by his neck, catching in his hair. The brown charger brushed shoulders with Lionheart and the little pony squealed in terror. Gil fought to hold him, turn him, steady his lance, raise his shield; and already the knight was thundering back, his lance aimed at Gil's heart.

Gil flung up his shield at the last moment and the steel point split the Pouncing Cat in two. Flinging the broken halves on the ground, he whirled Lionheart again. The knight laughed. Then he reached down and took the battle axe from his belt and hurled it in a flashing arc across the space between them. Gil threw himself flat on Lionheart's neck as it whistled over his head and Lionheart stretched out like a running cat and raced for the shelter of the briar hedge. *Don't run!* Gil cried. *He'll chase us!*

So? Lionheart shook his mane and plunged deeper into the maze of snow-laden briar. And then, suddenly, they were both at home. "Pony Chess!" Gil shouted exultantly. He whirled Lionheart and darted into a shadowy hollow. *Stand still!* Lionheart froze, small and silent, as the brown charger thundered past. *After him!* Obediently, Lionheart burst from his shelter and followed the brown horse's tracks. They caught the knight at a sudden cul-de-sac, so narrow that he struggled to turn his rearing charger. Gil drove at him and scored a glancing blow off the knight's helm, ringing it like a bell. *Run!*

Lionheart spun and ran, while the knight, shaking his head, fought to free his briar-tangled mount. *Under there!* Lionheart lowered his head and ducked beneath an overhanging tangle of thorns with Gil lying flat on his neck. Beyond lay an avenue, promising escape, but Gil pulled his pony around and waited, tantalizingly in sight, until the knight appeared on his puffing sweat-soaked charger. Lance lowered, Gil's pursuer charged, but the brown horse skidded to an indignant halt before the thorns. Cursing, the knight dismounted, hauling the big beast through the barrier as Gil and Lionheart cantered away.

Ahead, Gil saw, at last, what he sought: the avenue divided and became two. *That one.* He nudged Lionheart with his knee and the pony galloped to the left. At the first bend, Gil pulled him up. *Back.* With hill pony agility, Lionheart stepped backward until they stood again at the junction. Gil smiled at the tracks, jumbled and blurred, but all going one way. Hearing hoof beats behind them, he nudged Lionheart again and the pony galloped, snorting, down the corridor to the right. Around the first bend, Gil tugged the reins. *Here. Don't move. Not even an ear.*

Lionheart stood; a small, furry statue. Taking his lance in his hand, Gil carefully raised himself to his knees, and then stood, a foot on the jousting saddle and a foot on Lionheart's rump. He cast a quick glance over the briar to the avenue beyond and saw nothing but his pony's dark tracks. Then he ducked down out of sight as the brown charger's hooves sounded, warily pacing the muddied snow.

When the jingle of harness and the animal's breathing were a yard away, Gil rose to his full height. The eyes of the knight, blue like his own, met his, in utter astonishment, and for an instant, Gil hesitated. But the blue eyes flashed then with fury as the knight reached for his sword. Gil lunged across the briar and drove the lance into his throat. The knight seemed to freeze, hanging in mid-air. His eyes again met Gil's and he seemed to smile, but then slowly he faded into mist, and then into nothingness, and all that remained was the brown charger, standing alone. It dropped its head calmly, nuzzling in the snow for grass, and silence fell on the briar wood.

In the distance, Gil heard the voices of his friends, calling his name, and he put away his lance, and rode out to meet them, leading the brown charger behind him. A great cheer went up as he appeared and Janetta galloped to his side and flung herself onto Lionheart's back behind him, wrapping joyous arms around his waist, her silken hair enfolding them both. He turned in his saddle and kissed her, and then looked up and saw Floki standing, quietly watching, his arms wrapped around Percy and his rough hands yet ready to shield the boy's face. "The pleasures of Valhöll must wait," he said, with a small smile. "We are not yet done."

Gil was aware then of an aching weariness in his own body, the trembling of each sweat-soaked limb. His eyes fell on the white bones of the fallen knight and he knew that he, too, had fought some phantom of his own angry heart here until both he and his tormented mount met their deaths. Janetta slipped down from Lionheart's back and Gil followed her. The briarwood yet enclosed them. They stood at its very heart. He had crossed every inch of it, as Cat, and knew it well. He shook his head.

"But we are done," he said sadly. "It's a trick. It's all a trick.

Like Merlin's Tower. We were wrong. Palamedes was wrong. Aidan was wrong. There is no chapel. All that's left is that pile of stones." He pointed to the mossy heap, overgrown with rose briars, and a sound arose in his throat that was neither laughter nor weeping, but both.

"Wrong, Warrior," said Floki. "It is here."

Gil shook his head. "It can't be. I've seen…."

Floki released Percy and, keeping one arm yet over his hunched shoulders, he pointed to the sky. Above the frosty thicket, the eagle soared and circled on sunlit wings. "Go to the stones," Floki said. "The chapel is here."

Gil shook his head again, hopelessly, but he was too numb and tired to argue with anyone, much less Floki. Obediently, he stumbled toward the mossy rubble. A yard from it, he turned around and shrugged again. "What am I supposed to do?"

"Go," said Floki.

Gil sighed. "Sure." He took one more step, barely able to raise his aching leg high enough, and set his foot on the nearest stone. And in that instant, the briarwood exploded into flames. A wall of fire swept the length of the overgrown avenue, engulfing the rose-hedges, leaping skyward, billowing white smoke above their heads. Gil leapt back, his face scorched from the heat, and then, behind him, he heard an anguished scream. "The children! The children! Someone help the children!" And before he even turned, he knew who it was.

"Rachel!" he gasped. But she was running already toward the flames. He felt time slow, as if there wasn't any hurry at all; as if Danni, and then Ismail, and then Janetta would catch her easily. But one by one they reached out and she slipped from their hands. Then Floki crossed the clearing in two great bounds and caught her, wrapping her tight in his powerful arms.

"No, lass! No! No!"

But astonishingly, she found the strength, the mother-animal strength, to break his grip and with a look of pure, desperate love, she leapt past Gil and into the fire. Gil covered his face, the heat still blazing on the backs of his hands. He heard a stifled cry from Danni and whispered, "Don't watch. Don't watch." But then Percy squealed, not in fear, or horror, but in delight.

And Ismail murmured, "Beautiful. It is beautiful."

Slowly, Gil lowered his hands. His fingers jerked back from the heat of his chainmail hauberk, where it had faced the fire. And yet, there was no fire. Rachel stood alone where it had raged in the thorn thickets, as untouched by the flames as on the day she had stepped from the Wandering Pool. She stared at her hands and her clothing and then looked all around. "The children?" she asked in a quavering voice. But there were no children and no flames and no wall of snow-covered briar. Before Gil stood a low building like the church at Cille Aidan, its stone walls and turf roof whitened with frost. Seven arched windows lined the nearest wall and each flickered with candlelight so brilliant that it shone out into the fading day and cast bright shapes on the snow. At one end, a tall stone cross, like on the hill at Hy, stood beside an open door from which light flooded like a river of innocent fire.

"It is the holy chapel," Janetta whispered. "The Chapel of Pentecost." And she reverently marked Lord Yesu's sign across her heart. "We are here," she breathed. "The end of the quest."

Danni let out a shriek of irreverent glee, breaking the eerie hush of the briarwood. "We've done it!" she cried. "We've passed the Guardian." She turned and hugged Rachel, who was still looking around in confusion. "We've passed the test!"

But Floki studied the chapel with the same careful eye that he had fixed on Lancelot as they fought in the forest. "Ghosts and ghouls may be defeated. Real men with real swords yet ride this forest. And the hour grows late. Come." He led the way to the stone cross and the door, his hand on the hilt of his sword, as if expecting a trap. But just within the doorway he suddenly stopped. His fingers slipped away from the weapon as he stared for a long while in silence. Then he turned and laid a hand on Percy's shoulder and drew the boy forward. "Oh, child," he whispered. "Who now among us is the fool?" With a bewildered shrug, he turned to Gil. "Look," he said, and stepped aside.

For all the golden light pouring from the building, the interior was dark and shadowy, with but two thin candles standing on the simple white-draped altar, beneath a high round window piercing the gable wall. "But where was the light coming from?" Danni cried. "Outside, it's so bright and I can barely see in here."

Gil pointed to the altar. "From that," he said.

Between the two candles stood a cup, a golden chalice, adorned with a silver cross. Silver animals entwined around its base, and the cross and the beasts were studded with glowing jewels of red and green and deepest blue. So lustrous were the stones, so gleaming the metals that the chalice appeared to both pour out light, and absorb it, as if its very presence darkened the space around it. "Oh, Percy," Danni whispered. "It is beautiful. It is." She put her arm around his waist and pointed at the cup. Percy giggled and looked briefly at the chalice and then looked away.

"Perce," Gil said, puzzled. "Aren't you glad to see it?" Percy blinked innocently.

"Look, Perce," Danni said then. "Your cup."

"My cup?" Percy's face was one big question.

Danni sighed. "Right. Next time you throw yourself in the river for something, make sure you really want it." She grinned and shrugged. "Never mind," she took his hand, "Like it or not, it's coming with us."

Holding Percy's hand tightly, she stepped forward. But Ismail suddenly reached out an arm and barred her way. "If we pass Guardian of Chapel," he said, puzzled, "what is that?" He pointed to the base of the altar, where something barely visible lay breathing softly in the shadowy dusk. Gil peered into the shadows and saw the curving graceful outline of an animal's neck, slender and white, like a deer, with a mane like a horse. He followed the curve of its back to its tasseled tail, wrapped around its curled hind legs. The creature's forelegs were folded and its nose tucked in beneath its thigh; it was curled like a cat, asleep.

"A pony?" said Danni. "In here?"

"A deer," said Rachel. Gil thought of the white hind at Cille Aidan. But then Janetta clapped her hands together like a small, delighted child.

"It is him!" she cried. "It is my unicorn!" And she started forward, but then the creature awoke and raised its head and

Gil, too, saw beneath its white forelock, the gleaming perfect, impossible horn. The animal sprang to its feet with a clatter of hooves on stone, and, lowering its head, swung the horn back and forth, as if in warning. White as bone, and deadly as the polished prongs of a fighting stag, it seemed to pick them out, one by one.

"Here is Guardian?" whispered Ismail.

"Get back," Gil whispered to Danni who had moved, wonderingly closer. And he reached his arm to Janetta, and gently drew her back, too.

"But he delights me," she cried. "I know him!"

"It isn't a picture," Gil murmured, his eyes fixed on the beast. It swung the great horn again and the light of the candles glinted down its smooth length.

"It will charge?" Ismail whispered.

"Not sure." Gil studied it, seeking some clue to its intentions. It was the most uncanny thing he had seen, since the dragon, and, like the dragon, it was unquestionably, fiercely real. It stood its ground in front of the altar, and the chalice, which moments before had seemed within their grasp, might as well have been in the Golden Knight's citadel. Without taking his eyes fully off it, Gil turned to Floki, standing just behind him. "Do we fight it?" he whispered. There was no answer. Gil touched the Northman's arm, but he seemed paralyzed, his eyes locked on the beast, as if, at last, he had met something of which he was truly afraid.

"Gil," Rachel whispered. "You talk to horses. Talk to it."

"It is the unicorn," Janetta protested. "It is not a horse."

"It's a kind of horse," Rachel said impatiently. "Go on, Gil. At least you could try."

"Okay," Gil said uneasily, since he couldn't think of anything else to do. With his gaze fixed on the deep, black pools of the unicorn's eyes, he turned warily to the place within himself from which he spoke to Lionheart. At first, nothing happened. Then a darkness opened up inside him, a thousand times deeper and a thousand times darker than any night. He heard a sound like a rushing wind and then he was falling into a whirlpool of beautiful terror, as if he looked down to the center of the earth and saw the axis on which it turned. Then the blackness swallowed him and he was gone.

If time passed, he did not know, but he grew gradually aware of sound returning and then light. A girl was weeping quietly above him and then Percy cried loudly, "Gil? Are you dead?"

"Not dead," he mumbled.

Gil felt himself hauled up off the floor by the neck of his chain hauberk.

"I think we do not try that again," said Floki, setting him back on his feet.

"No," Gil answered quietly. And yet the thought of returning to the blackness, which should have filled him with terror, somehow did not. His vision cleared and the unicorn was still before him, still guarding the altar and the chalice. And then, out of the corner of his eye, he glimpsed a swift, sure movement as Janetta darted forward. "Stop her!" he cried.

"No!" she answered. "He is the companion of my captivity!" And then she was past them all, running to the uncanny beast, even as it reared up, shaking its glistening mane and flaunting its fierce horn. Its sharp hooves crashed to the ground, a foot from where she stood and the shining horn swung over her head.

"Janetta…." Gil pleaded.

She turned and smiled over her shoulder, her face lit with the radiance of the candles and the chalice. And then, as they all shrank back in horror, she leapt forward and flung her arms around the beast's great shining neck. For a moment, nothing moved. The beast was as motionless as its image in the tapestry and even the flickering of the candlelight was stilled. Then, very slowly, it bent its great head, carefully turning the fierce horn away. Folding its front legs, and curling its haunches beneath it, it lowered itself to the ground. Janetta slipped down, cross-legged, beside it, her fingers clinging to its silken mane. Then it silently turned, and lowering its beautiful head, rested it in the folds of her skirt and closed its fearsome eyes. "See?" she said. "His story is of love. How can he hurt me?"

Then, as quickly as it had knelt and bowed in submission,

the unicorn raised its head and, eyes flashing, sprang to its feet and bounded past them all, to the open door. Gil felt the silk of its mane brush his face and the darkness swept near. But then it retreated and was gone and the great beast was gone, too, leaving the chapel, and its treasure, to themselves.

"Now," said Ismail in a very small voice. "We pass test."

Gil ran to Janetta and clasped her in his arms, laughing and kissing her in the golden glow of the chalice. Releasing her, he turned to his friends in jubilation. But then, into the silence of the holy chapel, came the silver notes of the huntsman's horn. "One. Then two notes. Then four. Then one," Janetta whispered. "It is the death. The hunt is ended. We have no more time."

"Take the chalice," Floki ordered Gil. "We must ride."

"Only the Fool!" Janetta cried in warning. "None other may touch it!"

Gil turned to Danni and between them they led Percy back to the altar. Percy stared, unmoving, at the cup. "Take it," Danni urged.

"It's not mine," Percy said, hands in stubborn fists at his side. "Daddy said I shouldn't take things...."

Danni gripped his shoulders and shook him. "Take it, Slanty-Eyes." Percy's lip jutted out, but obediently he closed his fingers on the cup and lifted it from the altar, cradling the glittering treasure carefully in his arms. Danni sighed with relief and patted his head.

Floki put his arm around the child. "See," he smiled, "We make a Viking of you yet." Laughing softly, he looked up to the empty altar and the dusk-shrouded window above. Then the laughter froze on his lips. A great shadow fell over him and over the boy and a rush of great wings filled the air. Floki threw protecting arms around Percy and flung himself down to the floor. Still holding the boy, he looked up in astonishment as the eagle swept into the chapel through the circular window in the gable wall.

Brown wings transforming into grey-robed arms, feathered talons into monks' habit, it landed with easy grace. One hand rested lightly on the altar where the relic had stood, the other, outstretched, held the *bachall* of the Ab. Floki squinted up at the figure before him, as if looking at a ghost. "Mo'Aidan?" he whispered.

"Aidan?" Danni echoed in astonishment. Gil's mind reeled. Aidan, a Change-Thing? Aidan, here?"

But the grey-robed monk was as familiar as his presence was uncanny, and when he spoke, his voice was as gentle as always. "You have done well, Floki Magnusson," Aidan said. "And I will have that now."

Slowly, Floki got to his feet. His eyes still on Aidan, he lifted Percy upright, beside him. Percy clutched the heavy chalice to his chest and peered cautiously around it. Aidan smiled gently. He leaned the *bachall* against the altar and held out both hands. "Come, child," he said. Percy looked up at Floki, and when Floki nodded, he held the chalice out to Aidan, seeming almost relieved to be giving it away. Aidan took it, with another gentle smile, then set it back down in its place on the altar.

Gil gave Danni a quick, puzzled look, but she shrugged and returned her eyes trustingly to the Ab. He stood studying the chalice carefully, turning it one way and the other. Then he stepped back and with a movement as swift as his eagle's wings, grasped the *bachall* in both hands, raised it high, and brought it crashing down on the beautiful golden cup. Percy shrieked in fear and buried his face against Floki's arm. "Aidan!" Danni cried, astonished. "Aidan! What are you doing?" Aidan lifted the heavy staff again and struck a second blow. The soft, precious metals bent and twisted, and Gil saw exactly what Aidan was doing.

"No!" he shouted. "You won't destroy it! I never trusted you and I was right!" Rushing forward, he drew his sword and lunged, swinging wildly at the grey-robed figure of the Ab. The polished steel flashed through the candlelight and Aidan seemed barely to realize what was happening. His mouth formed the shape of Gil's name in gentle protest, but his eyes showed no fear and he made no move to defend himself.

Then something grabbed Gil from behind, pinning his arms and flinging the blade aside. Its fierce edge clawed through the sleeve of Aidan's robes but spared his flesh. "Let go the sword!" Floki whispered hoarsely, tightening his grip. "Let it fall."

Gil felt the bones of his forearms crunch together as Floki's fingers bit deep, but he fought back with all his strength. He heard the babble of protest of his friends and Percy's despairing wail as if from far away, as, wrenching his sword hand free, he struggled to turn the blade on his captor. "No one!" he gasped bitterly. "Trust no one! Why didn't I listen to you?"

Through a haze of tears, he saw Aidan strike a final blow on the battered chalice and saw it fall, in two broken halves, to the floor. "No!" he protested in anguish, and he renewed his efforts with ferocity, kicking out at Floki, and slicing at his imprisoning arm with the edge of the sword. Percy cried out again, and through his fury, he heard Floki shouting, "Look, Warrior! Look! *Look!*"

Percy squealed sharply, and Gil recognized his unbridled child's cry of joy. Turning his head from his battle with the Northman, he looked toward the sound. Percy sat on the stone chapel floor, his brown head bent over something clasped in his hands. He looked up, his eyes scrunched closed and his face a moon of bright happiness. "My cup! My cup!" he cried gleefully and held out to Gil his two hands lovingly clasping empty air.

The chapel fell silent and Gil was aware of a strengthening silvery light that revealed the puzzled faces of his companions like the aurora had shown him Floki in Merlin's Tower. Gil lowered his arms and the sword dropped from his fingers to the floor. Floki's grip eased and he drew back his hands until they rested gently on Gil's shoulders. "Look," he whispered softly again.

"What is it?" Danni cried, impatient and confused. "What does he think he's holding?"

Aidan laughed softly, "Oh, my restless daughter. He holds the treasure."

"The treasure?" Gil muttered. "But what's that?" He pointed to the broken gold vessel on the floor.

Aidan smiled. "Only a reliquary. As the body holds its greater treasure, the soul; so that but shields the greater worth." He clasped the *bachall* in both hands and looked down on the boy on the floor. "This," he said with wistful eyes on Percy's hands, "This is the grail, the holy treasure that all men seek, and none can see but the pure of heart."

Floki's grip tightened on Gil's shoulders and he said in a low murmur, "You are wrong. This cannot be."

Aidan tore his gaze from Percy and turned to the Northman with a wry affectionate smile. "So, the wisdom of Redbeard's stripling yet surpasses my own?" he said gently.

Floki released Gil and shook his head impatiently. He stepped closer to Percy and then he stumbled and sank to his knees as if suddenly too weak to stand. "Mo'Aidan," he whispered, staring at the emptiness in Percy's hands. "Mo'Aidan, I see it, too."

Startled cries swept around the company and Aidan's eyes opened wide with a look of stunned, child-like wonder, extraordinary on his weathered face. "'Blessed is he whom You choose,'" he murmured. Slowly, he shook his head. "Ah, Floki Magnusson," he said, "Your story is not what even you imagine." Floki seemed not to hear. He knelt, still as a statue, his gaze yet fixed on the nothingness in Percy's hands. Nor did he stir when the silver notes of the hunting horn rang out again. Gil looked in alarm to Janetta.

"The retreat," she whispered. "They return to the gate. We are trapped now. There is no escape."

But Ismail suddenly jumped forward, his dark eyes shining. "There is!" he said. "Morians tells me! There is other way. Other gate. They use North Gate. There is also gate to south."

"This is true!" Janetta cried. "Sir Alisander told me! Once there were four, but the gates east and west were walled closed. Still, to the south, one yet remains, since nothing but wilderness lies that way."

"But we can't go south," Danni said. "The Great Loch and the ships are north."

Gil smiled. "Yes. We can. Like at Hy."

They all turned to him, and Floki, seeming to wake from a kind of sleep, wrenched his gaze from Percy's treasure at last and got slowly to his feet. "How, Warrior?" he said distractedly.

"At Hy, we went north to go south. We circled the island. Here, you'll go south to go north."

"Circle the forest?" Rachel said. "But that will take...."

"Too long," Floki answered bleakly. "Even," he nodded to

Aidan, "following the eagle's flight. They will hold the road north before we can reach it. Our only chance is to be ahead of them."

"You will be ahead of them," said Gil. He crouched down on the floor and picked up the two halves of the reliquary. Carefully, he fitted them back together. Battered and misshapen, the vessel still looked whole. "If this is what men see, then this is what they will follow." He raised the golden cup high and suddenly grinned at Floki. "I will go out the North Gate and lead them a dance fit for a king's wedding!"

Floki smiled with sudden delight and gave Gil a bone-crushing hug. "Ah, now you are a Northman. Redbeard would be proud of you. As is his son," he said fondly. "Come, now," he released Gil and reached for the reliquary. "We do this thing. But I take that." Gil held onto the chalice and shook his head. Floki looked quickly around at the others, watching, and then appeared to decide that the time for discretion had run out. "They will kill you, Warrior," he said.

"They will kill you, too."

"Yes. But I will give them a glorious fight and I will enjoy it very much." Floki's eyes sparkled playfully, and he shrugged. "All men die, Warrior. And I live more in twenty years than most men live in sixty." He laughed gaily. "And look, this lovely creature will tend my grave!" He suddenly whirled and grasped Danni around the waist and swung her in a circle, laughing all the while. "Palamedes will see to it!"

"Floki, don't," she begged.

When she wouldn't join him in laughter, he said, "Ah, lass. A cold bed, but a bed all the same." Gently letting her go, he turned back to Gil. "Come, Warrior," he smiled. "This is my world." Gil shook his head again, and holding the chalice, he bolted out the door. Floki caught him five paces from Lionheart. For a moment, Gil expected punishment for his defiance, but the Northman only put a gentle but firmly restraining arm around his shoulders. "Warrior," he whispered, "Look, she there with the raven locks?" Gil turned instinctively to Janetta, who, with the others, had followed them out into the winter dusk. "She whose eyes melt when she looks at you? It is not just her eyes that melt, Warrior." Floki turned away, half-hiding a smile. "Oh, you will find pleasures there you have not even imagined," he said. "Go to her. Give me the chalice, and I will ride."

Gil looked up and was startled to realize he had grown so much in the months he had been here that he no longer had to crane his neck to meet the Northman's eyes. "No," he said. "This is for me to do."

Floki looked up at the dim sky. "Oh, Warrior," he cried in furious frustration. "Is this a time for that barren maiden, honor, when she could await you?"

Gil was suddenly so angry he didn't care what Floki did anymore. "You idiot," he whispered. "Do you think this wouldn't be in your stupid hands already if I could helm a longship?"

"If what?"

"The ship, dumbass. *Silver Dragon*. Your *Silver Dragon*. Who's going to take them to the Northlands if you're gloriously dead in this forest?"

"Erling," Floki answered at once. "Hakon will lead him. They are good seamen, Warrior," he said, suddenly calm.

"As good as you?"

"Sea-Friend is wiser."

"*As good as you?*"

Floki threw his hands in the air. "Warrior! *I am Floki Magnusson.*"

Gil laughed gleefully, aware of his friends staring at him as if he'd gone mad.

"Why do you laugh?" Floki's eyes narrowed dangerously.

"Because I win." Gil smiled and looked up into the Northman's eyes. "You are Floki Magnusson and I want Floki Magnusson to take them home. The best chance they can have," he finished solemnly.

Floki looked away and Gil knew he really had won. But then suddenly the Northman shook his head as if shaking away sleep. "I teach you," he said.

"Good idea," Gil grinned. "A little late."

"No. I teach you. You come back. I teach you."

"You just said...." Gil began, but he stopped, because

he knew from the look of dreamy confusion in his eyes that Floki understood his own words no better than he did himself. "Good," he said quietly. "You teach me."

"What say you?" Floki blinked, suddenly alert.

Gil shook his head. "Nothing."

The hunting horn sounded again and Floki suddenly leapt forward and grasped the monkish plough horse's rope bridle. "Take the big beast," he said to Gil. "He is a warhorse for all his holy vows. If there is any chance for you, it is with him."

"But Lionheart?" Gil said. He looked forlornly at the buff pony shaking his head with excitement as the others collected their mounts.

"I take him to Einar's Holm," Floki said gently. "To the hill where he was born."

Gil handed Lionheart's reins to the Northman, relief and misery warring within him for the beast who had carried him so bravely. He rested his forehead against Lionheart's mane. *He'll take you home,* he said, *back to your field. And your tree. Your own tree.*

Lionheart tossed his head, wild-eyed. *I don't know him! I don't know him!*

Floki threw the reins over his ears and said, aloud, "I lifted you to your feet, still wet from your mother's womb, you liar."

Gil said *See*? to Lionheart and then spun around and stared at Floki. "You heard him?"

Floki looked puzzled. "Why should I not hear him?"

I'll never understand this place, Gil thought wearily. He grinned at Floki. "No reason." He looked up and saw his friends all standing by their impatient horses, and Aidan watching gravely, his hands resting on the *bachall*. Rachel cried when he embraced her and he smiled and said, "All will be well, remember? All will be well!" She smiled back, brushing tears away, and nodded vigorously.

Danni flung her arms around his neck. "Oh, Gil!" she said miserably. "I got you into this! I'm so sorry. I'm so sorry!"

He held her close, startled to feel her grown up shape in his arms. "I'm not," he said fervently. "It's been the best time ever!" He kissed her and was startled again when she kissed him back. Letting her go, he realized he'd expected a punch.

Then he stood dumbly staring at Ismail. They tried thumping each other with their fists, then did a high-five, then fell forward and clasped each other in a bony boy-hug. "Good friend," Ismail whispered. "Best friend." Gil opened his mouth and tried to answer and then settled for a last high five.

Then, with his heart hurting so much he thought he would cry he turned to Janetta. She smiled radiantly. "Why say farewell, when we do not part?" she cried. "I shall go with you! Together, we ride. And together, we die. And so, we are together forever!" She flung herself into his arms and kissed him gaily.

Gil drew back and looked into her beautiful trusting eyes and felt suddenly a thousand years old. "Do you think," he said sadly, "that he would give us that?"

She froze in his arms and the joy went out of her eyes. "But then," she said numbly, "you truly leave me?"

He nodded, but then suddenly he whispered, "But I come back. I come back!" because he understood then that, like Aidan and the Ab of Hy, Floki Magnusson could see through time. And somehow, in some form, it would be true. "And, anyhow," he smiled and turned to Percy who stood, with his hawk on his shoulder and his hound at his feet, cradling the unseen cup in his arms. "I know you will be safe! You have your knight! Noble Sir Percy!" he bowed to the boy, "I bid you farewell." Percy dissolved in a wave of proud giggles. Gil looked up then and saw Aidan, leaning yet on his *bachall*. His eyes were gentle and his smile kind and he seemed to have no memory of Gil attacking him with a sword. Gil swallowed uncomfortably and said, "I'm really sorry...."

But Aidan shook his head. "It is a treasure well worth defending," he said simply, "Even for those like you and I, who only see its shadow." He beckoned Gil closer and when Gil stood before him, he smiled again, with great warmth. "Fearless men are easily brave," he said. "But there is nothing more powerful than the courage of a fearful heart. Come." He reached out and with his thumb firmly marked Lord Yesu's sign on Gil's forehead. "Ride, now, little brother. Ride."

Gil turned to where Floki waited with the monkish plough

horse. He laid a hand on Gil's shoulder and smiled, but his eyes stayed somber. "Godspeed, Warrior," he said quietly.

Gil grinned. "The last time someone said that to me, I got thrown off a horse."

"No!" Floki cried. "What rogue does this thing? Here! On his behalf, I apologize." He lunged forward, gripped Gil by the neck of his hauberk and the seat of his pants and flung him up onto the plough horse's back. Winded and gasping for breath, Gil pulled himself upright, got his leg over the animal's back, and clutched the reins with one hand and the chalice with the other. "Save me a seat in Valhöll," Floki shouted. "Should you find the place exists!" Then he brought his hand down hard on the great horse's rump. "Hee-yah, beast! Run!"

Then Gil was away, clinging to the huge animal, which, with his slight weight alone, ran as fast as Odin's mighty horse itself. He heard hoof beats behind him and the bark of Percy's hound and saw the eagle sweep past in the dusk. Then he was at the briarwood gate. The startled faces of Palamedes and the old couple flashed by. "Wait!" Gil shouted. "Follow them!" He waved over his shoulder and then he plunged into the forest, following the trail he knew well, back to the broken middle gate and through it into the outer forest, where he heard, at last, the baying of the hounds.

Every instinct said *run, flee!* But he mastered his fear and drew hard on the reins. When the first returning hound appeared, he grinned. From deep within his cat self he shouted, "Can't catch a pussycat! Yah! Nah! Yah, nah, nah!" and spun the big horse in a tantalizing ring. The hound skidded to a halt and four more piled up behind it. And then, behind them, Gil saw what he waited for; the first of the Golden Knight's huntsmen. *Don't let it be Morians!* he thought wildly. *He'll try to save me!* It wasn't. It was the harsh-tongued jailer who was spared Floki's sword at Merlin's Tower. "Pig face!" Gil shouted gleefully. The man stared, then recognized Gil with a howl of fury. Gil grinned, spun the plough horse again and raised the cup high. He waited long enough to see the shock in the man's eyes, then cried, "Hee-yah! Run, beast, run!" in as good a Viking shout as he could manage.

It ran. Ahead, he saw the great North Gate, standing open, as they'd left it, and thundered through it without slowing. Reining the animal left, he turned to the west and plunged into the wild forest, heading anywhere and nowhere. It did not matter, as long as they followed. *Seeking the place of my resurrection*, he thought, remembering the Ab of Hy. A calmness fell upon him, that even the baying of the hounds could not disturb, and as the dim forest closed around him, he loosened his grip on the hemp rope reins and let the beast itself choose the way.

Night fell and the great horse plunged on as if, like a cat, it could see in the dark. But soon there was no dark, for the sky filled again with the aurora, flinging great ribbons of silver across the heavens. He remembered the ride with Floki through the forest. And then, Lance'lot's forest dwelling. If he could reach it! And find his father there! But he shut his mind to the thought. He would never find it, and his father had left him, anyhow.

Gradually, the hounds fell back and he heard the horn calling, the call Janetta said was retreat. Had they given up? His heart surged. Was there still a chance? He drew on the reins and brought the tireless animal to a halt, listening intently. Far away, the cry of the hounds was a weary, homebound yapping. How much time had passed? He looked at the sky, but the aurora was so intense that even the guiding stars that Floki had shown him from the sea were paled. Besides, he'd never learned to read them well. *I teach you. You come back.* Again, he felt a flicker of hope as he imagined his friends, now far ahead on the road north, riding to safety.

North. But how did he find north? The light streamers covered the sky. *Odin's maidens dance tonight in the Hall of the Slain.* Gil grinned wryly. *If the place exists.* And then, as he swept his eyes all around the heavens, he saw something that took his breath away. In the quarter of the sky where the aurora pulsed strongest, suddenly three great bands rose skyward and stayed unmoving, like three standing pillars of light. North, he thought with the passion of pure trust. They're calling me home. Wherever home is. And he turned the brave plough horse and cantered gently toward the lights in the sky.

They never faded and the animal never tired and the night drew on. Twice he passed what he thought were familiar landmarks but still he kept his eyes on the sky, glimpsing the three pillars through gaps in trees, over sudden rises, down courses of streams. And then suddenly the beast's iron shoes rang on hard beaten, frozen snow. He looked down and saw the dark prints of horses. Many horses. The road. He was on the road north. "Hee-yah!" he shouted joyfully, and his mount leapt into a gallop. And then, behind him, he heard a sound he'd not heard before, a low, mournful howl, the fierce, deep voice of the wolfhound. And with it, the steady rhythm of the hooves of a single horse.

No. Not now, he begged. But somehow, he knew already which horse pursued him and who, gleaming golden in the Northern Lights, rode relentlessly on its gold-trapped back. "Go, beast!" he cried to the monkish plough horse. "Go! Go! Go!" Down the road to the north the great horse galloped. As if already scenting its far distant home, it needed no further urging, and Gil hunched down low, clinging to the golden chalice without knowing any longer why, his faced buried in the beast's rough mane. Ahead, his great pillars of light grew paler and he realized suddenly that the sky itself was paling into dawn.

Still, the horse and the hound pursued, neither gaining nor falling behind, as if, like the stars of the heavens, hunter and hunted wheeled across an earthbound sky. And then a new sound grew in Gil's consciousness, so faint he thought first it was but the echo of endless hoof beats in his weary ears. But it grew louder and took form, a great roaring that drowned out even the hooves of the pursuing charger and the deep voice of the hound.

"The Linn!" Gil whispered. "I'm there! The Linn of the Rainbow Bridge!" A dozen more strides and they burst into the clearing where the mighty cataract tumbled down. He slapped the horse's neck gleefully and it twitched its ears back and forth. But then, suddenly, it gave an angry snort. And then he, too, heard a low growling from within the forest, where night still lingered despite the greying sky. For a moment, Gil thought of the Questing Beast, come back again, but then the sound sharpened and drew near, a deep, fierce warning. He looked down from the horse into the golden eyes of the great grey wolfhound, standing waiting for them, at the edge of the clearing. Familiar with every tree of the forest, it had found another, shorter way.

Gil had barely time to cry out when it sprang. The horse reared, but the hound leapt by them and with two swift bounds launched itself into the round dark pool. With a great white splash that threw spray over the ice-bent rowan above, it disappeared into the black water. And then, in its place appeared the armor clad figure of a man. Hauberk and helm pouring streams of water, he climbed up from the pool. His sword was in his hand, and the Green Tree of Caledon, splintered by Floki's sword, yet grew bravely on his shield. Gil's hands dropped the reins and nearly the chalice as well. "Dad!"

"The horse! Give me the horse!"

"Dad, you have…."

"A Change-Thing. Yes. Twenty years is a long time, Gil. Please. The horse."

Then Gil, too, heard the Golden Knight galloping fiercely on the trail of his loyal wolfhound. Wordlessly, he jumped from the horse and his father, with an agility near to Floki's, leapt onto its back, in his place. He bent his heels into its flanks and in that moment, the plough horse became the war horse in its heart. The Golden Knight thundered out of the forest, his handsome face, beneath his helm, screwed up with hate. His eyes fell first on Gil, standing helplessly in the clearing, and lit with vengeful joy. Then the joy turned to astonishment, and then to fury, as, sword flashing Lance'lot bore down on him on the back of his borrowed mount.

"Traitor!" Guidbairn shouted.

"Your most loyal enemy," Lance'lot called back. "No man more devotedly despises you!" He laughed as his sword sliced a chunk from Guidbairn's shield and, again, he reminded Gil of Floki.

The clearing rang with clashing steel and Gil could barely force himself to watch. But his father seemed filled with a youthful vigor and he matched the Knight blow for blow. Then, breaking off, he cantered to the edge of the clearing and sent the plough horse galloping back. Unflinching, they bore down on the Knight's white charger and the two animals clashed, shoulder to shoulder, with a mighty thud of muscle and bone. The charger skidded on the icy ground and slid to his knees and the Golden Knight tumbled wildly over his head. Lance'lot was down and beside him before he could move. Wrenching off the Knight's helm, he drew back his head as if for the death stroke. But he stopped, holding the edge of the blade against Guidbairn's throat.

"Release the Bridge!" he shouted.

Guidbairn twisted an arm free and reached for his fallen sword, but Gil leapt in between and snatched it away. Then, with a stroke of inspired delight, he flung it, like he'd flung the key of Merlin's Tower, into the deepest pool he could find. It splashed gloriously beneath the ice bound rowan and sank into the depths.

"Excalibur!" Lance'lot laughed gleefully. Then he ceased laughing and pressed the steel against the Knight's throat. "The Bridge," he growled. "And I do not ask again. Release the Bridge!" Guidbairn paused a moment more and suddenly he smiled. Gil heard the approaching voices of pursuing hounds. Wildly, he looked to his father. "Release the Bridge or I'll fill your precious chalice with your own cursed blood!" Lance'lot shouted and Gil saw in the look on his father's face, the man this world had made of him.

Guidbairn saw it, too. With a bitter curse he reached within his golden hauberk and drew out a small, white stone. He held it up and the dawn shone through it and touched the tumbling waters of the linn with a soft bar of light. Spray swirled around the light and then suddenly gathered form and then sprang upward into a glorious, many-colored arch, a rainbow as tall as the heavens and as slim as the edge of a sword.

"Go, Gil!" Lance'lot cried. "Go! Think of home! Think of your mother! And nothing, nothing, nothing else. Now, Gil, they're coming."

"But you...."

"Now!"

Gil sprang forward and ran to the end of the arch, expecting it to move, or vanish as rainbows did. But his hand fell on something as cool and polished as ice. "Climb!" Lance'lot shouted. *Climb?* It was impossible. And yet, when he set a foot upon it, he found purchase at once. He took a step, and another. It was as easy as a staircase.

"Home!" Lance'lot called after. Gil turned and saw he was already high, high above the forest, and Lancelot and the defeated Knight and even the monkish plough horse were tiny below. Fear filled him, but he battered it down. *Home,* he thought. *Home.* And he pictured his mother's face, happy and smiling, by the window as he came home from school. *Home.* But then the face wavered for a moment and he saw instead sparkling, sea-green eyes, and hair like a raven's wing.

"No!" he cried. But already he was falling and the water was deep and dark below.

CHAPTER SIXTEEN

The Lookout Rock was warm and dappled with evening shadows. The river ran quietly beside it. The black waters of the Indian Kettle turned beneath a cloud of mosquitoes. The branch where the Stone-Pecker sat was empty. Hot and sticky in the warm summer air, Gil looked down at his feet, in his fur-trimmed boots, and his hands, still clutching the battered chalice. Then he looked up, across the pool, and saw a man with a yellow ponytail, sitting on the rocks.

The man raised his head suddenly and saw Gil. He got slowly to his feet, took something from his lips, studied it warily; then shrugged and tossed it in the water. Shading his eyes, he peered hard at the boy in Viking clothes, with a sword and a shield and a cup of silver and gold. Then his face broke into a slow baffled grin. "Looking good, dude," said Crazy Ivan.

About the Author

Alison Scott, the daughter of two writers, Alexander Leslie Scott, master of the western detective novel, and artist turned short story writer, Lily Kay Scott, was born in Manhattan. Her brother, Justin Scott, is a master of thrillers, mysteries, and sea stories, including the Isaac Bell Adventures. A Junior Year Abroad from her American university took her to Scotland, where she met her future husband, Clement Skelton--an actor, playwright, film cameraman, Battle of Britain Spitfire pilot, and monster hunter. She had her first baby while living on the shores of Loch Ness.

From an apprenticeship in Gothic romances, she went on to publish her first hardcover novel, A World Full of Secrets, writing as Alison Scott, while her husband became C.L. Skelton, writing successful family sagas. After she was widowed, she continued writing while raising their two sons, Professor Alasdair Skelton, geologist researching in climate change, and actor and gardener Justin Skelton.

As Alison Scott Skelton, she has published several works of contemporary and historical fiction in the US and Britain; among them, *Different Families, A Murderous Innocence, Saving Grace, An Older Woman*, and *Family Story*.

The Warriors of Tir nan Og, the six-book series that opens with *The Underwater Bridge*, is her first work for a young adult audience.

Curious about other Crossroad Press books?
Stop by our site:
http://store.crossroadpress.com
We offer quality writing
in digital, audio, and print formats.